The Seventh Life

Kris Tenn

Cover and Map Design - KTK Design

Editing - Kristen Hamilton, Kristen Corrects

Formatting - Tastec Ink, LLC

Epigraph

Seven times they fall, seven times they rise
If they forget the storm, the bond will die.
But if they meet beneath the sky's last blink,
The god may drink the curse like ink.

Part One

Present Day

Chapter 1

The Seventh Life

Ezra didn't mean to stop.

She was halfway out of the museum—coat on, bag packed, building empty behind her—when the weight of it finally hit.

At twenty-six, she'd expected more than this.

Five years at the museum. Gone. Her job. Her credibility. The one place that had let her chase the symbol without calling her obsessed. Without using words like "fixation" or "break from reality" the way her mother had before she died.

The director's voice still echoed: "The board thinks you've lost sight of the real world."

Maybe they were right. Maybe she had invented it all —the symbol, the dreams, the certainty that somewhere out there was proof she wasn't broken.

She got in her car and drove.

Seattle's gray sky pressed low as she merged onto I-5, then west toward the peninsula. Highway 101 unwound through forests that grew darker, denser, swallowing the road whole.

She caught her reflection in the rearview mirror—auburn curls wild from the rain, framing a pale face that looked younger than her years. Smaller too. At five-foot-three with a frame that had always made people underestimate her, she'd learned early that looking fragile didn't mean being weak.

But today, she felt both.

Rain hammered the windshield. Wipers beat a rhythm that matched her pulse—too fast, too unsteady.

Her mother had died thinking her daughter was sick. The museum had just fired her for the same reason. And now she was driving home with nothing. No job. No proof. No one left who believed her.

Except the symbol kept haunting her. The one she'd carved everywhere since childhood. The one in her dreams. Real or imagined?

But what if she'd invented it all? What if it was just a coping mechanism, something her desperate mind had created to make sense of the chaos?

The questions circled, tightening, until she couldn't breathe past them.

Ezra didn't remember deciding to pull over.

One moment she was driving, Highway 101 curving along Lake Crescent's shore. The next, she was parked at one of the overlooks, engine off, hands shaking on the wheel.

She opened the car door. Rain sliced sideways, cold and sharp.

The lake stretched below, impossibly deep. Six

hundred feet down, they said. Maybe more. Water so dark it looked like a void, black and endless, swallowing light and sound. Mist clung to the surface. The forest pressed close on all sides, ancient and indifferent.

She gripped the cold metal railing and leaned forward. Rain pelted her face, ran down her neck, soaked through her jacket. Below, the black water waited.

Twenty-one years. Twenty-one years of chasing shadows, of being called obsessed, delusional, sick. And for what? A symbol that might not even be real. Dreams that proved nothing.

The wind tore at her, tried to pull her back, but she leaned farther over the railing. The depth called to her—endless, quiet, final. No more questions. No more fighting to prove she wasn't crazy.

What if they were all right? What if she'd wasted her entire life on a delusion?

The exhaustion was crushing. The weight of it all—too heavy to carry anymore.

Her phone buzzed in her pocket.

Once. Insistent.

She almost ignored it. What did it matter? There was no one left to call, no one who cared whether she made it home.

But her hand moved anyway. Pulled out the phone.

A notification. A video recommendation.

"The Sacred Grounds of the Hoh Rain Forest."

Her thumb hovered over the screen. Why now? Why here?

Then opened it.

Drone footage. Trees. Moss. Ancient stone half-buried in ferns.

She barely breathed.

And there—carved into the rock—her symbol.

The phone slipped through her fingers. She caught it, gasping, and played the video again. And again.

Real.

The wind shifted again, gentler now, pushing her back toward the car.

Ezra looked out at the strait one more time. Then back at her phone. At the symbol glowing on the screen.

She had one more place to look. One more chance to prove she wasn't insane.

If the symbol was real, she was real.

And maybe—just maybe—she wasn't supposed to give up yet.

She got back in the car. Started the engine. Turned toward Forks.

The forest had called her back. And this time, she was going to answer.

The drive blurred—rain, trees, darkness pressing close. By the time she pulled into the driveway, exhaustion had settled deep into her bones. Her small two-bedroom cottage sat at the edge of town, tucked between towering Douglas firs. The house where she'd grown up. The kind of place tourists drove past without noticing. Perfect for someone who preferred solitude.

Inside, everything felt too normal. Too quiet.

Her mother's house. *Her* house now, though it had never felt that way. The kitchen still smelled faintly of coffee. Research books stacked on every surface—her obsession, not her mother's. The closet door in her childhood bedroom still bore the symbol she'd carved at fifteen, desperate proof she wasn't making it up.

Her mother had sanded it down twice. It always came back.

Ezra dropped her bag by the door and pulled out her laptop. Searched for the video again. Paused it on the stone, enlarged the frame until the symbol filled the screen.

Real. It had to be real.

But the exhaustion of the day pressed down on her. Her eyes burned. Her hands still trembled. Doubt crept in at the edges—what if it was just another dead end? Another carved rock that led nowhere?

She should sleep. Prepare. Go to the forest in daylight with a plan.

Instead, she curled beneath the quilt, phone facedown, laptop shut, but her mind wouldn't let go: Moss. Stone. Sigil. Not a replica. Not theory. A memory waiting.

The dreams had been coming since childhood—sometimes nightly, sometimes months apart, always triggered by stress or loss or moments when people didn't believe her.

But they'd never been this clear.

The dream came before dawn.

The forest drained of color. Trees bare, leaves scorched. The sky twisted, gray and blue pulling in opposite directions. A clearing opened: a pool, black and still, wide enough to swallow her whole. Fire sigils etched into obsidian rimmed its edges, glowing faintly like coals. From deep beneath, a heartbeat pulsed—ancient and alive.

Laughter drifted behind her.

Ezra turned. A figure stepped from the mist, scarred and shadowed, neither boy nor girl. Fifteen, maybe sixteen. Warrior-marks painted around their eyes that locked with hers.

"Veyar says, remember."

The name meant nothing to Ezra. Neither did the word that came next, unbidden from her own lips: "Ash."

But speaking it felt like unlocking something. The dream sharpened, vivid and terrible.

The warrior-marked kid shoved her backward with more force than she'd imagined they had, pushing her into the black pool—only she didn't fall. She was taken.

The kid's touch ignited her mind to open.

She knew without a doubt that this was more than a dream. It was a remembered past life. Her mother was right. She had lived before, and finally she was remembering again.

Memories flooded back—not just one death, but many. Six times before she'd lived and died. This was the seventh cycle, and she had yet to meet Ash in this life.

Was this symbol the clue to bringing them back together?

The first memory took shape around her.

She stood on a cliff's edge, wind tearing her hair, fire at her heels. Ash was beside her—no longer just the shadowy figure from her childhood nightmares, but real, solid, hers. A weapon incarnate. Sword in one hand, fire in the other.

His body blazed with power, yet his eyes remained wild and tender and fierce.

She reached for him. He kissed her, desperate and reverent, as the world shook. His pulse thundered against her lips. This was theirs.

"They are coming. We have ruined the entirety of the sacred valley because of Saav's rumors, but I will never let them take you. I have told them all it wasn't you, that it was I who was the murderer."

"No!" Ezra cried. "It was Saav, he was the one. Why can't we make them believe us?"

"Because it's too late and he is too powerful."

The mage's magic blasted an arrow through his back and pierced his heart. He collapsed onto Ezra, taking her down with him. His voice was rough with a slight gurgle. "Let them think they got you, too. Play dead."

Blood soaked her chest and hands. His breath rasped against her mouth.

His eyes found hers one last time. Through the pain, she saw recognition—not just of this death, but of the pact they'd made. Seven chances. Seven lives to find their way back to each other.

"Find me," he whispered, blood on his lips. "In the next life. Find me."

She kissed him as his life faded, tasting salt and copper and promise. "I will. Every time. I'll always find you."

Veyar's voice echoed in her mind, distant as thunder: The pact is sealed. Seven cycles. Seven chances.

Then he was gone, and her chest split with grief—a wound endless and older than time. But beneath the pain was something else: hope. This wasn't the end. It was only the first beginning.

The memory shifted. Another life. The sixth time they'd found and lost each other.

Smoke. Iron. The stench of death. The rain came crashing down.

Ezra lay broken, blood pooling fast from the wound at her neck. Ash dropped to his knees beside her, trembling. Trying to keep pressure on the wound, but it was useless. She had already bled out.

"No."

His voice cracked, grief shredding him raw. He shook her shoulders, pressed her cold hand to his cheek, but she didn't wake.

Rage erupted. The fire that she had tamed became a torrent, burning everything in its path. Not even the rain could stop his destruction of the Sacred Valley.

His eyes blazed with ruin. Fire consumed him—not life's flame but destruction itself. He rose screaming, his body incandescent, a force too wild for the world to hold.

A storm brewed, louder than the thunder. Ash vowed, "I will burn through every life until I find you again. The world will pay for taking you from me."

Kee, the shadow of death, appeared to take Ezra. "On to your next life."

"But what about Ash? You need to stop him. I can't let him destroy the world for me."

So Kee, taking the form of a battle-mage, struck him down—not because Kee could, but because Kee had to. If Ash lived, he would burn the world. Even as the blades pierced him, he screamed Ezra's name.

Even in death, his fury did not stop.

The battlefield dimmed. Darkness pressed in. His rage still burned.

The warrior-painted teen appeared again, standing above Ezra, hand extended.

Her eyes fluttered open. She recognized the teen this time—it was Kee, the shadow of death that had led her to this life. Grief flooded her veins, her heart heavy with what she had just lived through again.

"The madness from that death still burns in him," Kee whispered. "In this life, he doesn't remember you—but the rage remembers. And it's destroying him. He's become a killer. Special Ops. Always running, always hiding from a world he hates. The rage has to go somewhere."

Kee pulled her hand, guiding her up. "You're cursed, you know. Both of you. Six cycles—always dying, never together. He always dies first. Always. But in the sixth life, you died first, and—" Kee's eyes widened. "Oops. I've said too much. You weren't supposed to hear that yet."

Ezra's throat tightened. "What happens if we meet again?"

"You die. Both of you. The curse activates the moment you're in the same place." Kee's expression softened. "But if you don't meet, you die separately. Worse deaths. And the world he'll leave behind..." The kid shook their head. "He needs to see you're alive. Needs to know you're real."

"Then why show me this? Why make me remember if we're just going to die again?"

"Because this is the seventh life," Kee said quietly. "The last chance. If you fail this time—if you meet and the curse takes you, if you don't meet and die separately—there's no eighth life. No reunion in the stars. Just nothing. Forever."

The dream began to dissolve, but Kee's voice followed her into waking:

"You almost didn't make it. At the bridge." Kee's eyes held hers with uncomfortable intensity. "You were going to let go. That's why the video came when it did. Not coincidence. My intervention."

Kee's grip on her hand tightened. "This is the seventh life. The last chance. I couldn't let you give up before you even started."

A flicker of something—worry? guilt?—crossed Kee's face. "Don't tell anyone I did that. Go to the forest. He needs to see you're alive. Answers are waiting."

Ezra gasped awake, the name still burning in her chest: *Ash.*

The sky was still dark. Her skin damp. Breath ragged.

This dream had been different. Sharper. More complete than any before. She'd seen his face clearly for the first time, heard his name. And she understood with sudden, terrible clarity that these weren't just dreams.

They were memories.

Seeing the symbol in the video—knowing it was real, carved in ancient stone—had unlocked something. And Kee's words echoed in her skull: *This is the seventh life. The last chance.*

She'd spent her entire life searching for answers. She'd

lost her job, her credibility, everything—all for this symbol, this obsession, this bone-deep certainty that it meant something.

She wasn't going to wait anymore.

She moved on instinct. Jeans. Boots. Sweater. Journal. Flashlight. Camera. No map. No plan. Only the ache that told her he was real. Waiting. Dying inside from rage he couldn't control.

Coffee left cold. Laptop zipped. She scrawled a single word on the kitchen table—*Gone*—for the neighbors who checked on her. They'd worry if they didn't see her for a few days, but this wasn't something she could explain.

The drive to the Hoh Rainforest took less than an hour from Forks. Trees peeled open around her. Headlights split the dark. Fog clung to the canopy, softening the light until everything looked water-stained and ancient.

The forest did not welcome her. It watched.

Ezra pulled into a nearly empty lot. A weathered sign read:

HOH RAIN FOREST VISITOR CENTER

Trail placards pointed in neat directions: Hall of Mosses, Spruce Trail, Hoh River Loop.

Her eyes caught the broken rope fence, moss-slick, beside a fading warning:

TRAIL UNMAINTAINED – DO NOT ENTER
RECENT DISAPPEARANCES REPORTED

Her heart slowed. Louder. Louder.

The path beyond was barely visible, swallowed in green. Roots curled like ribs. Branches bent low as if whispering her name. The air thickened with cedar, wet earth, clove, and salt.

Ezra stepped past the rope.

The forest didn't welcome her. Didn't warn her. It simply recognized her, the way the symbol had, the way the dreams always did—as something that belonged to it, something it had been waiting to reclaim.

She didn't know what she'd find in that clearing. Didn't know if Ash was real or if she was walking into a trap. But she knew the symbol was real—she'd seen it carved in ancient stone. And if the symbol was real, maybe Ash was too. Maybe he needed her as desperately as Kee had said.

She didn't know if finding him would save them or destroy them both.

Six lives, Kee had shown her. Six times they'd met and died. Six cycles of blood and grief and loss that she couldn't fully remember but felt carved into her bones.

This was the seventh.

The last.

If they failed this time—if they met and the curse took them again, if they didn't meet and died separately—there would be no eighth chance. No reunion in the stars. Just nothing.

Forever.

And after a lifetime of searching, of dreaming, of being called crazy for believing in something no one else could see—she was done running from it.

She had two missions now: prove she wasn't insane, and save Ash from the rage that was destroying him.

She was going anyway.

Whatever waited in those sacred grounds, it was hers.

And she was going home.

Chapter 2

The Hunter

Ash's hands were still shaking from how close he'd come.

The bartender had bumped into him. Spilled a drink. Apologized.

And for three seconds—three fucking seconds—Ash had seen himself grab the man's skull and smash it into the bar until there was nothing left but pulp and bone.

He'd wanted to. God, he'd wanted to.

The only thing that stopped him was the memory. A flash—not his, but immediate. Undeniable. A woman's voice, urgent and familiar, *not this one. Not yet.*

Ash looked at his hands. At the scars that should be there but weren't. At the violence living just beneath his skin, patient and hungry.

He was running out of time.

One day soon, there'd be nothing left to stop him. And when that happened, he'd kill everyone. Start with the bar, move to the street, keep going until someone finally put him down or the whole fucking world burned.

Unless he understood what the memories meant.

The woman. The fire. The symbol he'd been drawing since he could hold a pencil.

All of it connected to something he'd lost. Something that had kept him human when nothing else could.

He stared into his whiskey, watching the amber liquid catch the dim light. The bar was half-empty—a few bikers near the pool table, the bartender wiping glasses at the far end. The TV above played muted sports highlights.

Somewhere in Oregon. He didn't remember the name of the town. Didn't matter. He'd been driving for days, running from the last job, trying to outrun the rage that threatened to consume him completely.

His phone sat facedown on the bar. Silent. No messages. No calls. He lived like a ghost—no ties, no connections, nothing that could be traced.

The first flash came when he was seven. Fire everywhere—his fire—wild and uncontrolled, wrapping around a woman he didn't know. He was older in the vision, a man, and the flames poured from his hands like they belonged there.

But she didn't burn.

She stood in the inferno, smiling. Not afraid. Like the fire was meant for her.

He'd drawn it in crayon on his bedroom wall—the woman surrounded by flames, untouched and smiling. His foster mother saw it and screamed. Locked him in the basement and called the police. Told them he was going to burn her alive. That he was dangerous. Possessed.

The cops took him away three days later.

At twelve, he woke gasping in the group home, rage burning so hot in his chest he couldn't breathe.

The vision had been clear this time. Brutally clear.

Someone he cared about was dying. Blood pooling beneath them, eyes going dim. He was a man again in the vision—older, stronger—but completely powerless. He'd reached for them, screaming, but they slipped away. Gone.

And the rage that followed wasn't human. It was annihilation. Fire everywhere. The world burning because he couldn't save them.

He'd woken clawing at sheets, throat raw from screaming a name he couldn't remember. The group home counselor found him destroying his room—mattress shredded, desk overturned, walls smeared with blood from his knuckles.

They sedated him. Called him violent. Uncontrollable.

But the rage didn't leave. It settled in his bones. And the fire symbol—the one that wouldn't burn the woman from his first vision, the one that meant something he couldn't name—it burned in his mind constantly now. Feeding the violence. Making it grow.

Each time he woke from the dreams, the wholeness shattered. Left him clawing at sheets, throat raw, the rage building with nowhere to go.

By sixteen, the rage needed an outlet.

The first kill came easy. A gang initiation. The man's name didn't matter—just that Ash could pull the trigger without flinching.

The gun kicked. The body dropped.

And for the first time in Ash's life, the symbol stopped burning behind his eyes.

No more flashes. No more dreams of the woman with fire in her hands. Just silence. Cold and complete.

He'd stood there in the alley, blood on his shoes, waiting for guilt that never came.

Freedom, he'd thought. Finally.

But the silence wasn't peace. It was erasure. Every night he didn't dream of her, he felt himself disappearing. Becoming less. Until all that remained was the rage and the violence and nothing else.

He'd thought killing set him free.

Instead, it buried the only thing that made him human.

But recently, the flashes had started coming back. Different this time.

Not the fire. Not her death. Not the rage that followed.

Her voice.

A woman's voice—urgent, familiar, real—whispering in his mind right when the violence threatened to take over. Right when his hands itched to kill.

Not this one. Not yet.

She was stopping him. Pulling him back from the edge every time he got close.

He didn't know how. Didn't know why. But somehow, she was reaching across whatever separated them, keeping him human when nothing else could.

The bartender tonight. The driver who cut him off last week. The man at the gas station who looked at him wrong.

Each time, right before Ash snapped, her voice cut through the rage: *Stop. Find me. I'm waiting.*

She was alive. A woman now, not just a memory. And she wanted him to find her.

It was the only thing that made sense. The only explanation for why the rage hadn't consumed him completely yet.

She was his cure. She'd always been his cure.

And if he didn't find her soon, there'd be nothing left of him to save.

His phone buzzed.

He almost ignored it. The burner only ever lit up for two reasons: job offers on encrypted channels or spam from whatever identity he'd stolen with the SIM card.

But something made him flip it over anyway.

A notification. YouTube. A video uploaded two days ago by a user named KEE.

"The Sacred Grounds of the Hoh Rain Forest."

Ash stared at the screen. He never subscribed to anything. Never searched for anything like this.

But his thumb moved anyway. Opened the video.

Drone footage. Trees. Mist rising from ancient stone.

The camera panned across moss-covered rock, half-buried in ferns—

And there.

Carved into the stone. Faint but unmistakable.

His symbol.

The one he'd drawn since he was a kid. The one that got him beaten in foster homes, called a demon, a freak, cursed. The symbol that brought the rage with it every time he tried to draw it—like it was feeding the fire inside him, making it grow until he couldn't control it anymore.

And now here it was. Real.

Ash's hands went cold. His breath stopped.

The symbol wasn't in his head. It was carved in stone, ancient and weathered, proof that he hadn't invented it. That maybe—just maybe—he wasn't crazy.

"Demon child," his mother had screamed, snatching the notebook where he'd drawn the symbol hundreds of times. She burned it in the sink. Her hands shook. "You're cursed. Cursed."

The third foster father found his sketchbook. Ash had filled every page with the symbol, obsessive and precise. The man ripped it apart. "Only psychopaths draw the same thing over and over with flames burning around it."

Ash broke the man's nose that night.

The court psychologist typed without looking up. "Patient exhibits no empathy. No remorse. Recommend institutional evaluation."

All because he couldn't stop drawing it. All because the symbol and fire burned in his mind, feeding the rage, making it grow until he couldn't breathe past it.

He read the description. The Sacred Grounds of the Hoh Rain Forest. Olympic Peninsula, Washington.

The symbol was real. And someone had left him a map.

Maybe finding it would give him answers. Maybe the angel he'd always thought was delusions of his subconscious was real too. Maybe he could finally understand why the rage had consumed him, why he'd never been able to feel normal, why he'd spent his entire life as a weapon instead of a person.

Or maybe finding it would make everything worse.

But he had to know.

Ash dropped cash on the bar and walked out.

The night air hit cold and damp. He got in the stolen sedan—a gray Honda he'd grabbed from a rest stop hours ago, plates already swapped—and started driving north. Highway 199 unwound through darkness, rain streaking the windshield. His mind circled around the video, the symbol, the impossible possibility that the angel might be real.

Two hours later, the gas gauge dropped to empty. He pulled into a truck stop, its sign buzzing under flickering bulbs.

Diesel fumes. Moths circling the lights. The hum of refrigerators through the station's open door.

He smelled them before he saw them.

Smoke. Leather. Cheap cologne. And something else —ammonia. The chemical stink of meth.

Two truckers stumbled out from the station's side door, laughing too loud. One lit a cigarette, the other knocked back an energy drink.

Ash kept his head down, watching them in his peripheral vision. Trouble, but not his problem.

Then a third man came around the pump—older, bearded, lips cracked and eyes red. He dragged someone by the arm.

Not someone. A kid.

Could've been thirteen. Could've been sixteen. Too-thin frame swallowed in a hoodie three sizes too big, cargo pants torn at one knee. The kid moved stiffly—like being forced too fast for too long. One eye already swelling. The trucker jerked the kid hard, muttering curses under his breath.

Ash stilled.

The pump clicked off.

"Hey!" the kid yelled. "I'm not going with you! I'm not for sale!"

Too loud. Too sharp.

Everything froze.

One of the other men turned. "Shut the hell up—"

Ash stepped forward.

Something in him shifted. Not rage this time. Something deeper. Protective.

A flash of memory—not from this life, but immediate. Visceral. Hands dragging him when he was small. Voices saying he was worthless, disposable. The first gang that took him at sixteen, promising protection but delivering only beatings and blood money.

And through it all, the angel's voice in his dreams, whispering that he mattered. That someone, somewhere, was waiting for him. That he wasn't alone.

He'd been that kid once. Taken. Beaten. Thrown into hell with no one to help him.

Whatever happened to this kid—the torture, the innocence stolen—he couldn't let it happen. Not when he was right here. Right now.

For once in his miserable life, he was in the right place at the right time.

The man dragging the kid didn't let go. "Mind your business."

"You just made it mine."

Ash didn't raise his voice. He didn't have to.

The kid's eyes widened. Not with fear—with hope. Like the kid had been waiting for him.

"Told you someone would come," the kid spat at the men.

Ash moved. Fast.

The fire in his chest roared to life—the same heat that came with the symbol, with the dreams, with the curse. Finally, a target that deserved it.

The punch landed square in the man's throat before he finished blinking. He crumpled, gasping, clutching his neck.

The other two lunged—one with a crowbar, the other with a knife.

Ash welcomed it.

The crowbar swung wide—easy to duck. Ash slammed his palm up into the man's elbow, then drove his fist into the man's face. Cartilage crunched. He dropped screaming.

The knife flashed.

Ash caught the wrist, twisted it. Hard. The blade clattered. He used the man's own momentum to throw him against the side of the pump. The metal dented. Bones cracked.

The last one was crawling to his knees when Ash kicked him in the ribs. The man rolled.

Then—

Sirens.

Shit.

Blue and red burst around the corner. Two cruisers. No warning.

One of the men still on the ground fumbled for something—a lighter, flicked with shaking fingers. Gasoline was pooling beneath the pump where Ash had thrown the knife-wielder. The spark caught.

The world lit up.

Flames roared up the pump, leaping across the hoses. The explosion threw Ash backward. Heat scorched his face. Glass shattered in the station windows. People dove for cover.

Ash didn't look back. The kid was already running.

He grabbed their arm and bolted.

The sedan was too close to the flames. No time.

"Back lot," Ash growled.

They cut behind the station, through a broken chain-link fence. A rusty toolshed sagged in the weeds, half-collapsed around a tarp-covered truck. The key was still in the visor.

"Get in," Ash ordered.

The kid dove across the seat.

Ash fired the engine. The truck shuddered to life. He threw it into reverse, backed through dry grass, and spun onto the side road just as the cops swarmed the station.

They didn't see him. Not yet.

But the sirens screamed louder.

Ash gunned it, tearing down the side road into darkness. The truck rattled, engine protesting, but it held. He kept his foot down, putting distance between them and the flames still lighting up the station behind them.

Twenty minutes later, somewhere past the outer neighborhoods of Eugene, the lights found them again.

A second unit appeared in the mirror—sharp grille, siren pulsing.

Ash didn't blink. Just downshifted. Pulled the wheel hard. The truck swung wide and hit gravel, bouncing rough.

"They're trying to box us in!" The kid twisted around, eyes sharp.

"No shit."

A third cruiser cut in from the left. Ash slammed the brakes, then cut hard right, fishtailing onto an unlit maintenance road. The truck screamed around the turn. Metal groaned. The engine coughed but didn't quit.

The road narrowed. Trees thickened.

Then the rain came—cold, sudden, blinding.

"You good?" Ash asked.

"I'm not dead," the kid muttered. "So yeah."

"Try to stay that way."

The last siren faded—smothered by distance or by the wall of trees. Ash kept driving blind, past broken trail signs and patches of moss swallowing the road.

Finally, he pulled off into a thicket deep enough that no cruiser could follow.

Steam rose from the hood. The engine clicked.

Kee slumped sideways, face pale and bruised. Ash leaned across and gently touched Kee's temple. The cut still leaked.

"You're going to pass out," he said.

"I already did," Kee mumbled. "I'm fine now."

"You're not."

But Kee was alive. And the worst of the chase was behind them.

"What's your name?" Ash asked.

"Kee."

Ash nodded. Strange name. But he didn't push.

He glanced at the kid again. "You a boy or a girl?"

Kee's expression didn't change. "Does it matter?"

Ash thought about it. "No. It really doesn't."

A tight smile crossed Kee's face. "Good answer."

Ash started the engine again. They had a long drive ahead.

The hours passed in silence. Ash kept to backroads, avoiding highways where patrol cars might be waiting. The truck's engine rattled but held. Kee dozed off sometime after midnight, head pressed against the window.

By the time they hit the coastal highway, the sky had started to shift. Not sunrise yet, but that deep pre-dawn blue that made everything look bruised.

Kee slept curled beside him, blood dried across Kee's brow. Ash had tied a rag there with water from a bottle he'd found in the truck.

He glanced at Kee again. Still breathing. Still here.

The road curved. Fir and spruce lined the shoulders now, tall enough to blot out everything but sky. The forest grew denser with each mile—older, too. Wilder.

The air shifted. Cooler. Wetter.

Ash cracked the window. Mist crept through. The trees loomed darker, trunks slick with moss. It wasn't like driving into a park. It was like entering a place that didn't want to be seen.

Then, there it was. A weathered wooden sign:

HOH RAIN FOREST – OLYMPIC NATIONAL PARK

But Ash didn't need the sign.

He knew this place.

Couldn't say how. Couldn't say why.

But something in him pulled toward it—like it had been waiting.

He felt it in his chest. Low. Steady. Like heat looking for air.

Not rage. Something else.

The road ended at a paved lot tucked between towering trees. A simple wooden building sat at the edge, with yellow light spilling from beneath its overhang. The sign above read:

HOH RAIN FOREST VISITOR CENTER

No rangers in sight. Just a plastic sandwich board listing trail conditions in faded print.

Only one car sat near the edge of the lot. An old, mud-streaked hatchback. Parked crooked.

Ash pulled in and cut the engine. The truck groaned, then went still.

Fog crept low across the concrete. The forest beyond loomed darker. Waiting.

Kee stirred beside him, rubbing their face. "We here?"

Ash nodded once. "Yeah."

Kee blinked at the window. "Smells like...home."

Ash didn't answer. But the kid was right. The place smelled clean and cold and living.

He stepped out, strapping his backpack tight. Knife back in his waistband. He left the truck unlocked, keys inside.

Let the cops find it. He wasn't driving it again.

Kee's boots hit gravel a moment later.

They stood side by side, breath fogging as they looked into the trees.

"You know where you're going?" Kee asked.

Ash didn't answer.

He didn't know the names. Didn't know the maps.

But something in him did. A weight behind the ribs. A heat that hummed low and steady.

Kee leaned toward a tree and whispered, "Tell Veyar we're finally here."

Ash turned. "What?"

The kid blinked fast. "Said it's...tail flare, deer's near. You know. Trail speak."

Ash narrowed his eyes. He'd heard what they said. And it hadn't been about deer.

Kee kicked a root and walked on. "It's a thing. You wouldn't get it."

Ash followed, veering right through a break in the trees where the moss grew thick. It didn't look like a path.

It was a deer trail.

Ash shook his head. Maybe that was it—why he let the kid stay close. Kee reminded him of himself, the version who might've survived if someone had ever walked beside him.

The forest pressed in—wet and alive. The canopy folded like a ceiling. Some trunks were wide enough to sleep inside.

Somewhere behind them, a bird screamed.

Kee exhaled slow, then mimicked the sound—sharp, low, familiar.

Ash shot the kid a look.

Kee shrugged. "Just letting the creatures know we're home. Kind of."

Ash didn't take to people. Definitely not kids. But ever since the gas station, something about Kee had stuck.

And the deeper Ash and Kee walked, the more his rage faded.

Slowly. Quietly.

Like something here was drawing it out of him.

The light thinned. The path narrowed.

Kee stopped suddenly, head tilted like listening to something Ash couldn't hear.

"What?" Ash asked.

"She's here." Kee's voice was barely a whisper. "The woman from your dreams. She came."

Ash's chest tightened. The rage that had been fading stirred again—not calming, but changing. Sharpening.

"How do you know?"

Kee's eyes met his, suddenly ancient, knowing. "Because the curse knows. It's been waiting for this. For both of you to be in the same place."

Ice ran through Ash's veins. "What curse?"

"The one that's killed you both. Six times." Kee's expression went serious, sad. "This is the seventh life. The last one. No more chances after this."

"What are you talking about?" Feeling his anger rise at Kee's words.

"You meet, you die. You don't meet, you die anyway."

Kee kicked at the moss, voice going soft. "But worse if you don't. You'll burn everything down. She'll... well. Neither of you wants to know."

The rage coiled tighter in Ash's chest. Not random anymore. Not senseless. It was waiting. For her. He didn't know why he believed the kid but somehow deep in his dark soul he felt Kee was telling the truth. And his instincts and gut never failed him.

"So what the fuck am I supposed to do?"

"Find her anyway." Kee started walking again. "Break the curse this time, or it breaks you both. Forever. No stars in the sky. No next life. Just gone."

Ash stood frozen, processing. The angel from his dreams was real. Was here. And if they met, one of them would die. Or both.

This was his last chance.

He could find her and risk destroying everything, or walk away and lose himself to the rage completely.

But at least if he found her, he'd know. He'd finally know if the dreams were real, if the angel had a face, if someone in this godforsaken world actually knew his name.

Ash started walking again, following Kee deeper into the forest. Each step took him closer to her, closer to an ending he couldn't see but felt waiting.

The curse wanted them together. The rage burned for her. And after a lifetime of killing, running, surviving in the shadows—he was finally going to face the one thing that terrified him more than death.

Her.

Whatever she was. Whatever they'd been. Whatever this curse demanded.

Because whatever waited out there was the woman who'd haunted every dream, every kill, every moment of silence in his blood-soaked life.

And it had never stopped waiting.

Neither had he.

He was done running.

Chapter 3

The Meeting

The forest closed behind her.

Ezra kept walking. No trail. No markers. Just mud, roots, and the pull in her chest that refused to let go.

She'd been walking for over an hour, guided by nothing but instinct and the certainty that Kee's dream had been real. Ash was here. He needed to see her alive. And somehow, finding the shrine would lead her to him.

The forest pressed in—ancient and watchful. Moss hung from branches like curtains. Ferns curled across the ground, hiding roots that caught at her boots. Everything felt alive in a way that had nothing to do with biology and everything to do with memory.

This place recognized her.

She recognized it.

Not from this life. From the others. Six times she'd walked through forests like this with fire at her back and Ash beside her. Six times she'd died.

Not this time.

Kee's words echoed in her skull: Seventh life. Last chance. He needs to see you're alive.

Then she saw it.

The shrine.

Collapsed. Swallowed in moss and vine. But unmistakable. The same broken stone from the video.

Ezra's breath caught.

Real.

Her knees buckled. She collapsed forward, hands slamming into the weathered stone as she fell. A sob tore from her throat—raw, desperate, relieved.

Real. Real. Real.

She wrapped her arms around the shrine, pressing her forehead against the ancient carvings. Tears streamed down her face, soaking into the moss. Twenty-one years. Two decades of being called crazy, obsessed, broken. All those years of losing everything—her job, her mother's faith, her credibility—all for this.

And it was real.

Her fingers traced the symbols through her tears— seven marks arranged in a circle, exactly as she'd seen in her dream. Fire. Eye. Lotus. Crescent with sound waves. Wind funnel. Mountain with tremors. Lock.

She knew them. Had drawn them. Had lived with them carved into her soul across seven lifetimes.

"Thank you," she whispered to the stone, to the forest, to whatever force had kept her believing when the whole world said she was insane. "Thank you."

She stayed there, clinging to the shrine, letting the relief wash through her. Letting herself believe.

Then—

A twig snapped behind her.

Ezra froze. Her breath stopped.

Footsteps. Careful. Deliberate.

Someone was here.

"You're here."

The voice came from behind her—rough, low, careful.

Ezra's heart stopped.

She turned slowly, still on her knees, hands braced against the stone.

And there he was.

Ash.

Taller than in her dreams. Broader. Real in a way that dreams could never capture. Brown skin gleaming with sweat, black hair tied back, eyes that carried death and something else—something desperate and lost.

He stood at the edge of the clearing, body tense like he was ready to run or fight. His gaze swept the forest behind her, as if searching for something—or someone.

"You're alive," Ezra whispered. Tears burned her eyes. "Kee said—I had to find you—"

Ash's entire body went rigid. "What did you say?"

"Kee. Kee told me you'd be here. That you needed to see I was alive—"

"How do you know Kee?" His voice was sharp, urgent. He took a step forward, eyes searching her face like he was trying to solve a puzzle. "How do you know that name?"

Ezra's heart pounded. "Kee came to me. In my dreams. Showed me our past lives. Told me about the curse, the seven lives—" She stopped, seeing his expression shift from confusion to something like fear. "How do you know Kee?"

"I—" Ash's hand moved to his chest, pressing against something that hurt. "I saved a kid at a gas station. Traffickers. The kid said their name was Kee. Led me here through the forest and then just—" He gestured at the empty clearing. "Vanished. The second I saw you."

They stared at each other, the impossible weight of it settling between them.

"Wait." Ezra's voice shook. "You're saying Kee was with you? Physically?"

"Yes. In the truck. Bleeding. I bandaged their head—" He stopped. "What do you mean, in your dreams?"

"Kee appeared in my dream last night. Showed me our past lives. All six deaths." Her hands trembled. "Kee's the shadow of death. The grim reaper. The one who guides souls between lives."

Ash went very still. His face drained of color. "The grim reaper."

"Ash—"

"I'm dead." His voice was flat, hollow. "I told Kee it might be my time. My chest—it's been burning since I got close to this place. And I don't feel pain. Ever. But this—" He pressed harder against the fire symbol. "That kid—Kee —death itself was sitting in my truck, and I didn't even know it."

"You're not dead—"

"How do you know?" His eyes were wild now, panicked. "The grim reaper led me here. To you. What if this is—what if I'm already gone and this is just—"

"Stop." Ezra crossed the distance between them,

grabbed his hand. Pressed it against her chest, over her racing heart. "Feel that? I'm alive. You're alive. We're both here."

His breath hitched. She could feel his pulse hammering against her palm.

"Kee guides souls between lives, yes. But we're still alive. Still in our seventh life. That's the whole point—this is our last chance to break this." She squeezed his hand. "Kee appeared to both of us. In different ways. To make sure we'd find each other."

"Different ways," Ash repeated slowly, trying to process. "You saw Kee in a dream. I picked up a bleeding kid on the side of the road."

"Same person. Same mission." Ezra's voice was stronger now. "Getting us here. Together."

"Then why disappear?" Ash looked around the clearing again, as if Kee might materialize. "Why not stay and explain?

"Maybe because this part—" Ezra gestured between them. "This is ours. Not Kee's."

Silence fell between them. Heavy. Weighted with her entire life spent searching on one side, a lifetime of rage on the other.

They were standing here. Together. The thing Kee said would trigger the curse.

Ash's jaw tightened. "Kee told me we'd die if we met. That the curse activates the moment we're in the same place."

Ezra's breath caught. "Kee told me the same thing. But also that if we don't meet, we die anyway. Separately. Worse deaths."

"So we're fucked either way." His voice was flat, but his hands were shaking.

"Unless we break it." Ezra took a step toward him. "Kee said this is the seventh life. The last chance. If we fail —if the curse takes us again—there's no eighth life. No reunion. Just nothing. Forever."

Ash looked at her—really looked. At the woman who'd haunted every dream, every moment of peace in his blood-soaked life. The one who'd kept him human when nothing else could.

"You're the one from my dreams," he said quietly. "The one who kept me..." He couldn't finish.

"Human." Ezra's voice broke. "I know. And you're Ash. I've watched you die six times. I can't—" Her hands curled into fists. "I can't watch it again."

"Then we break it." Ash's voice was fierce now, certain. "Whatever this curse is. We break it. Together."

"Kee said we'd meet Veyar. That he'd help us."

"Then we find him." Ash took another step closer. "But first—"

He stopped. Looked at her with something raw and desperate in his eyes.

"I need to know you're real. That this isn't just another dream that disappears when I wake up."

Ezra understood. She'd spent her whole life being called crazy for believing in him. He'd spent a lifetime searching for answers to dreams that made no sense.

Neither of them trusted that this moment wouldn't shatter.

"I'm real," she said.

"Prove it."

Ezra crossed the clearing. Stood in front of him. So close she could feel the heat radiating from his chest.

She reached up slowly, giving him time to pull away. "I've been searching for you my entire life."

"I've been dying without you." His voice was raw. Honest.

Her palm pressed against his chest.

The second her hand touched him, fire exploded beneath his skin.

Ash hissed, jerking back. "Fuck—"

The burning—the same burning that had been there since he entered the forest—erupted into something white-hot. Alive. Like his chest was being branded from the inside out.

His hands went to his shirt, yanking it open. Buttons scattered.

And there—

Blazing beneath his skin like living flame—the symbol.

Gold and red, pulsing with heat, etched into his flesh as if it had always been there, just waiting to ignite.

"What the hell," Ezra breathed.

She reached out, fingers trembling, and touched the symbol gently.

It was exactly like her dreams. Fire incarnate. Beautiful and terrible and real.

The heat didn't burn her. It called to her. Recognized her.

"Just like in my dreams," she whispered, tracing the lines with reverent fingers.

The rage—the constant, suffocating rage that had lived in him since childhood—vanished.

Not suppressed. Not controlled. Gone.

Peace flooded through Ash like cool water on scorched earth. His breathing steadied. His shoulders dropped. The constant tension that had lived in his muscles since he was five years old simply... released.

He stared at her, this woman with her hand on his burning chest, and for the first time in his life he felt human. Whole.

"You're it," he said, voice breaking. "You're the only thing that's ever made me feel like I'm not a monster."

And then he couldn't stand the distance anymore.

He pulled her against him and kissed her.

The world exploded around Ezra.

Not gentle. Not careful. Desperate and consuming and real.

His mouth on hers was fire and relief and every year of searching finally ending. His hands cupped her face like she was something precious, something he'd been searching for across lifetimes.

She kissed him back with everything—all the years of being called crazy, all the nights spent drawing his symbol, all the dreams where she watched him die and couldn't save him.

Heat surged through them both—searing, alive, consuming. The symbol flared brighter beneath his skin where her hand still pressed against his chest. The fire surged up her arm, not burning but fusing. Binding them.

She gasped against his mouth. "Ash—"

"I feel it," he breathed. "I feel everything."

He'd never felt like this. Never. The fire that had burned for violence his entire life—transformed. Not extinguished. Changed. Into something that felt like coming home.

She was shaking in his arms, overwhelmed, and he understood. He felt it too. The magnitude of this moment —six lifetimes of searching, of dying, of being torn apart.

And now—finally—together.

He pulled back just enough to see her face. To make sure this was real.

Her eyes were bright with tears, lips swollen from his kiss, and she was glowing. Actually glowing. Golden light wrapped around them both, pulsing in rhythm with their hearts.

"What's happening to us?" she whispered.

"I don't know." His thumb traced her cheekbone, reverent, like he was afraid she'd disappear. "But I feel whole. For the first time in my life, I feel whole."

"I feel it too." Her other hand came up to his face, cupping his jaw. "Like I've been missing half of myself and now it's back."

His hands slid into her hair, cradling her head like she was the most precious thing in the world.

"I don't know how to do this," he admitted quietly. "I don't know how to be... good."

"Neither do I." Her fingers curled into his shirt, holding him close. "But we figure it out. Together."

"Together," he breathed.

And then he kissed her again.

This time slower. Deeper. Like he was drowning and she was air. Like she was the only thing anchoring him to humanity.

Because she was. She'd always been. The woman from

his dreams. The voice that stopped him from killing. The fire that didn't burn. The only thing in his blood-soaked life that had ever felt right.

Ezra kissed him back with a lifetime of longing, of being called crazy, of knowing—knowing—he was out there somewhere waiting for her.

When they finally pulled apart, both gasping, foreheads pressed together, the golden light around them pulsed stronger.

The symbols on the shrine behind them blazed—all seven responding to their reunion.

The forest hummed with ancient power recognizing what it had been waiting for.

This was what the curse fought against. This was what someone wanted to destroy.

This connection that made them complete.

"Kee was right," Ezra whispered against his lips. "We're supposed to be together. We always have been."

"Then fuck the curse." Ash pulled her closer, his voice fierce. "We don't die this time. We break it."

But even as she said it, something cold settled in Ezra's stomach. A memory from the dreams. A shadow that was always there, always hunting.

She pulled back slightly, her expression shifting. "Ash, there's something you need to know."

He tensed immediately. "What?"

"In my dreams—in all the past lives—there was always someone else." Her voice tightened. "A third person. A man named Saav."

Ash went very still. "Who is he?"

"He's the one who kills us." The words came out

barely above a whisper. "Every time. Every life. He hunts us down and—" Her hands trembled. "He's there at every death. Watching. Sometimes he's the one who does it himself."

Ash's jaw clenched, his protective instinct flaring. "The curse is on him too?"

"I think so. Our names stay the same—mine, yours, his. Always Ezra, Ash, and Saav." She looked up at him, fear and confusion warring in her eyes. "But I don't understand why he keeps killing us. Why he's so driven to destroy what we have."

"Have you met him? In this life?"

"Not that I know of." She glanced around the clearing, suddenly hyperaware of how exposed they were. "But if the pattern holds, he's out there somewhere. And he'll find us."

"Never met anyone by that name." Ash's expression darkened, his hand moving instinctively to where a weapon would be. "And I'd remember."

"Maybe he hasn't found us yet. Or maybe..." She looked around the forest, fear creeping into her voice. "Maybe he's already here and we just don't recognize him."

Ash's hand moved back to his chest, to the fire symbol. "If he's cursed too, why does he keep killing us?"

"I don't know." Ezra's voice was barely a whisper. "In my dreams, he always looked... driven. Like he had to. Like he didn't have a choice either."

Something shifted in Ash's expression—recognition, empathy. "I know what that's like." His voice went quiet. "Spending your whole life being controlled by something inside you. Wanting to stop but not knowing how. Hurting people because that's all you know how to do."

Ezra went still. Took a small step back, her hand dropping from his chest. Her eyes searched his face—seeing him differently now. "You've... hurt people?"

He didn't look away. Didn't try to soften it. "Yes."

The word hung between them. Raw. Honest.

Ezra's breath caught. Fear flicked across her face—not of him hurting her, but of what this means. The man from her dreams, her other half, the one she's been searching for her entire life—he's also a killer. "How many?"

"Too many." His hands curled into fists at his sides. "I've been trying to stop. The rage—it's been there since I was a kid. I thought I was broken. Cursed. A monster." His voice cracked. "But when you touched me just now, it stopped. For the first time in my life, I felt... human."

She was trembling now, processing. In her dreams they were always lovers—passionate, desperate, dying together. But those were glimpses of adults meeting, falling, burning. She never saw what made him who he was. Never saw this.

The connection she'd felt moments ago—that overwhelming sense of wholeness—now warred with the reality standing in front of her. A stranger. A killer. Someone who'd just admitted to taking lives.

"I don't—" Her voice shook. "I don't know you. Not really. The dreams showed me who you were in other lives, but this life—" She gestured at him, at the space between them. "You're a stranger who just told me you've killed people."

He flinched but didn't argue. "You're right."

"And I just kissed you." The words came out strangled, half-laugh, half-sob. "I felt something real—something that terrified me with how right it felt—but I don't even know your last name. Don't know if you're telling the truth about wanting to change. Don't know if—"

"I'm not asking you to trust me." He took a careful step back, giving her space. "I'm not asking you to forgive what I've done. I know what I am. What I've been."

"But you want to change." It wasn't a question.

"I don't know if I can." His voice was raw. "But when you touched me, the rage stopped. For the first time in my life, I felt like maybe—maybe I could be something other than a weapon."

Ezra stared at him. At the pain in his eyes. At the way he'd stepped back, giving her room to run if she wanted to. At the fire symbol still glowing faintly on his chest— the same symbol she'd drawn her entire life.

At the man who, despite everything he'd done, had just stopped three traffickers from taking a child.

She took a breath. Then another.

"Kee said we need to break this curse together." Her voice was steadier now, but wary. "That means I need you alive. That means—" She swallowed hard. "That means I can't run. Even if part of me wants to."

"You should run." His jaw tightened. "I'm dangerous."

"So is Saav." She wrapped her arms around herself, suddenly cold despite the golden light still flickering around them. "He's the one who kills us. Every time. Every life. He hunts us down and—"

Ash's expression darkened. "Then we find him first." Ash's voice was flat, deadly. "Before he gets to us."

Her hands trembled. "He's cursed too. Just like us."

"We have to kill him."

"No." Ezra's voice was sharp. She placed her hand over his heart. "That's not the way—we can't just kill him. If he's cursed like us, maybe he doesn't have a choice. Maybe —" She stopped, thinking. "Maybe if we can break the curse together, all three of us—"

"I stop being a killer." Understanding flickered in Ash's eyes.

"We all do." She met his gaze.

Silence fell between them. The weight of what she was proposing—trusting not just Ash, a confessed killer, but also finding and saving the man who'd murdered them six times over.

"That's insane," Ash said quietly.

"So is everything else about this." Ezra's voice was steadier now. "But Kee said this is our last chance. If we fail—if we die again—there's no eighth life. Just nothing. Forever."

She took a tentative step toward him, not touching, but closer. "I felt something when we touched. Something real. But I also know you're a stranger who's done terrible things. And I don't know if I can trust you. Not yet."

"Fair."

"But I know the curse is real. I know we die if we don't break it. And I know—" Her voice softened slightly. "I know you saved a child tonight. That has to mean something."

"Or maybe I'm just good at pretending to be human when it matters."

"Maybe." She held his gaze. "But we're going to find out. Together. Because we don't have another choice."

The shrine answered.

A crack split the air like bone breaking. The stone trembled. Rain crashed through the canopy in sheets. Lightning seared the clearing white.

The seven symbols blazed—red, blue, green, gold, silver, violet, white. All seven gods responding to their reunion.

Ezra stumbled, but Ash caught her. Pulled her against him, moving in front of her instinctively. A shield.

"Ash—what's happening?"

The ground beneath them shifted. Not breaking—opening. Like the world was creating a doorway.

A voice echoed through the clearing—deep, masculine, ancient and patient:

You're being given a choice.

Ash looked down. Darkness swirled beneath their feet, shot through with stars. A pool of night. A threshold between worlds.

"Veyar," Ezra breathed. "It's him. The god Kee told me about."

The voice came again: Meet me in the space between, and I'll show you how to break what was never meant to be broken. Or stay, and let the curse decide.

Ash turned to face Ezra, still holding her close. The storm raged around them but he only saw her. "Together or stay?"

Ezra looked into his eyes. Saw the same desperate hope

she felt. The same bone-deep certainty that they were meant for this.

She'd spent her entire life searching for proof she wasn't crazy. She'd lost everything for this symbol, this obsession, this man.

And he'd spent his entire life being consumed by rage, trying not to become a monster, kept human only by dreams of her.

Kee had given them one last chance. Seventh life. Final chance to break the curse or be destroyed by it.

"Together?" Her voice wavered, uncertain.

She looked at him—this stranger who was also somehow her other half. This killer who'd saved a child. This man she'd just kissed who terrified her as much as he completed her.

Ash held out his hand. Palm up. Waiting.

Not demanding. Not taking. Offering.

Letting her choose.

"I can't promise I'm worth saving," he said quietly. "I can't promise I won't fail you. But I can promise I'll try. If you'll let me."

Ezra stared at his outstretched hand. At the symbol still glowing faintly on his chest. At the threshold opening beneath them, swirling with darkness and stars.

Kee's voice echoed in her mind: Seventh life. Last chance.

She could walk away. Let the curse take them separately. Die alone but at least die without having trusted a killer.

Or she could take his hand. Risk everything on the

hope that curses could be broken and monsters could be saved.

Her hand trembled as she reached out.

Their fingers touched.

"Together," she whispered.

Ash's grip tightened on her hand. Not crushing. Anchoring.

"Together."

The light swallowed them whole.

The shrine cracked open. The symbols blazed. The ground gave way beneath them and they fell—

Not down.

Through.

Into the space between moments, where time folded back on itself and a god of balance waited to explain what they'd forgotten.

Chapter 4

The Keeper

Ezra didn't scream.

She wanted to. But fear had no voice in that kind of silence—the kind that stripped sound before it could form.

The world folded inward. Heat and wind turning sideways. Her sketchbook tore from her bag and vanished. Hair lashed across her face.

She reached for Ash without thinking.

He caught her mid-fall. Twisted. Pulled her tight against him. Chest to chest. His arms locked around her like armor.

Then came the dark.

Not shadows. Not night.

Pitch—like the world had been erased.

Ezra couldn't see her own hands. Couldn't see Ash, though she felt his chest rising sharply against hers. The void pressed in on all sides, suffocating.

"Don't let go," she gasped.

"I won't." His voice was rough, strained.

The dark went on forever.

Then—impact.

Cold water swallowed them whole. The shock tore them apart. Ezra felt Ash's grip slip as the current pulled them in opposite directions.

She tumbled through liquid darkness, lungs burning, but this wasn't water—not really. It was something else. Something alive. The black pool—a viewing mirror of time itself—dragged her deeper.

Visions slammed into her. Not memories. Fragments.

Death. Over and over. Death.

His body in her arms. Blood. The arrow. His last breath.

Another life—poison. His eyes going dim while she screamed.

Fire consuming him. His hand reaching for her one final time before the flames took him.

Between the deaths, she sensed other moments—laughter, warmth, his hands gentle on her face—but they blurred past too fast, too distorted. The pool didn't want her to see those. It only wanted her to remember how it ended.

Always the same. Him dying. Her broken.

Then the sixth life. Different. Wrong.

Her blood pooling. His hands shaking as he tried to save her. His rage—fire erupting, consuming everything. The world burning because she was gone.

"I can't do this without you."

The words echoed from both their lips across six lifetimes.

She couldn't breathe. Couldn't think. The water pressed in from all sides and she couldn't tell which way was up—

Somewhere in the darkness, separated by the current, Ash was drowning too.

The pool dragged him down, deeper than physics allowed. His lungs screamed but he couldn't surface—couldn't move. The water held him like hands pressing from all sides.

Then the visions came.

Death. Only death.

The first life. The arrow piercing his chest. Her face above him, tears mixing with blood. Watching himself die in her arms.

Then what came after—what he'd never seen before. Her alone, holding his cold body. Time passing in flashes. Her walking to the cliff. Whispering his name. Stepping off the edge.

Second life. Third. Fourth. Fifth.

Different deaths. Blade. Poison. Fire. Each time he left her behind. Each time she survived long enough to choose death over living without him.

Rope. Drowning. Another cliff. A dagger to her own heart.

Between each death, he caught glimpses of something else—moments of light, of her smile, of peace—but they slipped away before he could grasp them. The pool wouldn't let him hold onto the good. Only the ending.

Then the sixth life—the one that broke the pattern.

Her dying first. His rage turning him into a monster.

Fire consuming the Sacred Valley. Kee striking him down before he could destroy the world.

Six lives. Five times his death destroyed her. One time her death turned him into something that had to be killed.

Every single time—his existence was poison.

The visions released him suddenly, violently. Ash surged upward, breaking the surface with a gasp that tore through his chest. His hands clawed at the edge of something solid—stone, ground, he couldn't tell. Everything was silver light and disorientation.

He hauled himself up, coughing, chest heaving—then froze.

His hands. Not his hands.

Younger. Unmarred by scars. The karambit calluses gone. The damage from years of killing—erased.

He looked down. The torn modern clothes were gone. In their place: loose pants, wrapped and tied at the waist. A simple tunic, open at the chest. Bare feet. And the fire symbol—no longer hidden beneath his skin but glowing against his chest, fully visible, pulsing with heat.

"What the hell?" His voice came out wrong—younger, sharper.

Then he remembered. Ezra.

His head whipped back to the pool. She was still under. The surface rippled but she hadn't surfaced.

Terror lanced through him—the same terror from the visions, watching her die over and over. Not again. Not this time.

Ash dove. The water was cold and thick, resisting him. He kicked deeper, eyes burning as he searched the murky darkness. There—a flash of red fabric. He reached, grabbed, pulled. His arms locked around her waist and he dragged her toward light.

Ezra broke the surface gasping, choking, clinging to whoever held her.

"I've got you." Ash's voice. Rough. Desperate. "Don't let go."

Her arms locked around his neck as he hauled them both to solid ground. She felt stone beneath her, felt him collapse beside her, both of them coughing and shaking.

"Ezra—" His hand found her face, turning her toward him. "Are you—"

She opened her eyes and froze.

Ash. But not Ash.

Younger. Twenty-two, maybe. Face leaner, hair longer, eyes the same storm-dark but without the weight of killing behind them. The fire symbol blazed on his bare chest, beautiful and terrifying.

Her breath caught. "What—"

Then she looked down at herself.

Red gown. Fitted at the top, flowing fabric over loose pants. Leather boots.

Her hands—younger, smoother, the self-harm scars from her teenage years erased like they'd never existed.

The clothing hit her like a punch to the chest. She knew this dress. Had seen it in her visions of the first life— the one where they'd stood on the cliff together, fire at their heels, before the arrow took him.

"What the hell?" she whispered.

Ash was staring at her with the same shock, then down at himself—at the simple tunic and wrapped pants. His eyes widened with recognition.

"This is what I was wearing," he said slowly. "In the first life. When I—" He couldn't finish. When I died.

"Me too." Ezra's voice shook. She touched the red fabric, feeling its weight, its reality. "I look eighteen. You look twenty."

The same ages they'd been when they first met. When they first loved. When they first died.

For a long moment, neither of them moved. The weight of what they'd seen pressed down like stone.

Ezra's hands trembled as she pressed them against her stomach, trying to hold herself together. She'd watched him die six times in those visions. Felt every loss. Every grief-soaked choice to follow him into darkness.

And he'd seen her do it. Seen her jump. Seen her choose the rope, the blade, the cliff.

Ash pushed himself to his feet abruptly, putting distance between them. His jaw was tight, eyes dark with something she couldn't read—guilt, horror, fear.

"What?" Ezra asked, still sitting on the stone, water dripping from her gown.

"I saw it all." His voice was rough, scraped raw. "Every time you followed me. Every cliff. Every rope. Every—" He stopped, fists clenching at his sides. "You chose death over living without me. Five times."

"You saw that?" Her voice came out small. Ashamed.

"All of it." He looked at her, and for the first time since they'd met, there was something like devastation in his eyes. "How am I supposed to—how do I live with knowing that every time I die, you destroy yourself?"

Ezra pushed herself to her feet, legs shaking beneath the unfamiliar weight of the gown. "The same way I live with knowing your death turned you into a monster that had to be killed." Her voice cracked. "I watched you burn the world, Ash. Watched Kee strike you down because you couldn't stop. Because I was gone and you—"

"I would've destroyed everything." His throat worked. "In the sixth life—when you died first—I burned everything. The Sacred Valley. The forests. Everything." He looked at his hands—young, unmarred, not yet stained with blood. "I couldn't stop. Even when Kee came, even when the blades pierced me—I screamed your name until there was nothing left."

Silence fell between them, heavy and suffocating.

"We're poison to each other," Ezra whispered. The truth of it sat in her chest like a stone. "We always have been."

"Yeah." Ash's voice was hollow. "We are."

He ran a hand through his hair—longer now, unfamiliar. His eyes swept their surroundings for the first time. The pool stretched behind them, but the forest around them was different—younger, simpler, as if time had folded back on itself. Silver light filtered through the trees, too thin, too strange.

"Where are we?" Ezra's voice came out smaller than she meant, following his gaze.

"I don't know." His jaw worked. Then his eyes found hers again, and something raw broke through. "But we can't keep doing this. You've seen what I become. What we become together. Maybe we shouldn't—"

"Don't." Ezra's voice cut sharp and desperate. "Don't say we shouldn't be together. We already made that choice at the shrine. We held hands and jumped into the void together." She took a step toward him. "The curse doesn't care if we're ready. We're here now. And I'm not—I can't—"

Her voice broke. Tears burned her eyes but she refused to let them fall.

"Why can't we ever just live one full life?" The words tore out of Ash, raw and desperate. "Loving each other? Why does it always end?"

The question hung between them, unanswered and unanswerable.

Then Ash pushed himself away. Abrupt. Cold. Catching himself before he sank too deep. His expression shifted—shuttering, hardening.

"You've seen lives where I'm some kind of...what? Lover? Protector?" His jaw locked, his words rough, cutting. "That's not me. Not now. Not ever. Today, I'm a killer. A hired blade since I was seventeen. The best at it. Paid in coin, blood, silence." He gestured at her, at the space between them. "You're innocent. You're light. And me..." He spat the word like it burned. "I'm poison."

Ezra's body went rigid. Then she tore herself away from him, stumbling back until her shoulders hit a tree.

Her breath came sharp, ragged. "God, I'm such an idiot," she whispered, almost to herself. "Every time I let myself believe...every time I let dreams rule the now—this is what I get."

Her eyes flicked up to his, blazing. "You think you're poison? Maybe you are. Because I can't even tell what's real anymore. I keep holding on to visions of us like they're promises, but all you give me is this..." Her voice cracked, angry at the sound. "This cruelty dressed up like protection."

Her hands fisted in the strange gown. She shook her head hard, as if to fling off the ache clawing through her chest. "Maybe I'm the fool for thinking we could ever have more than a moment."

Ash stayed silent, jaw tight, letting her fury burn. He wanted it—wanted her to hate him if that kept her safe.

But when the shadows shifted at the edge of the clearing, he moved without thought.

His body cut in front of hers, wide shoulders blocking her from whatever approached. His fists curled, muscles taut, ready to break whatever came for her.

Ezra froze. Her heart lurched in her chest. He had just shoved her away—called himself poison, cut her open with words meant to drive her off. But now—instinct put her behind him. Protected.

Confusion tangled with anger. *If he wants me gone, why guard me like I'm worth dying for?*

Her hand twitched, halfway to his back before she pulled it in. The contradiction scraped her raw—his cruelty and his care clashing until she couldn't tell which was truth.

And before she could demand an answer, a voice stirred the air.

Low. Patient. Almost amused.

"Ah. A lovers' quarrel. And you've only just crawled back into each other's arms."

Ezra startled, her pulse stumbling. The words had barely settled before the clearing seemed to breathe.

From the far edge, a figure eased forward—not

walking so much as letting the silver light decide he could be seen. Bare feet kissed the ground without sound. Loose white cloth draped his body, hanging in folds too simple for a king, too timeless for a beggar. His long hair, streaked silver, brushed his shoulders, catching the faint glow without reflecting it back.

But it was his eyes that rooted them. Black. Steady. Devouring. They didn't gleam—they absorbed.

Ash went taut, shifting wider, shoulders squared. His stance told a story: assassin, predator, weapon. But his body stayed angled in front of Ezra, instinct wrapping around her even as his words still rang sharp in the air.

The man tilted his head slightly, expression unreadable. A crease touched the corner of his mouth—almost humor, though it did nothing to ease the pressure crawling along their spines.

"Don't stop on my account," he said. His voice was soft, like stone worn smooth by water, but it carried through the space with ease. "You've fought here before. You'll fight here again."

Ezra's throat went tight. *Before?* The word rattled inside her like loose bones.

Ash's voice cut low, dangerous. "Who are you?"

The figure tilted his head, considering, then stepped closer, the white cloth of his robe shifting like mist. "Once, you asked me the same question. Once, you knew."

Ezra felt her stomach twist. The way he said it—like the weight of time pressed against her ribs.

She forced her voice steady. "That doesn't answer him."

The man's mouth curved. Not a smile. Not mockery. Something between. "I am Veyar," he said at last. "Keeper of what was forgotten. God of the places between."

The name pressed through the clearing like a ripple. Ezra's breath caught.

Veyar. The god Kee had told her about. The one who'd made the pact with them in the first life.

Veyar's gaze lingered on her, deeper than sight, like he was measuring not her body but the pieces of her soul. "You don't remember yet," he said softly, eyes shifting to Ash. "But you will. The pact was never meant to fade."

Ezra's chest tightened. She remembered. Kee had shown her in the dream—the first life, the first death, the deal they'd made with Veyar for seven chances.

But Ash didn't know.

His jaw locked, voice rough as gravel. "What pact?"

Ezra turned to him, guilt flickering across her face. "I —I should have told you. Kee showed me. In my dream." Her voice dropped. "In the first life, when we died, we made a deal with Veyar. Seven lives. Seven chances to find each other and break free."

Ash stared at her, something sharp flashing in his eyes. "You knew? This whole time you knew we had seven lives and you didn't—"

"I was going to tell you," she said quickly. "But every-thing happened so fast. The shrine, the fall—"

"Excuses," he bit out.

Veyar's voice cut through, patient as stone. "She carried the knowledge alone because it was given to her alone. Do not fault her for bearing what you could not."

Ash's fists clenched, but he said nothing.

Veyar's gaze shifted between them. "The pact was simple. Seven lives to find your way back to each other. To break the cycle of destruction. But you've spent six lives dying instead of living."

"And this is the seventh," Ezra whispered.

"The last," Veyar confirmed.

"Memory doesn't vanish," Veyar said. "It waits. You've carried every choice from every life—even the ones you tried to forget. They're still carved into your souls."

Ash's fists curled. His stance never eased, every inch of him a shield he didn't realize he was offering.

Ezra felt it—the contradiction twisting sharper inside her. His words had cut her raw. But his body was still between her and a god.

Ash's jaw tightened. "So we're stuck with them? Doomed to repeat it?"

A ghost of amusement flickered across Veyar's face. "You're already repeating it. He pushes you away to protect you. You chase him despite the pain. The same dance, different life."

Ezra's throat closed. She wanted to demand what he meant, but she could feel the truth of it.

Ash's voice scraped out low. "I didn't choose to love her. I never would've chosen this—not if I knew it meant watching her die."

The words struck her like a blade. Ezra's chest pinched, breath catching sharp. He didn't even look at her when he said it. And it wasn't the Ash she remembered— the ones in her visions, the ones who had loved her across lives. This was a stranger with his face, his voice, his arms still holding the shape of where he'd pulled her from the pool...but everything else, cold.

Her throat burned. The questions clawed at her—*Then why did I remember us? Why did you love me in every life but this one?*—but she swallowed them back. Not here. Not now. The ache was already lodged too deep, and if she let it out, it would shatter her.

Still, he stood in front of her. Shielding her. His body contradicting every cruel word.

It should've been terrifying—standing face to face with a god, hearing him speak of patterns and consequences like he'd watched them play out across lifetimes. By all rights she should've been screaming that she'd finally lost her mind.

But she wasn't.

Because Kee had been right. Veyar was real. The past lives were real. And standing here, watching Ash's body shield her even while his words pushed her away—this felt inevitable. Like she'd been walking toward this moment her entire life.

Veyar's gaze swept between them. He didn't smile. But something in his expression shifted—quiet recognition, as though their pain was familiar. His voice carried through the space, soft as stone worn down by water.

"You always resist," he said, eyes on Ash. Then, gentler, to Ezra: "And you always ache."

She flinched, the words striking too close. But she held her tongue. Not yet.

Veyar's presence filled the space without moving closer. The air bent around him—thick, weighted, patient.

Ash's fists clenched tighter. His voice dropped into a growl. "Then stop speaking in riddles. What do you want from us?"

"Want?" Veyar's head tilted, a faint crease at the corner of his mouth. "As if this were a bargain." His gaze lingered on Ash. "I want nothing. But you—you want to break free of this cycle. To live without watching each other die."

Ezra's pulse stumbled. "Can we?"

"There is a way," Veyar said slowly. "But it requires going back. To the first life. Before the curse was placed."

"Before Saav cursed us?" Ash's voice was sharp with suspicion.

"Yes. If you can prevent the curse from ever being cast, the six deaths you've suffered will never occur. You'll have a chance to live as you were meant to—light and fire, together, without destruction."

Ezra's breath caught. "But how? If we don't remember—"

"Kee and I will remember," Veyar interrupted gently. "We will guide you. But the choices must be yours. That is the consequence I speak of." His gaze sharpened on both of them. "You owe each other the truth. The trust. The willingness to choose love even when every instinct tells you to run."

Veyar turned his eyes on her, and it felt like standing too close to a cliff—dizzying, inevitable. "Of every life you've touched and broken. Every choice repeated."

Her lips parted, but no sound came. Tears crept to her eyes before she could stop them. She felt it in her marrow —Veyar was right. Every life she'd lived, she'd died broken. Her heart still cried out to Ash, but memory cut sharp: in the life before this one, she hadn't waited for him to leave her. She had taken her life into her own hands. She chose to walk away first.

Was that why this Ash was so angry? Was his soul mad at hers? Did he feel betrayed?

Good. He deserved it.

Ezra's arms crossed tight over her chest, as if to hold herself together. She was so tired of aching for him.

Then—

Ash stepped forward, blocking her again, anger sparking hard enough to cut through the dread. "We don't owe you anything."

"No," Veyar said softly. "Not me." His gaze sharpened on Ash, then flicked to Ezra. "But you owe each other."

The words dropped heavy into the silence, thick as stone.

Chapter 5

The Choice

Ezra's throat constricted. *Owe each other.* She wanted to demand what he meant—but the way Ash stiffened beside her told her he already hated the sound of it.

Her breath hitched. *Owe him what? Another broken heart? Another lifetime watching him fall away?*

Her arms locked harder across her chest, nails digging into her sleeves. "I don't owe him anything," she whispered. The words came sharper than she meant, edged with grief she couldn't hide.

Ash didn't look at her—but his jaw flexed like the words cut deep anyway.

Ezra's chest heaved. She jabbed a finger into his chest. "You know what."

Ash caught her hand, moved it aside. He could have snapped her finger with the smallest flick. Instead, he let it go.

She jabbed him again.

Her voice shook, rising. "You don't get to choose for me. Every life you swear you love me—but how can that be true if you keep pushing me away, calling yourself poison? What about me? You think I don't bleed every time you die? You think you're the only one cursed? You think I would choose to grieve the only man I've ever loved, ever wanted?"

Ash's jaw clenched. His voice came harsh, a low growl. "You have no right to die."

"I have every right to die."

"Better me than you. Better I carry it. I won't let you shatter on my account again." His hand ghosted to his hip—for the familiar curve of his karambit—only to find nothing. The blade was gone, like his clothes, stripped when they fell. His stomach turned. "Why am I even arguing? If this is death, or a dream, what does it matter?"

Ezra's eyes flashed through her tears. "You already have. Over and over. And I still—" Her voice cracked. "I still came back."

A single tear slid from her lashes. His chest twisted.

Unless—this was a test. Was his angel testing him?

The clearing shuddered. Veyar's voice rolled sharp as breaking stone.

"No more quarrelling over who hurt who. No more cries of cursed or not. Enough."

The words silenced them like a blade pressed to the throat.

"There are no more chances after this," Veyar said, his gaze hardening. "This is your last life. If you fail—if the curse takes you—there is no eighth cycle. No reunion beyond death. You will cease to exist. Both of you. Completely. Forever."

The ground groaned, roots straining overhead, silver light spilling through the trees like tears. Then Veyar lifted his hand, and the clearing itself seemed to peel open.

The silver dissolved into vision.

Ezra felt her breath still. She saw herself—kneeling before a stone shrine wrapped in vines and wildflowers. Not at Veyar's liminal space, but somewhere in the mortal world, ancient and sacred. Ash knelt across from her, their hands clasped between them.

They looked exactly as they did now—eighteen and twenty, fire mark glowing on his chest, light radiating from hers. But their faces held no fear. No weight of death. Only absolute adoration.

Ash staggered. He was seeing it too. His own eyes, his own hands, reaching for hers with a tenderness that made his current chest ache. This wasn't a stranger. This was him. Choosing her.

"I give you my fire," his past self said, voice rough with emotion. "Every flame, every spark. I am yours. In this life and every life that follows."

Ezra's past self smiled through tears. "I give you my light. Every dawn, every breath. I am yours. Until the stars burn out and beyond."

They leaned forward, foreheads touching, hands still clasped. The shrine glowed brighter, responding to their vow.

Then the vision shifted. A figure materialized beside the shrine—Veyar, but younger somehow, less worn by time. His expression held wonder, as if he'd been startled from a long sleep.

"It has been centuries since anyone found this place," Veyar said, his voice filled with something like awe. "To witness love this pure, this absolute..." He smiled, and it transformed his face. "It reminds me why I remain. Why I keep vigil over the places between."

Past-Ash and past-Ezra looked up at him, still holding each other.

"We want forever," past-Ezra whispered. "But the elders say our union will bring storms. That fire and light together will—"

"Destroy everything," past-Ash finished bitterly. "They're already planning to separate us. To send her away."

Veyar studied them both, seeing the desperation, the defiance, the love that wouldn't bend.

"There is a way," he said slowly. "If you are willing to accept the price."

They both straightened, hope flaring.

"Seven lives," Veyar said. "Seven chances to find your way back to each other. To prove that light and fire can burn together without consuming the world. But—" His expression darkened. "If you fail in the seventh life, if your love still unravels everything around you, I will break your bond. You will never meet again. You will exist on opposite ends of the sky, forever apart."

Past-Ezra's hand tightened on past-Ash's.

"Seven chances to get it right?"

"Seven chances to survive each other," Veyar corrected.

Past-Ash didn't hesitate. "I accept."

"As do I," past-Ezra breathed.

Veyar's eyes gleamed with something ancient and sad. "Then the pact is sealed. May you learn what I could not teach you. May you become what you were always meant to be."

The vision fractured, dissolving back into the clearing's silver silence.

Ash stumbled back, breath ragged. He couldn't hide this time. He had seen it—himself, not as a blade, but as a man begging a god for her. The same fire mark seared under his ribs, branding him again. Poison? Assassin? No. The truth scorched worse: He had chosen her.

The clearing shook again, echoing the weight of it.

Ezra's breath snagged. She wasn't mad. She wasn't alone. The past lives were real. Ash had loved her across lifetimes, just as she'd always known. But the look on Ash's face—haunted, wide with the certainty of it all— made her wish the truth didn't hurt so much.

Ash braced a hand against a tree, as if the wood could steady him. The vision still burned behind his eyes—the memory of a choice he couldn't deny, his own lips forming words he'd sworn he'd never say.

Ezra stepped toward him, hesitant. Her fingers twitched at her side, aching to reach for him but afraid he'd shove her away again. The silence between them wasn't empty—it was filled with everything they'd just seen, everything they couldn't take back.

"Ash..." Her voice cracked. "Do you see now? It wasn't just me. You chose this too."

He looked at her—haunted, torn wide open—and for a second, she thought he might deny it again. His jaw worked like he wanted to spit the word poison one more time. But no sound came.

The mark on his chest pulsed once, ember-deep, syncing with the ache in her ribs.

Ezra's heart lurched. "Why do you keep fighting it?" Her hands balled at her sides. "Even now—when it's right in front of you—why do you still fight me?"

Ash's throat worked. He wanted to tell her the truth: that loving her had never been the hard part. Surviving it was. But the words stuck, jagged and dangerous, and all he managed was a rough whisper.

"Because if I give in...you die." He pressed a hand to his chest, to the mark burning there. "I saw it. In the pool. Five times I died and left you behind. Five times you couldn't survive it. And the one time you died first—" His voice broke. "I became a monster. Either way, loving me destroys you."

The finality in it made her flinch.

Her tears blurred again, but she blinked them away, sharp and furious. "You don't get to decide that. Not for me. Not anymore."

He looked away, chest heaving, every muscle in him still trembling from the vision. He wanted to argue— gods, he wanted to push her back, keep her safe from him, from this—but the memory of his own hand clasping hers, begging a god for another chance, burned hotter than his excuses.

Ezra's voice softened, though it shook. "You weren't lying, Ash. You've loved me before. You've lost me before. But you chose me. Even when the world ended around us —you chose me each and every life."

Her hand hovered between them, trembling in the space just shy of his chest. He didn't move. Didn't stop her.

The clearing felt like it was holding its breath again, silver light humming with the after-echo of Veyar's riddle.

Finally—finally—her palm pressed over the mark searing beneath his tunic. Heat flared under her touch, not painful, but anchoring, pulling his breath out ragged.

His eyes shut. For the first time since the vision, he didn't step back.

Ezra swallowed hard, her voice small but fierce. "You're not poison, Ash. You're mine."

Ash's chest rose sharp, his breath thin as glass.

He hadn't moved since the vision dissolved, but his shoulders trembled, his fists flexing as if he could crush the silence between them.

Ezra's touch lingered, trembling. "You see it now," she whispered. "You felt it. It's real."

Ash's jaw locked. The muscle ticked, but he didn't push her hand away.

For a breath, he let her.

Her palm pressed against the mark, fragile and certain all at once, and he almost—almost—let himself lean into it.

Then he broke the moment, his voice low, fractured.

"Don't," he rasped. Not a command. A plea.

Ezra's throat burned. Her hand shook but she didn't drop it. "Why do you always fight me?"

His breath shuddered out, ragged. "Because if I don't —I won't stop."

The words hung there, dangerous and tender all at once.

Neither moved.

Her fingers stayed curled against his chest. His body stayed rigid, but every muscle betrayed the war inside him.

And in that suspended heartbeat, with gods watching and curses pressing in, they weren't enemies, weren't strangers, weren't lifetimes apart.

They were just two souls on the edge of breaking.

The silence bent.

Then Veyar's voice slid through it, low and certain, as if he'd been waiting for that single fragile heartbeat.

"You cling to what's broken," he said, his tone cutting but not unkind. "But there was a time before the shattering. Before the curse took root."

Ash's head jerked toward him, eyes narrowing. "What are you saying?"

Veyar's gaze lingered on Ezra's hand still pressed against Ash's mark. "The first life. Before Saav cursed you. Before death carved its pattern into your souls. I can send you back to the moment you first met—before the elders tried to separate you, before the storms came, before everything went wrong."

Ezra's breath caught. The mark beneath her palm pulsed hotter, as if it knew. "We could go back?" she whispered.

"You will go back," Veyar said, the clearing vibrating with the weight of it. "To the beginning. When you were only light and fire, meeting for the first time. Before choice turned to curse. Before death became your constant companion."

Ash's jaw tightened. His body stayed between Ezra and the god, even as his voice scraped out harsh, disbelieving. "Why? Why give us that?"

Veyar tilted his head, expression unreadable. "Because endings are written long before they arrive. But beginnings...beginnings can still be tested. And if there is even the smallest chance that light and fire can survive each other—then this is where it must start."

The ground shuddered beneath their feet. Behind Veyar, a new pool appeared—black and still, rimmed with the same seven symbols they'd seen at the shrine.

Ezra's chest rose sharply. "The first life," she breathed, eyes darting to Ash. "Before everything went wrong."

Ash met her gaze, torn raw, his voice low. "And if we fail again?"

Veyar's eyes darkened, the air thick with his answer.

"Then you will not fail again."

The clearing held its breath.

And the pool shimmered, silver now, like a mirror waiting to swallow them whole.

Ezra's throat tightened. The ache in her chest flared again, but this time it wasn't only grief. It was fear. It was hope. Both felt unbearable. "Ash..."

He didn't answer right away. His eyes were locked on the pool, jaw grinding hard. The assassin in him searched for escape, for a trap in the god's offer. But the fire beneath his skin pulsed hotter, steadier—like memory itself was forcing him forward.

At last, he looked at her. His voice was low, almost raw. "We go together. That's the only way this works."

Not a question. A statement. A promise.

A flash struck Ezra—not from the visions she'd just seen, but sharp and immediate. Starlight. His hand in hers. His voice rough with emotion: "I choose you. In every life, I choose you."

She looked at him now, in this transformed body, this impossible place between worlds. Saw the same memory flicker behind his eyes.

"I remember," she whispered.

His jaw tightened. "So do I."

She nodded, a shaky breath leaving her lips. "Always."

Veyar's gaze swept over them both. "Then begin."

The pool rippled. The silver sheen spread outward, climbing the trees, swallowing the clearing until the space itself seemed to dissolve. Roots stretched long and thin like veins of light. The air pulled, heavy and insistent, dragging them toward the water's edge.

Ezra's hand reached for Ash's. He hesitated only a fraction of a second before closing around hers. His palm was rough, his grip unyielding, but the tremor in it betrayed what he would never admit aloud.

The pull grew stronger. The pool glowed brighter. Their reflections wavered on its surface—not the broken, bleeding selves they knew, but younger, unmarked, waiting.

Ezra's heart lurched. Her voice cracked as she whispered, "The first life."

Ash swallowed hard, his chest burning like the mark was searing him from the inside out. He didn't know if this was a blessing or a trap. But he didn't let go.

They stepped to the edge together.

Ezra paused. Looked back at Veyar. "Will we remember? This life? Each other?"

Veyar's expression shifted—something between sympathy and warning. "No. When you enter the first life, you will have no memories of any life after it. You will only know what happened before the moment your seventh-life souls re-enter your original bodies."

Ezra's stomach dropped. "Then how—"

"But Kee and I will remember," Veyar continued. "We will retain all knowledge of what has happened, what will happen, what must change. We cannot alter your destiny or make your choices for you—those must remain yours alone. But we will be there. As advisors. As guides." His eyes darkened. "And if Saav attempts to curse you again, we will intervene where we can. That is all we are permitted to do to help correct this pact."

Ash's jaw tightened. "So we go in blind."

"You go in as you were," Veyar corrected. "Before the curse twisted you. Before six deaths carved scars into your souls. You will meet as light and fire, unburdened. Whether that is blindness or freedom depends on what you choose."

Ezra looked at Ash, fear and determination warring in her eyes. "We won't remember loving each other."

"No," Veyar said softly. "You'll have to fall in love again. Truly. Without the weight of memory forcing your hand. That is the gift and the test."

Ash's grip on her hand tightened. "And if we fail? If we don't—"

"Then Kee and I will guide you toward each other," Veyar said. "But the choice to love, to trust, to fight for each other—that must be yours. Made freely. Made new."

Ezra processed this. The weight of it. "We could forget everything," she whispered. "All of this. We could meet and not even recognize—"

"Then you'll recognize each other the way you were always meant to," Veyar interrupted gently. "Not through memory. Through choice."

The clearing held its breath.

Ezra looked at Ash. "I'm scared."

"Me too." His voice was rough. Honest.

"But we go together?"

"Together."

The pool shimmered, waiting.

Ezra looked at it one more time. Saw the darkness swirling with stars. "Will it hurt? Forgetting?"

"No." Veyar's voice was kind. "You'll simply be as you once were. Before any of this began. And Kee and I will be there, watching, guiding where we can."

She took a breath. "Then I'm ready."

"Are you?" Veyar studied her. "To meet him new? To fall in love without the safety of knowing he loved you first?"

Ezra thought of Ash at the shrine. The way he'd stood between her and danger even while calling himself poison. The way his rage had stopped the moment she touched him.

"Yes," she said. "I'm ready to choose him. Really choose him. Not because of dreams or memories or destiny—but because of who he is."

Veyar inclined his head. "Then go. And may light and

fire finally learn to burn together without consuming everything around them."

They jumped.

The pool swallowed them whole.

And the world turned inside out, pulling them back through time, through lives, through memory—

To the first life.

To the beginning.

Where everything had gone wrong.

And where, this time—with Kee and Veyar watching, guiding, protecting—they would have the chance to make it right.

Chapter 6

Pool Between Worlds

Veyar and Kee

Liminal Space

Kee balanced on a flat rock over the pool's glowing heart, knees drawn in, chewing on a peeled twig—far too casual for the weight of what was happening below.

"They've met," Kee said, mouth full of mischief. "Took them long enough. The stars are already shifting. Want to take bets?"

Across the pool, Veyar didn't look up. His weathered hands stirred the water slowly, coaxing ripples of light like a dream being woken.

Kee tapped a heel against stone. "You could smile, you know. This is supposed to be the good part."

"Good depends on what comes next," Veyar murmured.

A wind passed through the grove—dry, thin, almost

like breath. The branches above didn't stir, but in the water the stars twisted inward, spiraling slowly.

Kee leaned forward, squinting at the reflection. "I still don't understand your logic. You're putting them back at the exact same moment—the first meeting, the first life, when they were already unburdened. They already made their choices there. Without the seventh-life memories, how is this any different? Won't they just... do it all again? The same way?"

Veyar's fingers stilled mid-current. "It would seem that way, wouldn't it?"

"So enlighten me." Kee's tone was sharp with frustration. "What's the point of sending seventh-life souls back into first-life bodies if they don't remember being seventh-life souls?"

"Because," Veyar said slowly, "they will remember. Not consciously. Not in words or images. But in essence." He gestured to the pool where their reflections shimmered. "I am merging their seventh-life souls with their first-life selves. The consciousness belongs to the first life—young, unburdened, making choices freely. But the soul carries the weight of seven cycles."

Kee's eyes narrowed. "That's... that doesn't make sense. How can a soul remember what a mind doesn't know?"

"The same way your body remembers how to breathe without being taught. The same way a heart knows to beat." Veyar's voice took on the cadence of something ancient, something that predated language itself. "Memory is not only housed in the mind, Kee. The soul remembers everything. Every lifetime. Every choice. Every death. It's written into the essence of what they are."

"But they won't know they remember."

"Exactly." Veyar's eyes gleamed. "Their minds will be first-life—innocent, hopeful, unburdened by the weight of six deaths. But their souls..." He paused, letting the weight of it settle. "Their souls will recognize the patterns. Will feel the pull of choices they've made before. Will sense when something is wrong, even if they can't name why."

Kee shook their head. "You're talking about instinct."

"I'm talking about deeper truth. When Saav begins his manipulation, Ezra's soul will recognize the shape of it— even if her mind doesn't remember. When Ash feels rage building, his soul will know it's walked this path before, will fight harder to choose differently." Veyar's hands moved through the water, creating ripples. "And when they meet each other's eyes for the first time, their souls will know. Will remember. Even if their minds think it's the first hello."

Kee was quiet for a long moment, chewing the twig thoughtfully. "So you're... layering them. Seventh-life awareness buried under first-life innocence."

"I am giving them the wisdom of seven lives," Veyar corrected, "while allowing them the freedom of the first. It's a paradox. A contradiction. Which is why it's the only thing that might work."

"That's interference," Kee said flatly. "Massive interference. You said the pact forbids us from altering their choices."

"I am not altering their choices." Veyar's voice was firm. "I am altering their capacity to make them. There's a difference. Their seventh-life souls have earned wisdom through suffering. Why should that wisdom be erased simply because we're returning them to the beginning? The pact says they must choose freely—and they will. But this time, their souls will whisper warnings their minds cannot hear. This time, intuition will guide them where memory cannot."

Kee leaned back, considering. "And if it doesn't work? If their souls remember the pain but not the lesson?"

"Then we will have failed," Veyar said quietly. "But at least we will have given them every possible advantage within the bounds of what I am permitted to do."

"The paradox of time," Kee muttered. "You can't change the past, but you can change who experiences it."

"Precisely." Veyar's expression was grave. "I am sending seventh-life souls into a first-life timeline. It is interference enough. Any more, and I risk breaking the pact entirely— which would shatter them both immediately."

Silence stretched. The pool shimmered with possibilities.

Finally, Kee spoke, voice quieter. "So they'll feel like they know each other. Even though they're meeting for the first time."

"Yes."

"They'll sense danger before it arrives."

"Perhaps."

"And when they're faced with the same choices—to trust or fear, to stay or run—their souls will remember what happened last time, even if they don't know why they feel so strongly about it."

"That," Veyar said, "is my hope."

Kee bit the twig clean through, spitting it into the pool. "That's either genius or catastrophic."

"It's both," Veyar agreed. "Which is why we watch. And wait. And intervene only when the pact allows."

"No pressure," Kee muttered.

"None at all," Veyar said dryly.

"Right." Kee squinted at the pool again. "The last. The final. The end-of-everything-if-they-mess-it-up-again one."

Veyar said nothing.

Kee sighed. "Balance sucks."

"Some things do."

"Light and fire," Kee muttered. "They're supposed to meet in the middle. But he's all rage and she's all restraint. That's not balance—that's just two halves still broken."

"Which is why they must choose it," Veyar said softly. "Not inherit it."

The water shimmered, showing the first life unfolding. Ezra and Ash moving through their world, unaware they were being watched—unaware their seventh-life souls now resided within their first-life bodies.

In the reflection, Ash's fire symbol blazed on his chest, clear and expected. But beside him, something caught Veyar's attention. Ezra turned her head, eyes catching the light, and for just a moment—a flicker—her pupils gleamed with an otherworldly silver sheen. Not reflected light. Something deeper. Something seeing.

Veyar's brow furrowed. He leaned closer to the pool, watching as Ezra paused mid-step, her gaze unfocused as if looking through the world rather than at it.

Kee caught the shift in Veyar's attention. "What is it?"

Veyar hesitated. "Her Sight is changing."

Kee cocked their head. "Changing how?" They squinted at the pool. "I don't see anything different in her."

"You wouldn't. You were never with Visionary." Veyar's voice carried quiet reverence. "I, on the other hand, was. And Ezra has the silver reflection—the mark of someone who has more Sight than a typical oracle."

Kee's eyes widened slightly, the twig pausing mid-chew. "Silver reflection?"

"Not the kind of vision mortals inherit from their bloodlines." Veyar's voice quieted. "Most humans carry only echoes—instincts, fears, fragments. But this..." He gestured at the pool where Ezra's eyes still gleamed with that otherworldly sheen. "This is whole. Unbroken. As if someone gave her not just memory, but Sight itself."

Kee's twig paused mid-bite. "Older than you?"

"Older than all of us." Reverence hushed his tone. His eyes lingered on the pool, as if afraid to speak what he truly thought. "It should be impossible. Unless..."

Kee leaned forward, sharp grin dimming. "Unless what?"

Veyar shook his head, robe shifting in the draft. "I don't know. Merging seventh-life souls with first-life bodies may have... unexpected effects. Perhaps the weight of seven cycles awakened something dormant in her bloodline. Perhaps it's simply her soul remembering powers it once had." He paused. "If the Visionary were still among us, I would ask. But she's gone, and we work with what we have."

Kee leaned back. "So it's a side effect of what you did. The soul-merge thing."

"Possibly," Veyar said. His voice carried a weight that made the cavern feel smaller. "Or perhaps she always had this potential, and seven lives finally unlocked it. Either way, the spiral is already in motion. I began it. Now we must see it through."

The pool brightened, then dimmed. Below the surface, light and flame coiled toward each other—drawn, not merging.

"The world doesn't just need their love," Veyar said softly. "It needs their choice. When both burn with equal fire. When neither leads. When neither follows."

Kee snorted.

The twig cracked as Kee bit it clean through, spitting the nub into the pool. "You sure we can't nudge?"

Veyar's gaze stayed fixed on the water. "Nowhere in the pact does it say we must remain silent."

Kee's eyes lit up. "So...we can?"

"Nudge," Veyar said carefully. "Not push."

Kee's grin stretched wide. "I can nudge."

Veyar's glance lingered, unimpressed.

"...I can try."

The air shifted. Somewhere distant, a shrine groaned.

Kee swung legs over the water's edge. "I like them better this time," Kee said. "Their souls carry more weight. More fire. And did you see the recognition in their eyes when they first touched? Even without memory, they knew."

Veyar's mouth twitched, nearly a sigh. "You're meant to be watching for imbalance, not indulging your appetite for spectacle."

"I am watching. The boy's soul is a walking fault line. It's perfect."

"I doubt Ash would appreciate being called a boy—especially by someone who appears to be a child."

Kee hopped upright on the rock, arms folded tight. "I'm considered a young adult by their standards. Some even live alone. On the streets."

Veyar waved one dismissive hand. "Yes, yes. And your assessment of Ezra?"

Kee rocked back on heels, considering. "She's steadier. Quieter. A bit dull, like you." Then, after a shrug: "But still standing."

Veyar nodded once. "There is nothing more for us to do. Now we wait."

Kee crouched low again, chin nearly to knees, eyes fixed on the glowing surface.

Fire curled tighter around light—drawn like tides.

And beneath it all, something deeper shifted.

Not light. Not flame.

Something watching.

Something waiting.

The pool flared once—then stilled.

Veyar's voice came low, like the breath of the grove itself.

"The world is turning them back to the beginning."

Kee's head angled, eyes glinting. "The first life?"

Veyar nodded once. "Where the bond was forged. Where the curse began. Let us see...if they can survive the truth of their own origin."

The water darkened, swallowing the fire and light whole. When it opened again, the pool did not show the cavern.

It showed another world.

Part Two

The First Life

Chapter 7

The Shrine

The shrine rose from the riverbank—stone veined with moss, half-swallowed by ivy and time. No one came here anymore. The old gods had gone silent two centuries past, and the tribes of the Sacred Valley had learned to worship themselves.

But Ezra loved the quiet. Loved that this place was forgotten.

She sat cross-legged on sun-warmed stone, charcoal smudging her fingertips as she sketched the way light fell through leaves. The air tasted of cedar and smoke and the faint sweetness of wet stone. Birdsong threaded through the branches. The river whispered below.

Peace. Solitude. Freedom from the weight of visions she hadn't asked for and a future she couldn't escape.

Ezra closed her eyes for a moment, exhaling slowly. The familiar pressure building behind her temples—a vision trying to surface. She waited, breathing through it.

The charcoal snapped in her hand.

She opened her eyes, the vision, never came forward. She breathed a sigh of relief. She was hoping for a morning of solitude without interference.

She set the broken pieces aside, reaching for a new stick. The river hummed its quiet song. A breeze shifted through the leaves overhead. Her hand moved across the page again, tracing shadows and light.

Then the air changed.

Not wind. Not movement. Just a shift—like the forest itself had drawn breath and held it.

Ezra's hand stilled. Her pulse kicked sharp and sudden.

Someone was watching.

She rose slowly, charcoal falling forgotten to the stone. Her eyes scanned the tree line, the shadows between trunks, the places where sunlight didn't reach.

Nothing.

But her skin prickled with awareness. The hairs on her arms stood on end.

A twig snapped.

Ezra spun.

A man stood at the edge of the clearing. Tall. Broad-shouldered. Dressed in the dark leathers of the Fyr tribe, a blade strapped across his back. His skin was brown and sun-warmed, his black hair tied back from a face that was all sharp angles and harder edges. But it was his eyes that stopped her breath—storm-dark, burning with something that wasn't quite rage but felt just as dangerous.

Fyrwarden.

Her heart kicked against her ribs. She'd heard the

stories. Mercenaries. Killers. Warriors who felt nothing but the fire they wielded.

She should run.

She didn't.

Something in her today felt braver than normal. Steadier. Like she'd faced down danger before and survived it.

"This is Kireva land," she said, lifting her chin.

His mouth curved—not quite a smile, more like an acknowledgment of her audacity. "The seven shrines, although most are destroyed, belong to no tribe. They are sacred ground."

"Then we're both trespassing."

He took a step forward. Not aggressive. Testing. "What's a Kireva Oracle doing so far from her village alone?"

"Sketching." She gestured to her abandoned charcoal. "What's a Fyrwarden doing hunting this far south of Kireva?"

"I'm not hunting." Another step. "I'm looking."

"For what?"

His gaze locked with hers. The air between them thickened, charged. "I don't know yet."

"Well, you found an empty shrine." Ezra bent to gather her charcoal and sketchbook, movements deliberate. "I should go. My father will worry if I'm gone too long."

She moved to step past him, angling toward the path that led back through the trees.

He shifted. Not blocking her exactly—just occupying the space she needed to pass through.

Ezra stopped. Her pulse hammered. She should be

afraid. Everything about him screamed danger—the blade, the controlled violence in every movement, the fire she could sense coiled beneath his skin.

But fear wasn't what made her breath catch.

It was him. His presence. The way danger seemed to pull her closer instead of pushing her away. She didn't understand it—this stranger should terrify her, send her running back to the village. Instead, something in her chest tightened with recognition, like her body knew him even though they'd never met.

"You're in my way," she said, voice steadier than she felt.

"So move me."

The challenge hung between them.

But something flickered in his eyes—heat that had nothing to do with fire magic. His gaze dropped to her mouth for just a heartbeat before returning to her eyes. Like he was as caught off guard by whatever this was as she was.

Ezra didn't think. Her body moved on instinct—the training Torin, her adopted father, had drilled into her for years came to the surface. She darted right, low and fast, arm sweeping toward his ribs.

He caught her wrist.

Not hard. Not punishing. Just long enough for her to feel the strength before he let go.

Heat flared where his fingers had been.

Ezra came again, sharper this time. A twist of her hip, heel snapping toward his side. His boot met hers midair, slowing the force, sliding past in a way that left her calf dragging against leather.

Too brief to mean nothing. Too real to forget.

"You're untrained," he said.

Her teeth clenched. "I'm eighteen. I've trained, just never fought, that's not the same thing."

She spun, elbow slicing toward his chest. He shifted aside, palm brushing her shoulder as he guided her past. The contact burned.

"I'm not some sheltered village girl," she snapped, heat rising in her cheeks. "I've trained. I've seen things."

His eyes darkened—not mocking, but assessing. Like he was recalculating what she was.

He stepped into her reach, blocking her next strike with the flat of his arm. Their bodies pressed together, shoulder to chest. Close enough that she felt his breath stir her hair.

The Eye of Feeling opened without warning.

A flash—vision, raw and true. His hand cradling her face. Her fingers tangled in his hair. Laughter like sunlight. A kiss that tasted of smoke and want and coming home. The certainty of it slammed through her chest, undeniable as bone.

She gasped, stumbling back half a step.

"But have you lived them?" His voice rumbled low, dangerous, unaware of what she'd just seen.

She shoved back harder, trying to put distance between them. Her skin prickled with heat and something else—the vision still burning behind her eyes. His hands on her face. Her fingers in his hair. That impossible certainty

"You don't know anything about me," she said, voice sharper than she meant.

His eyes sparked—not offended, intrigued. "Twenty-two. Head Fyrwarden." A turn of his wrist caught her forearm, spun her past him, but without force. "I've lived more than you want to imagine."

"So have I." The words came out before she could stop them.

He paused mid-step, something shifting in his expression. "Have you?"

She didn't answer. Couldn't. Because the truth was she didn't know anymore—didn't know if that vision was future or past or something her mind had invented to make sense of this pull between them.

She turned the momentum into a kick. He deflected, his palm catching her ribs. The heat of it soaked through her tunic, steadying her instead of stopping her.

They circled. One step, then another. The river kept time.

He was faster than she'd anticipated—but he held back. Every block was careful. Every counter gave her space to breathe. Like he was testing her, not trying to win.

Like he was trying to see her.

And gods help her, she was letting him.

Every motion drew them closer. Every touch lingered longer than combat required. Her skin burned where his palm had steadied her ribs. Her pulse kicked faster with each near-miss.

She leapt, spinning, aiming high. He caught her midair, arm braced across her middle, pulling her back against his chest.

The world went still.

Her spine fit against him like it had always belonged there. His chest rose and fell against her back. His breath hitched—she felt it, rough and unguarded. His palm spread across her stomach, fingers splayed, burning through the fabric of her tunic.

Heat surged through her. Not fear. Not the fire she sensed in him. Something else. Something that felt like—

Like—

She elbowed him, hard enough to jar her own arm more than his stomach. His grip loosened. Instead of breaking away, she twisted—playful, dangerous—and sprang onto his back. Arms wound around his shoulders, her lips brushing his ear.

"Truce," she whispered.

The air shifted.

His body stilled beneath her—not in refusal, but in something that felt like surrender. His head tilted toward her, just slightly, and she felt the tension in his shoulders release.

Ezra dropped from his back, spinning to face him. Their eyes locked.

Then she struck.

Her palm pressed flat to his chest.

The moment her hand touched him, fire surged up her arm.

Not surface heat. Not simple warmth. A force that seized her blood, flooded muscle and marrow, rushed through her veins like molten gold.

The Fyr sigil blazed beneath her palm—red and gold and alive.

And Ash—

His whole body felt alive, yet every sensation was almost too intense. His eyes squeezed shut as though the fire under his ribs had been waiting to be tamed just for her.

What remained was raw. Wounded. Real.

"What are you?" His voice was barely more than a rasp.

She tried to pull her hand back, but his palm pressed over hers, holding her against him. His grip trembled.

"I feel everything." The words broke from him like confession. Like curse.

Ezra's breath caught.

She knew what that meant.

Fyrwardens didn't feel. Not pain, not joy, not tenderness. They were weapons forged in silence—trained to sense only what was useful in battle. But emotion? Love, sorrow, pleasure? Burned out of them until only discipline remained.

And now—here—Ash's voice was raw with it. Not chosen. Not learned.

Felt.

With her.

The fire around them didn't rise in fury. It curled low at their feet. Bowed.

Ezra swayed, heart pounding as though it wanted to tear free of her chest. She stared at him—the crack in his composure, the pain that looked too much like yearning, the way his grip trembled just enough to betray that he was holding on to more than her hand.

"What's your name?" he asked, voice rougher than before.

"Ezra." She said it simply, as if she'd been waiting for him to ask.

Something flickered across his face when she said it—like the name had struck him physically.

"I'm Ash."

"Ash." She tried it on her tongue, soft and reverent.

His breath caught. She saw it—the way his shoulders tensed, the slight shiver that ran through him.

For a moment they only stared at each other, the shrine hushed and holy around them.

His hand fell from hers.

He should have walked away.

He didn't.

Neither did she.

The silence between them was taut, electric. Not the silence of restraint, but of recognition.

"I should go," Ezra whispered, though her feet didn't move.

"You should," Ash agreed, though he didn't move either.

But neither of them left.

The space between them held. Bright. Dangerous. A line drawn straight through the air that neither had any name for.

At last—finally—Ezra stepped back. The loss of contact felt like cold water after fire.

She gathered her things with shaking hands. Charcoal. Sketchbook. The pieces of her solitude now irrevocably changed.

When she looked back, Ash was still watching her. Storm-dark eyes tracking every movement.

"Will I see you again?" The question escaped before she could stop it.

His jaw worked. Then, rough and honest: "Yes."

Not a promise. A certainty.

Ezra turned and fled into the trees, heart hammering, skin still burning where his hand had been.

The forest closed behind her, leaves settling back into silence. The shrine stood empty once more—or nearly so.

Ash remained in the clearing, chest heaving, fire bowing at his feet. He had come to the shrine looking for something.

He'd found her.

And nothing would ever be the same.

The walk back to Fyr should have cleared his head.

It didn't.

Every step burned. The mark on his chest pulsed hot beneath his tunic, syncing with a rhythm that wasn't his. The memory of her palm—small, certain, devastating— refused to fade.

I feel everything.

He'd said it out loud. Admitted the impossible.

And she'd known. He'd seen the recognition in her eyes, the wonder and fear tangled together.

Fyrwardens didn't feel.

Until her.

Ash was halfway through the pine grove when the air changed.

Not wind. Not movement. Just a shift—like the forest itself held its breath.

"Fyrwarden."

Saav stepped from the shadows between two ancient

cedars. Tall, lean, with the kind of face that looked carved rather than born. His robes were Kildra gray, edged in silver thread that caught the dying light. Mage markings spiraled up his forearms in patterns that seemed to shift when Ash wasn't looking directly at them.

Ash's hand went to his blade. "Mage."

"Easy." Saav's smile was slow, practiced. "I'm not here for trouble. Just passing through. The Veyona tribe sent word—their elder took ill, asked for protections on their fields." He gestured vaguely eastward, as if the errand explained everything.

Ash said nothing. The heat in his chest pulsed hotter.

Saav's eyes tracked over him, lingering on the flush still high in his cheeks, the way his chest rose too fast, the faint scorch marks on his tunic. His expression shifted to something like concern. "You look...unbalanced. Have you encountered something?"

"No."

"Are you certain?" Saav took a step closer, voice dropping. "By the looks of you, I'd say you crossed paths with the Oracle. The Kireva girl who wanders too far from her tribe."

Ash's jaw locked. The lie came swift and automatic. "I've seen no Oracle."

Saav had warned him weeks ago—tales of a Kireva girl who killed without remorse, whose visions drove men mad, whose touch corrupted fire itself. Ash had half-believed it then. Enough to investigate. Enough to track her to the shrine.

But the woman he'd just fought wasn't cruel. Wasn't

evil. She was light and laughter and belonging, and when she'd touched him, his fire had bowed.

Saav was lying. Or wrong. Either way, Ash wasn't letting him near her.

Saav studied him for a long beat. "Strange. Because the imbalance in your fyr is unmistakable..."

"No." Ash stepped back sharply, fire flaring beneath his ribs. Not in defense. In warning.

Saav's hand stilled, the glow fading. His expression didn't change, but something cold flickered behind his eyes. "You're refusing aid from a Kildra mage? That's...unwise."

"I'm fine," Ash said, voice flat. "Your protections are needed elsewhere. The Veyona fields, you said."

A pause. Then Saav's smile returned, thin and knowing. "Of course. Forgive my concern." He inclined his head—respectful, but with an edge of something darker beneath. "May your fire burn steady, Fyrwarden."

He turned and melted back into the trees.

Ash stood frozen, pulse hammering. The heat in his chest hadn't dimmed. If anything, it burned hotter—protective, possessive, refusing to be cleansed or corrected or touched by Kildra magic.

He'd lied to a mage.

He'd never refused tribal aid before.

And he'd do it again.

Because whatever had happened at the shrine—whatever she had done to him—was his. Not Saav's to fix. Not anyone's to take away.

Ash turned toward Fyr and walked faster, the memory of her name still burning on his tongue.

Ezra.

Chapter 8

The Aftermath

Ash didn't wake so much as come back into his body.

The room was still dim, cast in the lavender-gray of pre-dawn light that filtered through the ivy-draped slats of the citadel walls. Smoke trailed faintly from the hearth—a dying memory of last night's fire. His breath came slow and measured, like it belonged to someone else.

He should have been empty. Clean. The nightly burning should have taken everything—every ache, every longing, every unwanted feeling seared away in his sleep until nothing remained but useful sensation.

It always had before.

But tonight, he'd dreamed.

Not the cleansing void Fyrwardens were supposed to sink into—true dreams. Her face in firelight. Her laugh, bright and unexpected. The phantom weight of her hand still burning against his chest.

The burning hadn't touched it. Hadn't even tried.

Like his fire recognized her and refused.

Ash pressed a hand to his ribs, where the mark pulsed hot beneath his skin. The ache was still there. Deeper now. Sharper.

I feel everything.

The words he'd spoken yesterday at the shrine weren't supposed to survive the night. Fyrwardens didn't feel. That was the whole point. Every night, the pain of their bodies—every emotion that tried to root itself during the day—burned away in their dreams. Distance. Angles. The weight of a blade. The temperature of flame. Those remained. Everything else turned to ash by morning.

Not this.

Not the ache that pulsed beneath his ribs every time he thought her name.

Ezra.

Ash sat up slowly, the thin blanket slipping from his chest. His body moved without the usual numbness. There was a tightness in his shoulders, a subtle pull along his ribs.

He lifted a hand and flexed it. Red lines traced his knuckles, barely visible unless the light caught them—like veins of ember beneath his skin.

His fyr, reacting to her. Marking him.

It had never done that before. Fire answered to Fyrwardens, not the other way around. It didn't reach out. Didn't mark. Didn't choose.

But it had chosen her.

The mark on his chest throbbed warm beneath his

palm. Not painful. But present in a way it had never been before.

She confused him.

Saav had warned him weeks ago—at first just whispers. Rumors spreading through the tribes about a dangerous Oracle. A Kireva girl whose visions drove men mad, who killed without remorse, whose very touch corrupted fire.

As Head Fyrwarden, Ash had investigated. Watched from a distance. Followed her through the market plaza, saw how she moved—careful, quiet, like she was afraid of taking up too much space. Overheard her mention the shrine to a merchant selling charcoal.

He'd followed her there, expecting... he didn't know what he'd expected.

What he'd found was a girl who sketched in silence and moved through the world like she was afraid of breaking it.

Nothing like the warnings. Nothing like the danger Saav had described.

And yet—his fire had bowed to her. His body had responded to her touch in ways it never had before. The nightly burning had failed.

She confused him in ways that felt dangerous for entirely different reasons.

And yesterday, when Saav appeared on the path after the shrine—testing him, searching his face for signs of corruption—Ash had lied right back. Told him nothing. Protected her without fully understanding why.

He should have questioned it. Why Saav had been

there at all. The path from the shrine didn't lead to Veyona lands—Saav's excuse about protections on their fields didn't match his direction. And the timing was too convenient. Like he'd been watching. Waiting.

But Ash had been too focused on hiding what happened. On keeping Saav away from her.

The realization sat heavy in his gut: he'd chosen her over his own tribe's counsel. Over a mage who'd guided Fyrwardens for generations. Over everything he'd been taught about loyalty and duty.

He shouldn't want to see her again.

That was the first problem.

The second was worse—he was going to anyway.

Ash crossed the room barefoot, toes brushing worn floorboards, and splashed water onto his face from the clay basin near the window. Cold. Sharp. Grounding. He gripped the rim, let the water drip down his jawline, and stared out the slatted wall.

The mountain loomed to the west, jagged and sharp and veiled in mist. To the east, the valley yawned open— soft hills and long, sloping stretches of pine forest. Somewhere past that was the river. Somewhere beyond the river, Kireva land.

Somewhere out there, she was waking too.

The thought made his pulse kick in a way that should've been impossible.

He turned away, jaw tight, and dressed in silence. Black linen undershirt. Woven leather armor, cracked at the shoulders but still firm. Metal cuffs over his forearms, one dented from training. He didn't bother with the ceremonial cloth today. He wasn't in the mood to look like a priest.

When he stepped out onto the upper platform, the wind met him with a chill that tasted like smoke and coming rain.

Morning began the same way every day. First light rose behind the distant trees. The vines shimmered faintly with dew. A few of the elder apprentices moved along the sparring circle, sweeping away loose branches with long-handled brooms. In the central ring, Thorne was already stretching, shirtless, his long braid tossed over one shoulder as he moved through warm-up strikes.

"Look who didn't bleed out in his bed," Thorne called without looking.

Ash grunted and stepped onto the stone platform beside him. "Disappointed?"

Thorne smirked. "A little. I owe Anok five shards. He said you'd survive. I said you'd brood yourself to death."

"Sorry to disappoint."

"You don't look sorry." Thorne jabbed a hand in his direction. "You look like someone who just discovered fire for the first time. What happened yesterday?"

Ash dropped into a crouch, stretching his hamstrings. "Nothing."

"Right. Nothing." Thorne's grin sharpened. "That's why you're practically vibrating."

Ash didn't answer. Couldn't explain it. Couldn't put words to the way everything had shifted when her palm pressed against his chest. The way his fire—his own gods-damned fire—had bowed at her feet like it recognized something he didn't.

The ring was cool beneath their boots. The mountain wind swirled low around them. Ash took his stance. Focused. Breathed.

Thorne struck first, fast and loose. Ash parried, spun, blocked low. Their bodies moved through old patterns, but his limbs felt different today. Not slower—sharper. More aware.

Every sensation was amplified. The scrape of stone beneath his boots. The pull of muscle across his shoulders. The way air moved when Thorne's blade cut past his ribs.

He felt it all.

And it terrified him.

"See?" Thorne said between blows. "You're distracted. What's in your head?"

Her. Everything about her.

"Nothing," Ash lied.

Thorne knocked him to the ground. Ash rolled hard, planted a hand, and launched back up with a low sweep and sharp flip-kick, letting momentum drive a punch straight toward Thorne's chest—more force than finesse.

Thorne caught it—but just barely. The block landed with a dull crack against his forearm. "Damn. You trying to kill me or prove something?"

Ash didn't answer. He just needed to bleed off whatever this was. This fire lodged in his ribs ever since the Oracle touched him. This feeling that had no name and no place in a Fyrwarden's body.

He twisted, elbowed low, spun wide. Thorne ducked, pivoted, came back in with a knee aimed at Ash's side.

It connected. Hard.

Pain.

Sharp. Real. Immediate.

Not the dull awareness of impact he was used to. Not the distant knowledge that his body had been struck. Actual pain—nerves screaming what they'd been trained to ignore.

His breath hitched. For half a second, he froze.

Thorne noticed. His eyes narrowed. "You felt that."

It wasn't a question.

Ash stepped back, chest heaving. His hand moved to his ribs where the blow had landed. Warmth spread beneath his palm—not injury, but awareness. Sensation flooding back into places that had been numb for years.

"Ash." Thorne's voice went serious. He lowered his blade. "What's happening to you?"

"I don't know." The admission came out rough, reluctant.

Thorne studied him for a long moment. "This is about yesterday. About whoever you met." His expression shifted—surprise, then something like concern. "Did someone do this to you? A mage? A—"

"She didn't do anything." The words came out sharper than intended. Protective. "She just...touched me. And my fire responded."

"Your fire bowed to her."

Ash's silence was answer enough.

"Gods." Thorne scrubbed a hand over his face. "An Oracle?"

"It doesn't matter."

"It matters if she's breaking your fyr. You're feeling things, Ash. Pain. Emotion. That's not—" Thorne cut himself off, jaw working. His voice lowered, "That's dangerous. For all of us. If the elders find out you're compromised—"

"I'm not compromised."

"You're standing here arguing about a girl you met yesterday. That's the definition of compromised."

Ash turned toward the railing, gripping the worn wood. The valley spread out below, endless green and shadow. Somewhere out there, she was going about her day. Sketching, maybe. Moving through her village unaware that she'd upended his entire world.

Not thinking about him.

The thought sat bitter in his chest. Wrong. Sharp. He didn't know what to call this feeling—this gnawing certainty that she'd moved on while he stood here unable to think of anything else.

Was this what jealousy felt like? Inadequacy? He had no frame of reference. Fyrwardens didn't experience this. Didn't lie awake wondering if they'd made an impression. Didn't care.

But gods, he cared. About her. About whether yesterday had meant anything. About whether she felt even a fraction of what had torn through him when she touched his chest.

He hated it. This vulnerability. This need.

And he couldn't make it stop.

"So what are you going to do?" Thorne asked quietly.

Ash's knuckles went white against the wood. "Stay away from her."

Thorne was quiet for a long moment. Then: "You're a terrible liar."

Ash's mouth twitched despite himself.

Because Thorne was right. He was going to see her again. He had to. The alternative—never knowing if what he'd felt was real, never understanding what she'd woken inside him, never hearing her voice again—

That was unbearable.

And that terrified him more than any battlefield ever had.

The day passed in a haze of forced normalcy. Drills. Meals. Duties. Ash moved through them with mechanical precision, his body going through motions while his mind circled endlessly back to the shrine.

To the way she'd looked at him when their eyes met across the clearing. Not with fear or reverence, but recognition. Like she'd been searching for him without knowing it.

To the moment when her hand pressed against his chest and his fire bowed. The way she'd gasped and stumbled back, eyes wide with something he couldn't name. Shock, maybe. Or fear. Or wonder.

He wanted to know which.

He wanted to know everything about her—what made her laugh, what made her afraid, why her touch had unraveled something inside him he didn't know existed.

The wanting itself was dangerous. The fact that he couldn't stop it was worse.

By evening, he found himself on the outer ledge again —the place where the wind came cold and wild, where the stars stretched unbroken across the sky. This was where he always came when the burn inside got too loud.

He crouched, arms resting across his knees. Just breathing. Just trying to feel something steady.

"You've got that look again."

Ash didn't turn. "Kee."

"Nice to see you too, gloom prince."

Kee padded barefoot across the stone, twig clenched between teeth. Hair like a thunderstorm that never broke. Mischief in every step. Kee dropped down beside him, legs swinging over the edge without a care in the world.

"You've been brooding harder than usual," Kee said, voice pitched somewhere between amused and knowing. "Worried someone might've caught you smiling?"

"I didn't smile."

"You did. Yesterday. At the shrine." Kee's grin was sharp. "I was watching."

Ash's jaw tightened. Of course Kee had been watching. The gods saw everything—especially when mortals were trying to rewrite their own fates.

Kee nudged him with an elbow. "So. You liked meeting her."

He said nothing.

"You're thinking about seeing her again."

Still nothing.

Kee drew idle circles in the dust with one toe, voice going quieter. "Good. You should. But you need to move fast."

Ash's head turned sharply. "What does that mean?"

The playfulness drained from Kee's expression. "It

means those stories Saav's been spreading? The ones about the dangerous Oracle who corrupts fire?" Kee's voice lost its playful edge. "People are starting to believe them. Not just Fyrwardens. Kildra. Veyona. Even some of her own tribe are getting nervous."

Dread coiled cold in Ash's gut. "What kind of people?"

"The kind who think a dead Oracle is safer than a living one." Kee met his eyes. "Saav knows you lied to him yesterday. And he's patient. Saav doesn't need to curse her himself if someone else does the work first."

Ash's hands curled into fists. "She doesn't even know she's in danger."

"Exactly." Kee stood, brushing dust from legs. "She's out there sketching, completely unaware, while people sharpen their fear into something sharp enough to kill her with. Interesting problem, that. What someone might do about it."

"Why are you telling me this?"

Kee's grin flickered back, but it didn't reach eyes that suddenly looked older than time. "Because you've got a door inside you. And it's starting to open. What comes through that door—" Kee shrugged. "Well. That's up to you."

Then Kee was gone—not walking, not leaping. Just...no longer there.

Ash stayed long after, bones chilled, but fire still coiled beneath his ribs.

When he finally lay back on the stone, staring up at the stars, it wasn't fear that twisted in him.

It was purpose.

He'd see her again. Soon. Before Saav could poison any more minds against her.

Before it was too late.

And this time, he wouldn't just protect her from a distance.

He'd make sure she knew she wasn't alone in this.

Whatever *this* was.

Chapter 9

The Eye of Memory

Ezra woke with her hand still pressed to her ribs, as if feeling for his palm there.

Dawn had not broken. The window was a thin rectangle of dark blue, stars fading slow. Her skin burned where it should have been cool. She lay still, listening to her own pulse, the new rhythm it had taken.

Yesterday at the shrine, something had changed. Not just in Ash—though the way he'd looked at her, the way his fire had bowed at their feet, still made her breath catch. But in herself.

She had felt it the moment her palm touched his chest. Not just heat. Not just the surge of his fyr answering hers. Something deeper. Older. A door opening inside her that had always been locked.

The vision had come without warning—his hand cradling her face, her fingers tangled in his hair, laughter like sunlight, a kiss that tasted of smoke and want and coming home. The certainty of it had slammed through her chest, undeniable as bone.

A veil had lifted, revealing something that had always been there, waiting.

But this morning, lying in the pre-dawn darkness, something else stirred behind her eyes. A deeper awareness. A pull toward something she couldn't name.

Ezra sat up slowly, bare feet finding cool earth. The longhouse smelled of dye and lavender, the faint steam of morning fires just beginning to catch outside. Across the room, Sela rolled in her bedding, groaning.

"You're already up?" Her voice was scratchy with sleep. She squinted at Ezra, then sat up sharply. "You look different."

Ezra's hand went to her hair, smoothing it self-consciously. "I look the same."

"No." Sela swung her legs out of bed, eyes narrowing with the focus of someone who'd known Ezra since before either of them could walk. Since their families had lived side by side, mothers dyeing cloth together while their daughters chased each other through the bloomthistle fields.

Since the fever took Ezra's parents and Torin opened his home without hesitation, gathering Ezra into their family like she'd always belonged there.

Sela saw her. Really saw her. Always had.

"Your eyes. They're...brighter. And you're blushing." Her grin turned wicked. "You're thinking about him."

Heat flooded Ezra's cheeks. "I am not—"

"The Fyrwarden. The one you fought yesterday at the

shrine." Sela stood, crossing to Ezra with the easy confidence that had always come naturally to her—all the boldness Ezra had never quite managed to claim for herself. "I saw your face when you came back. You didn't look scared. You looked..."

"What?"

Sela's voice softened, and something shifted in her expression—affection, understanding, the fierce protectiveness of someone who'd held Ezra through nightmares about parents she could barely remember. "Alive. Like you finally stopped apologizing for taking up space."

The word settled between them, true and terrifying.

Ezra looked away, throat tight. Sela had always seen through her careful walls, had spent years trying to coax her into being bolder, louder, more herself.

"It was just a fight."

"Mmm." Sela didn't sound convinced. She moved closer, studying Ezra's face with the attention of a sister—not by blood, but by choice. By years of shared grief and shared laughter and shared secrets whispered in the dark. "Is that why you kept touching your chest last night? Like you could still feel his hand there?"

Ezra's breath caught. She had done that. Several times. Without meaning to, her palm had pressed where his had been, seeking that warmth, that connection that had made her feel—

Whole.

"Get dressed," Sela said, squeezing Ezra's shoulder—a gesture as familiar as breathing. "I'll cover for you with the dye work. You look like you need to think." Her smile turned gentle, knowing. "And maybe you need to stop running from whatever this is."

Ezra dressed quickly—pale blue wrap-dress, loose sleeves brushing her wrists. She slipped out before the village fully woke, before Orielle could assign her Oracle duties in the market square.

Her feet carried her down the narrow trail past the looms and cooling kilns, through bloomthistle and silver grasses, until the reflecting spring came into view.

The water lay wide and still, edged in pale stone. The surface shimmered faintly, as if the spring remembered everything poured into it—war, peace, vows, betrayals. That was what the elders said. That memory lived here.

Ezra knelt at the rim and pulled a crumpled scrap of paper from her pocket. Charcoal slipped from the braid at her temple, blackened her fingertips as she drew.

High cheekbones. Strong jaw. A straight nose, tilted slightly at the bridge. Lips too full to belong to a warrior, lashes so thick they shadowed when his eyes closed.

It wasn't perfect. It never was.

A breeze caught the page. Before she could pin it down, a voice startled her.

"Lovely drawing."

Her heart lurched. She pressed her hand to her chest and turned.

An old man stood at the clearing's edge. His robes were the color of stone and ash, his white hair tied in a loose knot, a sprig of sage tucked behind his ear as if forgotten there. His face was creased, weathered like bark left too long in the sun.

Not Kireva. She knew that at once.

Something about him bent the air, as though he carried another rhythm with him. He did not fidget or glance about like a traveler. He simply belonged—though not here.

"You startled me," Ezra said, forcing her voice steady.

"My apologies." His smile was faint, almost amused. "You were very intent on the Fyrwarden."

Her fingers tightened on the folded scrap. "You...know him?"

"I know him," the man said, "as well as I know you."

The air near the spring thickened, the way it did when truth pressed close. Ezra narrowed her gaze. "You're not from Kireva. Which tribe do you hail from?"

He dipped his fingers into the water as if greeting it. Ripples spread outward, unhurried. "I hail from many places. From none. Mostly, I am forgotten. But that is neither here nor there."

Ezra frowned. His words tangled like a riddle, yet something in them sank deep.

The man looked back at her. His eyes were gray-blue, the color of lakewater before a storm.

"I am Veyar," he said softly. "Minor god to the Visionary, who belongs to your people—the Kireva. I am keeper of the liminal—the space between moments, where memory clings and time flows unseen."

Ezra's breath caught. "The Visionary...she's my tribe's goddess."

"She is," Veyar confirmed. "And the shrine where you fought yesterday? That was mine. Built in her name, though few remember it now."

"You're a god." The words felt strange on her tongue.

"A minor one," he corrected gently. "Each of the great gods has a smaller voice to carry their work. I am hers."

Ezra studied his weathered face, trying to reconcile the stories she'd heard as a child with this man standing before her. "Forgive me, but...I've never met a god before. Any god. I thought—" She hesitated. "I thought you were all gone."

Veyar's expression shifted—something between sadness and understanding. "You are not wrong to think so. It has been very long since humans have looked for me. For any of the minor gods, really. Most have forgotten we exist at all." He gestured to the abandoned shrine behind them. "This place was once tended. Honored. Now the vines reclaim it."

"What happened?" Ezra asked softly.

"The gods vanished," Veyar said simply. "All at once. Major and minor alike. One moment they walked among mortals, the next..." He gestured to the empty air. "Gone. I do not know why. The knowledge of it has been taken from even my memory—scrubbed clean, as if someone does not wish us to remember."

"But you're still here."

"Because I am the god of space and time itself." His jaw tightened. "A major thing, though I am called minor because the Visionary is greater. It is hard to erase time, even for whatever force took the others. So I remain. Keeping the liminal spaces. Guarding the thresholds." A faint, tired smile touched his lips. "Continuing."

Ezra's mind raced. "Are you...are you the only one left?"

"No. There is one other." Veyar's expression softened slightly. "Kee. Shadow of life and death. The one who brings the dying to the other side. Kee remains because death, like time, cannot simply be removed. Even Phoenix's absence does not stop souls from crossing."

"Phoenix?" The name stirred something in Ezra's memory—old stories, barely remembered.

"The great god of life and death. Kee's major god." Veyar's voice quieted. "Gone now. Like the Visionary. Like the others. Kee and I do not know why the gods vanished. We cannot remember the reasons, only that we must remain."

Ezra wrapped her arms around herself. "The people of the Sacred Valley...we remember the major gods. The elders still speak their names. But we don't pray anymore. Not really. It's just...stories now."

"I know." Veyar's gaze was kind but sad. "No human living today has walked with gods as their great-grandparents once did. You are the first in generations to stand before me and know me for what I am."

The weight of it settled over Ezra like a heavy cloak. She was speaking with a remnant of a forgotten age. One of the last two gods in a world that had moved on without them.

Her hands trembled. A god. An actual god stood before her, speaking to her as if she mattered. As if she were more than just another Oracle girl selling visions in the market square.

"Why are you telling me this?" she whispered.

Veyar's gaze sharpened, focusing on her with sudden intensity. "Because you carry something that should not exist. A gift from a goddess who has been absent for two centuries. And I confess, child, I am astonished."

The word hung in the air between them. Astonished. A god, astonished by her.

Ezra's breath came faster. Her vision blurred at the edges. "I don't—I don't understand. How can I have a gift from a goddess who's gone? That doesn't make sense. None of this makes sense."

She stood abruptly, backing away from the spring, from him, her hands pressed to her chest as if she could hold herself together through sheer force. "You're saying I have something impossible. Something that hasn't existed in two hundred years. Something even you don't understand." Her voice rose, panic threading through it. "What does that mean? What's happening to me?"

Veyar stepped closer, his movements slow and deliberate. He studied her face as though seeing something written there in a language only he could read. When he spoke, his voice carried a weight that made the grove feel smaller.

"Yesterday, when you touched the Fyrwarden...something awakened in you. Something that should not be possible." He paused, and for the first time, she saw uncertainty flicker across his ancient features. "Tell me, child. Do you know how many eyes an Oracle carries?"

"Three," Ezra answered automatically. "The gifts of sight. We don't always name them, but—"

"But you know them," Veyar finished. "The eye that sees flesh, the eye that sees feeling, the eye that sees knowing." He tilted his head, watching her carefully. "And yet yesterday, I felt a fourth door open inside you."

Ezra's breath stopped. "That's...that's not possible."

"No," Veyar agreed quietly. "It should not be."

The spring's surface rippled, though no wind touched it.

"The Fourth Eye has not awakened in a mortal in over two hundred years," Veyar said, his voice hushed with something like awe. "Not since the Visionary herself walked these lands and blessed her chosen with the gift of Memory."

Ezra shook her head, instinct rising. "But the Visionary is gone. She's been gone for—"

"Two centuries," Veyar finished. His brow furrowed, confusion and wonder warring in his expression. "Which is why your awakening troubles me as much as it amazes me. The Fourth Eye—the Eye of Memory—is not inherited through bloodlines like the others. It is bestowed. A blessing from the Visionary herself."

He crouched down until he was eye-level with her, and she saw the genuine bewilderment in his ancient gaze.

"But she has been absent for two hundred years. Silent. Vanished beyond even my sight." His voice dropped to barely a whisper. "So how, child, do you carry her blessing?"

Ezra's hands trembled in her lap. "I don't...I don't understand. You're saying I have something that shouldn't exist? That comes from a goddess who isn't even here?"

"Yes." The single word carried the weight of centuries. "And I do not know why. Or how." He shook his head slowly, almost to himself. "When I saw it yesterday—when I felt the fourth door creak open inside you—I could scarcely believe it. I thought perhaps I was mistaken. That my sight had grown dim with age."

He reached out and touched the air near her temple,

not quite making contact. "But no. It is there. Growing. The Eye of Memory, waking in you like a seed long dormant finally touched by light."

"What does it do?" Ezra whispered.

Veyar's expression gentled. "The Eye of Memory does not look forward into what may be, nor does it simply observe what is. It pulls you into what was—into the moments that cling to places, to objects, to people. You don't merely see the past. You step into it. You become it, until the line between then and now grows so thin you can taste the truth of what happened."

Ezra's mind reeled. The vision during the fight—Ash's hand on her face, the kiss, the certainty of it—had felt more real than memory. More solid than dream.

"But why me?" The question came out small, afraid. "I'm not the strongest Oracle. Orielle, one of our elders, sees clearer than I ever have. Others are more skilled—"

"Strength is not measured in how many visions you sell in the market square," Veyar said firmly. "The Eye of Memory does not open with knowledge or skill. It opens with ache." He met her eyes. "With the hunger of a soul reaching for something it cannot name but knows it has lost."

The word ache settled in her chest like a coal, burning and bright.

"You said the Visionary was your goddess," she said, voice trembling. "That you were close to her. But you can't remember her?"

Veyar's expression shifted—something flickered across it, too fast to name. Pain, perhaps. Or loss. His gaze grew distant, focused on something she couldn't see. His hands trembled slightly as he raised them, then lowered them again, as if reaching for something that wasn't there.

"You know," he said slowly, haltingly, his voice rougher than before, "it's rather odd." He pressed a hand to his temple, frustrated. "I can tell you I knew her. I can feel the shape of her absence—like a missing tooth, or a word on the tip of your tongue that never comes."

His jaw worked. "But when I reach for her face, her voice, the way she moved through the world..." He trailed off, and his eyes met Ezra's. For a moment he looked lost. Ancient and alone and frightened in a way that made her chest ache.

"There is just...empty space where something precious should be." His voice dropped to barely a whisper. "I know I loved her. I can feel the love still burning inside me, bright as a star. But I cannot remember why. Cannot remember her smile, or her laugh, or the sound of my name in her voice."

His voice cracked. "It's like losing her over and over again. Every time I reach for the memory and find only absence."

Ezra's panic ebbed, replaced by something gentler. The pain in his voice was too raw, too real. Without thinking, she stepped forward and touched his shoulder. "I'm sorry."

His hand came up to cover hers—trembling, grateful —and held on for a moment longer than necessary. As if her touch was the only solid thing in a world that had forgotten him.

When he finally let go, his voice had steadied, but the confusion remained. "Another mystery to add to the growing pile. A goddess vanished beyond recall. A Fourth Eye awakening without her presence. And you, child, at the center of it all."

He stood slowly, brushing dust from his robes. "I do not have answers for you. Only this: what you carry is precious. Rare beyond measure. And dangerous, if the wrong people discover it."

"What should I do?" Ezra asked.

"Nothing," Veyar said, and something in his tone shifted—became gentle, almost protective. "Let it move you where it will. Do not force it. Do not fear it." He paused, then added more softly, "Stillness is not silence, child. And longing..." His gaze found hers. "Longing is not weakness. It is the spark that woke the eye in you. Without it, you would still be blind."

Ezra's eyes stung with tears she didn't fully understand.

Veyar's wrinkled finger tipped her chin up gently. "You are caught in something larger than yourself. Larger than me, even. I do not know what the Visionary intended—or if she intended anything at all. But I know this: you were not given this gift by accident."

"Then what am I supposed to do with it?"

His smile was faint, touched with kindness and sorrow both. "Survive. Learn. And when the memories come—" His voice dropped. "Trust them. The body remembers more cleanly than the mind ever could."

The grove went still.

No footfall, no shimmer of air. One heartbeat he stood before her, and the next—nothing.

Ezra sat frozen on the stone rim of the spring, hands

trembling in her lap. For a long moment she could only stare at the place where he had been.

Gone. Not walked away. Not slipped into the trees. Simply...gone.

The rational part of her mind tried to grasp for explanations—trick of the light, exhaustion, her eyes playing games. But the water still rippled where his fingers had touched it. The grove still held the weight of his presence like heat lingering after flame.

He was a god.

The certainty settled into her bones, terrifying and undeniable. One of only two left in all the world. And he had come to her. Told her she carried something impossible. A gift from a goddess who'd been gone for two hundred years.

Her chest felt too tight. Her breath came shallow and quick.

She needed to move. To think. To DO something other than sit here while the enormity of it pressed down on her.

Ezra stood on shaking legs and started back toward the village, her mind spinning with questions she had no answers for.

Chapter 10

The Reckoning

By the time Ezra returned to the village, the sun had climbed higher. Smoke curled from low chimneys, the scent of roasting grain drifting on the breeze. Children darted barefoot between huts, chasing a wooden hoop across the packed earth.

It all looked the same as it always did, yet nothing felt the same inside her.

Her feet carried her almost without thought toward the edge of the village, where the sparring yard rang with the sharp crack of wood against wood.

Torin stood in the center ring, broad and solid. He wasn't as tall as the Fyrwarden men—barely five-nine at most—but his frame was dense, carved with the kind of strength that filled space without needing height. His hair, streaked with gray through gold, caught the light when he moved, his trimmed beard glinting like iron in sun.

Sela faced him, breathless and laughing, her braid snapping bright as honey when she swung her staff. Her strikes came shallow, hesitant. Even after years of drills, her rhythm never sharpened. Fighting had never sat right with her, and Torin never stopped fussing at her stance.

"Feet, little bird," he said, tapping her ankle with his staff. The old nickname made Sela roll her eyes, but she was smiling.

"There you are!" Sela spotted her first, dropping her staff the instant she noticed Ezra. Her grin was pure wickedness. "I was about to drag you out of whatever hole you were hiding in."

Torin groaned, staff lowering. "Sela—"

"We weren't finished," he said.

"You're never finished," Sela said cheerfully. "You'd drill me until sundown if I let you."

"Because your stance is terrible."

"Because you worry too much." But she said it with affection, the kind of teasing that came from years of the same argument.

Ezra chuckled despite herself. "I wasn't hiding."

"Mm. Brooding, then." Sela's eyes sparkled with mischief. She knew. Of course she knew—Ezra had told her everything this morning. And now Sela was enjoying every second of watching Ezra try to keep it from their father.

"Come on. Take a staff and save me from being lectured into the ground."

Torin's gaze shifted, steady and appraising. "She could use the practice. A sharp mind needs a sharp body to match."

Ezra bent to lift the spare staff by the rail. The weight felt familiar—Torin had been putting weapons in her hands since she was seven. Not because he wanted her to fight, but because he'd lost too many people to leave her defenseless.

She could still hear his voice that first day, crouched down until they were eye-level: "The world took people from both of us. I can't bring them back. But I can make sure it never takes you from me."

He'd never treated her like fragile Oracle glass. He'd treated her like a daughter who needed to survive.

The staff felt heavier than she remembered.

Sela's eyes narrowed, a wicked grin spreading across her face. "Your grip's different. You've been practicing."

"I have not."

Torin's head lifted, sharp. His eyes—the same warm brown as Sela's—focused on Ezra with the intensity of a man who'd spent twenty years reading people's tells. "Practicing with who?"

Ezra froze. Heat rushed to her face.

Sela leaned against her staff, thoroughly delighted by the panic in Ezra's eyes.

"It was nothing. Just—sparring," Ezra tried.

"With who?" Torin pressed, voice like stone. But there was something else beneath it now. Concern.

Ezra's blush betrayed her. Her gaze darted to Sela, who only smirked.

Torin planted his staff in the dirt and stepped closer. "Ezra."

The truth burned in her throat. She forced it out, fast and small. "A Fyrwarden."

The sparring yard went still. The silence was louder than the crack of staffs.

Torin's eyes darkened, a storm breaking across his face. Not anger—not yet. Fear. "You did what?"

"I hadn't meant to," she said quickly. "I was just out by the border—sketching—"

The color drained from Torin's face. "The border." His voice went quiet. Dangerous.

Ezra's stomach dropped. She knew. She'd always known, deep down, that this was why she'd kept it from him. Not because she was afraid of getting in trouble, but because she couldn't bear to see that look on his face.

The same shrine where his wife had been killed.

"You went outside Kireva?" His voice rose, sharp with something between fury and terror. "Beyond the sacred land? Alone?"

Ezra's throat tightened. She couldn't look at him. "Just to the shrine. The old one. By the—"

"By the river." Torin's voice came out flat. Dead. "Just like she did."

The sparring yard went still.

Sela stepped forward quickly, her eyes darting apologetically to Ezra and her voice urgent. "Father, she's safe. She came back. She's right here—"

"That's not the point!" The words burst out of him, raw and ragged. He turned on Ezra, and she saw it then—not anger, but terror barely held in check. "There are rumors, Ezra. Stories spreading about an Oracle who corrupts fire. I've heard them in council meetings, whispered in the market." His voice dropped, shaking. "And if a Fyrwarden believed those lies—if he thought you were the one they're hunting for—do you have any idea what could have happened to you?"

Ezra's stomach dropped. "An Oracle who corrupts fire." The words tasted like ash in her mouth. "You think... you think they're talking about me?"

"I don't know," Torin said, and she could see the fear in his eyes that he did know. That he'd been worrying about this for days. "But if there's even a chance—if the Fyrwarden made the connection—"

"He didn't," Ezra said quickly. Too quickly.

Torin's eyes narrowed. "How do you know?"

Because he'd let her go. Because his fire had bowed. Because when she'd touched him, something had shifted in his eyes that wasn't hatred or fear.

"I just know," she whispered.

Torin stared at her for a long moment, and she saw the realization dawn across his face—that she was defending a Fyrwarden. That whatever had happened at that shrine went deeper than a simple fight.

His jaw worked, and for a terrible moment she thought he might ask. Might demand to know exactly what had passed between them.

Instead, she spoke first.

"I'm sorry." Her hands trembled. The words felt too small. Sorry for doing the one thing she knew would terrify him. Sorry for the rumors she hadn't known about. Sorry that even now, she couldn't promise she'd never go back.

"Kira went to that shrine." Torin's voice cracked. "She wanted to see it. To pray there. I told her it was useless, the gods abandoned us, that is was too far. Too dangerous. She kissed my cheek and said I worried too much." His jaw worked. "They found her body right outside our border near the river. Raiders. She'd been dead for hours, butchered, eaten by vultures before I even knew she was gone."

Sela's hand found Ezra's, squeezing tight. Neither of them had known the details. Not like this.

"And you—" Torin's voice broke completely. "You went to the same gods-damned place. Alone. And fought a Fyrwarden."

"He let me walk away," Ezra whispered.

Torin froze. Searching her face for anything childish, anything reckless. What he found only seemed to make it worse. His shoulders sagged.

"This time," he said quietly. Brokenly. "He let you walk away this time." He looked at her, and Ezra saw tears gathering in his eyes that he refused to let fall. "I wasn't there when Kira needed me most. And I won't lose you too. Either of you."

His voice dropped to barely a whisper. "So you're going to show me every move. From the beginning. And then I'm going to make sure that if you ever face a Fyrwarden again—if you ever go somewhere I can't protect you—you survive."

Then he saw them. Really saw them. Sela with tears streaming down her face, hand clasped white-knuckled in Ezra's. Ezra pale and trembling. Both of them looking at him with something close to fear.

His face crumpled. "Gods, I—" He stepped forward, pulling them both into his arms. "I'm sorry. I'm so sorry." His voice shook. "I shouldn't have—those details, I shouldn't have—"

He held them tighter, one hand cradling the back of

Sela's head, the other gripping Ezra's shoulder. When he pressed a kiss to the top of Sela's head, his breath hitched.

"No child should have to hear that about their mother," he whispered into her hair. "I'm sorry, little bird. I'm so sorry. I was just—" His voice cracked. "I was so scared."

He kissed the top of Ezra's head too, pulling back just enough to look at them both. "Fear makes us cruel sometimes. Even when we love someone. Especially then." His jaw worked. "But that's no excuse. I went too far."

Sela pressed her face into his chest, shoulders shaking with silent sobs. Ezra's eyes burned with tears she couldn't hold back.

Torin held them both a moment longer, then slowly released them.

His hands stayed on their shoulders, grounding.

"When did you two get so tall?" he said roughly, attempting lightness and failing. His thumb brushed Sela's cheek, wiping away a tear. "You were supposed to stay small forever."

"Too late," Sela managed, voice watery. "You fed us too well."

His laugh came out more like a sob. "Terrible planning on my part."

He cleared his throat roughly, wiping at his own eyes. Torin looked at Ezra, and his voice was hoarse but steady. "You're still going to show me that fight. Not because I'm punishing you. But because I need to know you can survive if it happens again."

He glanced at Sela, then back to Ezra. "I know you're not children anymore. I know you make your own choices. But you're still mine to protect. Both of you. And I won't apologize for that."

Ezra nodded, throat too tight to speak. Sela swiped at her eyes.

Torin shifted back into warrior mode like armor sliding into place, though gentler now. Tired. "Show me," he said to Ezra.

She set her stance, breath shallow, pulse thrumming in her throat. She replayed every step she remembered—the angled dodge, the leap that had nearly sent her sprawling, the way her knee slipped on damp soil. Her hand struck empty air where Ash's chest should have been.

When she finished, chest heaving, silence stretched long between them.

At last, Torin spoke. "You weren't ready."

Ezra's jaw tightened. She'd known. Even in the moment, she'd known Ash was holding back.

"But," he added, voice low and steady, "you're not weak. Just untaught. And that—" His mouth quirked, almost a smile. "That's my fault, not yours. I should've pushed harder. Trained you better."

"You trained me fine—"

"I trained you like you might face a drunk at the market. Not a Fyrwarden." He planted his staff in the dirt, firm and unyielding. "We'll fix that."

Her head snapped up. "You'll train me? For real?"

His gaze cut sharp as a blade. "I'll make sure you can stand against fire if it ever comes again. But hear me..." He stepped closer, and his voice dropped into something fierce and protective. "You will not leave Kireva. Not the shrine, not the boundary, not a single step past the market. Not again. I can't protect you out there."

Sela's hand found Ezra's, squeezing tight. A silent promise: *I've got you. Whatever you need.*

She wanted to promise. Wanted to mean it. But the shrine called to her—Veyar's words, the quiet, the way everything had shifted when she touched Ash. She couldn't promise never to return. Only that next time, she'd try to bring Sela. Next time, she'd be ready with knowledge.

Torin motioned for her to raise her staff. "Again. From the start. This time, I'll be him."

The spar lasted nearly an hour. Torin didn't go easy—he moved like the warrior he'd been before age and grief had settled into his bones. But every so often, he'd pause.

"Good. But drop your shoulder here—see? That's where he'll strike."

"Your footwork's sloppy. Plant your back foot." He nodded when she adjusted. "Better."

"Yes! That's the move that saves your life. Remember it."

By the end, Ezra's arms shook and sweat dripped down her spine.

Torin finally lowered his staff, breathing hard. He wasn't as young as he used to be, but his eyes were bright.

He watched her for a long moment—really watched her—and something shifted in his expression.

"You fought him well," he said quietly. "Better than you should have, with the training I gave you." A pause. "He must have been holding back significantly."

Ezra's throat tightened. "He was."

"And yet you survived. Not because he let you." Torin's voice was thoughtful now, not angry. "But because you read him. Adapted. That's instinct, Ezra. That's the kind of thing I can't teach."

He shook his head slowly, almost to himself. "I've been treating you like a child who needs protecting. But you're not a child anymore, are you?"

It wasn't really a question.

"No more half-lessons. No more holding back. From this day, you train as Sela trains." He reached out and squeezed her shoulder, brief but firm. "If you mean to survive, you'll need more than visions to save you."

Ezra nodded. This promise she could make. This one was true.

Torin's hand lingered a moment longer, then fell away. "Go. Both of you. I've terrorized you enough for one morning."

As he walked away toward the well, Ezra saw him pause. Saw his shoulders rise and fall with a deep breath, like a man steadying himself.

Sela slipped to her side, looping her arm through Ezra's. "Well," she said softly. "Now that Dad's properly terrified and we've all cried like babies, you can tell me what you did today."

Ezra told her. About the god at the spring. About the Fourth Eye. About being chosen by a goddess who'd been gone for two centuries. About not understanding any of it.

Sela listened, eyes growing wider with each word. When Ezra finished, Sela was quiet for a long moment.

Then she grinned. "A god and a Fyrwarden in the same week? You're having a much better time than I am."

Despite everything, Ezra laughed.

But as they walked back toward the longhouse, arms linked, Ezra's mind returned to the shrine. To Veyar's cryptic words about danger. To Ash's storm-dark eyes. To the way his fire had bowed when she touched him.

Torin had forbidden her from leaving Kireva.

But the Fourth Eye was waking whether she stayed or left. Veyar had called it precious and dangerous. And somewhere out there, Ash existed—the only person whose fire had responded to her touch instead of consuming her.

She needed answers. About what she was becoming. About why the goddess had chosen her. About what had passed between them at that shrine.

She'd promised Torin she'd train.

She hadn't promised she'd stay.

The thought should have frightened her.

It didn't.

Chapter 11

Market Plaza

The training had become routine—dawn sessions with Torin, afternoons helping with dye work, evenings with Sela who could talk of nothing else but the market. When would they go? Would he be there? What would Ezra wear? Sela's enthusiasm was relentless, her hope of catching a glimpse of Ezra's mysterious Fyrwarden bordering on obsession.

Three days since the shrine. Three days since she'd seen him. And finally they were allowed to go to Market Plaza.

The market spread across wooden platforms over slow water, bridges connecting the seven tribal roads in the only place where peace held. Smoke curled from cooking fires. Traders called low. Baskets swayed. The air was thick with cedar smoke, roasting roots, and the scent of crushed dye cakes.

Ezra carried her basket of jars—dye pigments for trade —but her thoughts were elsewhere.

Sela walked beside her, golden braid swinging, grin wicked. "You're doing it again."

"What?"

"That look. Like you're seeing something the rest of us can't."

Ezra forced herself to focus on the path ahead. "I'm just thinking."

"About him."

Ezra's pulse quickened as they crossed onto the main platform.

Somewhere in this crowd—

Her chest tightened. Torin had forbidden her from seeking him out. From leaving Kireva. From putting herself in danger.

But she hadn't left Kireva. The market was neutral ground. All seven tribes came here.

And she hadn't sought him out.

He was just...here.

If he happened to be here.

Her breath caught. There.

"What?" Sela followed her gaze. "What are you looking at?"

"Him." Ezra's voice came out barely a whisper. "The one by the spice merchant's stall. Long black hair. Arms crossed."

Ash stood with his shoulders rigid beneath his tunic. He wasn't looking at her. Not directly.

But she felt him anyway.

The air between them tightened, charged, as if their fight at the shrine had not ended but only shifted under awning and sunlight.

"Oh." Sela's voice went quiet, then immediately brightened. "Oh. *Oh my gods.*"

Ezra's heart stuttered. "Sela—"

"Who is the tall one standing next to him?" Sela made an exaggerated motion like wiping drool from her chin. "Please tell me you know him too."

"I—I don't. I've never—"

"I'm in love." Sela gripped Ezra's arm. "Look at those shoulders. Ezra. *Look at them.*"

Ezra barely heard her. Every part of her awareness had narrowed to Ash.

"Go talk to him," Sela urged.

"I can't just—"

"Why not? You fought him three days ago. Talking should be easy." Sela's grin turned wicked. "Besides, I need to meet his friend. So we're going."

"Sela—" Ezra grabbed her arm. "Wait. Fyrwardens don't feel. Not like us. They burn it out—joy, pain, tenderness."

Sela's grin didn't fade. "Then I guess I'll just have to change that." She squeezed Ezra's hand. "You did."

"I don't know if it works that way—"

"Only one way to find out." And she was already moving, pulling Ezra forward with the confidence of someone who'd never doubted a welcome in her life.

Ezra's feet moved because Sela gave her no choice. Her pulse hammered in her ears as they crossed the distance.

The tall Fyrwarden beside Ash shifted his weight—subtle, but Ezra recognized the movement. Protective. His hand didn't go to his blade, but his body angled slightly between Ash and the approaching strangers.

Ash's hand moved—a small gesture, barely visible. Stand down.

The tension in the other man's shoulders eased, but he didn't step away. Brothers in arms. Whatever came, they'd face it side by side.

Then Ash's gaze found hers, and everything else blurred at the edges.

"Hello!" Sela's voice cut through the moment, bright and shameless. She stopped directly in front of the tall Fyrwarden, tilting her head back to look up at him. "I'm Sela. And you are ridiculously tall."

Ezra's face flamed. "Sela—"

But the man's eyebrows rose, something like amusement flickering across his severe features. "Thorne."

"Thorne." Sela tested the name on her tongue, grinning. She stuck out her hand. "It's very nice to meet you, Thorne."

He hesitated, then clasped her hand briefly. Professional. Polite.

Sela didn't let go.

"You know," she said, eyes sparkling with mischief, "I need someone to help me carry something from the forge merchant. Very heavy. You look strong."

He blinked. "I—"

"Perfect!" Sela tugged on his hand. "Come on."

He didn't move. Just stared down at her like she was a puzzle he couldn't solve.

Sela tugged again, laughing. "Please? I promise I don't bite. Well—not hard, anyway."

Ezra wanted to disappear into the wooden planks beneath her feet.

His gaze flicked to Ash—some unspoken question passing between them.

Ash's mouth twitched. Almost a smile. A small nod.

Something shifted in the tall Fyrwarden's posture. Whatever silent communication had just passed between them, it seemed to settle the matter. Ezra had seen warriors do this before—speak entire conversations with nothing but glances and gestures. Years of fighting side by side, she supposed. Trust built in battle.

Thorne sighed, long-suffering, and let Sela pull him away. But not before positioning himself so he could still see Ash over his shoulder. "This is a terrible idea."

Even being dragged off by Sela, he kept Ash in his line of sight. Brothers in arms, Ezra realized. They didn't abandon each other.

"All the best ones are!" Sela called over her shoulder, already tugging him toward the forge stalls.

And then they were gone.

Ezra stood frozen, suddenly alone with Ash.

The market noise rushed back—voices, crackling fires, the slap of water against the platform supports. But it all felt distant. Muted.

The air between them tightened. Charged. As if their fight at the shrine had not ended but only shifted under awning and sunlight.

"Ezra." Her name on his lips sounded different than it had three days ago. Softer. Almost reverent.

"Ash." She barely managed the word.

Silence stretched between them—not awkward, but full. Heavy with everything unsaid.

Then Ezra's hand moved without permission. Her

palm found the center of his chest, pressing against the place where his fyr burned.

Heat surged up her arm—not surface warmth but a force that seized her blood, flooding muscle and marrow. Her breath caught.

Ash's whole body jolted. His eyes squeezed shut, jaw clenching as though the fire under his ribs had been struck. When he looked at her again, the control he always carried was gone.

"What are you doing to me?" His voice was raw, almost pained.

"I don't know," she whispered. Honest. Terrified. "But I can't stop."

His palm covered hers, pressing her hand harder against his chest. Heat bloomed beneath their joined hands—not from his skin but from something deeper. The Fyrwarden sigil. She'd felt it before, but now she could see it through the thin fabric of his tunic: intricate whorls of fire etched into his flesh, glowing like embers stirred to life. The lines pulsed with each beat of his heart. Alive. Part of him.

"I'm not asking you to stop."

The words hung between them, dangerous and true.

"At the shrine, when I touched you—"

"Everything changed," he finished. "I know. It's still—" His jaw worked. "I still feel it. Everything."

The certainty in his voice made Ezra's chest tighten. This was real. Three days, and the feeling hadn't faded.

Her touch had changed him.

But how? Why? Her mind raced back to the shrine— the moment her palm pressed to his chest, the Fourth Eye opening, the vision of their future together. Had her awakening power done this to him? Veyar said the Eye of Memory was a gift from a goddess who'd been gone for centuries. What if it didn't just let her see—what if it changed things? Changed people?

Fyrwardens didn't feel. They couldn't.

Until her.

His hand fell from hers, but he didn't step back. Instead, his voice dropped lower. "What's your favorite thing? Not as an Oracle. Just...you."

The question caught her off guard. "What?"

"Something small. Something that makes you feel ordinary."

Her lips parted in surprise. No one had ever asked her that. Not about visions or prophecies or what the gods wanted. Just...her.

"Honey cakes," she said slowly. "Still warm from the fire. I used to sneak them when I was small."

Ash's eyes crinkled at the corners—not quite a smile, but close. "I did the same. With bread."

"The baker always knew," Ezra continued, warmth spreading through her chest. "She'd leave an extra one out. Pretend not to notice."

"Mine too." Something shifted in Ash's expression. Softened. "The kitchen master. He'd turn his back just long enough."

"So someone let us have something," Ezra said quietly. "Even when we weren't supposed to ask."

"A kindness," Ash agreed. "When everything else was rules."

They stared at each other, the weight of recognition settling between them.

"Where did you go?" Ezra asked. "When you needed to be alone?"

Ash was quiet for a moment. "The barracks roof. Late at night. Everyone thought I was training."

"The shrine where you found me the other day," Ezra breathed. "Sela would cover for me. Tell Father I was meditating."

"Were you?"

"No. I was just...breathing."

"Me too." His voice was rough. "Just breathing."

The market noise faded. There was only his voice, low and careful, and the strange certainty that she'd had this conversation before. In another life. In a dream she couldn't quite remember.

"Do you ever feel like—" Ezra hesitated. "Like your whole life was decided before you even had a chance to choose it?"

Ash's jaw tightened. For a moment she thought she'd pushed too far. Then: "Every day."

Her throat tightened. "Me too."

Silence stretched between them. Not awkward. Full. Like there were a thousand things to say and all the time in the world to say them.

"I want to help people," Ezra said quietly. "I do. But sometimes I just want—"

"To be ordinary," Ash finished.

She blinked. "How did you—"

"Because I want the same thing."

Before she could stop herself, the words tumbled out: "Don't get me wrong—I want to help others."

At the same instant, Ash spoke the same words. "Don't get me wrong—I want to help others."

They froze.

Then Ezra laughed—bright and unguarded, her hand flying to her mouth.

Ash stared for a moment, stunned.

Then—slowly, reluctantly, as if he'd forgotten how— he smiled.

Not the faint curve of a warrior being polite. Something real. Radiant. His teeth flashed white, his whole face transforming.

And his fire answered.

It flared at his feet, curling up his legs in thin ribbons before bowing low again, as if even the flame itself had been startled into awe.

Ezra's laughter died into breathless silence.

Ash's smile softened but didn't fade. His voice was rough, wondering. "You make me feel ordinary. Even when I know I'm not." His flames pulled back into him just as quick as they came out.

The moment held—fragile, holy, enough to unravel them both—

Ash's expression shifted. His gaze snapped to something over her shoulder, body going rigid.

"What—"

His hand closed around hers—firm, urgent—and suddenly he was pulling her between two merchant stalls, into the narrow gap between buildings where the sunlight didn't quite reach.

Ezra stumbled, her back pressing against the rough wood. "Ash, what—"

"We're being watched." His voice was low, controlled, but she heard the tension beneath it. He positioned himself between her and the market, shielding her from view. "Dark robes. Silver threading. Kildra mage."

Her breath caught. "Why would a mage be watching us?"

Ash's jaw tightened, and for a moment she thought he wouldn't answer. Then: "We shouldn't be seen together like this. Not here. Not in the open."

"Why not?" But even as she asked, she knew. The rumors Torin had mentioned. The whispers about a dangerous Oracle.

Ash's hand still held hers, thumb brushing once across her knuckles—unconscious, protective. "There are rumors spreading. About Oracles and Fyrwardens. About...corruption." His eyes met hers, and she saw the war in them. The desire to tell her everything fighting against the need to keep her innocent. Safe. "We don't want to add fuel to that fire."

Ezra's throat tightened. "So we're supposed to pretend—"

"No." The word came out fierce. His free hand moved to the wall beside her head, caging her in, keeping her hidden. "But we need to be careful. For both our sakes."

The space between them was small, intimate, charged with more than just danger. She could feel the heat radiating from him, see the pulse jumping in his throat.

"Ash—"

"Where did they go?" Sela's voice cut through the market noise, higher than usual. Not playful—worried. "Ezra?"

Ash's eyes closed briefly. When he opened them again, something had shifted in his expression—something that looked like regret.

He stepped back, releasing her hand. The loss of contact felt almost painful.

He offered his arm formally, as if they were merely acquaintances. "We should return. Before your sister panics."

Ezra took his arm, understanding the game now. In public, propriety. In shadows, truth.

They stepped back into the sunlight together.

Sela stood on the edge of the crowd, head swiveling, cheeks flushed and lips swollen, her braid half-undone with wisps of golden hair clinging to her neck. Her eyes were wide, searching. Behind her, Thorne followed with steady calm, his hand resting lightly at the small of her back—guiding, grounding.

"There." His voice was low, carrying easily. "Told you they'd be fine."

Sela's breath left her in a rush. "You scared me," she said, turning on Ezra. "You just vanished—"

"We're fine." Ezra squeezed her hand. "Just needed a moment."

Sela's gaze darted between them, reading the tension, the careful distance Ash maintained. She opened her mouth, then closed it, something like understanding crossing her face.

Thorne's hand fell away from Sela's back, but his voice stayed steady, almost gentle. "Market's crowded. Easy to lose sight of people."

It was a lie, smoothly delivered. Cover for whatever had just happened.

Sela caught Ezra's wide-eyed stare and managed a wobbly grin. "Right. Crowded."

Ash made a sound—barely audible—that might have been approval. His gaze flicked toward Thorne, one eyebrow raised in silent acknowledgment.

Thorne's expression didn't change, but his chin dipped once. *Handled.*

A faint mark bloomed on his throat, just visible when he turned his head. Sela's doing, clearly. But if Thorne felt any discomfort about it, nothing showed.

Ash turned back to Ezra. His gaze lingered, something in him bending dangerously close to staying.

But then he stepped back. Bowed his head in a gesture more reverent than farewell.

"Ezra."

Then he turned and walked away. Thorne fell into step beside him automatically—same pace, same rhythm, the way they'd walked for years. Partners. Brothers.

"See you around, Thorne!" Sela called out, voice steadier now.

Thorne's shoulders remained relaxed. He didn't look back, but his hand lifted briefly—a small wave, deliberate and controlled.

Ash's hand moved—brief, barely visible—touching Thorne's elbow. Ezra couldn't hear what passed between them, but Thorne's posture eased. Approval, maybe. Or reassurance.

Thorne's jaw shifted, not quite a smile, but close.

They disappeared into the crowd together, side by side, the way Fyrwardens always moved. Never alone. Never unguarded.

Ezra watched until they were gone, her palm still burning where it had touched Ash's chest. But she'd also seen something else—the way Thorne had steadied Sela with quiet words and a guiding hand. The way Ash acknowledged it with silent approval.

Whatever else Fyrwardens had lost, they still had each other.

And maybe—just maybe—they were learning to have more.

As they walked home through the cooling dusk, Sela's fingers kept drifting to her lips, a dreamy smile playing at the corners of her mouth.

Ezra nudged her. "You look pleased with yourself."

"I am." Sela's grin was unrepentant. "Did you see him? All that seriousness just...melted."

"Sela..." Ezra hesitated. "You know what I told you before. About Fyrwardens not feeling—"

"I know what you said." Sela's voice was quieter now, thoughtful. "But Ezra, when I kissed him..." She touched her lips again. "He kissed me back. Not like someone going through motions. Like someone who wanted to."

"Maybe—"

"You changed Ash," Sela interrupted gently. "The moment you touched him at the shrine, something shifted. You saw it. I saw it." She squeezed Ezra's arm. "Maybe I can change Thorne too."

"I don't know if it works that way—"

"Or maybe," Sela continued, eyes bright with something fierce and hopeful, "they were never as broken as everyone said. Maybe they just needed someone to see them differently. As men, not weapons."

Ezra's throat tightened. "Maybe."

Sela's grin returned, wicked and warm. "Besides, did you see his shoulders? Totally worth the risk."

Despite everything—the danger, the uncertainty, the impossible situation they were walking into—Ezra laughed.

"We're both in so much trouble," she said.

"The best kind," Sela agreed, linking her arm through Ezra's. "The kind that's worth it.

Chapter 12

The Rite of Flame

Five days had passed since the market.

Ezra sat at the low table, steam from her bowl rising between her and the firelight. The stew smelled of root vegetables and wild herbs, rich enough to fill the small room with warmth, but she had barely touched it. Her spoon traced slow circles through the broth, her gaze somewhere past the flame.

Torin watched her from across the table, his weathered face softened by concern. Sela sat beside him, already halfway through her second serving, golden hair catching the firelight as she glanced between them.

"You're going to waste away," Sela said, nudging Ezra's knee with her foot beneath the table. "That's the third meal you've picked at like a bird."

Ezra blinked, pulled back into the moment. "I'm fine."

"You look exhausted," Torin said quietly. He set down his own spoon, leaning back against the woven wall. "I've been pushing you too hard."

"No." Ezra shook her head, forcing herself to take a bite. The stew was good—hearty and warm—but it settled in her stomach like a stone. "I can handle it."

Torin's eyes narrowed, not unkindly. He had the look of a man who had raised two daughters long enough to know when they were lying. "You've got shadows under your eyes dark enough to rival the night sky. Your hands are shaking."

Ezra glanced down. He was right. She tucked her fingers into her lap.

Sela leaned forward, grinning. "She's lovesick."

"I am not—"

"You are," Sela said, laughing. "You've met him twice and you look like someone stole the sun."

Heat crept up Ezra's neck. She opened her mouth to argue, but Torin shook his head, his expression softening into something both tender and serious.

"Stop that," he said quietly, looking at Sela. "You know very well some of us are soulbound and can find our match instantly." His gaze grew distant for a moment, touched by memory. "Look at your mother and me. We met and fell in love and had a commitment ceremony three months later. You were born the next year." His voice dropped, rough with old grief. "And even though she's been gone more years than we were together, there is no other woman for me. Soulbound."

He reached across the table and patted Ezra's hand, his palm warm and steady. "It's possible."

Sela's teasing grin softened. Her fingers touched her lips briefly—unconscious, telling. "Is that what it feels like?" Her voice was quieter now, almost wondering. "Like you found something you didn't know you were missing?"

Torin's eyes sharpened, catching the gesture. His gaze moved between his daughters, reading what they weren't saying. "Sela—"

"Just asking," she said quickly, but her cheeks flushed.

Ezra squeezed her hand under the table. *Later,* that touch said. *We'll talk later.*

Torin's jaw worked, but he let it go. For now.

He turned his attention back to Ezra, his expression shifting. "It's possible."

Ezra's throat tightened. For a moment, hope flickered.

Then Torin's expression shifted, protective and sad all at once. "But him being from a different tribe—that is the bigger issue." He paused, his thumb brushing over her knuckles once before pulling back. "Especially with all the tension between the tribes over the years. And he's a Fyrwarden. The head Fyrwarden. That's not something he can just pick up and leave to go live in the housing quarter in the market plaza. It's very rare that tribes intermarry, Ezra. Very rare."

The words settled over her like stones. The warmth that had bloomed in her chest a moment before withered, replaced by a hollow ache. She looked down at her bowl, her appetite gone entirely.

Sela's grin faltered. She glanced between them, then tried to pull the lightness back. "Well, you drew his face seventeen times in the dirt yesterday during water break. Seventeen. That has to count for something."

"I was practicing proportions," Ezra said quietly, but the words had no fight in them.

"You were sighing," Sela added, softer now.

Torin watched Ezra, his weathered face lined with concern. He saw the way her shoulders had curved inward, the way her fingers had gone still around her spoon. It was the kind of laugh that made the walls feel safer, the night less heavy. He shook his head, eyes crinkling at the corners. "All right, that's enough. Both of you."

He turned his attention back to Ezra, and his expression gentled. "You're taking tomorrow off. Sleep in. Rest."

Ezra straightened. "I don't need—"

"You do." His tone left no room for argument. "I've been working you too hard, and your body is telling you to stop. So you will."

Sela's spoon clattered into her bowl. "Not fair! What about me?"

Torin raised an eyebrow. "You haven't been practicing like Ezra. You'll get up and work like usual." He paused, his voice taking on a wry edge. "Plus, Orielle will be furious if you don't show up to the dyeing vat. She's already been on my case all week for keeping Ezra away and training her to fight."

Sela crossed her arms, pouting. "Well, what does Orielle know anyway?"

Ezra laughed—the first real sound of lightness she'd managed in days. "Everything. She's the best Oracle in our tribe."

Torin nodded, his expression shifting, the warmth fading into something more serious. He leaned forward, resting his forearms on the table. "Orielle knows more than most. And she's not fighting me on training you because she knows as well as I do that you girls aren't trained to fight. Not the way you need to be."

The air in the room changed. The teasing fell away, replaced by the weight of what they had been avoiding all evening.

Ezra set down her spoon. "What about the others? Shouldn't they be training too?"

Torin was quiet for a moment, his gaze dropping to the table. When he spoke, his voice was low, measured. "Orielle is leaving it to their families to decide. Most are being restricted. They can go to the village, to the market plaza, but never alone. Always in pairs."

"And the rumors?" Ezra's throat tightened. "Do they ever name the Oracle? Or who's spreading them?"

Torin's jaw worked. He set his spoon down carefully, the way he did when choosing his words. "No name for the Oracle. But there's been talk." He paused. "A Kildra mage has been visiting the tribes. Offering protections."

"Protections from what?" Sela asked.

Torin's voice went flat, disbelieving. "From corrupted fire, he says. Claims an Oracle's touch can twist a Fyrwarden's fyr, make it dangerous. Unstable." His eyes met Ezra's. "As if fire can be corrupted by touch."

Ezra's hands went cold beneath the table. The figure at the market. Dark robes. Silver threading. Watching them.

"Has he come to Kireva?" She kept her voice steady.

"Not yet." Torin's expression darkened. "But Orielle expects him within the week. She's already preparing how to respond." He reached across and covered Ezra's hand. "That's another reason for the training. If this mage convinces people you're dangerous..." He didn't finish. He didn't have to.

Ezra's mind raced, pieces sliding together like a puzzle she hadn't known she was solving.

An Oracle's touch corrupting fire.

Young Oracles being watched.

The rumors—

No. Wait. The rumors had been spreading before she met Ash. Torin had told her about them that first day in the sparring yard, right after she came back from the shrine. The whispers had already started. It couldn't be her.

Could it?

Her stomach dropped. She looked up and found Torin watching her, his eyes dark with something that looked like fear. He knew. He'd known since she told him about the Fyrwarden. Since she'd defended Ash in the sparring yard with that desperate certainty in her voice.

He thought she was the Oracle they were hunting.

But the timeline didn't make sense. Unless... unless something was changing in all the Fyrwardens. Or maybe the rumors had nothing to do with her at all and she was just one Oracle among many being watched.

Or maybe whoever was spreading the lies didn't need the truth. They just needed fear.

Still—she'd touched Ash and his fire had bowed. He'd said he felt everything—emotions Fyrwardens weren't supposed to feel. What if the mage was right? What if she had changed him? Corrupted him, even if it didn't feel like corruption.

What if every moment they spent together made it worse?

Her thoughts started spiraling.

Sela's hand found Ezra's beneath the table, squeezing hard. Her sister's touch pulled her back from the spiral.

"People in the market are looking at the younger ones," Torin continued quietly, voice rough. "You included." His jaw worked. "I don't feel comfortable with you girls going there until this blows over."

Especially not you, his eyes said. *Especially after you fought a Fyrwarden and walked away with stars in your eyes instead of fear.*

The words settled heavy between them.

"Orielle isn't stopping our training," Torin said, his gaze never leaving Ezra's. There was a fierceness there she had seen before—the look of a man who had lost someone and would not lose again. "She knows you're not safe. None of you are. And if something happens, I want you able to run. Or fight. Whichever keeps you breathing."

Ezra swallowed hard. She wanted to argue, to say she could handle herself, but the truth was she had felt the danger creeping closer. The stares in the market. The whispers that stopped when she passed. The way even the air seemed to hold its breath.

And now she understood why.

They were looking for an Oracle who corrupted fire.

They might be looking for her.

Torin reached across the table and covered her hand with his, rough palm warm and steady. "You rest tomorrow. Let your body recover. I'm not losing you to exhaustion or anything else."

Or to a mage's accusations, the unspoken words hung between them. *Or to whatever this is between you and that Fyrwarden.*

Sela squeezed her hand again, and Ezra nodded, her throat too tight to speak.

"Good." Torin pulled back, the sternness softening into something closer to a smile. "Now finish your stew before Sela eats it for you."

"I would never," Sela said, already reaching for the ladle.

Ezra laughed despite herself, and the sound broke the tension just enough to let the warmth creep back in. They finished the meal in quiet companionship, the fire crackling low, the night settling around them like a blanket.

When the bowls were cleared and the fire banked, Ezra followed Sela to their shared sleeping space. The pallet was thin but familiar, the coverlet worn soft from years of use. Sela crawled in first, already yawning, and Ezra lay down beside her.

For a moment, neither spoke. The fire crackled low. The night pressed close.

"You really do miss him," Sela murmured, her voice soft in the dark.

Ezra stared at the ceiling, at the faint shadows cast by the dying firelight. "I do."

Silence stretched between them, comfortable but weighted.

"Sela?" Ezra's voice came out quieter than she meant. "What if what Dad said at dinner is true? What if the mage is right—not about corruption exactly, but about

Oracle touch changing Fyrwardens? What if I did something to Ash without meaning to?"

Sela shifted beside her, and Ezra could feel her sister's attention sharpen even in the darkness.

"You're spiraling again."

"I'm serious." Ezra turned onto her side, facing her sister's silhouette. "Ash said he felt everything after I touched him. Everything Fyrwardens aren't supposed to feel. What if I broke something in him? What if every time we're together, I make it worse?"

Sela was quiet for a long moment. Then, carefully: "Did it feel like breaking? Or did it feel like... I don't know. Healing?"

Ezra's throat tightened. "I don't know the difference anymore."

"Well, I'm not an Oracle," Sela said, voice pragmatic, "so I can't corrupt anyone's fire. And Thorne still—" She paused. "At the market, when you and Ash disappeared and I panicked, he steadied me. Put his hand on my back. Told me they'd be fine." Her voice went softer. "It felt like care, Ezra. Real care. Not just manners."

"Or maybe it was just manners," Ezra said quietly. "Fyrwardens are trained to be... controlled. Professional. Maybe it wasn't care. Maybe it was just—"

"He kissed me back," Sela interrupted. "And that wasn't manners." A pause, then a wicked grin crept into her voice. "Also? Really good kisser. Like, exceptionally good. I didn't expect that level of skill from someone who's supposed to have no emotions."

Despite everything—the fear, the guilt, the weight of what Torin had said—Ezra laughed. "Sela."

"I'm just saying!" Sela's grin was audible now. "If that's what Fyrwardens are like when they're supposedly empty, I can't imagine what they're like when they actually feel things. You're in for a treat."

"Stop." But Ezra was smiling now, the heaviness in her chest loosening just slightly.

"I'm not." Sela bumped her shoulder against Ezra's. "And honestly? I want to see him again. Even if it was just manners. Even if he doesn't remember my name tomorrow. Because for five minutes at that market, I felt like the most interesting person in the world."

Her voice went quieter, more serious. "So if you're asking me if I think you should stay away from Ash to protect him? No. I think you should find out if what you have is real. Because if it is..." She squeezed Ezra's hand. "If it is, that's worth fighting for. Corruption rumors and angry mages be damned."

Ezra's eyes stung. "What if I hurt him?"

"What if you save him?" Sela countered. "What if both of you have been half-alive this whole time and didn't even know it?"

The words settled between them, too big and too true.

"Do you really think that?" Ezra whispered.

"I think," Sela said slowly, "that Ash's fire bowed to you. That's not corruption. That's recognition." She paused. "And I think if Thorne was just being polite, he wouldn't have kissed me like that."

Ezra huffed a quiet laugh despite herself. "You're impossible."

"I'm helpful." Sela's grin returned. "Also, his shoulders. Did I mention his shoulders?"

"Seventeen times."

"Well, they deserve eighteen." Sela yawned, already drifting. "Go to sleep, Ezra. Dream of your Fyrwarden. Maybe he'll dream of you too."

Sela's breath evened out quickly, her body going slack with sleep.

But Ezra lay awake, the quiet pressing in around her. She thought of Ash's smile. The way his fire had bowed when he looked at her. The warmth of his hand over hers.

And she thought of Sela's words. *What if you save him? What if both of you have been half-alive this whole time?*

She turned onto her side, fingers tucked beneath her cheek, and let herself sink into the memory of him.

Sleep found her slowly.

And then the fire did.

The clearing rose around her without footsteps. One breath, then another, and she was there—aware rather than present, held in a stillness that felt different than before. She did not move the air, did not bend a blade of grass. She simply arrived into heat and low sound and smoke.

This wasn't like the visions the Fourth Eye had shown her. Those had been fixed moments—memories crystallized, unchanging. This felt alive. Present. As if she'd been pulled not into the past, but into the now of someone else's experience.

Into Ash's now.

Heat pressed like a living thing. Seven bonfires towered in a wide ring, flames writhing upward like spires clawing the night. The Fyr chant pulsed from a hundred throats, deep and layered, then broke into piercing cries that climbed the dark and spilled down the stone spires in echoes. A low drumbeat hid beneath the voices—steady, relentless, like the earth itself was chanting with them. The ground was blackened, scored by old circles and older vows. Oil and pine sap burned clean. Smoke lifted blue.

Ash stood at the center.

Bare chest. The sigil over his heart burned like a brand brought to life, bright as fresh coals. A headdress of phoenix plumage crowned him, layered red, black, orange, yellow, white—each feather catching light so it seemed lit from within. Shadows of those feathers flickered against his shoulders, wings of fire and dark.

He moved with the rhythm of something older than language. Bare feet struck scorched earth. Palms carved air. Hips turned. His body carried both a warrior's discipline and a dancer's grace, each motion precise and fluid. With a sweep of his hand he pulled fire from one pyre and hurled it into another. Sparks leapt like scattered stars before the blaze devoured them.

The fire obeyed.

It bowed. It spun. It circled. Seven wheels of flame rose, perfect orbits shifting in time with his breath. Heat ran beneath his skin in luminous rivers, vein-bright, as though his blood carried embers. The marks along his arms glowed and dimmed with each change of breath. This was why he led at twenty-two. Not only for strength. For this command.

Ezra stood just beyond the circle. No footprint. No stirred ash. Aware rather than present, yet somehow more present than she'd ever been.

This wasn't the Fourth Eye. She knew that now, even if she couldn't name what had opened instead. Veyar had told her the Eye of Memory showed the past—fixed, unchanging, safe to observe without altering. But the chant struck her bones in real time. The sparks fell where she watched them fall. The heat on her skin didn't feel remembered. It felt now.

As if something deeper had awakened. Something that didn't just show her the past, but pulled her into the present of another soul.

Into his soul.

She tested that truth.

She breathed, slow and deliberate. Scent. Weight. Angle. Cedar and hot iron and pine. The pull of the circle under the soles of her awareness where her body did not tread. The angle of his shoulder as he turned—the tell that would bring his left palm high and his right low.

She stepped.

The flames nearest her parted as if wind had opened them. No burn. No sear. A corridor of heat made room. Ezra crossed the ring and stood within, just inside the perfect wheels, where the air thickened and the chanting rose. The fire did not challenge her entry. It recognized something and let her pass.

Veyar had not prepared her for this.

He had not said the Eye could slip through an hour as it happened. He had not said the living could sense the watcher.

Ash's eyes were closed. His head tipped back. His mouth shaped the words of the vow, low and certain, the cadence of the fire tribes rolling through his chest. The flame wheels tightened their orbits, then loosened on his exhale. He moved, and the blaze moved. He stilled, and a hush fell inside the roar.

Ezra pressed her palm to his sternum, over the place where his sigil burned. Warmth pulsed there in answer, not memory but echo, as if his sigil had hidden a flame in her.

The flames flared higher around them, and for a single breath the fire shaped itself into wings—vast and blazing, arching from his shoulders before collapsing back into formless heat. The sound it made was a crackling rush, wind and ember and something ancient. His fire felt her— recognition arriving before sight.

Then he opened his eyes.

Not surprise. Just the fractional change in breath, the minute shift through his ribs. He saw her. Saw through whatever veil should have kept her hidden. His gaze locked to hers with the clean surety of something already chosen.

Soul calling to soul.

The chant wavered. Not the pitch. The intent. A single ripple through a lake of sound.

Ash lifted both hands. Flames climbed into his palms, thick as poured gold. He turned one wrist and the wheel at his right spun faster, turned the other, and the left steadied. Finishing the ritual, mesmerizing her, never taking his eyes off of her. The flame burned in his eyes, reflecting the blaze.

Then a small motion that pulled heat into a bright line

between them, like the string of a bow. The flame passed through her. She closed her eyes, waiting for the heat, but it never came.

Ezra did not move.

She opened her eyes, and Ash was still watching her. The fire pressed close, curious and reverent. The headdress feathers trembled in the updraft. Light traced the hollow of his throat. Heat ran his forearms like lava in narrow valleys. The air tasted like lightning.

The tribe's voices rose, broke into high keens that made the hair lift on Ezra's arms. The sound shook her and steadied her in the same breath. She felt the urge to bow her head. She did not. She stood.

Seen.

His voice carried without force. Low. Resonant. The cadence of Fyr wrapped around the words as if they had belonged to the chant all along.

"Meet me at the shrine. Tomorrow."

The wheels of fire snapped outward in a shock of sparks and then collapsed inward. All seven pyres answered at once, dropping to a shudder of embers that painted the clearing in quiet red. Gasps rippled the ring. The chant stopped clean. No one moved.

A flamebearer lifted iron tongs, then stilled when an elder set a palm on a wrist and pressed down. The tribe held.

Ash lowered his hands. The blaze at his feet softened and lay low like an animal that knew its place. The sigil over his heart beat once, hard enough that Ezra felt the answer in her own chest. His eyes did not leave hers.

He did not bow. He did not kneel. His reverence took a different shape. He let her see the steadiness. He let her know the message was not a wish. It was a truth spoken aloud.

The shrine. Tomorrow.

Heat thinned. Smoke unraveled into the trees. One by one the Fyrwardens stroked their palms down their forearms, sealing light under skin. Marks dimmed. Ribs steadied. The headdress on Ash's head settled as if even the feathers had heard what the fire already knew.

The Eye began to loosen its hold on her. Not a tearing. An opening of fingers. Ezra let herself be carried back through the bright air to the thin skin of night. She kept the shape of him as she went. Bare feet on scorched earth. Flame in the hands. A leader because the fire chose him, not because men did.

Her body woke with a small start.

Moonlight cut the floor in a narrow stripe. Sela slept, one arm flung over her head, mouth soft. Ezra's palms burned—not with pain, with the echo of a sigil she did not wear.

The shrine waited, whole though worn, veined in ivy, ringed by open ground that asked for the press of bare feet. The river kept its low song for those who knew how to hear it.

Tomorrow.

She would go before the market woke. Before the elders stirred. Before Torin shaped the day with rules that made her a vessel. Water. Knife. Nothing else. The path would remember her feet.

She lay back and watched the window pale by slow

degrees. The night held her thoughts without smothering them. She did not hide from what had changed.

Ash had named her inside a circle where outsiders were not named. The fire had bowed. The elders had seen and kept their hands still.

Either a storm would break or a path would open.

Either way, she would meet him.

She turned to her side, watching Sela sleep. Her sister's face was peaceful in the moonlight, mouth soft, one arm flung over her head. Innocent. Unaware that tomorrow, Ezra would walk back into danger.

Back to the shrine where Torin's wife had died.

Back to the Fyrwarden who made her feel whole.

Torin's words echoed in her mind. *I'm not losing you. Either of you.* The fierceness in his voice. The grief that still lived in his eyes when he spoke of Kira. He'd made her promise to rest, to stay safe, to let her body recover.

He would be furious if he knew what she planned.

He would be terrified.

Guilt twisted in her chest, sharp and familiar. He had lost so much already. Given her a home when she had nothing. Trained her to survive. Loved her as his own.

And she was going to lie to him. Sneak out before dawn. Risk everything he'd tried to protect her from.

But Ash had summoned her. Not requested—summoned. And whatever had opened inside her tonight, whatever new eye had pulled her into his ritual, it wasn't something she could ignore. This wasn't recklessness. It was destiny pulling her forward, whether Torin understood it or not.

She would go. And she would deal with the consequences after.

Her chest tightened, but she didn't change her mind.

She closed her eyes, not to seek sleep, but to keep the shape of the clearing bright. Seven fires. Stone spires. A man the fire trusted. A voice that found her across heat and rules and distance. A summons that felt less like an order and more like truth spoken aloud.

She breathed in slow count. She breathed out the same.

Morning would come. She would go. And the world as she had understood it would need a new name.

I'm sorry, she thought, though she didn't know if she meant it for Torin or Sela or herself.

The dawn came anyway.

Chapter 13

Unclean

Smoke lingered after the rite.

Seven pyres had been reduced to glowing ribs of ember, their smoke drifting pale-blue into the night. The square was emptying, but unease clung heavier than the smoke itself. Even the drums had gone quiet, as though the earth didn't dare beat while fire was still watching.

Ash paced near the edge of the trampled circle, shoulders taut, the sigil at his chest still hot enough to burn through the sweat on his skin. He dragged a hand down his face, as if he could rub the flame out of him, but it stayed. It always stayed. His boots cut back and forth across the scorched ground, sparks crunching under heel.

A voice came from the edge of the circle, roughened with age but steady as iron.

"What was that about?"

Anok stepped into the glow of the embers. His hair, long and silver-gray, hung loose over weathered shoulders.

Skin darkened and lined from years of forge smoke and mountain sun. He carried himself with the patience of a healer, but the sorrow in his eyes belonged to a man who had buried too many he loved.

Ash didn't answer. His stride kept cutting, back and forth, like movement alone might burn the memory away.

"I've never seen fire bend like that." Anok's gaze lingered on the blackened earth, then lifted. "The others were in a trance, watching you. The elders are shaken." His jaw tightened. "And Saav stood with them, saying your flame burns unclean. That the Oracle cursed you."

Ash's hands curled into fists at his sides. People had seen them together at the market plaza days ago—Saav had wasted no time spreading his poison. The rumors had taken root fast.

"Saav is wrong."

Anok's voice softened, but the weight in it pressed heavier. "No. I think this time, you're wrong." His eyes dropped to Ash's chest, where the sigil pulsed with too much heat. "Your fire is different, Ash. I've watched you since you were eight years old. I knew your parents. I see the change."

Ash clenched his teeth, refusing to give the thought air.

"You may be fire," Anok said, quieter now, his voice thick with old grief, "but you're not a Forge. The ones who tried to burn hotter than they were meant to...they didn't last." His hand tightened over the scroll under his arm. "I buried two of them myself. Both swore they were fine. Lied with their last breath."

Ash's head snapped up, sharp. "You think I don't know that?"

Anok shook his head, gray hair shifting in the firelight. His expression carried the heaviness of someone who had carried Ash's father to the pyre, who had watched the boy grow into a man too fast, too fierce. "Then tell me what it is, if not her curse. Tell me why your fire bows to an Oracle when it should burn her."

"I don't know," Ash muttered, the lie sitting hot on his tongue. "But it isn't the Oracle."

Anok's face softened with something close to heartbreak. "I carried your father to flame, Ash. Don't make me carry you too."

Silence stretched. The square felt emptier, as though the shadows themselves had pulled back to listen.

Ash's jaw locked.

Saav had tried to poison him against her weeks ago—warning of a dangerous Oracle who corrupted fire, who searched deeper during her readings than people knew, judging them for thoughts they hadn't even acted on. The rumors had grown wilder since then. Drownings. A man struck dead by a falling planter from a third-story window. Stomach sickness sweeping through Veyona—all real tragedies, all twisted into weapons against her.

Ash had investigated on his own. The drownings were fisherfolk caught in a storm. The falling planter was an accident—rotten wood, nothing more. The sickness came from spoiled grain, not Oracle magic.

But Saav wove truth into lies so skillfully that even facts couldn't untangle them. Each tragedy became proof. Each coincidence, evidence.

And people believed him.

Part of Ash had still wondered—until Ezra touched him at the shrine, and instead of corruption, he had felt whole for the first time in his life.

Marked. The word still coiled like a brand in his mind.

A presence moved beside him.

Kee.

Silent as a stray wind, Kee matched his steps like they'd always been walking together. No announcement. No greeting. Just the sound of boots on packed earth and the soft crunch of fruit between teeth.

"Rough night?" The question came casual, followed by the pit of whatever had been chewed tossed carelessly into the dark. There was a grin in the words, mischief dancing at the edges like the whole situation was entertaining.

Ash didn't look over. "You saw it too?"

Kee hummed, swinging around to walk backward in front of Ash, arms spread wide in mock drama. "Hard not to. Whole field looked like a dream sequence. Very theatrical. I was *moved*." Kee clutched both hands over where a heart would be, then dropped them with a laugh.

Ash's shoulders stayed tense. "They think I'm cursed."

"Of course they do," Kee said, spinning back around to walk beside him. "It's easier than thinking you might be waking up. People hate change. Especially when it's happening to their shiny murder weapon." Kee poked Ash's bicep for emphasis.

Ash stopped walking. "Kee—what's happening to me?"

Kee sighed, the playfulness dimming just slightly. "You want the god answer or the friend answer?"

"Either. Both."

Kee tilted head, considering. "Alright. God answer: I'm a forgotten minor god of life and death—or what's left of it anyway. My role was to help humans have fun before they died. Not exactly in the business of curses." Kee paused, then shrugged. "Friend answer? Maybe your curse was being born a Fyrwarden in the first place."

Ash frowned.

Kee's grin returned, crooked and knowing. "Think about it. You've been numb since you were eight. Dead inside by design. But you felt her, didn't you? The fire responded. That's not madness, Ash." Kee leaned closer, voice dropping to something almost serious. "That's healing."

Ash stared at the ground, his fire reduced to a simmer.

Kee shrugged, spinning away again like the conversation was already boring. "Or maybe I'm wrong and you're doomed. But hey, at least it'll be entertaining to watch." A pause, then a glance back with a wink. "I'm rooting for the healing option, by the way. Much better story."

Silence stretched, then softer: "Night, gloom prince."

And then Kee was gone—not walking away, just... absent. The way gods did.

Ash didn't respond. Just kept walking back toward the barracks.

But the words stuck.

Not because of the doom part. He'd been marked for worse.

It was the other thing. The way Kee said *healing*, like maybe—just maybe—there was another path he hadn't seen. A way forward that didn't end with fire devouring everything he loved.

And gods, he wanted that to be true.

He tried to sleep. Laid on his side with one arm thrown over his eyes, as if pressure alone could shut out what he saw behind them. Her eyes. Her face. That stunned expression in the vision when he told her to meet him.

Had it even been a dream?

Had she really seen him?

The moment replayed again and again—fire curling around his hands, the chant rising, and her, suspended like breath over the flame. He hadn't just seen her. He had felt her—like a thread pulled tight through the hollow of his chest. The fire had responded. Like it knew her too.

He hadn't meant to say the words.

But they burned out of him anyway.

Meet me at the shrine.

The barracks settled into the deep quiet that came before the screaming started. Each Fyrwarden had their own chamber—small, stone-walled, just wide enough for a pallet and a narrow shelf. Soundproofed. Private. Necessary.

Every night, those who fell asleep first would begin. Raw, animal sounds ripping from throats as the pain they couldn't feel while awake tore free. The walls were thick enough that once you were under, you slept through your own screams. Had to sleep through them. It was the only way to keep the madness at bay, to release what their magic suppressed.

But you had to fall asleep first.

And Ash hadn't screamed since the shrine. Not once in the eight nights that had passed since she touched him.

He didn't know what that meant. Didn't know if the absence of screaming was healing or a different kind of breaking. The silence felt wrong. Like his body was holding something in that should have been let out.

Tonight, he didn't want to find out. Didn't want to sleep and discover whether the screams had finally returned, or whether whatever she'd done to him had changed even that.

He sat up.

He would not sleep. Not like this.

He swung his legs over the side of the pallet and pulled on his tunic. Quiet, fast. No armor. No markings. Just him.

He eased his door open—the hinges were oiled, silent —and stepped into the dim corridor. Oil lamps burned low at each end, casting just enough light to navigate by.

"You're going to her."

Ash stopped. Thorne stood in his doorway three chambers down, one shoulder against the frame. Arms crossed. Waiting. His door was open—had been open, Ash realized. Listening.

Ash's gaze darted down the corridor. Empty. But walls had ears, and Fyrwardens were trained to hear what others couldn't.

He crossed to Thorne quickly, caught his arm, and pulled him back into his chamber. The door shut with a soft click.

"Keep your voice down," Ash said, low and urgent.

Thorne didn't resist, just leaned back against the wall, arms still crossed. "Couldn't sleep. Been listening for you."

Ash's chest tightened. "Thorne, are you—?"

"I can see you worry now. That's new." Thorne's voice was flat, matter-of-fact. "Don't worry about me. I'm still screaming. Every night. Same as always. So whatever's happening to you, it's not happening to me." He paused, jaw working. "But something did change. A fraction."

Ash's focus sharpened on him.

"The kiss..." Thorne's voice went quieter. "The kiss was different. Better than any other kiss. Something more to it. Made me feel like Sela needed protection and only I could give it to her. I know it could be our training—we're supposed to protect women. Could be something else. But there was something different in the way I behaved when she got worried, not finding you where we left you."

He met Ash's eyes. "I know that's nothing like what you're feeling. But even this minuscule change has me up at night. I can't imagine what you're going through."

Ash placed his hand on Thorne's shoulder. "Maybe we're healing. At least that's what Kee thinks."

Thorne's expression went grim. "The elders won't see it that way. Not after the Rite." He paused. "Everyone was mesmerized. The entire tribe stood frozen, watching you. I wasn't. Neither was Kee." His jaw tightened. "Saav is already calling it corruption."

Ash's jaw tightened. "Anok already warned me.

Reminded me not to be another Fyrwarden he has to carry to the flames."

He gripped Thorne's shoulder harder. "Don't give them a reason to look at you. Be the perfect Fyrwarden. Follow every order. Show nothing."

"And what about you?"

Ash didn't respond.

"If you're not back by dawn," Thorne said, "I'm covering for you. One day. That's all I can give before they start asking questions."

Ash's throat tightened. "Thank you."

"Don't thank me yet." Thorne's expression went hard. Serious. "Because if it comes to them putting you on a pyre, we're not staying for that."

Ash went still. "Thorne—"

"I mean it." Thorne's voice was quiet but certain. "If they decide you're too corrupted to save, if they chain you up to burn you out—we run. Both of us. Become rogue. Live beyond the Sacred Valley. I'm not watching them burn you for falling in love."

The words hit Ash like a physical blow. "You'd give up everything—"

"For my brother?" Thorne's jaw set. "Yes. Without question."

Silence stretched between them, heavy with what that meant. Rogues were hunted. Killed on sight. They'd be betraying everything they'd been raised to be, everyone they'd sworn to protect.

But they'd be alive.

"It won't come to that," Ash said, though he didn't know if he believed it.

"Maybe not." Thorne pushed off the wall. "But if it does, we run. That's the deal. One day cover, and if things go wrong—" His voice dropped. "We run together."

Ash's chest ached. "I don't deserve—"

"Shut up." Thorne gripped his shoulder hard, the way warriors did before battle. "Go to her. Find out if this is healing or breaking. Just..." His voice roughened. "Come back. Because if you don't, I'll have to come find you. And I'd really rather not."

Ash nodded, not trusting his voice.

Thorne released him, stepped back. "One day, Ash. Dawn tomorrow. After that, you're on your own until the pyres."

"I'll be back."

"You'd better be." Thorne's mouth twisted into something that wasn't quite a smile. "Someone has to keep you from burning yourself alive."

Ash opened the door, checked the corridor. Still empty.

He looked back at Thorne once. His brother. His only person he called family left.

Then he left.

The stables were dark, save for a single oil lamp swinging near the far gate. Most of the horses slept standing, their tails flicking half-heartedly at night gnats. He chose the dullest one—the mare with uneven ears and a habit of chewing her reins. The kind nobody rode unless there were no other options.

Perfect.

He saddled her in silence, led her out with a click of his tongue.

No patrols saw him go.

Let them wonder. Let them stew.

By the time they noticed he was gone, he'd be halfway through the western pass. And if the elders questioned him—if they demanded to know where their Head Fyrwarden had vanished to in the middle of the night—

They'd think he was going mad.

Fyrwarden madness. The kind that came when the fire burned too hot, when the screaming stopped working, when a warrior started feeling things they shouldn't. The kind that ended with a pyre and Anok carrying another body to the flames.

Let them think it. Let them prepare his funeral.

He was going to her anyway.

And if he was wrong—if it hadn't been her in the vision—then he'd blame the fire, the moon, anything but the truth.

That he wanted it to be her.

That part scared him more than any curse.

The mare's hooves found the path without guidance, as though even she knew where they were headed. Ash didn't look back at the barracks, didn't let himself think about what would happen if the elders discovered he'd left.

Anok's warning echoed in his mind—*Don't make me carry you too.*

But Ash would rather burn trying to reach her than live another day as half a man.

Nothing could stop him.

Because for the first time since he'd been marked at

eight years old, since fire had burned the feeling from his veins, he had a reason to hope.

And hope, he was learning, burned hotter than any flame.

Chapter 14

What She Sees

Ezra slipped out before dawn.

She didn't dare take the main door—the hinges groaned too loudly—so she eased through the side window, boots wrapped in cloth to muffle the sound. On Sela's bedside table, she left a ribbon looped twice in the shape only they used. Their secret code since childhood. *Cover for me.*

The longhouse behind her stayed silent. Torin wouldn't know. Not yet. He'd given her the day to rest, to recover from the exhaustion that had been pulling at her for days. She felt a pang of guilt for using his kindness this way, but the vision had been too clear. Ash had called to her. She had to go.

Torin would be furious when he found out. And he would find out—he always did. She could already see the disappointment in his eyes, hear the fear in his voice.

I'm not losing you.

But she was already gone. Already crossing the line he'd drawn to keep her safe.

She pushed the guilt down. Dealt with it later. Right now, Ash was waiting.

The morning air was damp, gray, holding the hush before sunrise.

Ezra kept to the narrow path that wound toward the river. By the time the ridge lightened, mist had gathered low along the banks, curling white over the stones where she and Ash had fought weeks before. She stopped at the edge, remembering the way his fire had struck the water, the way steam had risen between them like a veil.

Her chest tightened.

She unlaced her boots and crossed barefoot, moving from stone to stone. The current tugged cold at her ankles, but the river remembered her steps. On the far side, she sat briefly to wipe her feet and pull her boots back on, then pressed deeper into the trees.

Beyond the river, the trees grew older. The path narrowed into something half-lost—overgrown and winding, moss draped like silk across stone ridges that had once been stairs. Her boots sank into wet leaves and softened earth, each step swallowed by the hush of old growth and mist.

A branch snagged her sleeve. She tugged it free, brushed the damp from her dress, then shifted the strap of her satchel higher on her shoulder. A smudge of charcoal had already darkened her fingers, and she wiped them absently against her skirt. Mundane gestures, small and human, in a place that was anything but.

Then she saw it.

The shrine.

The same place where they had first met. Where his fire had tested her and she had touched his chest and felt everything. The weathered stone structure rose from the forest floor, ancient and half-swallowed by the earth. Vines spilled from its rounded crown, trailing like water over the curve of its moss-laced roof. Lichen streaked the blocks with age-darkened green, and ferns clustered at its base.

The entrance yawned dark and silent. To the right, the squat stone pedestal still jutted from the ground, its top worn smooth from centuries of offerings.

Ezra stepped into the clearing, her cream cotton dress catching the wind, embroidered with soft blue flowers and cinched with a worn belt at the waist. Beneath it, darker trousers tucked into red boots. Practical. Not quiet. But enough.

She approached the stone altar and laid her palm flat on its surface. It was cold. Unyielding. But beneath it, something pulsed—not sound, not voice. Just a hum.

Ezra lowered herself to the ground, sketchbook balanced on one knee. She kept her hand moving, charcoal smudging across the page, though the lines blurred with nerves. Better to look busy than to look like she was waiting.

She was already sketching when he appeared.

Ash stepped from the trees like the forest had been keeping him. Dark shirt unlaced at the collar, sleeves rolled to his forearms, trousers tucked into worn black boots. No armor. No markings. Just him. Wild hair loose, hanging past his shoulders, half-damp with mist. A shadow of dirt at his cuffs as though he'd come by backroads.

Somewhere deeper in the trees, his horse—a dull mare with uneven ears—shifted and snorted softly.

Her charcoal stilled.

From the corner of her eye, she watched him pause— taking it all in: the altar, the trees, her. Then, with quiet purpose, he crossed the clearing.

He didn't speak at once. Didn't sit beside her. Didn't tower either. He crouched a few feet away, forearm braced on one knee, head tilted like he was listening to something she couldn't hear.

Ezra kept her eyes on the sketchbook. He wanted to see her; she'd let him speak first. She looked at the image of him she'd unconsciously been drawing and rubbed her thumb, trying to smudge the resemblance into someone else, but the shape became even closer to his likeness.

He watched her. Not like the others did. Not like a prophecy unraveling, not like a threat waiting to be named.

He watched her like he remembered her, just as much as she remembered him.

And that was more dangerous than his fire.

She glanced over her shoulder, scanning the tree line. Empty. But the weight of eyes lingered—real or imagined, she couldn't tell. Saav had been watching them at the market. And Torin had said the mage was expected in Kireva within the week.

They were running out of time.

The silence stretched. She kept sketching, but her hands trembled.

Finally: "You always this quiet when you show up?"

"I was trained to be quieter."

"Of course you were."

Ash's mouth shifted, a faint quirk that almost became a smile. Almost.

Silence stretched.

"You said tomorrow," she murmured.

"I didn't think you'd come."

"Then why ask?"

His pause carried weight. "I needed to know if it was real."

Her gaze lifted at last.

His eyes met hers—gods, it felt like falling. Not far, not fast. Just deep. Into something older than time, hotter than flame, and so familiar it hurt.

"It wasn't a dream," she said softly. "Last night."

"I know," he said. "I felt you." He placed his hand on his chest over his Fyr sigil, where she had placed her hand in the vision.

Her fingers tightened around the sketchpad. "My Sight...it's accelerating. I've been told there's more than the Third Eye."

Ash's brow furrowed. "I don't know much about Oracle Sight."

"I opened the Fourth," she said. "Used it for the second time last night. That's how I saw you during your rite."

He didn't interrupt. Just watched. Steady. Waiting.

"There are stages," she went on. "Visionary apprentices open them one by one. Three Eyes total—for physical truth, emotional truth, and intuition. No one ever had anything greater..." She shook her head. "Until now."

His expression sharpened. "Do you know what it means?"

She hesitated. "A god appeared to me. Once. Veyar—he was trained under the Visionary herself. He told me about the Fourth Eye, explained what was happening." Her voice dropped. "But I haven't seen him since. I don't know if he'll come back."

Ash's jaw shifted, but he didn't press.

"Your fire," she said. "It recognized me. Didn't it?"

He nodded. "It didn't just recognize you. It changed because of you."

Ezra's breath caught. "That's what they'll call corruption," she said quietly. "That's what the mage is telling people."

Ash's jaw tightened. "Saav."

"You know him?"

"He's been spreading lies about you for weeks. Blaming you for deaths that weren't your fault. Drownings, accidents, sickness—all twisted to make you look dangerous." His voice went hard. "I investigated. Found the truth. But people believe what they want to believe."

Ezra's hands went cold. "He's coming to my tribe. Torin said within the week."

The air between them grew heavier.

"Then we don't have much time," Ash said quietly.

Ezra looked at him—really looked. At the risk he was taking. At the way his fire had changed. At what Saav would do if he found out about them.

"No," she whispered. "We don't."

At last, she let herself look at him without flinching.

This was only the third time they'd met—first at this shrine weeks ago, then the market plaza, now here again. But it didn't feel like that. It felt like too many lifetimes trying to squeeze into a single breath.

"Can I ask you a silly question?"

He nodded.

"Do you have to try not to burn things?" She felt her cheeks heat.

His gaze slid to them, then back to her eyes. "All the time."

She swallowed that. She'd always wondered how the Fyrwardens carried fire in their veins and didn't lose themselves to it, how someone like him could hold that much heat and still look at her like she might break.

"Does it burn?"

"That depends." His voice was quiet, careful. "We don't feel pain like normal people. Not while we're awake. But each night when we sleep..." He paused. "We scream. It's the fire burning us from the inside out. All the pain we don't feel during the day comes out then. We don't feel it happening. Just know we're burning it out in our screams."

Ezra's throat tightened. "That must be frightening. Hearing so many nightly screams."

"We have a soundproof barracks."

"That's smart, I guess." But her chest ached at the thought of it. Of him lying down each night knowing what would come. Of fighting sleep just to stay normal a little longer.

"I haven't screamed in eight nights," he said quietly.

Ezra's breath caught. "What?"

"Not since you touched me at the shrine." His jaw tightened. "I don't know what it means. But Thorne noticed. He's covering for me today. One day. That's all he can give before the elders start asking questions."

Her stomach dropped. "You're risking everything to be here."

"So are you."

Their eyes met. Both of them defying their families. Both choosing this moment over safety.

Silence settled between them, weighted with what they'd both sacrificed to be here.

Ash's gaze dipped to her lap. "You draw people often?"

"Sometimes." A hesitation. "Lately...just one."

He nodded once. "May I see?"

"Didn't plan to show you."

"You don't have to."

Her hand faltered. Then she turned the book and held it out. "This is you. Sort of."

Her cheeks warmed again.

Ash reached for it. His fingers brushed hers—soft, charcoal-stained—and the touch sent heat racing up her arm straight to her chest.

He looked at the page for a long moment. She watched his face, trying to read his expression, but he gave nothing away. Just studied the half-finished lines and blurred shadows.

"I look peaceful."

Ezra shrugged, throat tight. "That's what I see when I'm with you."

His head tilted, and for a moment she thought he

might say something. But he didn't. Just looked at her like he was memorizing her face.

Then he leaned closer. Not enough to touch. Just enough for the air between them to heat.

His presence wrapped around her like forge warmth —pine, smoke, sweat, and something colder underneath. Snowmelt caught in flame.

Ezra pulled back. Not because she wanted to. Because if she didn't, she wouldn't stop.

Her hands shook. Her breath stuttered. The ache wasn't fear. It was want.

A want so deep it hurt.

She watched him give her space. Inch by inch. But his eyes never left hers. He didn't look away. Didn't pretend he hadn't felt it too.

Ezra looked up. Morning light filtered through the canopy, painting everything in shades of gold and green. Birds called from the high branches. The shrine felt patient around them, as it had for centuries, holding their moment like a cupped palm holds water.

Ash glanced at the sky, then back to her. "You should probably get back. Before they notice."

"Probably." But she didn't move.

Neither did he.

The silence between them wasn't empty. It was full of everything they hadn't said. Everything they were both too afraid to name.

"I don't want to go," she said quietly. The words slipped out before she could stop them.

His eyes found hers again. Something shifted in his

expression—she couldn't name it. Relief, maybe. Or recognition. Like he'd been hoping she'd say exactly that.

"Then don't."

The two words hung in the air between them like an offering. Like a choice only she could make.

Ezra's heart beat once, hard. She thought of Torin's warning about intertribal relationships. Of Sela's ribbon on the bedside table. Of all the reasons this was dangerous.

And then she thought of the way Ash looked at her. The way his fire had bowed. The way she felt whole when he was near.

"I'll stay," she whispered. "For a while."

Ash nodded slowly. Then he shifted, settling onto the ground beside her instead of crouching. Close enough that she could feel the warmth radiating from him. Far enough that they weren't touching.

Not yet.

He looked out at the clearing, at the ancient trees and the worn altar. His shoulders eased—she could see it in the way he exhaled, in the way tension bled from his frame. Like for the first time since she'd met him, he could breathe.

"Good," he said simply.

For a moment, neither of them moved. Then he settled more comfortably against the altar stone, and Ezra found herself mirroring him—close enough to feel his warmth, far enough that they weren't quite touching.

The day stretched out before them. One day. That's all Thorne could cover. That's all Sela's ribbon would buy her.

Tomorrow, there would be consequences. Torin's fury. The elders' suspicion. Saav's accusations.

But today—right now—was theirs.

Ezra let her sketchbook fall closed and tucked it beside her. "Tell me about the Rite," she said softly. "What it felt like when you saw me."

Ash's eyes found hers, and something in his expression shifted—opened. Vulnerable in a way she hadn't seen before.

"Like I'd been waiting for you," he said. "My whole life."

Her breath caught. The words settled into her chest, warm and certain and terrifying all at once.

And just like that, she felt the walls between them begin to fall.

Chapter 15

Daylight

The sun climbed higher, burning off the mist in slow ribbons.

Ezra sat with her back against the cool stone of the altar, sketchbook abandoned beside her. Ash had settled a respectable distance away—close enough to talk without raising their voices, far enough that propriety held. Barely.

"Tell me something," she said, tucking a loose strand of hair behind her ear. "Something no one else knows."

Ash's gaze stayed on the treeline, but his mouth quirked. "That's a dangerous question."

"I know." She pulled her knees up, wrapping her arms around them. "But I asked anyway."

He was quiet for a long moment. Then: "When I was ten, I used to sneak onto Nahrim land. By the Selish Sea."

"That's dangerous. The tribes don't—"

"I know." He shook his head, as if the memory embarrassed him. "But the other boys slept and I couldn't. Not with the screaming starting. So I'd slip past the patrols and hide in the rocks where I could see the water." His voice softened. "The Nahrim night-fish there. They sing to the ocean while they work. I'd count stars and listen to their songs until dawn."

Ezra's chest tightened. "Do you still?"

"Sometimes." His voice dropped. "When I need to feel like something other than what they made me. When I need to remember there's beauty in the world that isn't fire."

She understood that. The weight of being shaped by others' expectations. Of carrying a power that set you apart.

"Mine isn't as adventurous as yours," she said with a small smile. "I used to hide in the grain storage. Back corner, behind the big sacks. No one could find me there."

"Why hide?"

"Because everyone wanted something from me. A vision. A reading. Answers I didn't have." She picked at a loose thread on her sleeve. "In the grain storage, I was just Ezra. Not the Oracle. Just...me."

Ash turned to look at her then, really look. "Is that what you want? To be just Ezra?"

"Sometimes." She met his eyes. "But then I think about the Fourth Eye. About Veyar saying no one's had this gift in two hundred years. And I wonder if wanting to be ordinary is the same as running away."

"It's not running if you're trying to survive."

The words landed soft but sure. Ezra felt them settle in her chest like warm coals.

"Is that what you do?" she asked. "On the roof? By the sea? Survive?"

"I used to think so." He shifted, pulling one knee up and resting his forearm on it. "Can't risk Nahrim land anymore. Not as head Fyrwarden. So now it's just the roof." A pause. "But I'm not sure what I'm doing anymore."

The honesty in his voice made her brave. "When did it change?"

He didn't answer right away. A bird called overhead. Wind stirred the vines on the shrine's roof.

"When you touched me," he said finally. "When your hand went over my sigil and I felt something other than fire for the first time in fourteen years."

Ezra's breath caught. "What did you feel?"

"Whole." The word came out rough. "Like I'd been broken so long I forgot what it was like to be anything else."

She wanted to touch him again. Wanted to press her palm to that sigil and prove she could give him that feeling twice. But she stayed still.

"My turn," he said, shifting the weight before it grew too heavy. "Tell me something no one else knows."

Ezra bit her lip, thinking. Then: "I'm afraid of my own power."

His brow furrowed. "Why?"

"Because I don't understand it. Because Veyar disappeared after one conversation and I'm opening eyes that shouldn't exist and I don't know what happens when I can't control them." She pulled her knees tighter. "What if

I see something I'm not supposed to? What if I hurt someone?"

"You won't."

"You don't know that."

"I do." His certainty was absolute. "I've hurt more people than I can count, Ezra. I know what violence looks like. What cruelty looks like." He paused. "You don't have it in you."

"How can you be sure?"

"Because I felt you." He tapped his chest, over the sigil. "When you stepped into my rite. When you put your hand here. I felt what you are underneath all that fear." His voice dropped lower. "You're not a weapon. You're light that got lost in the dark and somehow found its way back."

Ezra's eyes burned. No one had ever said anything like that to her. Not Torin. Not Sela. Not even Orielle with all her wisdom.

"I don't feel like light," she whispered.

"You wouldn't." Ash's mouth curved, sad and knowing. "Light never does."

The morning gave way to afternoon. The sun reached its peak and began its slow descent.

They talked about small things. Ridiculous things. The kind of details people share when they're trying to memorize each other without being obvious about it.

Ezra told him about Sela's terrible singing voice and how she sang anyway, loud and off-key, whenever she was happy. About Torin teaching her to fight when she was seven because he knew Oracles weren't trained for violence and he wanted her to survive anyway.

"He lost his wife," she said quietly. "At this shrine, actually. Fifteen years ago."

Ash's expression darkened. "Raiders?"

"Yes. They..." She swallowed. "He told us about it recently. How they found her. What they did." Her voice wobbled. "He still loves her. After all this time. Says they were soulbound."

"Do you believe in that? Soulbinding?"

Ezra looked at him, really looked. At the sharp line of his jaw. The way his hair fell over his shoulders. The impossible heat in his eyes that should have burned but only ever warmed.

"I didn't," she said. "Until recently."

Something passed between them. Recognition. Understanding. The terrifying acknowledgment of what they were both starting to feel.

Ash cleared his throat, looking away. "Your turn. Ask me something ridiculous."

She laughed, grateful for the lifeline. "Alright. What's your favorite food?"

"Sweet date cakes from the Veyona market. The kind glazed with honey and topped with crushed almonds."

"You have a sweet tooth?"

"We're not supposed to taste much. Fire dulls it." He shrugged. "But the sweetness still gets through somehow. And the almonds add texture I can feel."

"I'll remember that."

"Why?"

Because I want to bring you some, she thought. Because I want to see your face when you taste them. Because I want to keep making you smile like this.

"Just will," she said instead.

Ash studied her, and she felt seen. Truly seen. Not the Oracle. Not the girl with the impossible power. Just Ezra, sitting in the dirt with charcoal on her fingers and hope in her chest.

"My turn," he said. "When did you start drawing?"

"Young. Six, maybe? Torin gave me charcoal and scraps of bark to practice on." She smiled at the memory. "I drew Sela first. Made her look like a angry bird. She threw a boot at me."

Ash laughed—a real laugh, sudden and warm. The sound transformed his face. Made him look younger. Less like a weapon and more like what he might have been if fire hadn't claimed him at eight.

Ezra wanted to sketch that expression. Wanted to capture the exact angle of his smile, the way his eyes crinkled at the corners.

"What?" he asked, catching her staring.

"Nothing. Just...you should laugh more."

"Hard to find reasons."

"I could give you some."

The words hung between them, heavier than she'd meant. Not a joke anymore. A promise.

Ash's smile faded, but his eyes stayed warm. "Yeah," he said quietly. "You could."

The afternoon light turned golden. Ezra had moved closer without meaning to—or maybe Ash had. Either way, the distance between them had shrunk to inches.

She could see the pulse at his throat. Could count the thin scars on his forearms where fire had marked him during training. Could feel the heat of him like standing near a forge.

"Can I ask you something serious?" she said.

"Always."

She twisted her fingers together in her lap. "The rumors. About an Oracle who judges people and...causes accidents." Her voice dropped. "Have you heard them?"

Ash's expression darkened. "Yes."

"Do you know..." She swallowed hard. "Do you know who they're about?"

Silence stretched between them. His jaw worked, and she saw the exact moment he decided to tell her the truth.

His hand covered hers, warm and steady over her twisting fingers.

"You," he said quietly. "They're about you."

The world tilted. Ezra stared at him, not understanding. "What?"

"Saav told me weeks ago. Before we met at the shrine. He said there was a dangerous Oracle who corrupted fire, who judged people for thoughts they hadn't even acted on." Ash's thumb brushed over her knuckles, grounding. "He sent me to test you. To kill you if you left your mark on me."

Her eyes filled with tears. "But I didn't—I would never—"

"I know." His voice was fierce. "I investigated. Found

the lies. But Saav saw us at the market plaza. He's been spreading it wider since then. Drownings. A man killed by a falling planter. Sickness in Veyona—whispers you were poisoning their land." His hands curled tighter around hers. "The rumors got wilder. More elaborate. Painting you as a monster who kills for unspoken crimes."

A tear slipped down her cheek. "Why?" Her voice broke. "Why would someone be so cruel? Say such horrible things about me? About any of my tribe?" She shook her head, more tears falling. "None of us would ever do something so horrible. We help people. We find lost things and offer guidance and—"

"I know," Ash said again, softer now. He shifted closer, his other hand coming up to cup her face, thumb catching the tears. "I know what you are, Ezra. I've felt it. Saav is lying."

"But why me?" she whispered. "I don't even know him. I've never done anything to him."

"I don't know." Ash's jaw tightened with barely controlled rage. "But he's not what he seems. For some reason I don't understand, he's after you. And now he's after me too. Telling the elders I'm cursed. That I have Fyr madness because I met you."

Ezra's hand came up to grip his wrist where he held her face. "What if he's right? What if I am changing you?"

"You are changing me." His eyes blazed. "But not the way he says. You're making me feel. Making me human again. That's not madness, Ezra. That's the only thing keeping me sane."

Ezra reached for him without thinking. Her hand

found his arm, fingers wrapping around scarred muscle. "Let me look. Please. I need to know you're not—"

He pulled back. Not harsh, but firm.

"You're afraid of me," she said, hurt bleeding into her voice.

"No." His tone was rough. "I'm afraid of what you'll see."

"What do you mean?"

Ash looked away, jaw working. Silent for so long she thought he wouldn't answer. Then: "I became head Fyrwarden at sixteen. Youngest ever." He dragged a hand through his hair. "You want to know why?"

She waited, her stomach already twisting.

"Because I'm the most proficient mercenary in the Fyr tribe." The words came out flat, brutal. "Because I have a higher body count than anyone else. Because I'm violent in ways most Fyrwardens aren't."

His jaw tightened. "Fyrwardens can't lie. So when the elders asked if I could do what needed to be done—if I could kill without hesitation, follow orders without question—I told them the truth. Yes. I could. I had." A pause. "That's why they chose me. Not despite what I am. Because of it."

Ezra's breath stopped. Her hand fell from his arm.

She stared at him—at the face she'd drawn as peaceful, at the man who'd talked about counting stars and listening to ocean songs. At the warrior who'd just confessed to being the tribe's best killer.

"How many?" The question slipped out before she could stop it.

Ash's eyes finally met hers, and the pain in them was raw. "I stopped counting after fifty."

Her hand went to her mouth. Fifty. And he'd stopped counting.

"Most of them deserved it," he said quietly, as if that mattered. "Raiders. Enemies of the tribe. People who threatened our borders." A pause. "But not all of them. Some were just...orders."

Ezra felt tears prick her eyes again, but different tears now. Not for herself. For him. For what they'd made him into at eight years old.

"You're horrified," he said. Statement, not question.

"I am," she whispered. Because lying would be worse. "But not—" She struggled to find words. "Not of you. Of what they did to you. Of what they turned you into."

His expression shuttered. "It's the same thing."

"No." Her voice strengthened. "It's not."

"Ezra—"

"You can't lie, right?" She leaned forward, forcing him to look at her. "So tell me this: When you killed those people, did you feel anything?"

His jaw clenched. "No."

"And now? When you think about it?"

"Now I—" He stopped. Swallowed hard. "Now I feel sick."

"Because you're waking up," she said fiercely. "Because whatever they burned out of you to make you a Fyrwarden is coming back. Because you're becoming human again."

"That doesn't change what I did."

"No," she agreed. "It doesn't. But it changes what you

are." She reached for his hand again, slower this time, giving him the chance to pull away. He didn't. "You say you're violent. That you're a monster. But if that were true —if that's all you were—you wouldn't count stars by the Selish Sea. You wouldn't feel sick thinking about what you've done. You wouldn't look at me the way you do."

"And how do I look at you?"

Her voice dropped to a whisper. "Like I'm the first good thing you've ever been allowed to have."

Ash's breath hitched.

"So yes," Ezra continued, tears slipping down her cheeks. "What you told me is horrible. It scares me. But not because I think you're evil." She squeezed his hand. "Because I think you've been suffering alone with this for years and I can't—" Her voice broke. "I can't bear the thought of you carrying that by yourself anymore."

Silence stretched between them, heavy and aching.

"I don't deserve you," Ash said finally, rough and broken.

"Maybe not." She gave him a watery smile. "But you're getting me anyway. Because I choose you. I choose to be here."

He pulled her hand into his. Looked into her eyes. "I choose to be with you, too. We will learn about each other together, but this feels right," as he laced his fingers into hers.

The sun dipped toward the horizon, painting the sky in shades of fire and bruised purple.

"I should get you home," Ash said quietly. "Before it's full dark."

Ezra nodded, though her chest ached at the thought of leaving. "I can get back on my own."

"I know you can." He stood, then offered his hand. "But I'd like to walk you to the border. Make sure you're safe."

She took his hand, letting him pull her to her feet. His warmth lingered even after he released her.

They gathered her things in silence—the sketchbook, her satchel. Then Ash led the way through the trees, taking a different path than she'd come. A faster route, he explained. One that would get her to Kireva land before full nightfall.

They didn't talk much. The day had been filled with words—confessions and fears and choices that still felt too big to hold. Now there was only the sound of their footsteps on soft earth, the rustle of wind through ancient branches, the distant call of birds settling for the night.

When they reached the river that marked the boundary, Ash stopped.

"This is far enough," he said. "Your village is just beyond the ridge. You'll be safe from here."

Ezra looked at the water, then back at him. The fading light caught in his hair, turned his eyes to amber. She wanted to memorize this moment. The way he looked at her. The way the forest held its breath around them.

"Ash," she started, but the words tangled in her throat.

He stepped closer. "I know."

"Do you?"

"You're afraid." His voice was soft. "Of what we chose. Of what it means."

"Aren't you?"

"Terrified." A pause. "But I meant what I said. I choose you."

Ezra's eyes burned. She wanted to cross the distance between them, wanted to touch him, but her feet stayed rooted.

"When will I see you again?" she asked, and hated how small her voice sounded.

Ash's expression tightened with frustration. "I don't know. My responsibilities—the patrols, the training, the council meetings. They will be watching me constantly now that Saav's leading them to believe I have the fyr madness."

His jaw worked. "And Thorne. He covered for me today. One day. That's all he could give before they started asking questions." His voice dropped. "When I go back tonight, I don't know what I'll find. If they believed him. If they're waiting for me."

Ezra's stomach dropped. "Will you be in trouble?"

"Probably." His thumb traced her knuckles, the gesture unconsciously soothing. "But I don't care. You're worth it."

Her eyes burned. "I don't want you to suffer because of me."

"I'm not suffering." His voice was fierce. "For the first time in fourteen years, I'm living. That's worth any consequence they throw at me."

"And I have readings, gatherings, Torin's training."

Ezra's voice dropped. "Orielle is keeping all the young Oracles close. We're not supposed to go anywhere alone."

Her chest tightened. "Sela covered for me today. The ribbon code—she'll tell Torin I was resting if he asks. But I can't ask her to lie for me again. Not when it puts her at risk too."

"The market plaza," Ash said suddenly. "It's neutral ground. I can make excuses to be there. Supply runs. Trade negotiations."

"I can too. Orielle sends me sometimes when no one else can go." Hope flickered in her chest. "It's not perfect, but—"

"But it's something." His hand reached for hers across the distance, fingers tangling. "We'll find each other there when we can. Even if it's just..."

"Just seeing you," she finished. "Even from across the plaza."

"It won't be enough."

"No." She smiled sadly. "But it's better than nothing."

His thumb brushed over her knuckles, and the simple touch sent heat racing through her veins. She stepped closer without meaning to, pulled by the same invisible thread that had bound them since the shrine.

"I can't promise tomorrow," he said, voice rough. "Or even next week. The elders are watching. Anok is worried. If I slip away too often—"

"I know." Ezra squeezed his hand. "I can't promise either. And if Torin finds out I've been sneaking away..." She swallowed. "But I'll keep trying. Whenever I can. However I can."

"Me too." His other hand came up, cupping her face.

"Even if I have to ride through the night. Even if I can only stay an hour."

"An hour is enough."

"It's not." His voice cracked. "But it'll have to be."

The space between them had shrunk to nothing. She could feel the warmth radiating from him, could count the scars on his forearms where fire had marked him during training. His hand trembled slightly against her cheek.

"Ezra," he whispered, and her name on his lips sounded like a prayer. Like a vow.

She tilted her face up to his. "Don't let go."

"Never."

And then he kissed her.

The world narrowed to the warmth of his lips against hers, the soft gasp that escaped her as his mouth claimed hers. It wasn't gentle. This was the kiss of a man who had burned with need, who had been hollowed out by longing, who had spent an entire day aching to do this and had held himself back through sheer force of will.

His lips moved over hers, demanding at first, searching, desperate. One hand cradled her face while the other slid to her waist, fingers digging in lightly, anchoring himself in the reality of her.

Ezra answered him with equal hunger. Her hands fisted in his shirt, dragging him closer. The taste of him—smoke and salt and something that was just Ash—made her dizzy.

He made a sound low in his throat, half groan, half plea, as he deepened the kiss. Then something shifted. The urgency melted into something slower, reverent. His thumb brushed her cheekbone with impossible tenderness as he kissed her like he was memorizing the shape of her mouth, the way she sighed against him, the small sound she made when his teeth grazed her lower lip.

Her fingers slid into his hair, and he shuddered at the touch. The fire mark on his chest pulsed hot between them, responding to her nearness, to the connection that had formed the moment she'd first touched him.

When they finally broke apart, both breathing hard, he pressed his forehead to hers. The sky had darkened to deep purple. Stars were beginning to appear overhead.

"I thought about doing that all day," he whispered, voice wrecked.

"Why didn't you?"

"Because I was afraid I wouldn't stop." His hands trembled where they held her. "And you deserve better than being kissed senseless by a river while the world tries to tear us apart."

Ezra's laugh was shaky, overwhelmed. "I don't want better. I want you."

Something in his expression cracked open—all the walls he'd built, all the control he'd maintained, shattered by those four words.

"I have to go," Ezra whispered, though every part of her rebelled at the thought.

"I know." But his hands didn't release her. Couldn't.

"This isn't goodbye," she said fiercely, needing to believe it.

"No." His thumb traced her jaw. "Just...until next time."

"However long that takes."

"However long." He kissed her forehead, her temple, the corner of her mouth. Small kisses, gentle ones, as if trying to memorize her through touch alone. "Be careful. Stay close to your people. Don't go anywhere alone."

"I won't. You be careful too." Her hands framed his face. "Saav is dangerous. And if the elders—"

"I'll handle them." His voice was certain. "Nothing is keeping me from you. Not Saav, not the elders, not the distance between our tribes."

She believed him. Saw it in his eyes, felt it in the way he held her like she was the most precious thing in the world.

One more kiss. Quick and fierce and full of promise.

Then she stepped back. Her hands fell away from him slowly, reluctantly.

She turned and started toward the river, boots finding the familiar stones. When she reached the far bank, she looked back.

Ash stood where she'd left him, silhouetted against the darkening trees. Watching. Making sure she made it across safely.

She raised her hand in goodbye.

He raised his in return.

Then she turned and climbed the ridge toward home, lips still tingling, heart still racing, carrying the warmth of his kiss like a coal in her chest.

The path remembered her feet. The night settled gentle around her shoulders.

Tomorrow, she'd face Torin. His questions. His fury when he realized she hadn't been resting in the longhouse.

The fear in his eyes when he understood she'd gone to Ash anyway.

I'm not losing you.

But she'd already chosen. And she'd choose again. As many times as it took.

She didn't know when she'd see Ash again—tomorrow, next week, maybe only glimpses across the market plaza.

But she would keep trying. Keep sneaking away. Keep choosing him.

Because they had chosen this. Chosen each other.

And nothing—not tribes, not rumors, not even the gods themselves—would make her regret it.

Chapter 16

What Cannot Be Unseen

The longhouse was warm when Ezra slipped through the door, the scent of banked coals and dried herbs wrapping around her like an old blanket. Her satchel hung heavy on her shoulder, charcoal-smudged and dirt-streaked from a day spent sitting on stone and moss.

And her lips still tingled from his kiss.

Sela looked up from where she sat mending a torn sleeve, needle paused mid-stitch. Her eyes swept over Ezra —disheveled hair, flushed cheeks, swollen lips, the unmistakable glow of someone who'd spent the day somewhere they shouldn't have been.

Sela's mouth dropped open. "You kissed him."

It wasn't a question.

Heat flooded Ezra's face. She dropped her satchel by her pallet and sank onto the edge of her bed, unable to stop the smile that spread across her face. "I kissed him."

"Ezra!" Sela threw her mending aside and launched

herself across the space between them, grabbing Ezra's hands. "Tell me everything. Right now. Every single detail."

"Sela—"

"Was it good? Of course it was good, look at your face. You look like—" Sela stopped, squinting at her. "Wait. Your lips are swollen. How long were you kissing him?"

Ezra buried her face in her hands, laughing despite her embarrassment. "Long enough."

Sela made a gleeful sound. "I knew it! I knew the moment you came back from that shrine the first time that something was going to happen. The way you talked about him, the way you drew his face over and over—" She pulled Ezra's hands away from her face, grinning wickedly. "So? How was it? And don't you dare give me some vague romantic nonsense. I want details."

"I do." The admission came easily now. No hesitation. No fear. "I love him, Sela. And he loves me. He said it. He chose me."

Sela's expression shifted—joy mixed with something deeper. Understanding, maybe. Or recognition.

"Is it weird?" Ezra's voice dropped, suddenly uncertain. "Am I crazy? We've only met three times."

"You're not crazy." Sela squeezed her hands harder, fierce and certain.

"But three times, Sela. Three times and I feel like—like I can't breathe without him. Like I've known him my whole life." Ezra's voice cracked. "I've never felt anything like this before. Never wanted anyone before. What if I'm just—what if it's just because he's the first person who ever—"

"Stop." Sela's voice was firm. "I think Dad's right. I think you're soulbound."

Ezra's breath caught. "But Dad said—"

"I know what Dad said. That he and Mom were soulbound." Sela's voice softened, thoughtful. "And maybe they were. But honestly? I think he just loved her that much. Loved her so deeply it felt like destiny." She paused. "Soulbinding isn't typical. It's rare. Really rare. The kind of thing that happens once in a generation, if that."

She leaned closer, her grip tightening on Ezra's hands. "But this? What you're feeling—this overwhelming, impossible certainty after only three meetings? When you've never wanted anyone before in your entire life?" Her eyes were fierce. "That's not normal love, Ez. That's not even extraordinary love. That has to be soulbinding. It has to be a gift from the gods, even though they vanished centuries ago. That's the only thing that makes sense."

"You really think so?" Ezra whispered.

"I do." Sela's voice dropped, almost reverent. "Because you're not someone who falls easily. You never have been. People have tried—plenty of them—and you never even looked twice." She smiled sadly. "And then you meet him once at a shrine, and suddenly you can't stop drawing his face. That's not coincidence, Ez. That's destiny."

Ezra laughed through the tears, wiping at her cheeks. "We don't know when we'll see each other again. The tribes, the rumors, everything between us—"

"You'll find a way." Sela's voice was certain. "Love like that doesn't just disappear because it's inconvenient."

"You sound like Dad. When he talks about your mother."

"Good." Sela smiled. "Then maybe he'll understand when he finds out."

Ezra's stomach dropped. "We can't tell him. Not yet. Not with everything—"

"I know." Sela sighed. "But he's going to figure it out eventually. You came home with kiss-swollen lips and stars in your eyes. He's not blind, Ez."

Ezra's stomach dropped. "Wait—where is Dad?"

"Tribunal." Sela waved a hand. "He was gone before dawn. I heard him leave while you were still asleep."

Relief flooded through Ezra so fast her knees nearly buckled. "He didn't see me come back?"

"Didn't see you leave, either." Sela grinned. "I found your ribbon on my table this morning, but by the time I got up to check on you, you were already gone, and so was he. Emergency tribunal—border dispute with one of the northern tribes."

"When will he be back?"

"Late tonight. Maybe tomorrow if it goes badly." Sela's grin widened. "So luck was definitely on your side today."

Ezra let out a shaky breath. When she'd woken this morning, she'd been terrified—certain Torin would be waiting with questions she couldn't answer, disappointment in his eyes, fear in his voice. The ribbon code hadn't even been necessary.

But her relief was short-lived. "I can't keep doing this. He's going to figure it out eventually."

"I know." Sela's expression softened. "But you're safe for now. That's what matters." She pulled Ezra into a hug. "I'm happy for you. You got your first kiss. Even if the timing of it all terrifies me."

Ezra held her tight, grateful beyond words for Sela's fierce loyalty, her unwavering support.

When they pulled apart, Sela's grin had returned. "So. On a scale of 'pleasant' to 'I forgot my own name,' how was the kiss?"

Ezra threw a pillow at her. "Sela!"

"What? I'm your sister! I deserve to know these things!"

Despite everything—the fear, the uncertainty, the dangers ahead—Ezra laughed.

"It was perfect," she admitted softly. "He was perfect."

Sela's expression turned serious for a moment. "Then hold onto that. Whatever comes next, remember how this felt. Remember that he chose you and you chose him."

"I will."

"Good." Sela stood, brushing off her skirt. "Now come on. I'm starving, and you look like you haven't eaten all day."

"I haven't."

"Then let's fix that."

The night air was cool against Ezra's skin as they walked toward the communal fire pit. Lanterns swung from low branches, casting dappled light across the packed earth. The scent of roasted roots and spiced bread drifted on the breeze, mingling with laughter and the low hum of conversation.

Members of Kireva still lingered despite the late hour—elders sharing stories by the fire, children chasing each other between tents, families gathering for evening meals.

They'd just filled their bowls when a familiar figure emerged from the shadows between the longhouses.

Orielle.

Ezra's stomach dropped. The head Oracle moved with quiet purpose, her weathered face grave in the firelight. She carried a small bundle wrapped in cloth, held close to her chest like something precious. Or dangerous.

"Ezra." Orielle's voice was low, meant only for them. "Walk with me."

It wasn't a request.

Sela squeezed Ezra's hand once—a silent question. Ezra nodded. *It's fine.* Sela hesitated, then stepped back, giving them space but staying close enough to watch.

Orielle led her away from the fire, toward the edge of the village where the torchlight didn't reach. When she was certain no one could overhear, she stopped.

"I came back early from the tribunal," Orielle said without preamble. "The border dispute was settled quickly. But the rest..." Her jaw tightened. "The tribunal spent hours discussing the Fyrwarden and Oracle rumors. You and the head Fyrwarden were seen together at the market plaza."

Ezra's breath stopped. Her heart hammered against her ribs.

"The focus is on you now," Orielle continued, her voice flat. "They're calling you the corrupted Oracle. The one who poisons Fyrwarden fire."

"I didn't—" Ezra's voice cracked. "I would never—"

"I know." Orielle's hand came up, firm and certain. "Torin knows. We've raised you. We know what you are and what you're not." Her eyes softened slightly. "We don't believe the rumors. Neither of us."

Relief flooded through Ezra so fast her knees weakened.

"But there's something else." Orielle's expression darkened. "One of the Veyona elders pulled me aside after the main session ended. Made sure no one else was around—not even the other tribunal members." She paused, choosing her words carefully. "They don't believe the rumors either. They think there's foul play."

"Foul play?"

"Teyna is dead." Orielle's voice dropped to barely above a whisper. "She was one of their most powerful elders. A Rootsinger."

Ezra's breath caught. Rootsingers were rare—Veyonians who could sing life into the land, coax growth from barren soil, heal withered crops. Losing one was devastating.

"Her Rootsong is gone," Orielle continued. "Ripped out of her. And without it, the fields around Veyona are dying. Not from poison or blight—from absence. The land is grieving." Her hands tightened on the bundle. "The Veyona elders need to know what happened. But they can't ask openly. Not with the tribunal focused on blaming Oracles for everything."

She held out the bundle.

Ezra stared at it, heart pounding. "What is that?"

"Teyna's scarf. The last thing she wore before she died." Orielle's eyes met hers, sharp and assessing. "Your visions are sharper than mine, Ezra. Clearer. You see things the rest of us can't." A pause. "I don't want to show favoritism. I don't want the others thinking I'm putting you above them. But if anyone can see the truth of what happened to Teyna, it's you."

Ezra's hands trembled as she took the bundle. The fabric was soft through the cloth wrapping, and even covered, she could smell it—lavender and something earthier beneath. Sweat. Soil. Smoke.

Memory clung to it like cobwebs.

"This is dangerous," Ezra whispered. "If the tribunal finds out—"

"They won't. The Veyona elder gave this to me in secret. No one else knows." Orielle's grip on Ezra's shoulder was firm. "But I need to know what we're facing. If someone is killing Oracles and stealing their gifts..." Her voice hardened. "I need to protect our tribe. I need to protect you."

Ezra looked down at the bundle in her hands. It felt heavier than it should. Weighted with more than fabric and memory.

"I'll try," she said, though her stomach had already begun to twist. "I'll see what I can."

Orielle nodded, relief flickering across her face. "Don't do this alone. Keep Sela with you. Or come find me if you need an anchor." She paused. "And Ezra—if you see something terrible, don't carry it by yourself. Come to me. Do you understand?"

"I understand."

"Good." Orielle squeezed her shoulder once more, then stepped back into the shadows, disappearing as quietly as she'd come.

Ezra stood alone in the darkness, the scarf heavy in her hands.

When she returned to the fire, Sela was waiting. One look at Ezra's face and she was on her feet.

"What did she want?"

"I'll tell you later." Ezra's voice was barely above a whisper. "Let's just...eat. Please."

They ate in silence—roasted roots sweetened with honey, spiced bread still warm from the ovens, pickled vegetables sharp enough to make Ezra's eyes water. But Ezra barely tasted any of it. Her mind kept returning to the bundle in her satchel, to the weight of what Orielle had asked.

When the fire burned low and Sela's yawns grew frequent, they returned to the longhouse. Sela crawled into bed, but her eyes stayed on Ezra.

"You going to tell me what that was about?" Sela asked softly.

"Tomorrow," Ezra whispered. "I promise."

Sela studied her for a long moment, then nodded. Within minutes, her breathing evened out into sleep.

But Ezra couldn't settle. Her skin felt too tight, her thoughts too loud. The scarf seemed to pulse in her satchel, calling to something deeper than sleep.

She slipped from bed and out into the night.

The grove beyond the village was silent save for the whisper of wind through ancient branches. Moonlight filtered through the canopy in pale shafts, painting the moss-covered stones in silver.

Ezra walked until the sounds of the village faded, until there was only the hush of her own breathing and the distant call of a night bird.

Then the air shifted.

"I was wondering when you'd show," she said without turning.

Veyar stepped from the trees as if he'd always been there, barefoot and silent. His bone-white robes whispered at his ankles, the hems shimmering faintly as though they carried their own light.

He said nothing at first, only fell into step beside her, his presence heavy as cedar smoke.

Ezra's throat tightened. She'd been holding the words in since the Rite of Flame, but they spilled out now in a rush. "I saw him. Ash. In the flames during his ritual."

Veyar's head turned slowly. "You entered a Fyrwarden's vision?"

"No." Her breath quickened. "I was there. It wasn't a dream—it wasn't memory. He spoke to me. He told me to meet him."

Veyar stopped walking. The grove bent quiet around them, as if even the trees were listening. His eyes—dark as wet stone—narrowed. "Impossible."

Ezra turned to face him, desperate for him to understand. "I felt him. His fire felt me. The flame changed because of it."

Veyar studied her with an intensity that made her skin prickle. When he spoke, his voice was blade-sharp with disbelief. "The Fourth Eye shows the past. Memory. Fixed and unchanging." He paused, eyes boring into hers. "But what you describe—stepping into the present, being seen, being felt—that was not the Fourth."

Ezra's breath caught. "Then what—"

"The Seventh." His voice dropped, almost reverent. "The Eye of Soul. It allows you to see soul connections in present time, to step into another's soul-space when the bond is strong enough." He circled her slowly, as if seeing her for the first time. "That's why the Fyrwarden felt you. Why his fire recognized you. Why you could interact with his ritual instead of merely observing."

Her stomach dropped. "Seventh? But you told me about the Fourth—"

"Because I expected you to open them in order. First, Second, Third, then Fourth." His expression was unreadable, but his stillness pressed heavier than words. "You skipped ahead. Opened the Seventh before the Fourth, Fifth, or Sixth. That should be impossible."

Ezra's hands trembled. "How many are there? How many Eyes?"

Veyar's silence stretched, then cracked. "Nine."

The world tilted. "Nine? All this time I thought...I thought there were only three."

"Most Oracles never open beyond the Third. But you..." His voice lowered, almost reverent. "You've opened the Seventh. You have no idea the storm you've invited. The Ninth belongs only to the Goddess Visionary herself."

"How many have you opened?" Ezra asked, fear threading through her voice.

His gaze did not waver. "Seven. I am liminal—caught between god and memory. But even I will never touch the final two. They are not for me. They are not for anyone living."

Her head spun. Nine Eyes. Nine ways to see. Nine doors she didn't know how to close. "What do they all do?"

"The first three you know—Flesh, Feeling, and Knowing. The Fourth is Memory." He began to pace, moonlight catching in the folds of his robes. "The Fifth is Empathy—to feel what others feel, to step into their skin. To become them."

Ezra's stomach dropped at the description. To become them. She had a feeling she'd find out what that meant soon enough.

"The Sixth is Shadow—to see what is hidden, what is obscured. The Seventh reveals the Soul's Desire—the one you opened for your Fyrwarden."

Soul. Ash. The Rite. She'd opened the Seventh without even knowing. Had stepped into his soul-space and been recognized.

"The Eighth shows the Living Thread that binds all things. And the Ninth..." His eyes darkened. "The Ninth is Omniscience. To see all that was, all that is, all that could be."

Too much. It was too much to hold. Ezra's stomach turned. "I can't—this is too much."

"Which is why you must be careful." Veyar's voice gentled, but the weight did not lift. "You are moving faster than I expected. Faster than I've ever seen. The Seventh Eye alone should have taken years to open. And the faster you open, the thinner the walls will become. If you lose yourself in the Eyes, they will not give you back."

Panic clawed at her throat. "Then tell me how to stay grounded."

Veyar stepped closer, his presence thick as smoke. "You will need anchors. Two. No more. No less. One for your body. One for your mind. Choose those you trust without question. If either betrays you, you will not return."

The answer came immediately, as if her heart had already known. "Sela," she whispered. "And Torin."

Veyar inclined his head. "Then make them your anchors. Let them know their role. They must stay by your side when you wander—watch over your body, call you back if you drift too deep. If you lose yourself in the Eyes, they are the tether that pulls you home."

Ezra nodded, though her pulse trembled. "And you mentioned...objects?"

"Objects remember," Veyar said. "Keep close something bound to the one you seek—a scarf, a blade, a stone warmed by years of touch. Memory clings to matter. It can steady the Eye and draw you deeper when you call."

Understanding bloomed in her chest. Teyna's scarf—that's why Orielle had given it to her. The object would help her see.

And Ash. She'd touched his sigil. His fire. Objects tied to his very soul.

That's why the Seventh Eye had opened for him.

"There's something else you should know," Veyar said, his voice darker now. "The Kildra mage—Saav. He's coming to Kireva."

Ezra's stomach dropped. "I know. Orielle told me. The tribunal—"

"The tribunal is the least of your concerns." Veyar's expression was grave. "Saav is a blood mage. He deals in curses, rot, death. He's been leaving a trail of bodies across the tribes—elders dying in agony, their gifts stolen." His eyes bored into hers. "Stay away from him. If he comes to

Kireva, do not let him near you. Do not touch anything he's touched. Do not trust a word from his mouth."

"Why?" Ezra whispered. "Why is he doing this?"

"I don't know. But he's searching for something. Someone." Veyar's jaw tightened. "And I fear you're part of whatever he's planning."

Her hands trembled around the scarf bundle. "Teyna. The Veyona elder who died. Her Rootsong was stolen."

Veyar's expression darkened further. "Then it's worse than I thought. Rootsong is powerful—one of the rarest Oracle gifts. If he's collecting them..." He didn't finish, but the implication hung heavy between them.

"Orielle gave me Teyna's scarf. She wants me to see what happened."

"Then be careful." Veyar's hand came to her shoulder, heavy and warm. "What you see may break you. The Fifth Eye—Empathy—doesn't just show you what happened. It makes you become the person in that moment. You will feel what they felt. Think what they thought. If the person you step into is a killer..." His voice dropped. "You will feel their pleasure. Their satisfaction. And you won't be able to stop it."

Ezra's throat closed. "I have to try. The Veyona elders need answers. Orielle needs to know what we're facing."

"I know." Veyar's grip tightened. "Just remember—no matter what you see, no matter what you feel in that moment—it's not you. You are not the monster. You're only witnessing." His eyes softened slightly. "And when it's over, come find me if you need to. Don't carry that darkness alone."

He released her shoulder and stepped back.

"You are safer now than you were this morning," he said softly. "But only because you know how close danger walks. And because you know what you're capable of."

Ezra looked back toward the village, where lantern light glowed faintly through the trees. When she turned to thank him—

Veyar was already gone.

She exhaled slowly, then walked the rest of the way alone.

The longhouse was quiet when she returned. Sela slept curled on her side, one arm draped over her blanket, mouth slightly open.

Ezra crawled into bed and pulled Teyna's scarf close, lavender filling her lungs.

Veyar's words echoed in her mind. *Objects remember. You will become them.*

If she held tight to herself, maybe she could walk through the memory without losing herself completely. Maybe she could see the truth without being destroyed by it.

But even as she thought it, dread pooled in her stomach.

Sleep came swiftly.

And the vision rose to meet it.

She stood inside someone else's eyes.

Not beside. Not watching. *Inside.*

A clearing spread before her, a stone well at its heart. An old woman knelt in the dirt, hands trembling as she carved sigils into soil salted and ashed. The air pressed heavy with burnt sage, scorched lavender, bitter smoke that scalded Ezra's lungs.

Teyna. She knew the name without being told.

The woman looked up, hope cracking through weariness. "Saav. Are the wards finished?"

Ezra's lips parted to answer—

But the sound that came wasn't hers.

"Oh yes." The voice was warped, slick as oil, rising through her mouth like it had crawled from the bottom of a drowned well. "The wards are finished. Completely."

Pleasure. Hot and vicious. It pulsed through Ezra's chest like a second heartbeat—*his* heartbeat—and she wanted to vomit but her body wouldn't obey.

Teyna froze. Confusion first. Then horror.

No no no please— Ezra screamed inside the prison of his skull but nothing came out. She tried to jerk her hands back, to run, to do anything, but her body moved without her. His body. His will.

Her hands—*his* hands—lifted.

Power spilled from her fingertips, black and shimmering, oily as tar across water. It stank of rot and copper and something sweet-sick underneath, like fruit left too long in the sun. The smell coated the back of her throat, made bile rise.

Her skin blackened with it. Shadow uncoiled like hunger, lashing outward, choking the air.

It struck Teyna.

The old woman's mouth opened in a scream that never finished. Her body convulsed, spine arching so hard Ezra heard the vertebrae crack. Teyna's hands clawed at her own throat, fingernails tearing skin, blood welling dark beneath them. Her eyes went wide—so wide the whites showed all around—and then they started to bleed.

Not tears. Blood. Thick and black, pouring from the corners like ink.

Ezra felt it. Felt the curse sink into Teyna's flesh like hooks, felt the woman's terror crash into her own. Felt Teyna's heart stutter and lurch, felt the air rip from her lungs and refuse to return.

And worse—*worse*—she felt his satisfaction. Saav's pleasure rolled through her like heat, like the first bite of a perfect meal, like scratching an itch that had festered for days. He *enjoyed* this.

Teyna collapsed to her knees, whimpering. The sound was animal. Broken. Her skin began to blacken from the inside out, veins turning dark beneath papery flesh. The scent of decay bloomed thick—rotting meat and turned earth and human waste.

Ezra sobbed soundlessly inside his body. She was drowning in him, in his thoughts, in the vicious glee that made her want to claw her own eyes out just to stop seeing.

Stop stop STOP—

But it didn't stop.

Teyna's hair fell out in clumps. Her teeth loosened in her gums. She tried to speak but only blood came out, bubbling past her lips in thick gouts. Her fingers scrabbled at the dirt, nails breaking, leaving red smears.

"Shhh," Saav's voice crooned through Ezra's mouth, gentle as a lullaby. "It won't hurt much longer."

Liar. Ezra felt every second of Teyna's agony like it was her own.

Teyna's eyes found his, disbelieving, accusing. Her lips moved, blood bubbling between them. The words came out broken, barely audible: "The gods...are dead..."

Rage erupted through him—through Ezra. "NO!"

The word ripped out like a scream, like a prayer denied. His hands—her hands—slammed down on either side of Teyna's head, fingers digging into the poisoned earth.

"Only because of a curse!" Spittle flew from his mouth. "I need the Rootsong. I need it to bring her back. My goddess. My Visionary." His voice dropped to something reverent, obsessed. "She is alive. She will be mine."

Teyna's eyes went wide with horror. Understanding. She tried to shake her head, tried to pull away, but the curse had her pinned.

Then Saav's hands moved to hover over her chest, and Ezra felt him pull.

Not with his hands. With something deeper. Darker.

Light rose from Teyna's chest—golden-green, threaded with the essence of growth and life and earth. Her Rootsong. The gift that let her sing to the land, coax crops from barren soil, heal withered fields.

It struggled. Twisted. Tried to return to its owner.

But Saav pulled harder, and the light tore free with a sound like roots ripping from soil. Teyna's mouth opened in a soundless scream as her gift was wrenched from her very soul.

The golden-green light writhed in the air between them, still fighting, still trying to return. Saav's hands closed around it, and where it touched his skin, it began to blacken. Rot spreading through beauty. Death consuming life.

He absorbed it into himself, and Ezra felt the rush of stolen power flood through him. Felt his satisfaction. His triumph.

Teyna's body went slack. Her eyes stared at nothing. The woman who had sung life into the earth was empty. Hollow. Dead.

"Thank you,"

The roots carried the rot into the ground. Trees shuddered, bark splitting open to weep black sap. The air itself soured, thick enough to choke on. Crops withered in seconds—stalks collapsing like broken bones, grain turning to ash. Shadows bled into the river, and Ezra heard the fish dying, belly-up, their scales sloughing off into the poisoned water.

Everything he touched turned to rot.

Everything *she* touched.

Because she was him. She was the hands that had done this. The mouth that had lied. The pleasure that had savored every scream.

The vision released her with a violence that felt like being ripped in half.

Ezra woke choking.

Her throat was raw, torn from screaming she didn't remember starting. Her body shook so violently the pallet rattled beneath her. She couldn't breathe—couldn't get air past the phantom taste of rot and copper coating her tongue.

She gagged, rolling to her side, and vomited.

Nothing came up but bile and spit, but her body kept heaving anyway, ribs seizing, stomach clenching until her vision went white at the edges. The stench of decay was still in her nose. Teyna's blood still sticky on her fingers even though her hands were clean.

Clean, clean, they're clean, it wasn't me—

But it had been. She'd felt it, done it, *enjoyed* it.

"Ezra!"

Hands grabbed her shoulders, and she flinched so hard she cracked her head against the wall. Pain exploded bright and sharp, but it didn't matter because Teyna's face was still burned into her eyelids, mouth open, eyes bleeding—

"Ezra, look at me!"

Sela shook her. Hard. "Ezra!"

The sound cut through. Ezra's eyes snapped to Sela's face—pale, frightened, *alive*. Alive.

"I—" Ezra tried to speak, but the words tangled, came out broken. "I killed—I didn't—his hands—"

"You're not making sense." Sela's voice was tight, trying to stay calm and failing. "Ez, you were screaming. You woke up screaming, and you won't stop shaking—"

"I was him." The words ripped out of Ezra like confession, like purging poison. "I was *inside* him. Saav. I—" She gagged again, pressed her fist to her mouth. "I felt what he felt. When he—when he killed her—"

Her whole body convulsed. She doubled over, forehead pressed to her knees, hands fisted in her hair hard enough to hurt. She needed the pain. Needed something real to anchor to because she could still feel the curse crawling under her skin, still feel Teyna's heart stopping, still feel the *pleasure*—

"I killed her," Ezra whispered, and the words broke on a sob. "I killed her with his hands, and I *felt* it, Sela. I felt her die. I felt him enjoy it."

The sobs came then, wrenching and ugly, tearing out of her chest like something dying. She clung to Sela and shook apart, and even Sela's arms around her couldn't make her feel clean.

Because she could still smell the rot.

Still taste the blood.

Still feel the hooks sinking in.

She thought of Ash. Of the way he'd looked at her by the river, the way he'd called her light. But she didn't feel like light now. She felt stained. Dirtied by what she'd seen, what she'd felt, what she'd been forced to become—even for a moment.

Saav had killed Teyna with pleasure. With satisfaction. Had stolen her Rootsong to bring back his goddess. And he was coming to Kireva.

Coming for her.

Coming for the Oracle he'd spent weeks framing for murders.

And for the first time in her life, Ezra was terrified of what her power could make her see.

Chapter 17

The Choosing

Two days had passed since the vision.

The morning after, Ezra had gone to Orielle. She'd found the head Oracle in the herb garden behind the longhouse, hands deep in soil, face lined with the kind of worry that came from carrying too many secrets. When Orielle looked up and saw Ezra's tear-stained face, her trembling hands, she'd known immediately.

"You saw."

Ezra had nodded, throat too tight to speak.

They'd talked for hours. Ezra described everything—Saav's pleasure as he killed, Teyna's agony as the curse took her, the golden-green light of her Rootsong torn from her soul like roots ripped from earth. She'd told Orielle about his words: *My goddess. My Visionary. She will be mine.*

Orielle had gone pale, then hard as stone.

"He's coming here," Orielle had said, voice flat and deadly. "The Veyona elders were right to suspect foul play.

This wasn't random violence. This was orchestrated. Planned." Her grip on Ezra's shoulder had been fierce enough to bruise. "When he arrives, you stay close to me. You don't speak to him. You don't let him touch you or anything he's touched. Do you understand?"

"What will you tell the tribe?"

"The truth. That Teyna was murdered by a blood mage who steals Oracle gifts. That her Rootsong was taken to fuel his obsession with resurrecting a dead goddess." Orielle's eyes had burned with cold fury. "And that anyone who trusts the Kildra mage is a fool who will get us all killed."

She'd sent word to the other Oracles that same day. Called an emergency gathering. Warned them all to be vigilant, to travel in pairs, to trust no strangers bearing gifts or promises.

But whispers traveled faster than warnings. By the second day, the whole village knew. An Oracle had been murdered. Her gift stolen. And the killer was coming to Kireva.

Fear had settled over the tribe like frost.

Torin still hadn't returned from the tribunal. The border dispute had resolved quickly, but new complications had emerged—something about water rights and trade agreements with the northern tribes. Sela had received word he'd be delayed another few days.

Part of Ezra was relieved. When he came home, when he learned what she'd done, where she'd been going...

But that was a problem for another day.

This morning, Ash had sent word through a traveling merchant: *Market plaza. Noon. I need to see you.*

She'd read the note three times, her heart both lifting and breaking. She needed to see him too—desperately. Needed his warmth to drive back the cold that had lived in her bones since the vision. But she also needed to tell him what she'd seen. Warn him that Saav wasn't just after her.

He was after anyone who stood in his way.

The Market Plaza hummed with its usual chaos—merchants hawking wares, children weaving between stalls, the mingled scents of spiced cider and roasted nuts. Ezra stood beside Sela at a fabric merchant's table, pretending to examine bolts of dyed wool while trying to ignore the nausea that had been her constant companion since the vision two nights ago.

She'd barely slept after seeing Teyna's death. Every time she closed her eyes, she felt Saav's hands—her hands—lifting to cast that terrible curse. Felt his pleasure rolling through her like poison.

"You look awful," Sela murmured, not looking up from the indigo cloth she was inspecting.

"I feel awful."

"Maybe we should go home. You don't have to—"

"No." The word came out strained. "He sent word to meet here. I need to see him." She stopped, pressing a hand to her stomach. How could she explain that Ash's fire and warmth was the only thing that would drive back the memory of rot and decay? That even thinking about him made the cold recede?

Sela's hand found hers, squeezing gently. "Okay. But if you need to leave—"

"I'll tell you."

Two familiar figures on horseback crested the rise at the plaza's edge, and despite everything—the exhaustion, the lingering horror—Ezra's heart lifted.

Ash sat his horse with that same controlled intensity, his long dark hair loose down his back, shimmering black as midnight in the morning light. When his eyes found hers across the crowded plaza, something in her chest settled. Warmth bloomed where cold had taken root.

The memory of their first kiss rushed back, and heat crept into her cheeks. This was the first time seeing him since.

Beside him, Thorne looked more alert than usual, his gaze immediately seeking and finding Sela.

"There they are," Sela said, her voice brightening. She raised her hand in greeting. "Ready?"

Ezra nodded, though her legs felt unsteady as they crossed the plaza.

Ash dismounted smoothly, but his expression shifted the moment he got a closer look at her. His eyes tracked over her face—the shadows beneath her eyes, the pallor of her skin, the way she held herself like someone trying not to break.

"Ezra." Her name came out rough with concern. He started toward her, then stopped himself, glancing at the crowd around them. Too many eyes. Too many witnesses.

"I'm fine," she said automatically.

His jaw tightened. Even without a bond between them, he would have known she was lying. "You're not."

Sela cleared her throat meaningfully. "You know, Thorne, I've been dying to check out that new weapons merchant on the south platform. Very important. Could take hours."

Thorne's eyebrows rose slightly. He turned to Ash, who gave a subtle nod of approval.

"Excellent." Sela grabbed Thorne's arm, though her eyes stayed on Ezra. "Why don't you two go to the shrine? We'll take our time here. And Ez?" She squeezed her sister's hand once, grounding. "Remember what we talked about."

"I know." Ezra managed a small smile. "Thank you."

They disappeared into the crowd, Thorne's head bent toward Sela as she chattered about blade techniques she clearly knew nothing about.

The moment they had relative privacy, Ash stepped closer and pulled her into a long, warm embrace. She melted into him, absorbing his heat, letting it chase away the chill that had lived in her bones since the vision. His hand found hers as they walked to his horse.

He lifted her up with careful strength, then climbed behind her, surrounding her with his presence. As they headed out of the Market Plaza toward Kireva, Ezra leaned back into him, wrapped in his arms. The gentle sway of the horse and the solid warmth of his body was a balm to her soul.

They rode in comfortable silence along the road that led south from the plaza. Kireva wasn't far—barely more than a mile—and the trail that led to the shrine branched off just past her village. When they were on the quiet stretch beyond Kireva's edge, approaching the river crossing near the shrine, Ash finally broke the silence.

"What happened?" His voice was low, meant only for her. "You look like you haven't slept."

"I haven't. Not really." She wrapped her arms tighter around herself despite his warmth. "I had a vision. Two nights ago, after we last met."

His body tensed behind her. Had she changed her mind about him? He'd been feeling so many intense sensations with her pressed against him—her warmth, her scent, the softness of her—and he'd been grateful for the silence at first, needing time to simply absorb the wonder of it.

His body went rigid behind her. The warmth that usually radiated from him flickered, dimmed. When he spoke again, his voice was tight with something she'd never heard from him before.

Fear.

"Tell me," he managed, though the words sounded strangled.

Was he afraid she'd changed her mind? That the vision had made her see him differently?

They crossed the shallow river, water splashing softly around the horse's hooves, and continued up the winding trail. The shrine finally appeared through the trees—ancient stone wrapped in vines, slate roof missing half its tiles. Even through her distress, Ezra felt something in her chest loosen.

Safe. This place felt safe. Ash felt safe.

He dismounted and helped her down, hands lingering at her waist. He needed to know what she'd seen, needed to hear whatever had put that haunted look in her eyes—even if it meant hearing she regretted their kiss.

Her legs wobbled when her feet hit the ground. The nausea surged, and she swayed.

"Ezra—" His arm came around her immediately, supporting her weight. "Gods, you're burning up." His expression twisted with guilt. "I should have noticed. I was so—" He stopped, jaw clenching. "I'm sorry."

"Am I?" She pressed her hand to her forehead. It felt normal to her, but then again, everything felt wrong right now.

He guided her to sit on the grass near the altar while he tended to the horse. She watched him work—loosening the girth, pulling the saddle blanket free with practiced efficiency. The simple, practical motions steadied her somehow. Reminded her that the world still worked in normal ways. That not everything was cursed visions and shadow magic.

He shook out the blanket and laid it on the grass beside her, then sat close enough that their shoulders nearly touched.

"Tell me," he said quietly. "What did you see?"

Ezra pulled her knees up, wrapping her arms around them. The words came slowly at first, then faster, tumbling out in a rush. She told him about Teyna's scarf. About the vision that pulled her in so deep she'd lost herself in it. About being inside Saav's body, feeling his pleasure as he murdered an old woman who'd trusted him.

"I felt him enjoy it," she whispered, voice breaking. "I felt the curse go into her. Felt her heart stop. And I couldn't—I couldn't do anything to stop it because I wasn't me anymore. I was him."

Something shifted in his expression—relief flooding his features, then fury darkening them. She could see both warring across his face as he processed what she'd told him.

His hand found hers on the blanket, fingers threading through hers. "You're not him. You know that, right? What you saw—what you felt—that wasn't you."

"But it felt like me." Tears slipped down her cheeks. "My hands. My mouth. His pleasure. How do I know where he ends and I begin?"

"I know we've only known each other for days, but I swear it feels as if we've known each other for lifetimes." His other hand came up to cup her face, turning her to look at him. "And there's nothing of him in you. Nothing."

"How can you be sure?"

"Because I've felt you." He tapped his chest, over the sigil. "Remember? When you touched me, I felt everything you are. Light and warmth and kindness and love." His thumb brushed away her tears. "Saav is none of those things. You are all of them."

The certainty in his voice cracked something open in her chest. She turned into his touch, letting herself lean against him. His arms came around her immediately, holding her close.

"I'm scared," she whispered against his shoulder. "What if I see something worse? What if I lose myself completely?"

"You won't." His hand stroked her hair, slow and

soothing. "Because you're stronger than you know." His voice roughened. "And because I won't let that happen. Even if I have to burn the whole world down to bring you back."

Despite everything, she almost smiled. "That's very dramatic."

"I'm a Fyrwarden. We specialize in dramatic."

This time she did smile, just a little. She stayed there in his arms, breathing in the scent of him—smoke and cedar and something uniquely Ash—until the trembling finally stopped. Until the warmth of him drove back the cold that Saav's vision had left behind.

When she finally pulled back to look at him, his expression was fierce and tender at once.

"Better?" he asked.

"Better?" he asked.

"Better." And she meant it. The nausea had eased. The exhaustion still pulled at her, but the horror had receded to something manageable. Something she could carry.

Because of him.

"Thank you," she said softly. "For this. For everything."

"You don't have to thank me." His hand came up to tuck a strand of hair behind her ear, fingers lingering against her cheek. "I told you before—I choose you. That means all of it. The visions, the fear, the days when you can barely stand. All of it."

Her throat tightened with emotion. "I choose you too. Even when—" She stopped, swallowing hard. "Even when I know about the things they made you do. I'm not going anywhere."

His eyes burned with too much feeling to name. "You're going to ruin me."

"Good." She smiled through her tears. "You've already ruined me."

The space between them had shrunk to nothing. She could feel his breath against her lips, could see the exact moment he stopped fighting what they both wanted.

"Ezra," he whispered, her name a question and a prayer.

"Yes," she answered, and closed the distance.

The kiss was different from their first one. Slower. Deeper. Weighted with everything they'd confessed since then—his violence, her visions, the impossible choice they'd already made to walk this path together.

His mouth moved against hers with careful intensity, like he was memorizing the shape of her, the taste of her. When his teeth grazed her lower lip, she gasped, and he swallowed the sound.

Her fingers slid into his hair, pulling him closer. His hand splayed across her lower back, drawing her flush against him. Heat bloomed between them—not his fire, not Oracle sight, just the warmth of two bodies finally, finally allowed to touch without fear.

When they broke apart, both breathing hard, his forehead pressed to hers.

"I needed that," he admitted roughly. "Needed you."

"Me too." She kissed him again, softer this time. "You make everything better. Even the worst days."

"You do the same for me." His hands framed her face, thumbs brushing her cheekbones. "Every night since we met, I sleep better. The screaming is less. The fire burns quieter." His voice dropped to a whisper. "After our kiss—you're healing me, Ezra."

"Don't thank me." She covered his hands with hers. "Just stay. Keep being here. That's all I need."

"Always." He kissed her forehead, her temple, the corner of her mouth. Small kisses, gentle ones, full of promises they hadn't spoken yet. "For as long as you'll have me."

"Then you're in trouble," she said with a watery laugh. "Because I'm never letting you go."

Something shifted in his expression—wonder mixing with hunger, tenderness bleeding into need. But he didn't move. Didn't close the distance. She could see him fighting it, every muscle locked tight, holding back a storm.

So she chose for both of them.

Ezra kissed him, fierce and claiming. Not the tentative exploration of their first kiss, but something deeper. A declaration.

The sound he made was guttural, almost a growl. His hands came up to her waist, gripping hard enough to leave marks. When she bit his lower lip, his control shattered like glass.

He kissed her back with a hunger that stole her breath. His mouth moved against hers—demanding, devouring. One hand fisted in her hair, angling her head to deepen the kiss. The other splayed across her lower back, crushing her against him.

"Ezra—" Her name came out ragged. "I don't know if I can—" His whole body was shaking, but not with weakness. With restraint. Like he was holding back a wildfire with his bare hands. "Everything I'm feeling—it's too much. You're too much."

"Good." She pressed against him deliberately, and he groaned, forehead dropping to her shoulder. She felt the heat radiating off him—his Fyrwarden fire responding to his desire, making the air around them shimmer.

"I need this," she whispered against his ear. "I need you to burn away everything else. Make me forget the cold."

His breath came harsh against her throat. When he lifted his head, his eyes had darkened—pupils blown wide, the brown nearly swallowed by black. Heat flickered at their edges.

"If I start—" His voice was barely human. "I don't know if I can stop."

"Then don't." She pulled him down onto the blanket, and he came willingly, powerfully, covering her with his body. The ancient shrine kept watch. The sky vast and blue above.

Her hands found the laces of her dress, working quickly. "Help me."

Ash's hands joined hers, and where she fumbled, he tore. Fabric parted beneath his grip—not violent, but urgent. Desperate.

When her skin was bared to the afternoon light, when his shirt was cast aside and her hands met the bare heat of his chest, they both knew there was no going back.

"Ezra—" Her name was a question and a prayer.

"Yes," she answered. "Yes to all of it."

And then there were no more words.

Chapter 18

The Binding

There was no going back now.

The ancient shrine kept watch. The sky stretched vast and blue above them. The blanket was soft beneath her back, and his body—warm and solid and trembling with restraint—covered her.

This was her choice. Her need. Her want.

And she had never been more certain of anything in her life.

"Gods—" The word fell from his lips like prayer and blasphemy at once. His hands moved over her bare skin, possessive and reverent. Everywhere he touched, heat followed. Not burning, but close. So close. "I can feel everything. Your pulse. The way your skin flushes. The—" He shook his head, words failing him.

She reached for his shirt, and he helped her this time, yanking it over his head and throwing it aside. When her hands met the bare skin of his chest, he shuddered violently. His Fyrwarden sigil blazed beneath her palm.

With absolute focus. With hunger that had been denied too long.

"I've wanted—" His voice was gravel and smoke. "Since the first time you touched me, I've wanted—" Another shudder. "This is madness. You're driving me mad."

"Good." She pulled him down into a kiss that was all heat and need. When his weight settled fully over her, she felt the barely-leashed power in him. The fire burning just beneath his skin, demanding release.

He kissed her throat, her collarbone, each touch searing. His hands mapped her body like he was memorizing her through touch alone—learning her the way he'd learned to master flame. With absolute focus. With hunger that had been denied too long.

"You're so soft," he breathed against her skin. "So alive. I can feel your heart racing. Feel the heat between—" He groaned, low and rough. "Tell me how. Tell me what you need."

"You." Her hands slid into his hair, gripping tight. "Just you. All of you."

His laugh was broken, desperate. "You already have me. You've had me since the shrine. Since—" He kissed her again, harder this time. "I'm yours. Completely. And I don't know what to do with how much I want you."

"Then let me show you." She guided his hand lower, over her ribs, her stomach. Showed him where she ached for him. "Let me help you burn."

His hands trembled, sliding over her ribs, her stomach, lower. When his fingers found the heat between her thighs, they both gasped—him at the slick evidence of her desire, her at the first electric touch.

"Yes—" The word broke on a moan as he stroked, tentative at first, then bolder. Learning what made her gasp, what made her arch.

She reached for him, fingers working the laces of his trousers with fumbling haste. When she freed him—thick and hard and burning hot—he groaned like she'd wounded him.

"Ezra—I don't—" His hips jerked involuntarily into her touch. "Gods, what are you doing to me?"

"Showing you what I want." She stroked him once, and fire literally sparked at his fingertips. He buried his face against her throat, panting. Sweat rising, trying to contain his fire.

"I'm going to lose control," he warned, voice breaking. "I can feel the fire—it wants out—"

"Then let it." She guided him between her thighs, and they both froze at the contact. "Let it burn."

He entered her slowly, carefully, despite the inferno raging inside him. The stretch made her gasp—pain and pleasure and fullness all at once. He stilled immediately, trembling with the effort of holding back, breathing hard.

"Don't stop," she breathed. "Please don't stop."

"You're—" His voice was wrecked. "So tight. So perfect. I can feel everything—"

He pressed deeper, and she cried out, nails digging into his shoulders. When he was fully seated inside her, they both struggled to breathe. The intimacy of it—the connection—was overwhelming.

"Move," she whispered. "Ash, please—"

He obeyed, pulling back and thrusting slowly. Testing. Learning. Each movement drew gasps from them both. The pleasure built gradually, then faster, spiraling higher with every rock of his hips.

Fire began to leak from his skin. Small flames dancing across his shoulders, down his arms. He tried to pull back, panicked, but she held him fast.

"Don't—" She arched against him. "It doesn't burn. It feels—gods, it feels like—"

The flames spread, encasing them both in a cocoon of golden light. But where they touched her skin, instead of burning, they caressed. Stroked. Like a thousand heated fingers worshiping every inch of her.

The blanket beneath them should have caught fire. The grass around them should have withered. But the flames moved with purpose, with consciousness—touching only her, warming without destroying. As if his fire knew the difference between what it should consume and what it should cherish.

"Ezra—" Her name was a prayer torn from his throat. He thrust harder, deeper, losing himself in the sensation. The fire burned brighter, hotter, responding to his need. His lips pressed down on hers in a kiss, swallowing her moans.

She was drowning in sensation—him inside her, moving with increasingly desperate rhythm, and the flames dancing across her skin, teasing her breasts, her throat, everywhere. The pleasure built impossibly high, threatening to break her apart.

"I can't—" Ash's voice broke. "I can't hold—"

Their hands found each other beside her head, fingers

lacing together without thought. Palm to palm. A connection as natural as breathing.

The moment their hands touched, light erupted between them.

Not his fire. Something else. Something ancient.

Lines of brilliant light began etching themselves into their joined palms. An eye wreathed in flames on hers. A flame curved like an eye on his. The marks burned as they formed, searing into flesh and bone and soul.

The pleasure crested higher. Impossibly higher.

Ash thrust harder, flames roaring around them in response. She could feel him everywhere—inside her, around her, the fire an extension of his touch. It stroked between her thighs, circled her breasts, until she was writhing beneath him, sobbing with the intensity of it.

"Ezra—I'm—gods, I'm—"

"Yes—" She could barely speak. "Yes, with me—"

The marks blazed brighter, and suddenly she felt him. Not just physically, but deeper. His wonder. His desperation. His love. His soul pressed against hers like their palms, merging, becoming one.

And he felt her. Her warmth. Her light. Her choice to be his. Her soul choosing his in return.

The realization struck them both at once—this wasn't just pleasure. This was binding. A vow made without words. A choice sealed in fire and flesh.

I choose you, her soul whispered to his.

I choose you, his answered back. *Always. Forever.*

The marks flared one final time, and they shattered together.

Ezra's climax tore through her like lightning—white-hot and all-consuming. She screamed his name as waves of pleasure crashed over her, each one higher than the last. The fire around them surged in response, flames reaching toward the sky.

Ash roared, the sound primal and raw. His release hit like a breaking dam—overwhelming, unstoppable. He thrust deep and stayed there, body locked against hers, as he spilled himself inside her. The flames exploded outward in a brilliant sphere of golden light.

For one perfect moment, they burned together. Two souls. One fire. Completely joined.

Then the flames collapsed inward, rushing back into Ash's skin. The light faded, leaving only the gentle warmth of afternoon sun and the marks glowing softly on their palms.

Ash collapsed over her, braced on trembling arms, forehead pressed to hers. Their joined hands still blazed between them—the marks sealed, permanent, undeniable.

"What—" His voice was hoarse, barely above a whisper. "What did we—"

"A vow," Ezra breathed, tears slipping down her temples. "We made a vow. Our souls—they chose. It was as if they'd been waiting to do this forever."

He stared at their hands, at the matching marks that had branded them irrevocably. The eye-and-flame sigil, split between them. Ancient. Forbidden. Perfect.

"I felt you," he said, wonder threading through his voice. "Inside me. Your soul touched mine."

"I felt you too." She brought their joined hands to her lips, kissing the mark on his palm. "You're mine now. In every way that matters."

"And you're mine." He kissed her, soft and reverent, a different kind of claiming than before. "For as long as souls endure."

The marks pulsed once more in agreement, then settled into a steady glow.

Chosen.

Bound.

Eternal.

They returned to the Market Plaza as the sun dipped toward the horizon, painting the sky in shades of copper and gold. The ride back had been quiet, both of them still processing what had happened, the marks on their palms glowing faintly with each touch.

As they approached the plaza, Ezra spotted Sela first. Her sister's smile started bright—the teasing grin Ezra knew too well—but it faded as her eyes tracked over Ezra's face. Down to where she and Ash stood close but not quite touching, tethered somehow. Sela's gaze caught on Ezra's throat, and her eyes widened slightly.

She knows, Ezra realized. Or suspects.

Ash and Ezra separated reluctantly as they dismounted. He walked toward Thorne, and Sela immediately closed the distance to Ezra, eyes sharp with concern and curiosity.

"What happened?" Sela asked, pulling Ezra aside while Thorne engaged Ash in quiet conversation near the horses. "You look—" She gestured vaguely at her sister's face, the way she held herself. "Different. Like something fundamental changed."

Ezra's throat tightened. She couldn't find the words, so instead she simply opened her palm.

The mark blazed softly in the fading light—an eye wreathed in flames, intricate and undeniable. Beautiful. Terrifying.

Sela's eyes went wide. Her hand flew to her mouth. "What is that?" She grabbed Ezra's wrist, pulling her hand closer to examine the mark. "Ez, what—is that a brand? Did someone—"

"No." Ezra's voice was steady despite her racing pulse. "It formed on its own. When we—" She stopped, cheeks flushing deeper. "When we were together."

Sela's eyes went even wider. "Together. You mean—" She glanced toward Ash, then back to her sister. "You slept with him."

Ezra nodded, unable to speak past the sudden lump in her throat.

"And this appeared?" Sela stared at the mark, something like awe creeping into her expression. "During?"

"At the moment we..." Ezra swallowed. "At the moment our souls touched. We were joined, and light erupted between our palms. The marks burned themselves into our skin. His is the same—a flame shaped like an eye."

Sela was quiet for a long moment, studying the mark, the way it pulsed faintly with light. When she spoke, her voice was hushed. "I've never seen anything like this. Never even heard of anything like this."

"Neither have we." Ezra's hand trembled slightly. "But Sela, when it happened—when the marks formed—I felt his soul. He felt mine. Like we were choosing each other not just with our bodies or our words, but with something deeper. Something eternal."

"Soul binding." Sela's voice was barely a whisper. "True soul binding. Not the metaphor Dad uses about Mom, but the real thing." She looked up, eyes shining with unshed tears. "Ez, this is—" She stopped, shaking her head. "The elders are going to lose their minds."

"Why?" Ezra's stomach dropped. "What will they do?"

"I don't know." Sela gripped her shoulders, urgent and afraid. "Because this kind of bond—a mark that appears, that glows, that connects souls—I don't think anyone alive has seen it before. They'll either call it a miracle or they'll call it dark magic." Her voice dropped. "And right now, with all the rumors about Oracles corrupting Fyrwardens, which do you think they'll choose?"

Ezra's breath caught. She hadn't thought—hadn't considered—

"We need to hide that mark," Sela said firmly. "At least until we figure out what it means and how to explain it without getting you both killed."

Sela stared at her for a long moment, reading the certainty in her expression, the way she seemed more solid somehow. More present than she'd been since the vision. Then, slowly, her fierce grip softened and she pulled Ezra into a crushing hug.

"Then I'm happy for you," Sela whispered against her hair. "Terrified out of my mind, but happy."

"That seems to be the consensus," Ezra managed with a watery laugh.

When they pulled apart, Sela brushed away a stray tear

from her own cheek. "We need to hide that mark. At least until we figure out how to tell Dad without him having an apoplectic fit."

"How exactly do I hide a glowing sigil on my palm?"

"Gloves. Bandages. I don't know—we'll figure something out." Sela grabbed her hand, studying the mark more closely. "It's beautiful though. Terrifying, but beautiful."

Across the plaza, Thorne's voice rose slightly. Not angry, but shocked. They both turned to see Ash showing him the matching mark on his palm.

Thorne's expression cycled through shock, concern, then something like awe. He gripped Ash's shoulder, saying something too low to hear. Whatever it was made Ash's jaw tighten, made him nod once, sharp and certain.

Then, as if feeling her gaze, Ash looked up.

Their eyes met across the plaza.

The bond hummed to life between them—not overwhelming, but present. Warm. Real. She felt the echo of his emotions: wonder, possessive satisfaction, fierce protectiveness. And underneath it all, love so intense it stole her breath.

His lips curved into the smallest smile. Just for her.

"Come on," Sela said gently, tugging her toward their horses. "Let's get you home. We'll figure out the rest tomorrow."

But even as they mounted and began the ride back to Kireva, even as Ash and Thorne headed north toward Fyr, Ezra felt the connection holding strong. Distance meant nothing now. The marks on their palms pulsed in time with their heartbeats, a constant reminder of what they'd become.

Bound.

Chosen.

And Ezra knew, with absolute certainty, that whatever came next—whatever the tribunal decided, whatever Saav planned, whatever darkness waited in the days ahead— they would face it together.

They had chosen each other.

Soul to soul.

Fire to light.

And nothing—not the tribes, not the elders, not even the gods themselves—could unmake that choice.

Ahead, Kireva's lanterns glowed in the dusk. Some- where in that village, Torin would return soon. Orielle waited for updates. Saav drew closer with each passing day.

But tonight, Ezra carried warmth in her chest and a mark on her palm that said she was no longer alone.

Tonight, that was enough.

Chapter 19

What the Water Showed Them

Veyar and Kee

Liminal Space

The Pool of Seeing lay still beneath the moon's pale eye, its surface dark as obsidian and veined with thin gold threads that pulsed faintly, as if the world's heartbeat had been trapped beneath stone. Moss rimmed the basin, damp with night, and the hush of the shrine pressed close, as though even air was forbidden to move.

Kee crouched near the edge, one hand hovering above the water. Cold breathed upward, clinging to skin, pulling like a tether. Every time it tempted touch. Every time it warned against it.

Kee broke the silence first, voice low, too sharp to be casual. "We wait, and nothing changes. The spiral twists the same way, over and over. But this..." Kee's jaw tightened. "This feels worse. Stronger. Like the pattern itself is rotting."

Veyar stood motionless, robe stirring faintly in the draft. His long white hair caught the starlight like frost, but his eyes remained shadowed, weighed by centuries.

"We are bound by the pact," he said at last. The words dragged, reluctant, sour. "No hand upon the weave. Only warnings given. I have stayed apart—watching from the shadows of the pool. Ezra's sight grows keener than expected. Too much contact and she would know what I am. What we risk."

Kee's fingers curled into fists against the stone rim. "And what about me? Am I meant to watch Ash walk blindly again? Pretend I don't want to tell him everything?"

The pool's light flickered faintly, gold veins stuttering like embers fighting for breath.

Kee leaned closer, voice rough. "I always find him. Every life, every cycle—Ash becomes my friend, even when I'm not looking for him. Like I can't help it." A hollow laugh caught in Kee's throat, unfinished. "But this spiral doesn't look like the others. I don't know this shape."

The pool's surface rippled without touch, golden threads pulsing brighter for a breath—then flaring, brilliant and strange, a pattern neither of them had seen before.

Kee's hand jerked back from the water. "What was that?"

Veyar's eyes narrowed, fixed on the pool. "Show me," he commanded, staff dipping into the water.

The vision shifted. The shrine. Afternoon light. Two figures tangled together on a blanket, fire burning gold around them—and then light, searing and sudden, erupting between their joined palms.

Marks burned into flesh. An eye wreathed in flames. A flame curved like an eye.

The vision faded, but the echo of it lingered in the pool's depths—golden threads now wound differently, twisted into a shape that hadn't existed before.

"No," Veyar breathed, and for the first time in centuries, his voice shook. "That's not possible."

Kee stared at the water, at the new pattern writhing through the spiral. "What did they do?"

"A Life Sigil." Veyar's knuckles whitened on his staff. "It bound them. Soul to soul. Life to life." His voice dropped to barely a whisper. "This has never happened before. Not in the first life. Not in any cycle. This is something new."

"New?" Kee's breath caught. "How can it be new? We've watched them for—"

"I don't know." Veyar's admission came reluctant, frightened. "From what I can feel through the weave—through life and death itself—the sigil didn't just bind their souls. It merged their lives. Inextricably. Deeper than anything we've seen." His jaw clenched. "If one dies, the other—" He stopped. Couldn't finish.

Kee stood abruptly, fists clenched. "Then we have to—"

"We can do nothing." Veyar's voice was stone, but his eyes betrayed him—grief and fury warring beneath. "The pact binds us. We cannot interfere. We can only watch as they walk into—"

"Into what?" Kee demanded. "You saw the sigil form. You know what it means. What aren't you saying?"

Veyar turned back to the pool, stirring it again. The water darkened, showing different visions—Saav, kneeling over Teyna's corpse. Saav, speaking to shadows in a darkened room. Saav, eyes fixed on a crude drawing of Ezra's face.

"He doesn't just want to kill Oracles," Veyar said slowly, each word pulled from him like a blade from a wound. "He's channeling something. I've felt it in the weave—power that tastes like Bastillion, but wrong. Sickened. Corrupted."

Kee's eyes widened. "Bastillion? But he's—"

"Gone. Like the rest of the gods." Veyar's expression hardened. "But Saav is trying to channel what remains. He thinks—" Veyar stopped, studying the visions playing across the water. Saav killing. Saav stealing gifts. Saav watching Ezra from shadows.

"He thinks Ezra is Visionary," Kee said, horror dawning. "In human form."

"Yes." Veyar's voice was flat, dead.

The pool rippled again, showing more: Saav standing over the bodies of dead Oracles, their gifts stolen. Saav at the edge of Kireva, watching Ezra through the trees. Saav in a dark room, surrounded by stolen light—Rootsongs and other gifts, all corrupted to sickly red.

"Look at the pattern," Veyar said, gesturing to the visions. "He doesn't kill randomly. Every Oracle he targets is near Ezra. Every tribe he poisons is one she might turn to for help." His hands trembled on his staff. "He's isolating her. Destroying everyone around her."

Kee stared at the pool, understanding dawning with horror. "He thinks if she has no one else—"

"She'll turn to him." Veyar's jaw clenched. "And he's channeling Bastillion's power—corrupted, yes, but power nonetheless. He believes that if he can channel the god of fire and destruction, he can—" He stopped, the thought too terrible.

"Become Bastillion through her." Kee's voice was hollow. "If she's Visionary, and he brings her back to divine state..."

"He thinks he can ascend with her. Through her." Veyar closed his eyes. "Watch."

The pool showed Saav again, this time kneeling before a makeshift altar. Crude drawings of the Visionary goddess. Offerings of stolen Oracle gifts. His lips moving in prayer—not to the goddess, but speaking to her as if she could hear him. As if she were already present.

"Delusion," Veyar whispered. "He truly believes she'll love him for this. That every murder is an act of devotion—stripping away what he sees as human weakness so the goddess can emerge."

Kee's fists clenched. "That's not love. That's—"

"Obsession. Narcissism woven with sociopathy." Veyar's eyes were ancient and tired. "He believes he's saving her. And that makes him more dangerous than any curse."

The pool showed more: Oracles dead, their gifts stolen. Tribes turning on each other. Fear spreading like poison. And at the center of it all—Ezra, unaware, carrying marks that made her a beacon for something she didn't understand.

"And now the Life Sigil," Kee whispered. "It makes them—"

"More of a target." Veyar's voice was hollow. "Because if Saav discovers what they've done—that they've bound themselves in a way that's never been done before—he'll see it as proof. Proof that Ezra is the Visionary. That she's accessing divine power." His grip on the staff tightened until it creaked. "And he'll move faster. Harder. He'll destroy everything to get to her."

"Then we have to warn them—"

"I have warned Ezra. As much as I can without breaking the pact." Veyar's voice was taut with restraint. "But I cannot tell her what I see. Cannot explain that the blood mage hunting her believes she's a goddess. Cannot reveal that his obsession will drive him to murder everyone she loves." His eyes closed. "That is the curse of the pact. Knowledge without the ability to act."

Kee's jaw clenched, every muscle rigid with fury barely contained.

Kee pressed harder against the stone rim, trembling with fury. "We gave them a choice, remember? To come back to the first life. To try to mend what shattered before Saav cursed them, before they signed the pact with you. That was supposed to be the hope. The clean beginning." Kee's voice cracked. "Only this time it's worse. Nothing is like the first life. Saav is more brutal. Ash and Ezra are more volatile. And technically..." Kee's gaze cut toward Veyar, sharp as a blade. "Technically, the pact doesn't even exist yet in this timeline. So why can't we interfere?"

Veyar's grip whitened on his staff. "Because to act now

is to bind them tighter. Do you think I don't feel it? The spiral frays with each passing moment." His voice dropped. "But the moment we step beyond warning, we unmake their choice. That is the true curse, Kee—not Saav's, but ours, if we forget."

Kee's mouth tightened, words catching. For a moment it looked as if more might spill out. Instead, Kee folded arms across chest, jaw set in hard defiance. "You sound so certain. But I think you're just afraid."

"I am," Veyar admitted, eyes heavy with grief too old to disguise. "And that is why I will not move beyond what the pact allows. Fear drives interference. Love demands restraint."

Kee held his gaze for a long moment, then looked away. Arms stayed crossed, shoulders stiff, posture locked in fuming silence. Every part of Kee bristled with refusal, yet beneath the heat lingered something quieter, unspoken—trust. Not in the pact. Not in the spiral. In Veyar.

At last, Veyar dipped his staff into the pool and stirred the water in a single sweep. Ripples spread outward, and vision rose like breath breaking the surface.

The pool revealed open fields, their crops bowed heavy under moonlight. A well stood at the clearing's center, its stones damp with moss, water seeping dark from the cracks.

Beside it lay Teyna. Her body was already collapsing inward, shriveled like bark after fire, skin clinging to bone. Veins that once sang with Rootsong stretched unnaturally out of her limbs—blackened cords of root and blood pulled tight into the earth around the well, pinning her to the soil as if the land itself had swallowed her alive.

Kee sucked in a breath, sharp and furious. "Teyna..."

"She bore the Rootsong," Veyar whispered, grief threading every word. "The eldest of Veyona. The strongest. Her gift was meant to pass to the next generation when death came naturally—to keep the earth magic flowing through their tribe. Their crops. Their trade. Their very survival." His voice hardened. "And now—"

Saav knelt at the well, hood shadowing his face, gloved hands dripping black oil. His blade flashed, cutting deeper into Teyna's chest. Roots and sinew split with the sound of tearing cloth. He reached inside, fingers closing around what pulsed there—light, fragile, ancient. The Rootsong itself, torn from its vessel.

Kee's fists hammered against the stone rim. "He's stealing it—"

The light flickered once in Saav's grasp before he crushed it with fingers slick with shadow. The glow twisted, corrupted—green turning to sickly red, life magic inverted into rot. He drove it into the well's stones, smearing symbols with blood and sap. His chant rose guttural, harsh, wrong—words scraping like bone dragged across stone.

The earth bucked. The well shuddered. Teyna's body jolted as the veins still tethered to her were driven deeper into the soil, binding her death to the land. Blackness rippled outward in waves, seeping through roots and waterlines, poisoning what she had spent a lifetime nurturing.

The vision widened. Fields withered in heartbeats,

stalks collapsing to ash. The river darkened, fish rising belly-up. Villagers clutched their chests—not in pain, but confusion. Then suspicion. Rage blooming where trust had lived. Fear rippling through them like rot through grain.

"He doesn't just kill," Veyar said, voice like stone. "He inverts the gift. Binds her death to the land and poisons it. Turns the Rootsong itself into a weapon. Veyona will starve. Their magic will wither. And the other tribes..." He closed his eyes. "They will see only the sickness. The blight. They will blame each other."

"Ezra touched that vision," Kee said, voice breaking with fury. "She saw through his eyes. Felt him kill Teyna. Felt his pleasure." Kee's hands shook. "But she didn't see this—the theft. The binding. She doesn't know he stole the Rootsong and weaponized her death. She thinks she was the monster who enjoyed it."

"And Saav knows what she doesn't," Veyar said, voice heavy as stone. "He knows the spiral. Knows what should happen. And he's changing it—corrupting each step to ensure they break before they can heal what was shattered."

The pool's light trembled, the golden spiral in its depths stuttering like a thread pulled too tight.

"We are bound," Veyar said at last, voice heavy. "Until they choose their path. Until the spiral breaks—or binds anew."

The water stilled. The moon's reflection returned, perfect and cold.

Kee stared at it for a long moment, then stood. Arms still crossed, jaw set with defiance barely leashed.

"The pact binds you," Kee said softly, dangerously. "But I am made of shadows, and not bound at all."

Veyar's eyes snapped to Kee, a warning forming on his lips—

But Kee was already gone, melted into darkness like mist at dawn.

Chapter 20

The Night Kireva Fell

The sickness came back worse.

Ezra had felt better after being with Ash—his fire had driven back the cold, the Life Sigil on her palm had pulsed warm with their connection. For one perfect day, she'd felt whole.

But the next morning, the vision returned.

Not a new one. The same one. Teyna's death replaying behind her eyelids every time she blinked. Saav's pleasure rolling through her like poison. The curse sinking into flesh, the woman's heart stopping, the rot spreading through the land.

Over and over and over.

"It won't stop," Ezra whispered, pressing her gloved palms to her eyes. The thin silk couldn't hide the heat—the Life Sigil blazed through the fabric, a constant reminder of what she'd become. But even that couldn't drive back the images. "I keep seeing it. Feeling it."

Sela pressed a cool cloth to her forehead. "The vision from before? The one with Teyna?"

"Yes." Ezra's body shook. The fever had returned with a vengeance—burning and freezing in alternating waves. Her head split with pain that made vision blur, made thoughts scatter like leaves in wind. "It's like it's happening again. Like I'm trapped in his body, doing it over and over—"

"You're not him," Sela said firmly, gripping her hand. "You're here. With me. Safe."

But Ezra didn't feel safe. She felt like she was drowning. And worse—she couldn't feel Ash anymore.

The bond that had hummed between them since the Life Sigil formed had gone quiet. Not severed—she would have felt that like a blade through her chest. But muffled, as if someone had wrapped it in thick wool and buried it deep.

"Something's wrong," she gasped, clutching at the mark on her palm. "I can't feel him. Sela, I can't feel him at all."

"Maybe he's just far away. He went back to Fyr yesterday—"

"No." Ezra shook her head frantically. "It's not distance. It's like—like he's not there. Like he's—" She couldn't finish the thought. Terror closed her throat.

What if Saav had done something to him? What if the tribunal had already—

"Don't," Sela said, reading the panic in her face. "Don't go there. He's alive. You'd know if he wasn't."

Would she? The bond was so new, so untested. What if she was wrong?

The day crawled past. Ezra drifted in and out of consciousness, the vision playing on repeat. Each time she woke, she reached for the bond—for any sense of Ash on the other end—and found only silence.

By the second day, she was too weak to leave her pallet.

Sela never left her side. True to the promise she'd made after Veyar's warning, she'd become Ezra's anchor—one of two protectors for body and mind. She pressed cool cloths to Ezra's brow, whispered stories to keep her tethered to the waking world, held her hand through the worst of the visions.

"He's coming," Ezra whispered through cracked lips, trying to convince herself. "I can feel him. He's trying."

But she couldn't feel him. That was the worst part. The bond lay dormant, and she was alone with Saav's memory eating her alive.

Sela's hand tightened on hers. "I know. But Ez, you need to eat something. Drink something. You're wasting away."

Ezra tried. Gods, she tried. But everything tasted of ash and copper, of Teyna's death replaying on her tongue. The visions came harder now, sharper. Not just the memory anymore—prophecies bleeding through, futures she didn't want to see.

She saw Ash chained. Saw fire consuming him from within. Saw the Phoenix rising, terrible and beautiful. Saw herself reaching for him across an impossible distance, fingers falling just short.

"No," she gasped, jerking upright, Sela catching her before she fell. "No, they can't—they're going to—"

"Shh, you're safe. You're here with me." Sela's voice

was steady, grounding. "I promised I wouldn't leave you. Remember?"

"I remember." Ezra's fingers clutched at Sela's hand like a lifeline. "You're my anchor. You and Torin."

"That's right. And we're not going anywhere."

But Ezra knew better. Safety was an illusion. Saav's curse—the one he'd planted when she'd stepped into his memory—had taken root. It was spreading through her like poison through water, and without Ash's fire to burn it out, she was running out of time.

The market brought news on the third day of her relapse.

Torin returned at dusk, his expression grim. He sat heavily on the bench by the hearth, dirt still caking his boots, exhaustion carved into every line of his face.

"The tribunal met," he said without preamble. "All seven tribes. They've made their decision."

Ezra's stomach dropped. She knew—she'd seen fragments in her fevered visions—but hearing it spoken aloud made it real.

"You've been spared," Torin continued, voice rough. "The Life Sigil on your palm was noted, but they've ruled it a manipulation—Fyrwarden magic used to seduce and corrupt an Oracle. They blame Ash entirely." His jaw tightened. "They condemned the Fyrwarden who burns with madness. He will be exiled to the Shattered Vale beyond the Sacred Valley."

Sela's face went white. "That's a death sentence."

"It's meant to be." Torin's hands curled into fists. "Saav

convinced them. Showed them 'evidence' of the poisoned lands, the dying crops, the sickness spreading through Veyona. Blamed it all on your bond breaking the balance between tribes."

"But it's him!" Ezra tried to sit up, but her body wouldn't cooperate. "I saw him kill Teyna. I felt him poison the land. Why won't anyone believe—"

"Because he's a respected mage from Kildra," Torin said heavily. "And you're a young Oracle who's been having visions no one else can verify. And Ash is a Fyrwarden who nearly burned down his own tribe during a ritual."

The words hit like blows. True, all of them. And damning.

"What about Ash?" Ezra's voice broke. "Where is he?"

Torin's expression darkened further. "Locked in Fyr's dungeons. They drugged him the moment he returned from the market plaza three days ago—the elders were waiting. He's been unconscious since. That's why—" He stopped, understanding dawning in his eyes as he looked at where the glove couldn't quite hide the glow. "That's why you can't feel him through your bond. He's not conscious to feel."

Everything suddenly made terrible sense. The silence. The emptiness where Ash should be.

And the fever. The relapse. The visions returning with vicious strength. It wasn't just Teyna's curse. It was Ash, unconscious and drugged, their merged lives pulling at each other across the distance. His forced sleep dragging her down with him.

He wasn't ignoring her. He wasn't abandoning her.

He was drugged. Imprisoned. Helpless.

And she was dying with him.

"The charges against him are severe," Torin continued, voice heavy. "They're blaming him for Teyna's death. For the blight spreading through Veyona's lands."

Ezra's blood ran cold. "What?"

"Three days ago, massive fires erupted across Veyona's fields—Fyrwarden fire, they say. Ash's signature." Torin's expression was grim. "It took all of Nahrim, Seyathi, and Morilan working together to contain it. Saav was there too, creating protection barriers, helping coordinate the effort. When he returned to the tribunal, he testified that the fire was deliberate. Targeted. The work of a Fyrwarden who'd lost all control."

"No." The word tore from Ezra's throat. "No, that's impossible. Ash was with me three days ago. We were at the shrine, we—" She stopped, cheeks flushing despite her fever. She couldn't tell them about the Life Sigil forming. About what they'd done.

But Torin's eyes dropped to her palm, to where the thin silk glove couldn't quite hide the glow beneath. The Life Sigil pulsed faintly through the fabric—visible if you knew what to look for. Understanding flickered across his face, then darkened into something harder. Worry.

"The timing doesn't help your case," he said quietly. "Saav told the tribunal that Ash's madness escalated after forming a forbidden bond with you. That the Life Sigil itself is proof of his corruption—using Fyrwarden magic to seduce and bind an Oracle against the natural order."

Sela made a sound of outrage. "That's a lie. You can't

force a Life Sigil. It requires—" She stopped, looking at Ezra. "It requires choice. From both of them."

"I know what it requires." Torin's voice was gentle but firm. "But the tribunal doesn't care about the truth. They care about what they can see—and what they see is Veyona's fields burning with Fyrwarden fire, Teyna dead, the Rootsong stolen, and a mage they trust telling them it's all connected to one mad Fyrwarden and his forbidden bond with an Oracle."

Ezra's vision doubled. Even through the muffled bond, she could feel echoes—Ash's rage, his pain, his desperation. But also something else. Something darker, writhing beneath his fire like an infection.

"It's a lie," Ezra said, voice shaking with fury despite her weakness. "All of it. I saw Saav kill Teyna. I was inside his memory—I felt him do it. I felt him poison the land, steal the Rootsong, corrupt it." She looked between Torin and Sela, desperate for them to understand. "He must have found a way to mimic Ash's fire signature. To make it look like Fyrwarden flames when it was his shadow magic all along."

"Making Ash the perfect scapegoat," Sela finished softly, horror dawning in her eyes.

"But why?" Torin's brow furrowed. "Why go to such lengths? Why frame a Fyrwarden? Why destroy Veyona's crops and then—" He stopped, realization flickering. "He's targeting the tribes. Systematically."

Ezra's mind raced despite the fever clouding her thoughts. "Veyona first. He stole their Rootsong—their earth magic. Without it, they'll starve. Their trade will collapse."

"And now he's gone after Fyr," Sela added, her voice tight. "If they strip Ash of his fire and exile him, if the elders believe one of their strongest Fyrwardens went mad..." She looked at her sister. "It'll create fear. Distrust. What if their other warriors are unstable too?"

"It weakens them," Torin said grimly. "Makes them doubt their own power. Their own people." His hands curled into fists. "But to what end? What does Saav gain from destroying the tribes one by one?"

"Power," Ezra whispered. "It has to be power. But what kind?" She pressed her palm—the one with the Life Sigil—against her forehead, trying to think through the fever. "The Rootsong was ancient magic. Passed down through generations. What if—what if he's collecting it somehow? Taking the tribes' magic for himself?"

"But Fyrwardens don't have transferable power like that," Sela protested. "Their fire is bound to them. When they die, it dies with them."

"Unless there's a way to take it before they die," Torin said slowly, his expression darkening. "The ritual to strip a Fyrwarden's power—it doesn't destroy the fire. It removes it. Seals it away."

Ezra's blood ran cold. "You think Saav wants them to strip Ash's fire so he can steal it?"

"I don't know." Torin shook his head, frustration clear in his voice. "I'm just a warrior. I don't understand mage craft or ancient rituals. But something about this feels deliberate. Planned. Like he's working toward something specific."

"But what?" Sela demanded. "What could be worth destroying entire tribes? Worth framing Ash and stealing the Rootsong and—" She stopped, looking at Ezra. "And pursuing you. He's been after you since the beginning. The rumors he spread, the way he poisoned your reputation—" Her voice dropped. "What if it's not just about the tribes? What if it's about you and Ash specifically?"

"The Life Sigil," Ezra breathed. "We formed something that hasn't existed in over a century. Something forbidden. What if—" Her thoughts scattered, fever making it hard to hold onto the thread. "What if he needs it for something? Or fears it?"

"Or wants to corrupt it the way he corrupted the Rootsong," Torin said darkly.

They fell silent, the weight of unknowing pressing down on them. Somewhere out there, Saav was executing a plan none of them fully understood, and Ash—drugged, imprisoned, blamed for atrocities he didn't commit—was powerless to stop it.

Ezra grabbed Torin's arm with what little strength she had left. "When they wake him—when the tribunal sentences him—you have to get word to him. Tell him I know the truth. Tell him not to fight it alone. Tell him I'm —" Her voice cracked. "Tell him I'm still here. Still waiting. That I can barely feel him but I know he's there. That I believe him."

Torin covered her hand with his, careful not to press against the Life Sigil. "I'll try. But Ez, you need to understand—they're going to strip his fire. The tribunal has already decided. Exile to the Shattered Vale, powerless. They believe he's too dangerous to let him keep his abilities."

"He'll die there." Sela's voice was flat. "Without his fire, without his strength—the Vale will kill him in days."

"I know." Torin's jaw tightened. "That's the point. They want him dead, but they want to look merciful doing it."

Ezra pressed her Life Sigil to her chest, trying desperately to push something—anything—through the bond. *I know it wasn't you. I know. Hold on. Please hold on.*

But the bond remained silent. Muffled by drugs and distance and the weight of Saav's cursed lies.

The day stretched endlessly. Ezra drifted in and out of consciousness, each waking moment bringing fresh pain. Sela stayed beside her, one hand always touching—shoulder, arm, hand—maintaining the anchor Veyar had said she needed.

"Tell me about when we were children," Ezra murmured during one of her clearer moments. "When things were simple."

Sela's smile was sad but genuine. "You mean when you convinced me we could fly if we jumped off the grain storage roof?"

Despite everything, Ezra's lips curved. "We were six. Everything seemed possible."

"I broke my arm. You cried harder than I did."

"Because it was my idea. My fault."

"And I'd do it again." Sela squeezed her hand. "That's what sisters do. We jump together, break together, heal together."

Tears slipped down Ezra's temples. "I'm scared, Sela. What if Ash doesn't wake up in time? What if Saav already cursed him, and he dies? Does that mean I die too?"

"I won't let that happen. You and I will barge in and save him if we have to." Sela's voice was fierce. "We fight our demons together. Like we always have."

By evening, most of the village had gathered for the communal meal. The scent of roasted vegetables and fresh bread drifted through the longhouse, making Ezra's stomach churn.

"Come on, Ez," Sela coaxed gently. "We need to go eat. You need your strength."

"I can't." Ezra turned her head away, pressing her face into the pillow. Even the smell was too much.

Torin stepped away from the door. "Let her rest. The communal meal will be too heavy for her anyway. I'll make something here."

Sela nodded, settling back beside Ezra's pallet. "That will be better anyway. Too much gossip in the dining hall tonight. Better just us three."

So they stayed in while the rest of Kireva gathered at the communal fire pit. Laughter and conversation drifted through the open windows—the sounds of a village at peace, unaware of the poison spreading through their evening meal.

Ezra's eyes were already closing. She heard them move around the longhouse—Torin at the hearth, the quiet clatter of a pot, Sela's gentle humming. Voices and laughter drifted from somewhere distant. The communal meal, she thought hazily. Everyone gathering. Everyone but them.

Some time later, warmth touched her lips. "Just a little," Sela's voice coaxed. "A few sips."

Ezra swallowed without thinking. Broth. Mild and warm. It didn't taste like ash. She managed a few more sips before exhaustion pulled her under again.

Darkness.

The fever dreams came—Teyna's face, Saav's hands, rot spreading through roots. She whimpered, twisting in the blankets.

Cool fingers on her forehead. Sela's voice, distant. "Shh. I'm here. Sleep."

More darkness.

Then—

Wrong.

Something was wrong.

Ezra surfaced from sleep like breaking through ice. Her Oracle sight flared without permission, showing her shadows where there shouldn't be shadows. The air felt thick. Oily. Wrong.

And silent.

Too silent.

Her eyes snapped open, heart hammering. The long-house was dark except for the dying embers in the hearth. Beside her, Sela slept peacefully. By the door, Torin's silhouette was still, sword across his lap.

But outside—nothing. No footsteps. No quiet conversations. No dogs. No night sounds at all.

The wrongness pressed against her skin like a physical weight.

"Sela—" Her voice came out as a rasp.

Beside her, Sela stirred. "Mmm?"

The door exploded inward.

Saav stepped through, beautiful and terrible in the firelight, dark magic coiling around him like living smoke. His eyes found Ezra's, and his smile was gentle. Poisonously gentle.

"Hello, little Oracle. I've come to take you home."

Torin moved faster than his age should allow, blade singing free. "Get away from her!"

Saav's hand flicked almost lazily. A strand of black magic shot forward, wrapping around Torin's throat. The older man choked, dropping his sword, hands clawing at the shadowed binding crushing his windpipe.

"Dad!" Sela lunged from the pallet, but another dark tendril caught her, slamming her against the wall. She gasped, struggling, the magic tightening with each movement.

"Stop!" Ezra tried to rise, but her body wouldn't respond. The fever had her locked in place, too weak to do anything but watch in horror.

"I'm not here to kill them," Saav said calmly, as if discussing the weather. "Just ensuring they don't interfere." He moved closer to Ezra, the shadowed strands maintaining their grip on Torin and Sela. "Though I should thank them for taking such good care of you. You're exactly where I need you to be—weak enough to move, strong enough to survive the journey."

"What did you do?" Ezra's voice came out barely a whisper.

Saav knelt beside her, gathering her into his arms. She tried to fight, but had no strength. "I made you the last surviving person from Kireva. They're gone, and you are mine now."

The words didn't make sense. Couldn't make sense.

"No," Ezra breathed. "No, you didn't—"

"The communal meal," Saav said simply, almost conversationally. "A sleeping draught mixed into tonight's stew. Strong enough to ensure no one wakes until morning." His smile turned sad, mocking sympathy. "By then—well. There won't be a morning for them."

Horror crashed through Ezra like ice water. "The whole tribe—"

"Everyone who ate at the communal fire tonight. Which was everyone." His eyes flickered to Torin and Sela, still pinned by his magic. "Except you three. How fortunate that your illness kept you away. How unfortunate that it won't save you." He stood, cradling her like a child. "They won't feel anything when the fire comes. I'm doing them a mercy, really. Better a quick end than the slow death Kireva faced anyway. Your tribe was dying—no warriors to defend it, no future to speak of. I'm simply hastening the inevitable."

"You're a monster," Ezra choked out.

"I'm practical." Saav turned toward the door, and Ezra saw over his shoulder—Sela and Torin still pinned by the darkness, eyes wide with terror and rage, fighting uselessly against the bindings holding them. "We're going to your new home now. Kildra. Where you'll learn what you could become with proper guidance."

"Please," Ezra gasped. "Please don't hurt them. Don't—"

"I told you. I'm not going to hurt them." Saav's voice was almost kind. "The fire will do that for me."

He carried her into the night.

Ezra's last sight of the longhouse was Sela and Torin struggling against the shadows, mouths open in screams Ezra couldn't hear over the roaring in her ears.

Outside, the village lay in unnatural silence. Bodies sprawled everywhere—in doorways, on benches near the communal fire pit, slumped against walls. All breathing. All sleeping. All condemned.

And then she saw Orielle.

The head Oracle lay near her dwelling, eyes wide and staring at nothing. Not sleeping like the others. Dead. Her mouth was frozen in a silent scream, hands clawed against her chest as if trying to pull something back inside.

No. No, not Orielle—

Ezra's vision blurred with tears, but she couldn't look away. Orielle, who had warned the tribe. Who had trusted Ezra with Teyna's scarf. Who had believed in her when no one else did.

Gone.

"She fought me," Saav said conversationally, following Ezra's gaze. "More than the others. Her gift was strong—visions, like yours, though not nearly as powerful. She saw me coming, tried to warn the others before the sleeping draught took hold." His voice held a note of admiration. "I had to silence her permanently. Couldn't risk her waking anyone."

Ezra's throat closed. She tried to scream, to rage, to do anything—but the binding magic held her voice trapped.

Saav paused beside Orielle's body, studying it with clinical interest. "The Oracle gift is always fascinating when it's torn free. Like pulling thread from a tapestry—if you're careful, it comes out whole. If you're not..." He gestured at Orielle's twisted form. "Well. She made me hurry."

Horror crashed through Ezra. He'd stolen Orielle's gift. Just like he'd stolen Teyna's Rootsong. Just like he was stealing everything.

"Don't worry," Saav continued, moving past the body. "I'll put it to better use than she ever did. Her visions were wasted on warning this dying tribe. I'll use them to see what's coming. To prepare for when you finally remember who you are."

Plates and cups still sat beside the sleeping bodies, the remnants of their last meal congealing in the night air.

"What have you done," Ezra sobbed through the binding that barely let sound escape. "What have you done."

"What was necessary." Saav carried her past the sleeping forms, toward the village edge. "The tribunal needed a final push. Proof that the Fyrwarden's madness had gone too far. And what better proof than a village burned to ash by his fire?"

Understanding hit like a physical blow. "You're going to frame Ash."

"Of course. By morning, when the smoke is spotted,

when they find the remains—" Saav's smile was terrible. "They'll see Fyrwarden fire. Ash's signature all over it. The elders will have no choice but to strip his power. Execute him, probably. One less obstacle in my way."

He paused at the village boundary, setting Ezra down just long enough to work his magic. Darkness and flame twisted together in his hands—not the clean fire of Fyrwardens, but something corrupted, tainted with Ash's signature but wrong underneath.

"No," Ezra whispered. "Please, no—"

Saav bound Ezra with dark magic, forcing her voice to silence and her body rigid as if wrapped in chains. Then he released the spell.

Fire erupted behind them, consuming thatch and wood with terrible efficiency. Not the wild conflagration of true madness, but controlled. Deliberate. Designed to look like a targeted attack—the work of a Fyrwarden who'd chosen his victims carefully.

Screams began—those closest to the flames waking just long enough to understand they were dying.

Ezra's heart shattered.

Her tribe. Her people. The children who'd played in the square, the elders who'd taught her, the weavers and hunters and healers who'd been her community since birth. The families who'd gathered tonight for their evening meal, laughing and sharing stories, never knowing it would be their last.

All burning.

All dying.

Because of her.

"This is your fault, you know," Saav said gently,

throwing her over his shoulder. "If you'd come willingly when I first asked you to be my bride, none of this would have been necessary. But you always chose the Fyrwarden over reason. Chose that filthy love over security and power."

The words pierced through her shock like a blade of ice.

Always. He'd said always. As if this had happened before. As if she'd made this choice a hundred times and he was tired of being rejected.

"You don't understand yet," Saav continued, voice almost tender. "But you will. You ARE her—the Visionary. You just don't remember. Trapped in this human form, this weak flesh, these mortal memories." His grip tightened. "I'm freeing you. Making you what you were always meant to be. What you've always been, beneath the curse of mortality."

But that was impossible. This was the first time. The only time.

Unless—

The thought scattered as he started walking, carrying her away from the burning village.

"Every cycle, you choose him," Saav whispered, almost to himself. "Every life, you turn away from me. But not this time. This time, I'll strip away everything that blinds you—your tribe, your family, your false love—until only the goddess remains." His voice hardened. "Now you'll learn the cost of that eternal choice. And when you finally remember what you are, you'll thank me."

She didn't know him—they'd barely spoken beyond that one encounter at the market. He'd never asked her to marry him. Never courted her. Never even hinted at wanting her as anything other than a weapon to use against Ash.

Yet he spoke as if they had a history. As if he'd rejected him a thousand times. As if he'd loved her across lifetimes and she'd always, always chosen Ash instead.

The wrongness of it terrified her more than the flames. The wrongness meant he was delusional—and delusions that deep couldn't be reasoned with.

Behind them, Kireva burned.

Ezra watched through tears as the flames consumed everything. The longhouse where she'd grown up. The market square where she'd laughed with Sela. The herb garden where Orielle had taught her to read visions in tea leaves. The children's play area. The weaving hall. The shrine.

All of it. Gone.

And the people—

The weavers who'd made her first Oracle robes. The hunters who'd taught her to track. The healers who'd delivered half the village's babies. The elders who'd told stories by the fire. The children who'd chased each other through the square just yesterday, their laughter bright and careless.

Dead. All dead.

The sleeping draught hadn't been mercy. She understood that now. Saav had said they wouldn't feel the fire—but that was a lie. She could hear them. Faint screams carrying on the wind as the flames woke them too late. As they died choking on smoke, burned alive, trapped in their own homes.

Her people. Her tribe. Her entire world.

Gone.

And Sela—Sela and Torin, pinned by shadow magic in a burning longhouse. The flames would reach them. Would consume them. And Ezra wasn't there. Couldn't save them. Couldn't even scream their names.

Her anchors. The two people who were supposed to keep her tethered to reality. Both dying because of her.

Because she'd loved Ash. Because Saav wanted her and she'd never even known.

This was her fault.

All of it.

Every. Single. Death.

Something broke inside her.

Not her body—that had already been broken by fever and binding magic. Not her mind—that had shattered the moment she'd seen Orielle's body.

Her soul.

The grief rose from somewhere deeper than bone, deeper than blood. It came from the place where the Life Sigil blazed—from the part of her that was bound to Ash, soul to soul, life to life.

And it ripped out of her like a scream made of light.

She couldn't make sound—the binding held her voice trapped. But the wail that tore from her soul didn't need sound. It was pure feeling, pure anguish, pure loss.

It howled through the Life Sigil like fire through a dry field.

Ash—

Not words. Not thought. Just grief. Overwhelming,

soul-destroying grief that she couldn't contain, couldn't control, couldn't silence.

They're gone, they're all gone, everyone I love is dead or dying, and I couldn't stop it, I couldn't save them. I watched them burn. I'm alone, I'm so alone—

The bond—silent for days, muffled and distant—stirred.

Not responding. Not answering. Just there, buried and dormant like embers under ash.

But she couldn't reach gently anymore. Couldn't be quiet. Couldn't be careful.

Her soul was screaming.

It tore through the Life Sigil like lightning through a storm—raw, desperate, clawing.

WAKE UP. WAKE UP. WAKE UP.

Everything she had left—every shred of strength, every ounce of will, every fragment of her breaking soul—she poured into that bond. Into the mark on her palm that blazed like a brand against her heart.

Please. Please wake up. Please come for me. I have no one left. Nothing left. You're all that remains. Please don't leave me alone in this. Please—

The bond stayed silent. Muffled. Distant.

He couldn't hear her. Or he was too deep in drugged sleep to answer. Or the binding was too strong, the distance too far, the connection too new to carry the weight of her grief.

She was alone.

Completely, devastatingly alone.

Ash—

The world grayed at the edges. Consciousness slipping away despite her desperate grip on it.

The last thing Ezra managed before darkness took her was one final, soul-shredding scream through the bond:

PLEASE.

Then the darkness swallowed her whole.

And she fell into it alone, not knowing if he'd heard.

Not knowing if anyone would ever hear her again.

Chapter 21

Phoenix Rising

Darkness.

Cold.

Ash drifted in the drugged haze they'd forced down his throat three days ago—thick, suffocating, keeping him locked in his own mind while his body lay helpless in Fyr's dungeons.

The bond had been whispering for days. Distant. Muffled. Ezra's terror bleeding through in fragments he couldn't answer, couldn't soothe, couldn't reach.

And then—

Pain. Sharp and sudden, lancing through the bond like lightning through storm clouds.

Not physical pain. Soul pain.

The kind that came from watching everything you loved burn.

He tried to wake. Tried to claw his way up through the drugs, through the darkness, through the weight pressing him down—

But he was trapped. Locked in a cage of his own making, the drugs holding him under no matter how hard he fought.

Until her scream shattered everything.

The bond flared white-hot.

Ezra's scream tore through him—not sound, but soul. Terror. Agony. Grief so vast it threatened to drown the world.

PLEASE.

The word—her final, desperate wail—hit him like a fist to the chest.

And something inside Ash broke.

The bond flared white-hot.

The chains wrapped around his soul since birth— since BEFORE birth—shattered.

Heat erupted from his core, molten and divine, racing through his veins like wildfire through dry grass. His chest split open with light, the Fyrwarden sigil blazing so bright the elders threw up their hands to shield their eyes.

Ash's scream ripped from his throat—primal, inhuman, eternal.

The sound shook the ritual chamber. Dust rained from the ceiling. The blessed chains meant to suppress his fire exploded outward in a spray of molten metal, droplets hissing as they hit stone.

NO.

The word came from everywhere and nowhere—his voice layered with something older, vaster, something that had been SCREAMING inside a cage for eighteen years and was done.

Anok stumbled backward, face going white. "Impossible—"

The other elders scrambled away as light poured from Ash's body—not red-orange Fyrwarden flame, but GOLD. Pure. Radiant. Divine.

His back arched. Bones cracked and reformed. His scream pitched higher, agony and fury and something like rapture all tangled together as his shoulder blades split open—

And wings erupted.

Not fire shaped like wings. Not illusion or magic trick.

Wings. Massive and terrible and beautiful, spanning the width of the chamber, each feather wrought from living flame that burned without consuming, radiated heat that felt like standing at the heart of a star.

Not physical. Not flesh and bone. These wings existed halfway between the mortal world and the divine—visible when the Phoenix surged forward, fading to translucence when Ash's human side took control. Spiritual fire given form, burning brightest when his power was at its peak.

Right now, newly awakened and burning with fury, they were solid as stone and twice as deadly.

The elders fell to their knees—not in worship, but because their legs wouldn't hold them. Because something DIVINE had just ripped its way into the mortal world and the weight of it pressed down like the hand of creation itself.

Ash rose.

Not standing. Rising—lifted by wings that beat once, scattering embers like stars, filling the chamber with light that hadn't existed since the gods walked freely.

His eyes opened.

Gold. Molten. Burning with power that should have been impossible, that WAS impossible, that every law of magic said couldn't exist in a mortal body.

But Ash wasn't just mortal anymore.

She needs us, the presence inside him roared—not separate, not foreign, but HIM. The part of himself that had been locked away, buried, CAGED by forces he didn't understand. *They hurt her. They DARE—*

The wings flared wider, and the stone walls cracked.

"Ash—" Anok's voice shook. "What have you—what ARE you—"

Ash's head turned toward him, movements too fluid, too perfect, human motion blended with something far older. When he spoke, his voice resonated—layered, harmonic, the sound of a god and a man speaking as ONE.

"I am vengeance for what was stolen. I am fire that will not be caged. I am the answer to her scream across the dark."

The ritual brand that had been meant to strip his power melted, iron running like water across the chamber floor.

The blessed water meant to suppress him evaporated before it could touch his skin, steam hissing upward in clouds.

Every flame in the chamber—candles, torches, the ritual fire itself—bowed. The fire bent TOWARD him like flowers turning to the sun, recognizing its source, its origin, its god.

"And nothing—not chains, not fear, not the weight of all seven tribes—will keep me from her."

The words weren't a threat.

They were a promise written in fire and starlight and power that made the air itself tremble.

One of the younger elders sobbed. Another pressed his forehead to the stone floor, trembling.

Anok stood frozen, tears streaming down his weathered face—not from fear, but from AWE. From witnessing something that shouldn't exist, that COULDN'T exist, that was happening anyway.

"Phoenix," he breathed. "The god himself. After all this time—"

Ash's wings folded slightly, and even that small movement sent waves of heat rippling through the chamber. He looked at his hands—still his, still scarred from years of training, but limned now in gold, burning with power he'd never been meant to touch.

We don't understand, the god-part whispered inside him, confused, angry, desperate. *Why her? Why does this mortal matter so much? Why does her pain feel like OUR pain?*

But Ash—human, mortal, ALIVE with love—knew.

"Because she's mine," he said aloud, voice his own again but still touched with flame. "Because I would burn eternity itself before I let her die alone."

The Phoenix inside him didn't understand.

But it didn't need to.

It felt Ash's love—fierce and desperate and absolute—and that was enough.

Then we burn, it agreed. *Together.*

Then we burn, it agreed. *Together.*

And with that agreement came something else—knowledge. Not memories, exactly, but understanding flooding through Ash like water through a broken dam.

Rituals. Ancient ones, from before the gods vanished. Magic that hadn't been spoken in centuries. The true names of fire, the way to call starlight down, how to walk between life and death without losing yourself.

The Phoenix had been locked away for eighteen years —since before Ash's birth, since the moment his soul had been chosen as vessel. But before that? The god had existed for millennia. Had watched the world turn, had guided souls, had burned and been reborn countless times.

All of that knowledge—sleeping, dormant, caged—was Ash's now.

We remember, the Phoenix whispered. *We remember what was lost. What was stolen. What must be reclaimed.*

Ash's breath caught. "You know things. Things I don't. Things no mortal should know."

We are not separate. What we know, you know. What you feel, we feel. A pause, almost tentative. *We are one now. For better or worse.*

"Then teach me," Ash said, wings spreading wide. "Teach me how to save her."

We will. But first— The Phoenix's presence surged, urgent. *First, we must leave this place. She needs us. And time is running out.*

Ash's hand pressed to his chest, to the Life Sigil that pulsed faint and desperate against his palm. He poured everything he had into the bond—every ounce of fury, every fragment of love, every promise his soul could make.

I'm coming. I heard you. I'm coming.

He didn't know if she could hear him. Didn't know if the bond could carry his voice across the distance while she was unconscious, captive, broken.

But he sent it anyway. Over and over.

Hold on. I'm coming. You're not alone.

The wings spread wide again, and this time when they beat, the chamber doors exploded outward in a shower of splinters and divine fire.

Ash launched through the opening, wings propelling him faster than any horse, any warrior, any mortal thing could move.

Behind him, the elders stared at the empty space where their prisoner had been.

At the melted chains and scorched stone and the lingering taste of divinity in the air.

"May the gods have mercy," one whispered.

Anok shook his head slowly, eyes still wet. "The gods aren't the ones who need to fear him."

He looked toward Kildra, where smoke still rose from Kireva's ashes.

"Saav is."

Thorne waited outside, sword drawn, ready to fight beside his brother one last time.

"The gates are sealed," he said. "They won't let you leave."

"They can't stop me." Ash's voice was certain. "Not anymore."

Together, they headed for the gates.

And behind them, the ritual chamber smoldered with the ashes of what Ash had been.

What remained was something new. Something fierce.

Something that would burn the world to save the woman he loved.

The gates of Fyr exploded outward in a shower of golden flame.

Ash didn't slow, didn't look back at the guards scrambling away from the divine fire that rolled off him in waves. The Phoenix burned inside him—not separate, not controlling, but sharing. Two consciousnesses occupying one body, both driven by the same desperate purpose.

Find her. Save her. Burn anything that stands in the way.

Thorne kept pace on horseback, having grabbed mounts while Ash dealt with the ritual chamber. He tossed the reins of the second horse to Ash, who swung up without breaking stride, wings folding tight against his back.

"The shrine?" Thorne asked.

"First." Ash's voice was layered, human and divine both. "But I need to—" He stopped, jaw clenching. "No. To Kireva first."

Thorne's expression darkened, but he nodded. They both knew why. Ash needed to see what Saav had done, needed to understand the full scope of the monster he was hunting.

The ride took less than an hour, pushed hard. But they smelled the smoke long before they saw the flames.

Kireva was still burning.

Not the wild conflagration of a village caught by

surprise, but the methodical burn of a controlled fire. Buildings collapsed in sequence, flames spreading in patterns too deliberate to be accidental.

Ash's hands clenched on the reins so hard the leather groaned.

Bodies lay everywhere.

Not burned—not yet. The flames hadn't reached most of the village center. But the people lay where they'd fallen, sleeping peacefully even as death crept closer.

Ash and Thorne reached Ezra's longhouse. Inside, Sela and Torin lay collapsed, barely breathing—their pulses so faint Ash had to press hard to feel them at all.

"They're alive," Ash breathed, relief crashing through him. "Barely, but alive."

The Phoenix stirred inside him. *Near death we can pull back. But only if the soul hasn't left. Only if there's still a spark.*

Ash didn't know what he was doing, but the Phoenix did.

Light surged from his fingers, golden and pure, striking both their chests. Their bodies jerked, backs arching as divine fire jolted through them like lightning to a stopped heart.

Sela gasped first, eyes flying open, gulping air like drowning. Torin followed seconds later, coughing, disoriented, hand going to his bruised throat.

Thorne steadied them as they struggled upright, both dizzy and shaking.

The Phoenix whispered: *If we'd been minutes later, they would have been beyond reach. True death is not ours to reverse.*

Ash's hands shook. Minutes. They'd been that close to losing them.

Flames crept closer to the longhouse, smoke thickening. "Where is Ezra?" Ash demanded.

"Gone." Torin's voice was raw, damaged. His hand went to his bruised throat. "Saav—he used shadow magic. Choked us. When I woke, she was gone and the fires had started."

Fury blazed through Ash, wings bursting free and scattering embers across the small room.

Sela grabbed his arm, her grip desperate. "We need to save them! The village—everyone's still out there—"

The four of them raced toward the village center. Ash went to the nearest figure—an old woman collapsed near the well. He dropped to his knees, pressing fingers to her throat.

Nothing. No pulse. No warmth. Gone.

He tried anyway, desperate, channeling the golden light—

The Phoenix recoiled. *She's been dead for hours. The poison took her long before the flames. Her soul is gone. There's nothing left to heal.*

"No," Ash whispered. "No, please—"

He scrambled to the next. A young man sprawled in a doorway.

Cold. Dead. Soul long departed.

A child curled beside her mother.

Both cold. Both dead. Both far beyond his reach.

The Phoenix's grief echoed through him: *We cannot bring back what has already left. We are not gods of resur-*

rection. Only of rebirth—and only when the soul remains to be guided.

"They're all gone," Thorne said quietly, voice thick. "Poisoned before the fire ever started. There was nothing you could have done."

Ash's vision blurred red. The Phoenix screamed for vengeance, for blood, for Saav's heart torn from his chest and fed to the flames.

But underneath the rage—grief. Pure, devastating grief.

These were Ezra's people. Her family, her community, everyone she'd ever known. And they were dead because of him. Because Saav needed to frame him, needed to turn the tribunal against him, needed to break Ezra completely.

"I didn't do this," Ash said, voice breaking. "I didn't—"

"I know." Thorne's hand landed on his shoulder, grounding.

Sela was crying, quiet sobs shaking her shoulders.

And Torin stepped forward, placing a hand on Ash's back. "Everyone who matters knows."

"Do they?" Ash looked up, eyes blazing. "The elders believed me capable. By morning it will have spread that we escaped Fyr, that the Phoenix descended upon me out of madness and destroyed this land. The tribunal will believe it. By morning, every tribe in the Sacred Valley will be hunting me for this." He looked at each of them in turn. "They were already taking my power away, sending me to be exiled. Now is your time to turn back. Once you're associated with me, you'll be sentenced to death as well."

"Then we make sure they know the truth before morning comes," Torin said firmly.

The air shimmered.

But this time, it wasn't Saav's shadow magic or Phoenix fire.

This was something else. Something ancient and liminal, belonging to neither life nor death but the space between.

Kee stepped from the shadows—not playful now, not grinning. Made of darkness and starlight, solemn in a way Ash had never seen them.

"Kee," Ash breathed.

The minor god's eyes swept over the burning village, the bodies, the devastation. For once, their usual irreverence was gone.

"So many," Kee said quietly. "All at once. The liminal spaces are... crowded." They looked at Ash, and their expression was unreadable—something between grief and anticipation. "Normally, I'd guide them. Shadow of death—it's my duty. I walk them through the dark, show them the paths, let them choose."

They gestured, and suddenly Ash could see them—

Translucent figures rising from the bodies scattered throughout the village. Souls. Hundreds of them, drifting like smoke, confused and lost and grieving.

They turned toward Ash as one, sensing the divine fire inside him.

"But you're here," Kee continued, voice soft with something like reverence. "Phoenix. God of rebirth and renewal. And that changes everything."

"I don't understand," Ash said.

"I can guide them through shadow to their next choice —rest or rebirth." Kee's expression turned solemn. "But if Phoenix leads them to the light first? If divine fire purifies their passage, burns away the trauma of their deaths, gives them peace before they even reach the crossroads?" They looked at the souls, then back at Ash. "That's a gift I can't give them. An honor beyond what shadow can offer."

"The Phoenix is barely awake," Ash said, desperation bleeding through. "I don't know if I can—"

"You can." Kee's voice was firm but gentle. "We'll do it together. You call the light. I'll walk them through it. They'll have both—your fire to cleanse them, my guidance to see them home. It's how it was meant to be, back when gods walked freely and worked in harmony."

The words settled into Ash like an old memory, something the Phoenix recognized even if he didn't.

Yes, the Phoenix whispered inside him, exhausted but stirring. *This is right. This is proper. Death and rebirth working as one.*

Ash closed his eyes, reaching deep inside where the Phoenix lay dormant.

They're Ezra's people. They died because of me—because Saav framed me, because I exist. The least I can do is give them this. Please.

The Phoenix's response was weak but certain.

One time. Then I must sleep. Recover. This body... it can't sustain divine power the way our true form could. We're burning it out. But for them—for her people—we'll give them light.

Ash opened his eyes and nodded to Kee. "Together."

"Together," Kee agreed.

Light erupted from the sigil blazing on Ash's chest—golden, pure, fierce. It swept outward in waves, washing over the gathered souls. Where it touched, darkness fell away. Pain lifted. Fear dissolved. The trauma of poison and fire and betrayal burned away like mist in sunlight.

The souls turned toward Ash—and their expressions transformed. Confusion became clarity. Fear became peace. Grief became gratitude.

Thank you, their voices whispered through his mind. *For this gift. For this light. For letting us go gently.*

Kee stepped forward, made of shadow and starlight, and extended their hands. The souls responded, drifting toward the minor god even as Phoenix fire still bathed them in gold.

"Come," Kee said softly, voice carrying the weight of ages. "The light has cleansed you. Now I'll show you the paths. Eternal rest in the starfields, or rebirth into new lives. The choice, as always, is yours."

The souls began to rise—not just toward light, but through a doorway only Ash and Kee could see. A threshold between life and death, shadow and flame, where Phoenix fire met liminal darkness and made something beautiful.

Kee walked with them, guiding them through the passage even as Ash's light continued to burn away the last remnants of their mortal pain.

One by one, they crossed over.

One by one, they made their choices—some flowing toward distant stars (eternal rest), others spiraling down toward the mortal world again (rebirth into new forms, new lives, new chances).

And through it all, Phoenix fire and death's shadow worked in perfect harmony.

When the last soul crossed over, when the final choice was made, Kee turned back to Ash. The minor god's expression was softer than Ash had ever seen it.

"That," Kee said quietly, "was how it was meant to be. Before the gods vanished. Before everything broke." They tilted their head. "Thank you. For remembering, even if you don't remember."

Ash staggered. The Phoenix whispered inside him, exhausted: *Hundreds. We gave rebirth to hundreds. The cost is heavy.*

His knees buckled. Would have fallen if Thorne hadn't caught him.

"What did you see?" Sela asked, voice hushed with something like awe. "We saw light—so much light, sweeping through the village like peace itself. And we felt them leave. Felt their gratitude." Tears streamed down her face. "They're at rest now, aren't they?"

"Yes." Ash's voice was hoarse. "They're free."

Torin's hand landed on his shoulder—heavy, grounding. "You gave them that. Whatever else happens, you gave them peace."

But Ash barely heard him. His eyes locked on Kee, who stood watching with an expression Ash had never seen before.

Sorrow. And concern.

"The Phoenix," Kee said quietly, "is fading. Not gone, but... sleeping. Deeply. It used almost everything it had just awakening. And now this—" They gestured at the village, at the hundreds of souls just guided. "It won't be able to help you for a while."

"How long?" Ash demanded.

"Hours. Days. I don't know." Kee's expression turned serious. "You're not a god anymore, Ash. You're a mortal body trying to contain divine fire. The vessel can't sustain that kind of power. Not yet. Maybe not ever."

The words settled like lead in Ash's stomach.

"Then I fight without it," he said flatly. "Where is she? Where did Saav take Ezra?"

Kee's expression flickered—frustration, anger, helplessness. "I don't know."

"What?" Thorne stepped forward. "You're a god. You can travel the liminal spaces. How can you not—"

"Because Saav is hiding her." Kee's voice was sharp. "Shadow magic. Binding spells. He's wrapped her location in so much concealment magic that even I can't track her. The only thing I can sense is..."

Kee stopped, tilting their head as if listening to something the others couldn't hear. "Terror. Hers. Coming from somewhere far. Somewhere protected. But WHERE? I can't tell."

Ash's hand flew to the Life Sigil, he'd been feeling Ezra's terror pulse faint and desperate through the bond as well.

"Then how—" Ash's voice cracked. "How do I find her?"

Kee was silent for a long moment, expression troubled. Then something shifted in the god's eyes—realization, or perhaps remembrance.

"The shrine," they said slowly. "Veyar's realm beneath

it. There's a pool there—the Pool of Reflected Truths. Ancient. Divine. Created before the gods vanished." They looked at Ash. "It shows what's hidden. What's concealed. What shadow magic tries to bury."

"You think it can find her?" Thorne asked.

"Maybe." Kee's voice was cautious. "Scrying through divine means rather than liminal travel—that's different. Saav can hide from me because he moves through shadows, uses binding magic I can't penetrate. But the pool..." They nodded slowly. "The pool sees through ALL veils. Even the deepest shadow magic. It might be able to pierce his concealment and show you where he's taken her."

"Then that's where we're going." Ash tried to stand, but his legs wouldn't hold him. The exhaustion was catching up—three days drugged, Phoenix awakening, giving rebirth to hundreds of souls. His body was past its limit.

"You can barely stand," Torin said carefully.

"I don't care." Ash's voice was flat, dangerous. "Every moment I waste, she's with him. Alone. Terrified. I'm going to the shrine. Now."

"Then we're coming with you," Sela said fiercely.

Kee watched them with something that might have been approval. "You won't make it on foot. Not in your condition. And time..." They glanced at the sky, where pre-dawn light was just starting to touch the horizon. "Time is not on your side."

"What do you mean?" Thorne asked.

"I can feel something building. Power gathering in a place that shouldn't exist anymore." Kee's expression darkened. "Vana'Sul. The gods' home. It's... waking.

Responding to divine presence." They looked at Ash. "Bastillion is there. I can feel him now—his power signature, his divine essence. And he's preparing something. Something that requires darkness. Starlight. The hour before dawn."

"A ritual," Ash breathed.

"Yes." Kee's voice was grim. "And whatever it is, it's tied to Ezra. I can feel her terror bleeding through the spaces between. She's there. In Vana'Sul. And you're running out of time to reach her."

Ash forced himself upright, wings spreading despite their translucent flickering. "How long?"

"Until dawn. Maybe three hours. Maybe less." Kee's eyes were serious. "The shrine first. Find out exactly where in Vana'Sul he's taken her. Then you'll need someone who can open the liminal ways to the gods' home." Their expression turned wry. "That's not me. I'm powerful, but I'm not THAT powerful. You'll need—"

"Veyar," Thorne finished.

"Yes." Kee nodded. "He's the only one who can get you there fast enough. But first—the pool. Learn what you're walking into."

They looked at Ash, Thorne, Sela, Torin. This impossible alliance.

Kee looked at Ash—at his exhaustion, his determination, the wings that barely flickered with translucent fire.

"You won't make it on foot," the minor god said flatly. "Not in your condition. Not with time running out."

Kee gestured, and the air between them rippled. Shadows coalesced, starlight twisted, and a doorway formed—shimmering, impossible, made of darkness and divine power.

The portal led somewhere else. Somewhere between.

"The shrine," Kee said. "This will take you there. Fast." The god's grin flickered back, sharp and dangerous. "And when you need me again—when the real fight starts—I'll find you. Wouldn't miss the final confrontation for anything."

Ash looked at the portal, then at the others. Thorne, Sela, Torin. This found family, blood-bound by choice and grief and love.

"Together?" he asked.

"To the end," Thorne said.

"For Ezra," Sela added, hand on her sword.

"For all of them," Torin finished, looking back at Kireva's ashes. "For everyone we've lost."

Ash stepped toward the portal, wings spreading despite their weakness. One step. Then another.

Behind them, Kireva burned—a pyre for the dead, a promise for the living.

Ash was coming.

And nothing—not distance, not exhaustion, not the weight of seven tribes—would stop him.

They reached the threshold. Ash's hand extended toward the shimmering doorway—

And the air EXPLODED.

Not with fire. Not with shadow.

With presence.

Something vast crashed through reality itself, tearing through the liminal space like a stone through water. The portal Kee had created shuddered, destabilized, and through it stumbled—

Veyar.

The ancient god nearly fell, staff planted hard to keep from collapsing. His face was pale, eyes wide with something between terror and awe. His usual composure—that timeless, weathered calm—was gone, replaced by frantic urgency.

"Good," he gasped, looking at all of them—Ash, Thorne, Sela, Torin, and Kee. "Good. You're all together. I was afraid I wouldn't—that I'd be too—"

He stopped, chest heaving, and his ancient eyes locked on Ash.

On the golden wings.

On the sigil blazing on his chest.

On the divine fire that still flickered in his gaze despite the exhaustion.

Veyar's face went slack with shock.

"Two," he breathed. "There are two."

Chapter 22

Race Against Dawn

"What are you talking about?" Ash demanded, wings flaring instinctively despite their weakness.

But Veyar wasn't listening. He stepped closer, circling Ash like a man trying to confirm something impossible. The air around him shimmered as he reached out with senses mortals didn't possess, testing the divine resonance.

"Phoenix," Veyar whispered. "You're Phoenix. Not blessed by the god. Not carrying borrowed power." His voice cracked. "You ARE the god. Reborn. Awakened."

Thorne's hand went to his sword despite knowing it would be useless. "Veyar, what—"

"Bastillion rose first," Veyar interrupted, speaking faster now, words tumbling over each other. "I felt him wake in Vana'Sul—felt divine power I hadn't sensed in two centuries flood back into the world. I came here to warn you—to tell you that you're not just fighting a mage anymore." His gaze snapped back to Ash. "But then I got close and felt YOU. Felt Phoenix burning inside mortal flesh and I—"

He stopped, staff trembling. "Two gods have returned. In one night. After two hundred years of silence."

Kee, still standing near the portal, grinned despite the gravity. "About time."

"Kee!" Veyar turned on the minor god. "Did you know? Did you know what they were?"

"Suspected." Kee's grin didn't fade. "Life Sigil that shouldn't exist? Oracle with the Fourth Eye? Fyrwarden who makes fire bow? Pretty obvious something divine was happening."

Veyar sank onto a charred piece of timber, pressing both hands to his face. "No more hiding. No more half-truths." He dropped his hands. "The gods didn't vanish. They were imprisoned. Divine essences stripped away, souls forced into mortal bodies, memories erased."

Sela made a choked sound. "That's impossible. Who could—"

"The Visionary," Veyar said. "My goddess. The one I served for millennia. She had the power—the Ninth Eye, omniscience itself if she chose this——"

"I don't care." Ash's voice cut through like a blade.

Everyone stopped. Turned.

Ash stood with wings half-spread, golden fire crackling weakly across the feathers. His eyes burned—mortal brown layered with divine gold—and his hand pressed against his chest where the Life Sigil pulsed.

"I don't care about gods or imprisonment or what

happened two hundred years ago." His voice was flat, dangerous. "Where is Ezra? How do I get to her?"

Veyar opened his mouth—

"NOW." The word cracked with desperation and command both. "She's terrified. I can feel it through the bond. Every second we stand here talking, she's alone with him. Dying. So either open a portal to where she is, or get out of my way and I'll find her myself."

"Ash—" Thorne started.

"No." Ash turned on him. "You want to know why I'm not asking questions? Why I'm not demanding explanations?" His hand pressed harder against his chest. "Because I can FEEL her. Slipping away. Every moment we waste, the bond gets weaker. She gets weaker. So we're done talking and we're MOVING. Now."

Through the bond, Ezra's terror spiked—and then faded, weaker than before.

The Life Sigil burned against his palm.

Veyar and Kee exchanged a glance.

"He's right," Kee said quietly. "If we wait much longer—"

"Then we don't wait." Veyar stood, gripping his staff. "But Ash—you're walking into Vana'Sul. The gods' home. Not just Bastillion's—it was home to ALL the gods once. And now he's twisted it, claimed it as his own."

"Then tell me while we walk." Ash's wings spread wider despite their translucence. "But we're moving. Now."

"Stubborn mortal," Veyar muttered, but he was already raising his staff. The air split open—not the portal Kee had created earlier, but something different. A path made of starlight and shadow, twisting through impossible angles that hurt to look at.

"The liminal way," Veyar said. "It will take us to the edge of Vana'Sul. Fast." His ancient eyes locked on Ash. "Normally, mortals must cross the Shattered Vale on foot—a test for the worthy, where wolves and spirits hunt the undeserving. But we don't have time for tests. The liminal way bypasses that trial entirely. And I'll tell you what you need to know on the way. But LISTEN. Because if you go in blind, you'll lose her and yourself and everyone else."

Ash looked at the others—Thorne, Sela, Torin. His found family.

"Coming?"

"To the end," Thorne said, hand on his sword.

"For Ezra," Sela said fiercely.

"For my daughter," Torin added, jaw set.

Ash didn't wait for more. He stepped into the liminal way, wings propelling him forward faster than human legs could follow.

Behind him, the others hurried to keep pace.

Reality twisted.

Time and space bent in ways that made mortal minds rebel. Stars streaked past like tears. Shadows coiled and uncoiled. The path beneath their feet was solid and not-solid, existing in multiple moments at once.

Ash pushed forward, wings beating despite exhaustion, every fiber of his being focused on the bond—on Ezra's fading presence at the other end.

Hold on. I'm coming. Almost there.

Veyar's voice resonated through the liminal space, following him even as Ash flew ahead.

"The mage you know as Saav is actually Bastillion," Veyar called, words echoing strangely. "God of Light, Order, Form, and Wards. One of the most powerful gods to ever walk the divine realm."

"But he uses shadow magic," Sela's voice came from behind, breathless as she ran. "Darkness. Corruption—"

"Because he's fallen that far," Veyar said. "God of Light turned to Shadow. God of Order embracing Chaos. Everything he was, he's inverted."

Inside Ash, the Phoenix stirred—weak, but listening.

That shouldn't be possible, it whispered, confused and troubled. *The balance... when Light falls to Shadow, Shadow must rise to Light to maintain equilibrium. That's the order of things. The way the divine realm stays stable.*

Ash felt the god's unease bleed through their connection.

But I feel no corresponding shift. No dark god turning toward light to balance Bastillion's fall. The scales are tipping. Reality itself is destabilizing because he's broken the fundamental order.

"What does that mean?" Ash asked aloud, not realizing he'd spoken.

"What does what mean?" Thorne called from behind.

"The Phoenix says—" Ash stopped, trying to process the god's wordless knowing. "Bastillion changing from Light to Shadow should have triggered a balance. Some dark god turning toward light. But it didn't happen."

Veyar's expression went pale. "Gods above. I didn't

even think— That's why the Sacred Valley is weakening. Why everything feels wrong. The divine balance is broken. And if it's not restored—"

"The collapse accelerates," Kee finished grimly. "Even if we stop Bastillion, even if we save Ezra and Ash, the imbalance alone could tear everything apart."

Ash's wings beat harder. One more reason to end this. Fast.

Ash didn't slow. Through the bond, Ezra's terror pulsed—weaker, more distant.

How much time had passed? Five minutes? Ten?

Too long. Every second was too long.

"How do I fight him?" Ash demanded without looking back.

"You don't," Veyar said bluntly. "Not directly. But you might be able to disrupt his ritual—"

"Then tell me how."

Thorne's footsteps pounded behind him. "Why does he want Ezra?"

"I think he thinks she's the Visionary reborn," Kee's voice drifted forward, unusually serious. "Because she has the Fourth Eye. Because she formed a Life Sigil with Ash —who is Phoenix. Because of patterns that made him certain."

"Fourth Eye?" Veyar muttered, voice troubled. "Fifth and Seventh too, probably. If he's seeing what I think he's seeing..." He shook his head. "Bastillion has always been about patterns. Order. Structure. If he recognized a pattern across lifetimes..."

"What are you talking about?" Sela demanded. "Fifth? Seventh?"

"The Oracle gifts," Veyar said. "There are seven eyes of sight. Most Oracles only manifest one or two in their lifetime. The Fourth Eye—seeing truth through lies—is rare enough. But if Ezra has others awakening..." His voice dropped. "That's not just power. That's a signature. Something that might repeat across incarnations if the soul is old enough."

"You think she's had these gifts before?" Torin asked. "In past lives?"

"I don't know," Veyar admitted. "But if Bastillion thinks he recognizes a pattern—gifts that appear together, a soul that keeps manifesting the same abilities—that's the kind of evidence that would convince a god of order and structure."

"Is she?" Torin demanded, voice tight.

"No." Veyar's voice was firm. "She CAN'T be. The Visionary in mortal flesh would destroy everything. Her power—the Ninth Eye—it would tear reality apart. The Sacred Valley would collapse."

Inside Ash, the Phoenix recoiled.

Then where is she? If she can't be in mortal flesh, where—

Grief crashed through him—god's anguish layered with human desperation.

Lost. She's lost. How can my love be gone forever—

Ash tried to shake off the Phoenix's grief, but the god's anguish only made his own worse. The loss, the longing, the desperate love for someone who might be gone forever—it crashed through him in waves.

"I don't care if she is Visionary or not," Ash said aloud, voice cracking with layered pain—mortal and divine both.

"I don't care what Saav thinks she is. I only care that he HAS her. And I need to get her back. So tell me what to do."

The path twisted. Stars wheeled overhead. Shadows pressed close.

"Sela. Torin." Veyar's voice cut through. "You're her anchors, yes? Protectors for body and mind?"

"We are," Sela called back.

"Then you're the key. If you can reach her during the transformation, if you can maintain physical contact, you can anchor her to herself. Keep her from being lost. Keep her MORTAL."

"And then?" Ash demanded.

"Then you burn it out," Veyar said. "The transformation. The curse. The spell. Everything Bastillion's trying to force into her. Your fire—Phoenix fire, or whatever you can manage—burns it away."

Ash's hand went to his chest where the sigil pulsed warm but weak.

The Phoenix was dormant. Sleeping. He'd have to do this with mortal fire alone.

"Will it work?" Thorne asked.

"I don't know," Veyar admitted. "But it's the only chance. The alternative—"

"Don't." Ash's voice was sharp. "Don't tell me the alternative. Just tell me it's possible to save her."

Silence stretched.

"It's possible," Veyar said finally. "But Ash—the fire won't discriminate. It will burn the transformation, yes. But also everything connected to Bastillion's magic.

Including the Fourth Eye. You'll save her life but destroy the gift that makes her special."

"I don't care." The words came without hesitation. "As long as she's alive."

"She might not feel the same when she wakes," Veyar warned.

"Then I'll spend the rest of my life making it up to her. But at least she'll BE alive to be angry at me."

The path shifted. Through the shimmer of starlight and shadow ahead, something vast loomed—mountains of impossible height, sky the color of dying stars, architecture that shouldn't exist.

Vana'Sul. The gods' home.

"How much time?" Ash asked, voice tight.

"When dawn breaks over Vana'Sul," Veyar said, "Bastillion's power becomes absolute. The ritual completes. Whatever he's trying to make her become—it will be irreversible."

"HOW. MUCH. TIME."

"Maybe three hours," Kee said quietly. "Maybe less. The stars are already shifting. Dawn comes fast to places outside normal time."

Ash's wings beat harder despite the pain, despite the exhaustion, despite the way his mortal body screamed that it couldn't sustain this.

Three hours. Maybe less.

To cross the Shattered Vale. Storm a god's fortress. Disrupt a divine ritual. Save the woman he loved from a fate worse than death.

And if he failed—

"If the ritual completes," Veyar said, as if reading his

thoughts, "Ezra dies. The mortal body can't contain what Bastillion's trying to force into it. And when she dies—"

"I die," Ash finished. "Life Sigil. I know."

"And when you die," Veyar continued, voice heavy, "Phoenix dies. Trapped in mortal flesh with no escape. And when Phoenix dies—"

"The gods destabilize," Kee finished. "The Sacred Valley collapses. Everything—mortal and divine—ceases to exist."

The words settled like stones.

Apocalypse.

Save Ezra, or the world ends.

No pressure.

Inside Ash's mind, the Phoenix stirred one last time before retreating to dormant rest:

The humans must live. If they fail—if this curse takes them in this seventh life—we ALL die. You, the mortal girl, me, and Visionary.

The god's voice cracked with renewed anguish.

Wherever she is. Whatever form she wears. If she even EXISTS anymore. I don't know if she's lost, if she's dead, if she's scattered across the stars. All I know is that I've been without her. And if saving your mortal ensures my goddess —even if she's gone, even if she's nothing but memory now— doesn't cease to exist entirely...

A pause, heavy with desperate, aching love.

Then save her. Your Ezra. Love her with everything you have. Because right now, your human heart is the only thing keeping us all from oblivion. And because I understand now —truly understand—what it means to love someone you'd burn the world to save.

I don't know if my Visionary still exists. But you KNOW yours does. You can feel her through the bond. So fight for that. Fight for the certainty I lost.

Bastillion has gone mad. God of Light turned to Shadow. He thinks the Oracle is Visionary. He's wrong. He has to be wrong. But sane or insane, he'll destroy everything if we don't stop him.

So destroy him. Destroy the human shell he wears. Break this curse. Let the mortals live.

Because if they don't, neither do we. And I'll lose her—truly, finally, eternally—all over again.

Then the Phoenix was gone, leaving only the faint warmth of divine fire in Ash's chest and the desperate beating of his wings.

"One more thing," Veyar called as the path began to stabilize ahead. "I don't know what Bastillion is capable of now. He was the God of Light and Order once—direct, structured, clear. But now he wields shadows..." Veyar's expression turned troubled. "Shadow magic can deceive. Twist perception. I don't know if he'll use it, but be wary. Trust what you know to be true, not what you see or hear in his domain."

The landscape was solidifying now—no longer pure liminal space but something between. Mountains loomed. Valleys gaped. And ahead, through a veil of shadow and starlight, Vana'Sul waited.

"Trust each other," Veyar said. "Hold fast to what you know is true. That's the only way you'll survive this."

Ash looked at the Life Sigil on his palm—glowing faintly, pulsing with Ezra's weakening heartbeat.

"I know she chose me," he said quietly. "Three days

ago. With full knowledge of what I was. What I'd done. She touched me anyway. That's the truth I'm holding onto."

The path twisted ahead, still deep in the liminal way. The landscape flickered around them—sometimes stone, sometimes starlight, sometimes nothing at all.

Ash's wings spread wide, catching the last flickers of golden fire.

"Then let's go get her," Sela said fiercely, drawing her sword.

"For Ezra," Torin added, gripping his weapon.

"For everyone," Thorne finished, falling into step beside his brother.

Veyar planted his staff. "For what remains of the world we once knew."

Kee's grin flickered back—sharp, dangerous. "And for what comes after."

Together, they moved forward.

Deeper into the liminal way.

Toward the edge of Vana'Sul.

Toward Bastillion.

Toward Ezra.

The path twisted around them—stars wheeling, shadows pressing close. But through it all, Ash felt the pull. The bond drawing him forward like a compass needle toward north.

"How much longer?" he demanded.

"Soon," Veyar said. "We're close. When the path opens, we'll be at the edge. And then—"

"Then we fight," Ash finished.

Through the bond, faint and desperate, Ash sent one final message:

Hold on. I'm here. I'm coming. Just hold on a little longer.

The path twisted one more time.

And ahead, through the shimmer of starlight and shadow, something vast began to take shape.

They were almost there.

Chapter 23

The Black Sun

Through the shimmer of starlight and shadow ahead, the liminal way began to thin.

Ash could see it now—reality bleeding through the between-space. Stone. Sky. The sharp scent of dust and ancient magic growing stronger with every wing-beat forward.

And carved into the mountain before them, descending into the earth like a colossal wound: Vana'Sul.

The city descended in circles—vast rings spiraling down and down into darkness. The outermost ring bore bones of a village long dead. Half-buried houses leaning against each other. Collapsed market stalls showing hints of faded color. Deeper in, grander ruins: toppled colon-nades, fractured mosaics, the ribs of banquet halls. And deeper still, the third ring opening into compounds hewn from living rock. God-homes, cold and waiting.

Too far to see clearly. Too deep to reach quickly.

But somewhere down there, past obsidian arches and spiraling descent, the Sanctum waited.

Where Ezra was dying.

Ash felt it through the bond—distant, weakening, her terror a drumbeat against his ribs.

The path ahead solidified. The liminal way's entrance split open like a seam in reality, depositing them directly at Vana'Sul's outer gates.

Ash's wings beat once as he passed through, feet hitting ancient stone. Behind him, the others followed— Thorne with hand on sword hilt, Torin leaning on his staff, Sela favoring her good leg, Veyar's robes settling, and Kee flickering as the liminal magic released its hold.

The gates rose before them—massive, weathered, carved with symbols that had watched gods walk as mortals two centuries ago.

Open.

Waiting.

"We're here," Veyar said quietly.

Ash turned to look at the path ahead—the descending rings, the ruins, the impossible distance between them and the Sanctum—

"This isn't good." Thorne's voice cut through, tight with urgency. "Look."

He pointed not ahead, but up. East.

Ash's gaze snapped to the sky above Vana'Sul's center, and his heart stopped.

The sky was wrong.

Dawn was rising. Not the gentle blue-gold of natural sunrise, but something corrupted. The horizon burned sickly purple, light bleeding upward like infection through flesh. Time itself twisted visible, pulling morning forward, dragging the sun toward Vana'Sul hours too early.

"He's accelerating it," Veyar breathed. "Bastillion is pulling dawn toward himself. Forcing the sun to rise NOW."

"How long?" Sela demanded.

"Minutes." Veyar's knuckles went white on his staff. "Maybe less. When true sunlight touches the Sanctum, the ritual completes. Ezra becomes whatever he's trying to make her. And if she's not the Visionary—if she's just mortal flesh forced to contain divine power—"

"She dies," Ash finished. His hands curled into fists. "And I die with her."

Through the bond: Ezra's scream. Silent in his ears but deafening in his soul.

They'd never make it. A mile through a dead city, descending through rings of ruin, while dawn raced toward them like a predator.

They'd never reach her in time.

NO.

The word came from deep inside—from the place where the Phoenix slept.

Not a suggestion. A command.

Dawn will not come.

Ash gasped as divine consciousness surged upward, no longer asking permission, no longer waiting for Ash's mortal will to align with divine purpose. The Phoenix simply TOOK control, flooding his mind with power and fury and absolute certainty.

Not while I have strength to hold it back.

"Ash?" Thorne stepped toward him. "What's—"

But Ash was already burning.

Golden fire erupted from his chest—the Phoenix sigil blazing like a star being born. It spread outward in tendrils of light, wrapping around his arms, his legs, crawling up his throat like living flame.

His wings flared wide, no longer translucent and weak but blazing with power that made the others shield their eyes.

"ASH!" Sela shouted.

He didn't answer. Couldn't. The Phoenix had seized every part of him—mortal and divine merged so completely there was no separation, no distinction between Ash's desperation and the god's fury.

Fire erupted from his hands. From his eyes. From his mouth when he opened it to scream.

Not pain. Purpose.

The flames streamed outward, golden and terrible and beautiful, shooting toward the corrupted dawn like spears of condensed sunlight. They wrapped around the rising sun—coiling, tightening, a serpent made of divine fire constricting around stolen morning.

Distantly, as if from the bottom of a well, Ash heard voices below.

"What is he doing?" Torin's voice, small and afraid.

"He's stopping it." Veyar's voice shook. "He's stopping the dawn."

The fire around the sun pulsed once. Twice.

Then—

Ash INHALED.

Not breath. Not air.

Light itself.

The sun's radiance—every ray, every photon, every particle of stolen morning—flowed backward. Into the golden fire. Into Ash. Into the Phoenix burning inside him.

He drank the dawn.

His body blazed brighter, brighter, too bright to look at directly. The Phoenix sigil on his chest cracked, light bleeding through the fissures like magma through stone.

And the sun turned black.

Not void-absence like Bastillion's corruption. Not shadow-darkness.

This was presence inverted. Light turned inside-out. Divine fire made manifest in cold radiance that swallowed rather than gave.

The Black Sun hung on the eastern horizon—frozen, eternal, terrible in its wrongness.

And Ash—

Ash was burning.

Not with fire anymore. With transformation.

His body couldn't contain what he'd taken in. The sun's light. Dawn itself. Divine power meant for the sky now trapped in mortal flesh.

He could feel it happening.

Feel his skin cracking like dried clay. Feel his bones turning brittle as burned wood. Feel everything that made him solid, everything that made him real, beginning to UNMAKE.

The Phoenix's voice resonated through him—not words but knowing, ancient and absolute:

This is the price. To stop dawn, I must become it. And to become it, we must burn.

Ash tried to answer, tried to hold on, but there was nothing left to hold.

His body exploded into ash.

One moment: flesh, bone, blood.

The next: ember and particle, suspended in air, held together only by the Phoenix's will and the last dregs of Ash's consciousness.

He was falling. Drifting. Scattered.

He drifted downward like snow made of fire.

And as he fell—disintegrated, scattered, barely aware —the Phoenix spoke:

I give you what I have left.

The words resonated through every particle, every fragment of what Ash had been.

Not death. Rebirth. The sun's light burns in you now— absorbed, transformed, yours to carry. When you reform, I will sleep. Not gone. Never gone. Dormant, weak, a spark sheltered in your mortal flame.

The ash drifted lower. Ash could feel each piece of himself separately—thousands of embers, each one holding a fragment of consciousness, a splinter of memory.

I will grow again through you, with you, fed by the life you live and the love you fight for. You are no longer just vessel or god. You are both and neither—something new. Something that might survive what we could not.

Closer to the ground. The embers swirling, beginning

to coalesce, drawn together by something deeper than gravity.

The golden fire in your eyes—that will be my promise. Proof I remain. When you need me and I have strength to answer, I will rise.

The first embers touched stone.

And ignited.

Not with destruction. With creation.

Ash reformed.

Particle by particle, ember by ember, his body reconstructed itself from nothing. Bones knitting from ash. Flesh weaving from fire. Blood flowing like molten gold before cooling to mortal red.

Until then: run. Save her. Show me what mortal determination can accomplish when gods have given all they have.

Ash hit the ground whole.

He gasped—a full-body convulsion, lungs remembering how to breathe, heart slamming against ribs like it was trying to escape.

Live, Ash. For both of us.

Then the Phoenix was gone. Not dead. Not absent. But distant—so far down in the depths of Ash's soul it was barely a whisper. A warmth at his core. A spark buried beneath ash, dormant and dreaming.

Growing. Incubating. Fed by Ash's mortal life like a seed planted in fertile soil.

Still there.

Always there.

Ash pushed himself upright, hands shaking, body

weak but whole. He looked down at himself—same skin, same scars, same body he'd worn his entire life.

But different.

He could feel it. The Phoenix sleeping inside him, smaller now. Vulnerable. A baby god curled in the garden of his soul, drawing strength from Ash's heartbeat, his breath, his stubborn refusal to die.

And when he lifted his eyes—

Golden light blazed in his brown irises. Not replacing the color. Layered beneath it. Like sunlight filtered through amber, divine fire banked but present.

Proof that the Phoenix remained.

"Ash!" Thorne reached him first, dropping to his knees, hands hovering like he was afraid to touch. "You—I thought—we saw you—"

"I'm okay." Ash's voice was rough, smoke-damaged, but his. "The Phoenix burned out. Gave everything to create the Black Sun. It's sleeping now. Weak. But..." He pressed a hand to his chest, feeling the warmth there. "Still here. Still with me."

Sela stumbled over, limping badly, eyes wide. "Your eyes. They're—"

"Golden," Ash finished. He pushed to his feet, legs trembling but holding. "I absorbed the sun's light. It's part of me now. Part of..." He looked up at the Black Sun hanging cold on the horizon. "That."

Veyar approached slowly, staff raised as if testing for danger. "The Black Sun is stable. Time is frozen over Vana'Sul. Dawn cannot break while it holds." His ancient gaze fixed on Ash. "How long?"

"I don't know." Ash called fire to his palm—not golden god-fire, but red-orange Fyrwarden flame. His flame. Mortal and familiar and still strong. "The Phoenix said minutes. Maybe an hour. When it burns out completely, when the Black Sun fails—" He looked at the distant city. "Time will resume. Dawn will break. The ritual will complete."

"Then we're racing your burnout," Torin said quietly. "Not the sun."

"Yes." Ash looked at each of them—exhausted, injured, terrified, but still standing. "And we don't have time to rest. The Black Sun is already flickering. I can feel it. Every second we stand here is a second closer to—"

Through the bond: Ezra's pain. Sharper now. More desperate. Being closer to her again, their bond surged—he felt her pain as Saav did whatever he was doing. And for the first time in days, he heard her voice aloud.

A scream. Tortured. Breaking.

"RUN!" Ash was already moving.

No more words. No more explanations.

Just movement.

They sprinted through the gates into Vana'Sul's outer ring.

The air changed the moment they entered—heavier, colder, magic so old it left a taste like copper and ashes on Ash's tongue. The village ruins blurred past. Buildings half-buried in sand. Market stalls collapsed. Empty doorways watching.

Ash didn't slow. Couldn't. Ezra's scream still echoed in his mind.

The second ring opened before them—grander ruins, colonnades fallen, mosaics fractured. They leaped over rubble, ducked under broken arches, boots pounding on stone that hadn't felt footsteps in two centuries.

"Keep up!" Thorne shouted, sword drawn despite having nothing to fight yet.

Torin limped but didn't fall behind. Sela pushed through her injured hip. Veyar's robes billowed as he moved faster than any ancient should. Kee flickered ahead, scouting.

The third ring: god-compounds carved from living rock. Massive doorways yawning into darkness. Ash's lungs burned. His legs screamed. But the bond pulled him forward like a rope around his chest, and he followed it without thinking.

Faster.

Obsidian arches rose ahead—the Inner Gate, twin monoliths carved with spirals.

They didn't slow. Passed through at a dead run.

The Sanctum opened below.

Vast. Ancient. Untouched by decay.

An arena carved from black stone, spiraling down to a center where water darker than night waited—the Veil Pool, surface glass-still, swallowing even the Black Sun's light.

Rising from the pool's center: a temple platform. Stone steps. An altar of obsidian.

And on that altar—

Ezra.

Bound by golden-brown vines that pulsed with corrupted magic. The Rootsong wrapped around her like living chains. Sickly purple light blazed from her forehead where the Fourth Eye burned. Her body convulsed. Her mouth moved in silent screams—spelled voiceless, robbed even of that release.

Beside her stood Bastillion.

Still wearing Saav's face, but the god was eating the man from inside. Sallow skin stretched too tight. Dark veins spiderwebbing across his neck. Eyes burning purple with two centuries of madness.

He held a bone-carved vessel, tilting it toward Ezra's mouth.

Forcing visions down her throat. Dead Oracle souls. Kireva's stolen dreams.

"NO!" Ash didn't stop running.

He launched himself off the Sanctum's edge, dropping twenty feet to the next level, rolling, coming up still moving. Fire erupted from his hands—red-orange Fyrwarden flame, mortal and deadly.

Bastillion looked up.

And smiled.

"Ah," he said pleasantly. "You made it."

His gaze found Ash's golden eyes. Saav looked up to the open sky over the Sanctum. Fury flickered in his gaze, giving Ash a moment of satisfaction.

"You stopped the dawn. Impossible." An accusation.

Ash hit the bottom level, boots splashing in the shallow water surrounding the Veil Pool. The temple platform rose ahead. Ezra convulsing on the altar above.

"You aren't the only god who returned," Ash snarled. "And it's staying stopped until I get her back."

He didn't wait for a response. Didn't give Bastillion time to speak.

Ash ran for the temple steps.

Behind him, the others spread out—Thorne going left, Torin right, Sela and Veyar circling wide. Kee vanished into shadow.

Above, the Black Sun flickered.

And Bastillion's smile widened.

"Then let's see how long your mortal fire can last," he said.

Shadow erupted from the ground.

Chapter 24

The Sanctum

Shadow erupted from the ground.

Not formless darkness—shapes. Twisting, coiling shapes that rose like smoke given substance, oily black magic forming into creatures with too many limbs and eyes that burned purple.

Bastillion's constructs.

They materialized between Ash and the platform where Ezra hung convulsing—a wall of living shadow, blocking any approach.

"Move!" Ash's fire blazed to life in both hands, red-orange flames painting the Sanctum in flickering light.

They all scattered.

Thorne dove left, sword in one hand, fire erupting from the other—Fyrwarden flames matching Ash's, brothers who'd trained together since childhood moving in perfect synchronization.

Torin went right, staff whirling despite his injured leg.

Sela limped after him, knife drawn, refusing to fall behind even as her hip screamed protest.

Veyar's staff blazed with pale liminal light. Kee flickered in and out of visibility, death-shadows gathering around the minor god like a cloak.

The constructs attacked.

One lunged at Ash—humanoid but wrong, limbs too long, joints bending backward. He met it with fire, flames washing over shadow-flesh. The creature shrieked and fell apart, dissolving into oily smoke.

But before the smoke even hit the ground, it was reforming. Coalescing. Rising again.

"They're not dying!" Thorne shouted, blade carving through another construct only to watch it pull itself back together seconds later.

"Bastillion's will!" Veyar called back, staff slamming down to freeze a construct mid-leap. Liminal energy trapped it between moments—but only for seconds before divine will broke through and it lunged again. "They're made of him! As long as he maintains them, they won't stop!"

Ash snarled and pushed forward, fire streaming from both hands. Two constructs intercepted him, claws extended, purple eyes blazing. He ducked under one's swipe, drove his fist into the second's chest, fire exploding on impact.

The construct shattered. Reformed. Attacked again.

Behind the wall of shadow, on the platform over the Veil Pool, Bastillion continued his work.

He stood beside the altar where Ezra lay bound, golden-brown Rootsong vines wrapped around her body like serpents. In his hands: another bone-carved vessel, tilting toward her spelled-silent mouth.

Though their bond he could sense her trapped in stolen visions from her tribe being forced down her throat.

Ezra's body convulsed. Light blazed beneath her skin—too bright, too much. An Eye sigil that she never had before burned on her forehead like a brand, searing deeper as she consumed each vision.

"Almost ready, my Visionary," Bastillion crooned, voice layered with divine resonance and human decay. Still Saav's voice, but wrong. Sick. "Just a little more. Soon you'll remember what you truly are."

"Get through them!" Ash roared at the others. "We have to reach her!"

Thorne was already moving, fire and blade working together to carve a path. A construct lunged at him—he met it with flame, blade following to scatter the pieces before they could reform.

But there were too many. For every one they destroyed, two more rose from the shadows.

Torin's staff cracked across a construct's skull. The creature's head snapped sideways, neck breaking—but shadow had no bones to break. It twisted back, lunged, jaws opening impossibly wide.

"Dad!" Sela threw her knife. It buried itself in the construct's eye, and the creature shrieked—a sound like wind through a graveyard—stumbling back.

But still reforming. Still coming.

Kee flickered between them, death-shadows lashing

out. "I can disrupt them!" the minor god called. "But only for seconds! His will is too strong!"

"Then we use those seconds!" Ash dove through a gap Kee created, rolled, came up running. Three more constructs materialized in his path. He didn't slow—just poured fire forward, creating a wall of flame they had to pass through.

They did. Burning. Shrieking. Reforming on the other side.

Veyar appeared beside Ash in a flash of liminal light, staff blazing. "The platform! If we can reach it—"

A construct's claws raked across Veyar's shoulder. The ancient god stumbled, blood soaking his robes. Another construct lunged—

Torin's staff intercepted it, sending the creature flying. "Keep moving! We'll hold them!"

But they were being pushed back. Worn down. For every step forward, the constructs forced them two steps back.

And on the platform, Bastillion emptied another vessel into Ezra's mouth.

Her body arched, convulsing harder. The Rootsong tightened, forcing her to swallow. Patterns spread beneath her skin—not quite veins, not quite roots, something between. Wrong. Corrupted.

Through the bond, Ash felt her pain like it was his own. Felt something being ripped from her soul piece by piece. Felt her breaking.

NO.

He pushed harder, fire blazing brighter. Thorne fell in beside him without a word, their flames combining, doubling in intensity. They'd fought like this a hundred times—coordinated, instinctive, brothers who knew each other's movements before they happened.

They carved through the constructs together, Ash creating openings and Thorne exploiting them, fire and steel moving as one.

But it wasn't enough.

A construct's claws caught Ash's ribs, tearing through jacket and flesh. He hissed in pain but drove his elbow into its face, fire erupting. The creature fell apart. Reformed.

Thorne took a hit across the shoulder, blood spraying. He spun, blade removing the construct's arm—which dissolved and regrew in seconds.

They were bleeding. Exhausted. Losing.

And above the Sanctum, something changed.

The ceiling near the skylight cracked.

Not from the battle. From Bastillion's magic.

Stone split like an eggshell. The Black Sun hung cold on the horizon, partially visible to where the light of the sun was to hit the stone, only now it was frozen and immovable.

Bastillion looked up, and his decaying face twisted with fury.

"BREAK!" he screamed at the Black Sun, arms raised, divine power gathering. "BREAK, DAMN YOU!"

Shadow magic lashed upward, striking at the impossible sun. Trying to shatter it. Trying to pull dawn through by force.

The Black Sun held.

Cold. Eternal. Unmovable.

Bastillion poured more power into the assault. His human body shuddered, sallow skin going paler, dark veins spreading further. The god was consuming the man from inside, burning through mortal flesh to fuel divine fury.

The Black Sun flickered.

Just for a heartbeat. But enough to show it was weakening.

Bastillion felt it. Saw his chance. Gathered everything he had and struck again—

And the Black Sun pushed back.

Bastillion staggered, divine power rebounding. His rage exploded outward in a shockwave of shadow magic that made the air itself scream.

The constructs dissolved.

Not dismissed. Ripped apart by their master's uncontrolled fury, unable to maintain form in the face of divine rage unleashed.

Ash saw the opening.

"NOW!"

He sprinted across the Sanctum floor, boots splashing through shallow water surrounding the Veil Pool. The platform rose ahead—solid stone covering the dark water, temple steps leading up to the altar where Ezra hung trapped.

Bastillion turned, saw him coming.

And smiled through his fury.

"Come then, little Fyrwarden," he purred, shadow magic coiling around his fingers. "Let me show you what happens when mortals defy gods."

Ash didn't answer. Just ran faster, fire blazing in both hands.

He hit the temple steps at a dead sprint, leaping up three at a time. Bastillion raised his hands, shadow lashing out—

Ash rolled under it, came up swinging. His fist, wreathed in flame, connected with Bastillion's jaw.

The god stumbled back, actually stumbled, surprise flashing across his decaying face.

Ash pressed the advantage. Another strike, fire erupting. Bastillion blocked with shadow, but Ash was already moving, kicking low, sweeping the god's legs.

Bastillion went down.

For just a moment—just a heartbeat—the fallen god of Light crashed to the platform's stone.

Ash dove for the altar, reaching for Ezra—

Shadow magic exploded beneath him.

It hit like a physical blow, lifting Ash off his feet and hurling him backward. He flew through the air, arms pinwheeling, and crashed into a pillar at the Sanctum's edge hard enough to crater stone.

Pain exploded through his back, his ribs, everywhere. He slid to the ground, gasping.

And Bastillion stood, brushing off his robes with hands that trembled with barely contained fury.

"Impressive," the god said quietly. Too quietly. "You actually knocked me down. The last time a mortal managed that..." He paused, considering. "Well. There was no last time."

He raised both hands.

"And I'm afraid—" His smile turned cruel. "—yours just ran out."

Shadow magic gathered above Ash. Not a construct. Not an attack.

The ceiling itself.

Stone groaned. Cracked. A massive section—tons of rock—began to fall.

Directly toward where Ash lay dazed and bleeding.

Ash tried to move. His body wouldn't respond fast enough. Legs trembling. Arms weak. He looked up and saw death falling toward him—

Movement from the left.

A figure running. Torin.

"NO!" Sela's scream cut through the air.

But Torin was already there, already moving. His body slammed into Ash, shoving him sideways, out of the path of falling stone.

And the ceiling came down.

The impact shook the entire Sanctum.

When the dust cleared, Torin lay in the rubble.

His upper body was visible—head, shoulders, chest. The rest buried beneath tons of stone. Blood spreading across the platform in a dark pool.

"Dad!" Sela was running, stumbling. "DAD!"

Ash scrambled to Torin's side, hands shaking. The older man's eyes were open. Still aware. But fading.

"Torin—" Ash's voice broke.

"No time." Torin's hand found Ash's, gripping with what little strength remained. Blood bubbled at the corner of his mouth. "Get... her..."

"I will," Ash promised. "I will, I—"

Torin's grip tightened for just a moment. His eyes found Ash's—and there was no fear there. No regret. Just fierce, absolute certainty.

"For Ezra," he whispered.

Then the light went out of his eyes.

Sela reached them, collapsed beside her father's body, hands reaching for his face. "Dad, no, no, no—" Her voice broke into sobs. "Please, Dad, please—"

Ash heard his last breath whisper out "Little bird."

Then he was gone.

On the platform, Bastillion laughed.

"One less obstacle," he said pleasantly, already turning back to the altar. "Now. Where were we?"

Something inside Ash broke.

Not shattered. Not destroyed.

Unlocked.

He stood slowly, Torin's blood on his hands, Sela's sobs echoing in his ears. The golden fire in his eyes blazed brighter—not divine power, not Phoenix stirring, just the light of absorbed sunlight reflecting pure, cold fury.

This was the warrior he'd been before Ezra.

The mercenary. The killer. The Fyrwarden who fought without mercy because mercy was weakness and weakness got you killed.

Cold. Efficient. Deadly.

But now—

Now there was something more.

Love.

Hot, fierce, burning love for the people around him. For Torin who'd trusted him. For Sela who'd fought beside him. For Thorne who'd never left his side. For Ezra who'd chosen him despite everything he was.

The cold warrior powered by hot love.

The combination was devastating.

Ash moved.

Not running. Not charging. Just moving with the terrible inevitability of an avalanche, of a wildfire, of death itself approaching.

Fire blazed to life in both hands. Not wild. Not desperate. Controlled. Focused. Deadly.

He crossed the platform in seconds, boots splashing through shallow water, temple steps blurring beneath him.

Bastillion turned, vessel raised toward Ezra's mouth—

Ash hit him like a battering ram.

His hands closed on Bastillion's robes, fire erupting where flesh met fabric. He yanked the god away from the altar, away from Ezra, and drove his fist into Saav's decaying face.

Once. Twice. Three times.

The vessel flew from Bastillion's hands, bone carving spinning through the air.

It hit the edge of the platform and tumbled into the Veil Pool.

The last of the stolen Oracle visions—hundreds of dead souls, Kireva's dreams, all of it—vanished into water darker than night.

Gone forever.

Bastillion shrieked.

"NO! She is MINE!"

Ash's fire cut him off. Flames washing over the god's

face, his chest, his arms. Bastillion stumbled back, shadow magic lashing out in wild defense.

But something was wrong.

The god moved slower. His shadow magic flickered. The purple light in his eyes dimmed and brightened erratically.

The human body was failing.

Too much divine power. Too much fury. Too much god forced through mortal flesh that was never meant to contain it.

Bastillion's skin had gone translucent in places, dark veins visible beneath like cracks in porcelain. Blood dripped from his nose, his ears. The god was eating the man, and there was barely any man left to consume.

Ash didn't hesitate. Didn't give Bastillion time to recover.

He drove forward, fists and fire, brutal and efficient. Every strike calculated to hurt, to weaken, to force the god back step by step.

And Bastillion—weakened, his mortal shell breaking—couldn't hold the assault.

He went down.

Hard. Crashing to the platform's stone, eyes rolling back. The purple light flickered once, twice—

And went out.

Unconscious.

Ash didn't wait to see if he'd stay down. He spun and ran for the altar.

Ezra hung there, Rootsong vines wrapped around her body like living chains. Her eyes were closed, face pale, lips moving soundlessly. The Fourth Eye on her forehead still blazed—corrupted visions burning through her mind even with Bastillion unconscious.

"Hold on," Ash breathed, reaching for the vines. "I've got you. Just hold on."

The Rootsong resisted his touch, corrupted magic making the vines pulse and tighten. But Ash worked carefully, fingers finding where each vine wrapped around her —chest, arms, throat—and pulling them loose one by one.

He couldn't burn them. Couldn't destroy them. The Rootsong belonged to the Veyona people, and they'd need it returned whole.

So he pulled. Unwrapped. Loosened each coil despite the way the corrupted magic fought him, despite the way it tried to dig deeper into her flesh.

The last vine came free.

Ezra eyes fluttered open. Unfocused. Dazed.

She looked at him—really looked, seeing him despite the visions still burning through her mind—and her lips moved.

"You came."

Just a whisper. Barely audible. But it hit Ash like a physical blow.

"Always," he said, voice breaking. "Always."

Tears streamed down her face.

He pulled her into his arms, hugging her tight, feeling her heart beat against his chest. Alive. She was alive. They'd made it. They'd—

Behind them, something moved.

Ash felt it a heartbeat before it struck—oily black

magic wrapping around his legs like tentacles, like chains, cold and wrong and furious.

He tried to pull away, tried to break free, but the cords tightened and yanked backward.

Bastillion was awake. On his knees, one hand extended, purple eyes burning with madness and desperation. Blood running from his nose, his mouth, his ears. Human body breaking apart but divine will still there, still fighting.

"If I can't have her," Bastillion rasped, "NO ONE CAN!"

The cords whipped Ash backward, pulling him toward the platform's edge. Toward the Veil Pool's dark water.

Everything slowed.

Ash felt the cords pulling. Felt his balance tipping. Felt the cold emanating from the pool behind him.

His arms tightened around Ezra. He wouldn't let go. Couldn't. Whatever happened—

They fell together.

Bastillion lunged after them, shadow magic extending, trying to drag them down.

And all three—Fyrwarden, Oracle, and fallen god—tumbled over the platform's edge into the Veil Pool.

The water was cold beyond cold.

Dark beyond dark.

It swallowed them completely, and the world went black.

Ash held Ezra tighter, felt her arms wrap around him in return, felt Bastillion's shadow magic coiling around them both, dragging them down—

Down—

Down—

Into the Veil itself.

And somewhere in the darkness, something ancient stirred.

Something that had been waiting.

Something that had been watching.

Something that remembered when gods walked free, when the Visionary made her choice, when everything broke and was buried in mortal flesh.

The Veil opened its arms.

And pulled them deeper still.

Chapter 25

The Fall

The water swallowed them whole.

Not water—not really. Ezra couldn't breathe, couldn't scream. Cold pressed in from all sides, thick and resistant, like falling through honey made of midnight. She felt Ash's arms tight around her, felt Bastillion's oily black cords wrapped around them both, dragging them down into impossible darkness.

Down.

Down.

Deeper into the Veil Pool.

Her lungs burned. Her vision darkened at the edges. She was drowning, dying, and Ash's grip was the only thing tethering her to—

Light.

Dim. Golden. Impossible.

The water changed. Still thick, still strange, but suddenly Ezra could breathe it. Her lungs pulled in something that wasn't air but sustained her anyway—

like breathing liquid starlight, cool and sweet and wrong.

She gasped, body convulsing as it remembered how to function.

Beside her, Ash's grip loosened slightly. She heard him gasp too, heard him pull in the strange not-water.

But something else was happening.

Golden light blazed from his chest—the Phoenix sigil erupting with power. His eyes snapped open, no longer brown, no longer his.

Pure gold. Divine. Ancient.

"Ash?" Her voice came out strange in the not-water, but audible.

He looked at her, and she saw the layering—mortal man and god consciousness both present, but the divine leading now. When he spoke, his voice resonated with power that made her bones hum.

"I'm here. The god-body—it's near. Proximity triggered the awakening. I'm whole again."

Even as he spoke, wings erupted from his back.

Ezra's breath stopped.

Wings. Golden and blazing and impossible. Each feather burned with divine fire, limned with light that shouldn't exist. They spread wide in the strange water-space, massive and terrible and utterly magnificent.

She'd never seen anything like them. Had never imagined they could be real.

But they were. And they were part of him.

Ezra couldn't breathe—and not because of the water.

He was devastating. God and man layered together, divine power radiating from every line of him. The wings spread wide, golden eyes blazing, Phoenix sigil burning like a star on his chest.

But it wasn't just seeing him that stole her breath.

It was feeling him.

The presence of a god. Ancient. Vast. Power that made the water around them hum with energy. It pressed against her like heat from a bonfire, like standing too close to the sun.

And beneath it—woven through it—her love for Ash.

The two sensations crashed together: mortal love for the man she'd chosen, and awe at the divine being he carried. Both overwhelming. Both true.

She loved him. The man.

But gods, the god was beautiful too.

"Ezra?" His voice—layered now, human and divine both—pulled her back.

She realized she was staring. Mouth open. Eyes wide.

"Sorry, I—" She swallowed hard. "I've never seen anything like this. Like you."

"A lot's happened since I last saw you," she managed.

Ash—Phoenix—smiled. Not his usual smile. Something wilder. More dangerous. Divine amusement mixed with mortal affection, and his smirk was pure Ash despite the god wearing his face.

"No kidding."

Ezra's throat tightened, still caught in the presence, in the beauty, in the impossible reality of what he was.

"You're beautiful," she whispered.

The smile softened. Something human breaking through the divine. "So are you."

Then his expression shifted, golden eyes focusing past her, and the warmth vanished. "But we're not alone."

Above them, Bastillion's roar of fury shook the Veil itself. Then he descended, shadow magic propelling him downward like a spear of darkness.

They were falling through layers of reality.

The darkness gave way completely to golden light, and suddenly Ezra could see.

The realm between life and death. Between mortal world and divine prison.

Gods.

The Seven Gaurdian Gods of the Sacred Valley and five minor gods. Floating in the golden-dark like stars suspended in amber, each one wrapped in chains of light that pulsed with slow, steady power.

Their forms were beautiful. All frozen in perfect stasis and faces peaceful in eternal sleep.

Ezra's breath caught in her throat. "The sigil on her forehead blazed, showing her the truth beneath—the chains weren't just light, they were will. Divine will woven through every link, holding this prison together through sheer force of determination.

And there at the center of it all, surrounded by the other sleeping forms, was the goddess. The one Saav thought she was.

The Visionary.

The goddess floated in her chains, draped in a hooded gown of deep midnight blue. Her face was covered by a golden mask—smooth, featureless except for a single carved symbol: the Visionary's Eye, etched in relief across where her eyes would be. Below the mask, blue-cold lips.

Her skin, visible at throat and hands, was pale like marble and just as spirit like as the other gods.

Not far from the Visionary, another form floated. A spirit that looked like Ash. Wings folded tight. Face serene.

Phoenix.

The god-body hung in its chains, and it was ghost-like too. Pale. Translucent. Empty.

Because the soul that should fill it was here. Beside her. In Ash's flesh.

"Your true form," she whispered.

Ash—Phoenix—nodded slowly, golden eyes locked on his sleeping body. "Yes. The body sleeps. I walk." His gaze shifted to the Visionary's empty form, and something broke in his expression.

Ezra looked around at the other sleeping gods. All of them ghost-like. Translucent. Empty.

"All of the gods' souls are missing," she breathed.

"That is what Veyar was saying," Ash said, Phoenix's voice layered beneath. "He thinks somehow all the souls were placed in human bodies except for Visionary. He says she can't become human because the Ninth Eye is too powerful."

Ezra looked at the Visionary's empty form. The translucent body. The absence.

"I'm not sure he's right," she said quietly. "Because Visionary is just as empty as the rest."

Phoenix's expression shifted. Grief. Recognition. But he said nothing.

Just looked at the empty goddess with longing so vast it made Ezra's chest ache.

Behind them, Bastillion burst into the realm with a shriek of fury.

He looked worse here. Still Saav's face, but the decay had accelerated. Gray skin, nearly translucent. Dark veins everywhere, pulsing with shadow magic. Blood dripping from his nose, his ears. The human shell was collapsing.

But his eyes—those burned with purple madness, undimmed.

"Two hundred years!" he screamed, swimming past them toward the Visionary's empty form. "If only I had known—but now—"

He reached the goddess, hands trembling as they touched her masked face with terrible tenderness.

"Finally," he breathed. "Finally within reach."

Ezra watched in horror as Bastillion's fingers found the edge of the golden mask, trying to pry it free.

"I'll prove it to you," he snarled over his shoulder at them. "Prove that Ezra is mine. That she IS the Visionary."

He pulled at the mask. Clawed at it.

It didn't move. Didn't budge. Sealed by divine will stronger than any god.

"Come OFF!" Bastillion screamed, yanking harder. "COME OFF!"

Nothing. The mask remained fixed, immovable.

Bastillion released the Visionary with a shriek of fury. "BITCH!"

He spun toward Ezra, eyes blazing with madness and rage. "What did you do to her?"

Ezra backed up into Ash, who immediately pushed her behind him, wings spreading protectively.

Saav growled at Ash. "She was mine!" Shadow magic

erupted around him. "Until YOU tainted her with darkness!" He spat the words. "She was pure! Perfect—and you RUINED her!" Then he lunged.

Not at Ash. At Ezra.

Shadow magic wrapped around her like chains, yanking her away from Ash's protection. She felt herself being dragged toward the Visionary's sleeping form, felt Bastillion's mad intention—

He was trying to push her INTO the goddess's body. Trying to force Ezra's soul into the empty vessel. Trying to make her become what he believed she'd always been.

"She chose wrong!" Bastillion screamed as Ezra fought against his grip. "But I'll make her understand! When I wake her—when I free her—she'll be grateful! She'll WANT me!"

"You're mad!" Ezra gasped, the Eye sigil blazing as she struggled. "She'll never choose you! She chose him—across eternity, across every life—she chose Phoenix!"

Bastillion's expression twisted into something monstrous. "Then she'll learn to choose differently."

Shadow erupted from his hands, lashing toward them both.

The oily black magic wrapped around them like web —thick, sticky, suffocating. Ezra felt it pulling at her limbs, dragging her down, separating her from Ash.

She couldn't move. Couldn't break free.

Ash's wings beat frantically, fire blazing, but the shadow web held them both trapped.

"Stay close to me," Ash gasped, reaching for her.

Ezra's hand found his—not to be protected, but to fight.

"No," she said, gripping tight. "We fight together."

Her Life Sigil blazed on her left palm. His on his right. Their marks connected.

And everything changed.

Power surged between them—not just Phoenix fire, but something deeper. Something that hummed with the frequency of choice, of love freely given, of two souls bound so completely that not even death could break them.

The Life Sigil flared white-gold, brilliant and defiant.

The oily shadow web disintegrated.

Bastillion shrieked as his magic burned away under the force of their connection. "IMPOSSIBLE!"

But it wasn't. Because they weren't just mortal and god anymore. They were BOTH. Together. Amplified.

The battle exploded through the golden-dark.

They moved as one—Ezra holding Ash's right hand with her left, their Life Sigils blazing where palm met palm. They floated and spun through the strange not-water, propelled by Ash's wings and the power flowing between them.

Bastillion's shadow magic lashed out from every direction—above, below, from the sides. Amplified by his sleeping god-body, the darkness was devastating, trying to crush them, bind them, tear them apart.

But every time shadow came close, the Life Sigil pulsed.

Pure light erupted from their joined hands, pushing back darkness, burning through Bastillion's web before it could trap them. Fire and defiance made manifest. Love as weapon.

Ash's wings beat hard, carrying them around sleeping gods, through impossible currents in the not-water. Ezra held tight, feeling the power flow through their connection—her Oracle sight guiding them, showing openings, while his fire struck wherever she pointed.

They weren't fighting separately anymore.

They were one weapon. One purpose. One absolutely unbreakable bond.

And Bastillion couldn't touch them.

They spiraled around a massive sleeping god—scaled, winged—and came up behind Bastillion.

Ash struck. Fire washed over Bastillion's back. The god screamed, shadow magic thrashing.

"You can't win!" Bastillion roared. "I am a god!"

"Then let's see what a fragmented god can do," Ash growled.

His wings beat hard, propelling them forward. Bastillion raised his hands—

And Ash crashed into him.

Body to body. Hand-to-hand.

They grappled in the golden-dark, spinning through the not-water, and Ezra had to release Ash's hand to avoid being caught in the violence.

She watched, heart in throat, as Bastillion's hands found Ash's throat, squeezing with shadow-amplified strength.

Ash couldn't breathe. His wings beat frantically, trying to break free.

Then fire erupted from his palms, directly into Bastillion's chest.

The god screamed and released him, stumbling backward.

Ash didn't give him time to recover. He dove forward, fists blazing, and drove them into Bastillion's face.

Once. Twice. Three times.

Fire underwater—impossible, but Phoenix fire didn't care. It burned because it chose to, because love and fury were fuel enough.

And Bastillion's skin cracked.

Ezra watched in horror and fascination as his face split like porcelain under stress. Light bled through the fissures —purple and sick and wrong.

"NO!" Bastillion shrieked, clutching at his breaking face.

But the cracks spread. Down his neck. Across his chest. His hands.

The human body was failing. His god in chains was starting to merge into the cracks.

Ezra saw her chance.

"NO!" she screamed at Bastillion's breaking form. "You will NOT become a full god!"

She pushed.

Pushed his fragmenting soul toward the chained god-body, pushed with Oracle sight and desperate fury and the absolute certainty that he could not be allowed to reunite while free.

Bastillion's mortal shell disintegrated as light exploded outward as Saav's body finally shattered, dissolving into motes of purple radiance that scattered through the golden-dark.

His god soul—pure divine essence, no longer

anchored to the human form—shot toward the chained god-body like an arrow finding its mark.

It struck.

The god-body convulsed. The chains blazed, tightening.

And the pale ghost-like form solidified.

From translucent to real. From spirit to flesh.

But still asleep.

The chains held, pulsing with divine will that would not be denied, sealing Bastillion's reunited form in perfect stasis.

The first god to reunite soul with body.

But still trapped. Still imprisoned. Still sealed away.

"Is it over?" she whispered.

Light exploded from Ash's chest before he could answer.

Not fire. Something deeper. The Phoenix sigil blazing so bright Ezra had to shield her eyes.

When she looked again, Ash's eyes had gone pure gold. The divine consciousness that had been present but cooperative surged forward, taking full control.

"The battle is won," Phoenix said, voice layered and vast. He looked around at the sleeping gods, at Bastillion's sealed form. "But the work is not finished."

Ezra's throat tightened. "What do you mean?"

Phoenix looked at the sleeping gods. At the Visionary's empty form. At his own pale ghost-like body floating in chains.

Understanding settled across his features. Grief. Love. Choice.

"These gods were imprisoned for a reason," he said

quietly. "The Visionary saw something—some future, some catastrophe—that made her choose this. Lock us all away." His voice softened with sorrow. "She sacrificed everything."

"So they can't wake," Ezra breathed. "Not yet."

"Not until the world is ready." Phoenix's gaze lingered on the Visionary's translucent form. On the body that slept without a soul.

He stared at it for a long moment, golden eyes showing recognition, grief, understanding. But he said nothing. Just looked at the empty goddess with longing that had no words.

Then he turned back to Ezra.

"Bastillion is sealed. But these gods need a guardian. Someone to keep watch. To ensure they sleep peacefully." His voice gentled. "To protect the Visionary most of all."

Understanding crashed through Ezra. "You're going to stay."

"Yes." Phoenix looked at his own sleeping body, at the chains holding it. "I should return to that form. Seal myself away. But there's another way."

He turned to where Ash's human consciousness waited, buried beneath the divine.

"You will live your mortal life," Phoenix said, speaking to the man he'd been sharing flesh with. "You must love her with everything you are—not everything I am."

The spirit turned one last time to look at the Visionary's empty form.

"She will return and I will be her waiting for her," he said, so quietly Ezra almost didn't hear. "However long it takes."

Ezra felt Ash's human grief through their connection, felt his desperate protest.

But Phoenix was already moving.

He placed a hand over Ash's heart—over his own heart. "After seven lives of dying for love, you've earned the chance to live for it."

Golden light pulsed.

And Phoenix stepped back.

No—stepped OUT.

Ezra watched in awe and horror as divine consciousness separated from mortal flesh, as god-soul pulled free from human form. It should have been violent, should have torn Ash apart.

But instead it was gentle. Careful. Like a spirit emerging from a chrysalis, leaving the shell intact and whole.

Phoenix's form materialized beside Ash.

Translucent. Pale. Ghost-like—just like the sleeping body in chains, but free-floating. Spirit without anchor.

Ash gasped, body convulsing as the separation completed. His wings—those beautiful golden wings—flickered.

And vanished.

Ash gulped and swallowed water. His eyes went wide—brown now, fully mortal—panic flashing across his face as his lungs burned.

Ezra sensed it immediately. He could no longer breathe here.

Phoenix's voice echoed urgently. "Hurry—he can't breathe here any longer."

It was Ezra's turn to save him. She grabbed his arm,

pulled it over her shoulder, and started kicking upward, propelling them through the water. Phoenix's spirit gave them a push from below, moving them faster toward the surface.

A current formed, gentle but insistent, pulling them upward. "Hang on, I feel the Veil is releasing us," Ezra said.

Higher. Higher still.

Until the golden-dark began to fade, the realm of sleeping gods growing distant below them.

Ezra looked down one last time.

At Phoenix's spirit-form standing watch among the chained gods.

At Bastillion sealed away forever.

At the Visionary's empty body, masked and waiting.

Then the current pulled them through another layer, and the realm disappeared from view.

Just cold water and the desperate need to reach air remained.

Ezra's hand found Ash's in the dark. Squeezed once.

Together. Always together.

He squeezed back.

And they swam toward the surface, toward whatever waited above, toward the choice they would have to make.

The water grew lighter.

Almost there.

Almost—

Chapter 26

The Choice

Ezra broke the surface gasping.

Water streamed down her face, into her eyes, choking her as she tried to breathe and understand where she was at the same time. Strong hands caught her waist, steadying her.

"I've got you," Ash said, voice rough. "I've got you."

He pulled her through the water toward the edge of the pool, both of them coughing, disoriented. Ezra's fingers found stone—cool, damp, covered in moss. She hauled herself up onto the ledge and collapsed, chest heaving.

Ash pulled himself up beside her, water pouring off him in rivulets.

For a long moment, they just breathed. Just existed. Just tried to process what had happened.

Ezra's hands moved over herself frantically—checking for injuries, for the Rootsong vines, for any sign of Bastillion's ritual still clinging to her flesh.

Nothing.

She was whole. Unharmed. Wearing—

"Jeans," she breathed, looking down at herself in shock.

Her modern jeans. Her jacket. Her boots from the museum. All soaking wet, plastered to her skin, but undeniably the clothes she'd been wearing when she fell into this pool.

Or was it weeks ago?

Or seven lifetimes?

Beside her, Ash was staring at his own hands, at the leather jacket that clung to his shoulders, at the jeans and boots that belonged to a construction worker in Seattle, not a warrior from the Sacred Valley.

"Where—" His voice cracked. "Ezra, where are we?"

She looked around, recognition hitting her like cold water.

The underground chamber. The one beneath the shrine in the Hoh Rainforest. The Black Pool above them scattered fractured light across dark stone, ripples playing across the ceiling like breath on glass.

They were back where it all began.

In the modern world.

The place where it all started, in the shrine at the black pool in the Hoh Rainforest.

"No," Ezra whispered. "No, this isn't—this can't be—"

"Was it real?" Ash's hands were shaking. "Ezra, tell me it was real. Tell me we didn't just—"

"I don't know." Panic clawed at her throat. "I remember all of it. Every life. Every death. Every choice.

But—" She looked down at her hands, searching for proof. "The sigil, it should—"

Both their gazes dropped to their palms at the same moment.

And there it was.

Faint, delicate, like henna drawn across their skin—the mirrored flame mark. The Life Sigil that had bound them across seven lifetimes, that had blazed with divine fire in the Veil, that had been forged in choice and love and impossible power.

Here in the modern world, without divine presence nearby, it looked almost... ordinary. Beautiful, yes. Intricate. But mortal. Subdued.

Ezra's breath caught. "It's still there."

"Then it was real," Ash said, voice gaining strength. He reached for her hand, lacing their fingers together.

The moment their palms touched, the marks flared.

Not the blinding gold of divine fire. But warm. Present. Undeniable.

Real.

"It was real," Ezra breathed, half sob, half laugh. "All of it. We really—"

"We did it," Ash finished, pulling her into his arms. "We broke the curse. We're here. We're alive. We can finally —" His voice broke with relief. "We can finally have a life that doesn't end in tragedy."

Ezra laughed against his chest, the sound watery but genuine. "Seven lifetimes. It took us seven lifetimes."

"Worth it," Ash said fiercely, holding her tighter. "Every single one was worth it to get here."

They clung to each other for a long moment, both

shaking, both overwhelmed by the enormity of what they'd survived.

"Gods, you two are dramatic."

They both jolted, spinning toward the voice.

Kee sat perched on a ledge above the pool, one leg swinging, grin sharp as ever. They looked exactly as they had in the first life—young, androgynous, eyes gleaming with mischief and ancient knowledge.

"Kee!" Ezra gasped.

"The one and only." Kee hopped down, landing in a crouch that sent ripples across the pool's surface. "Seriously, though. Seven lives, one Life Sigil, multiple god battles, and you STILL can't figure out when you're dreaming versus when you're awake. It's almost adorable."

Ash was on his feet in an instant, water dripping from his clothes. "What's happening? Where are we? Is the first life gone?"

"Breathe, gloom prince or should I now call you Phoenix-boy." Kee joked.

Ash opened his mouth to speak but Kee held up a hand. "Nothing's lost. Everything's exactly where it should be."

Veyar emerged from the shimmer of light and shadow.

"Veyar." Ezra said the moment she saw him.

He seemed older—so much older. His white robes hung in tatters, and his face bore lines that spoke of exhaustion beyond measure. But his eyes were kind, and when he smiled at them, it was genuine.

"You did it," Veyar said simply. "You saved the Sacred Valley. You trapped Bastillion. You broke the curse that has killed you six times before. And we are all alive."

Relief crashed through Ezra so hard her knees went weak. Ash caught her, holding her upright.

"The gods," Ash said urgently. "Phoenix stayed behind. To guard them. To keep them sleeping. Is he—"

"He's exactly where he needs to be," Veyar confirmed. "I learned of this only moments before you surfaced. Phoenix safely guards the sleeping gods in the Veil. Bastillion is trapped in his divine form, unable to ever return as human. The Visionary sleeps peacefully, her imprisonment holding until the world is ready for her returne and the gods to wake." He paused. "And the mortal vessels—those who carried fragments of divine essence without knowing—they live on, free to be human without the weight of godhood until this human life is over or Visionary returns."

"So it's over," Ezra breathed. "We actually did it."

"You did," Kee said, and for once their voice held no mockery. Just respect. "You crazy kids actually pulled it off. Broke a curse that should have been unbreakable. Defeated a god. Saved multiple worlds." They grinned. "Pretty impressive for a couple of mortals."

"We're not just mortals," Ash said quietly, looking at the Life Sigil on his palm. "Are we?"

"No," Veyar agreed. "You're something new. Something that's never existed before. The Life Sigil made you... more."

Ezra's throat tightened. "And Torin? Sela? Thorne? Are they—"

Kee's expression softened. "They're waiting for you. In the first life. At Vana'Sul. Wondering if you're ever going to surface from that pool you've been glowing in for the past two hours."

Hope flared in Ezra's chest. "They're alive? They're okay?"

"Define okay," Kee said. "Sela's got a nasty hip wound. Thorne's beaten to hell. They're exhausted, grieving, and terrified they lost you both forever." A pause. "But yeah. They're alive."

Ash's breath left him in a rush. "Thorne's alive."

"Your brother's fine," Kee confirmed. "Stubborn as ever. Pretty sure he threatened to dive into the Veil Pool about fifteen times before Veyar convinced him it would just kill him."

"And Torin?" Ezra asked, though part of her already knew. Ash's grip tightened in her hand. He turned his head away from her. She turne to Kee and a sad smile fade away. In the grief that flickered across Veyar's ancient face.

Kee walked to her, shadows curling gently around their feet. When they spoke, their voice was gentle. Reverent.

"Torin didn't make it."

Ezra's world tilted.

"He gave his life to make sure you both had a chance at one," Kee continued softly. "Threw himself in front of falling stone. Saved Ash from Bastillion's attack. Gave his life so you could defeat the god, so every god sleeping in the Veil could remain safe, and so every mortal in the Sacred Valley could live." Their hand found hers, squeezing gently. "His sacrifice was your blessing. And he knew it. Chose it. Would do it again without hesitation."

Tears streamed down Ezra's face. "He's really gone?"

"From the mortal world, yes." Kee's voice carried weight. "But not from existence. Torin chose—when the moment came, when I offered him the choice—not to return in another life. He asked to go to the other side. To be with his wife for eternity."

Ash made a choked sound. "His wife. The one who died when Sela was young."

"He's with her now," Veyar said gently. "At peace. At rest. No more war. No more loss. Just love, eternal and unbreakable."

Ezra pressed both hands to her face, sobbing. Ash pulled her close, his own tears falling into her hair. They held each other, grieving the man who'd been father to them both, who'd given everything so they could have this moment.

"Sela," Ezra gasped between sobs. "Oh gods, Sela. She must be—"

"Devastated," Kee confirmed. "But she has Thorne. And she's waiting for you. For her sister to come back and help her through this."

That broke something in Ezra. She pulled back from Ash, wiping her eyes with shaking hands. "We have to go back. To the first life. To Sela and Thorne. We have to—"

"That's why we're here," Veyar interrupted gently. "To give you a choice."

Ezra and Ash both turned to him.

"A choice?" Ash repeated.

"You've earned it," Veyar said. "You broke the curse. Saved both worlds—the first life and this seventh one. Now you get to decide: Where do you want to finish your seventh life? Here, in the modern world where everything is 'fixed'?" He gestured around the chamber. "Or back in the first life, where your family waits and the work of rebuilding needs to begin?"

Silence fell, heavy with implication.

Ezra looked around the underground chamber. Thought about the modern world waiting above—her cottage in Forks, the museum job she'd been fired from, the normal life she'd dreamed about when the symbol drove her half-mad with obsession.

Everything she'd wanted for years.

And it felt... empty.

"I don't want to stay here," Ash said quietly. "In the modern world, I had nothing. No family. No purpose. Just... existence. Going through the motions. Empty. Angry at the world." He looked at Ezra. "But now I have peace. I have you. And in the first life, I also have Thorne —a brother who'd die for me. Who fought beside me against a god and didn't hesitate."

"I don't want to stay either," Ezra admitted. Her voice shook. "I thought I did. Thought the modern world was home. But—" Her throat closed. "In the first life, I have family. I have a sister. And Torin—" She couldn't finish. Just pressed a hand to her chest where grief sat like a stone.

"Torin taught you to fight," Veyar said softly. "Took you in. Called you daughter."

"He did," Ezra whispered. "And I never got to say goodbye. Never got to tell him—" She looked up at Veyar, at Kee. "If we go back, will we be there? Will we be able to honor him properly?"

"You'll be there," Kee promised. "Right when you left.

Well, two hours later. But time moves differently between worlds. Between liminal spaces."

Ash's hand found Ezra's. "Are we in agreement, then? We go back to the first life? To our family?"

Ezra looked at him—at the face she'd loved across seven lifetimes, at the man who'd given up godhood to be human with her, at her soulmate and anchor and choice.

"Yes," she said firmly. "We go back. Together. To our family. To help Sela through her grief. To rebuild."

"Together," Ash echoed.

Veyar smiled—sad and proud and ancient. "Then here's what you need to know before you go."

He stepped closer, staff planted between them, and the weight of his words settled like prophecy.

"Ash, when you die—and you will die, eventually, at hopefully a ripe old human age—you will return to your god-body in the realm of sleeping gods. Phoenix will remain dormant, guarding the others, until the world is ready for the divine to wake again." He met Ash's eyes. "But you will have lived a full mortal life first. With her. Free of the curse."

Ash nodded, throat tight. "I understand."

Veyar turned to Ezra. "And you, my child. When your time comes, you will finally be able to move on to the ever-after of rest. No more cycles. No more rebirth. Just peace." His smile gentled. "You've earned it. Seven lives of loving and losing. You deserve rest."

"But—" Ezra's voice cracked. "But if I go to rest, and Ash returns to his god-body, we'll be—"

"Separated," Veyar confirmed. "For a time. Maybe a very long time. But not forever." He glanced at Kee, who nodded. "The gods will wake eventually. And when they do, when Phoenix wakes, he'll carry the memory of Ash. Of this life. Of you."

"And who knows?" Kee added with a grin. "Maybe the Visionary will wake too. Maybe she'll remember you. Maybe love finds a way even between rest and godhood." They shrugged. "We've seen crazier things. Like, for instance, two mortals defeating a god with nothing but a Life Sigil and audacity."

Despite everything, Ezra laughed. It came out watery, broken, but real.

"Okay," she said. "Okay. We go back. We live our lives. We love each other for as long as we have. And then..." She looked at Ash. "Then we trust that whatever comes next, we'll find each other again."

"We always do," Ash said, squeezing her hand. "Seven lives proved that."

Veyar gestured to the pool. "Then go. Jump back in. The Black Pool here connects to the Veil Pool in Vana'-Sul's Sanctum. When you surface, you'll be in the first life. Sela and Thorne are waiting."

Ezra and Ash moved to the edge together, hands still joined.

"Thank you," Ezra said, looking back at Veyar and Kee. "For everything. For guiding us. For saving us. For—"

"For being insufferably cryptic and annoyingly helpful?" Kee interrupted with a grin. "You're welcome."

"Go," Veyar said gently. "Your family needs you."

Ezra took a breath, looked at Ash one more time, and together they jumped.

The water swallowed them.

Cold. Dark. Infinite.

But this time, Ezra wasn't afraid. Because Ash's hand was in hers, and they were going home.

They were going to family.

They were going to the life they'd earned.

The water shifted around them—not the cold modern pool, but something warmer. Heavier. Charged with divine residue.

The Veil Pool.

Ezra kicked toward the surface, Ash beside her, both of them rising through liquid darkness toward light.

They broke through gasping.

Air hit their faces—not the damp forest air of the Hoh, but the dry stone-scented air of Vana'Sul's sanctum.

"There!" A voice shouted from above. "Ash is bringing Ezra up!"

Thorne.

Hands reached down—multiple pairs, grabbing for them, hauling them toward the edge of the Veil Pool.

Ezra's fingers found stone. She pulled herself up with the last of her strength, and then someone was grabbing her, yanking her fully out of the water.

"Ezra!" Sela's voice, raw and broken. "Oh gods, Ezra, you're alive!"

Arms wrapped around her—desperate, shaking, holding so tight it hurt. Ezra collapsed into the embrace, both of them soaking wet, both sobbing.

"I thought I lost you," Sela gasped. "The pool was glowing and you were just gone and we couldn't— couldn't reach you—"

"I'm here," Ezra managed, holding her sister tight. "I'm okay. We're okay. We're home."

Beside them, Thorne had pulled Ash from the pool, and the brothers embraced—hard, brief, the kind of contact that said everything without words.

"You crazy bastard," Thorne said, voice rough. "Thought you were gone for good."

"Can't get rid of me that easy," Ash replied, but his voice shook.

Ezra pulled back slightly from Sela, taking in her sister's face—pale, exhausted, eyes red from crying. Her hip was bandaged, blood seeping through.

"Dad," Ezra whispered. "Sela, I'm so sorry. I'm so—"

Sela's face crumpled. "He saved you. Both of you. He —" She couldn't finish, just buried her face in Ezra's shoulder and wept.

Ezra held her sister and cried with her, grieving the man who'd been father to them both, who'd given them a home, who'd taught them to be strong.

Around them, the sanctum was in ruins. Stone rubble everywhere. Scorch marks on the walls. The aftermath of a battle that had shaken the foundations of the world.

But they were alive.

Together.

And they would rebuild.

They would honor Torin's sacrifice.

They would live the lives they'd been given.

Ezra looked up and found Ash's eyes across the space. He was still holding Thorne, but his gaze was on her. Brown eyes—fully human now, no gold, no god—looking at her with love so vast it hurt.

She smiled through her tears.
He smiled back.
And in that moment, Ezra knew:
They had finally broken the curse.
They were finally free.
And whatever came next—rebuilding the Sacred Valley, helping Sela heal, living mortal lives that would eventually end—they would face it together.

The Seventh Life

A few days later, Ezra stood at the Sanctum in Vana'Sul, at the place where Torin had fallen reminiscing.

The massive boulder that had crushed him was no longer just stone. Green ivy climbed every surface, weaving across the rock like eager fingers reaching for sky. Wildflowers bloomed impossibly bright—vivid yellows and deep purples and whites that glowed faintly even in shadow. The transformation had happened three days ago, when Ezra and Sela stood sobbing over their father's memorial, their tears soaking into the blessed earth where his body had dissolved to ash.

Ezra could still see it. The moment the ivy had erupted from cracks in stone, unfurling in seconds. Flowers blooming. Life from death. Beauty from grief.

They'd all stepped back in wonder, and Veyar had been the first to speak, voice quiet with realization. "It appears you may have absorbed some Rootsong as well as all the Oracles' power we discussed."

Now, standing here with Sela's hand in hers and Ash close beside her, Ezra touched her forehead where the Eye sigil burned permanent—the mark Saav had forced upon her. The artificial Oracle gift that would never fade. A scar and a power both.

She was changing. Becoming something new. The Rootsong—earth-magic, the Veyona tribe's gift—was growing inside her alongside the Oracle visions. And through her Life Sigil bond with Ash, she could feel flickers of his Fyr too, heat bleeding through their connection when they touched.

Three tribes' powers. Three impossible gifts that shouldn't coexist in one person.

But they did. In her.

Veyar interrupted her melancholy. "The Veyona elders are waiting for us," he said gently pulling her from her thoughts. He stood at the edge of the memorial, staff in hand, looking exhausted but at peace. "They know we're coming. They're eager to have the Rootsong home."

Ash lifted the cloth-wrapped bundle they'd retrieved from the platform in this very Sanctum—the place where Ezra had been chained, where Bastillion had tried to transform her into something she wasn't. The Rootsong hummed beneath the fabric, golden-brown and still carrying earth-magic despite its corruption.

"I'm ready," Ezra said.

Thorne moved closer to Ash, and Sela stepped beside Ezra. The four of them together, bound by more than blood now. Bound by choice and loss and impossible survival.

Kee appeared from the shadows, grinning as they always did. "Road trip! Well, liminal passage trip. Much faster. Less scenic. But the company's better."

Despite the grief still heavy in her chest, Ezra smiled.

Veyar raised his staff, and the air around them shimmered. Reality bent and folded like cloth being gathered, and suddenly they were stepping through into somewhere else entirely. The transition was seamless—one moment standing in Vana'Sul's Sanctum, the next emerging into a valley thick with ancient trees.

The Veyona settlement spread before them, and Ezra's heart clenched at what she saw. Burned sections of forest. Hastily rebuilt structures. Faces marked with grief. The tribe had suffered under Bastillion's destruction, and the scars were everywhere.

But they'd survived.

When the elders saw them approach, when they saw what Ash carried, something shifted. Hope flickered across weathered faces like the first light of dawn.

An elderly woman stepped forward, and Ezra's breath caught. She recognized her from one of the visions Bastillion had forced into her mind—the woman who'd brought Tenya's scarf to Orielle.

The elder's eyes widened as they met Ezra's, and understanding passed between them. She knew. Somehow, she knew that Ezra had seen that moment. Had carried it with her.

Ash unwrapped the Rootsong with reverence and held it out. The golden-brown length of it seemed to pulse with life, humming with earth-magic that made the ground beneath their feet vibrate softly.

The elder took it with shaking hands, tears streaming down her weathered face. "You brought it back," she whispered, voice breaking. "After everything. After what that monster did. You brought it home."

"We're so sorry," Ezra said, her own voice cracking. "For what Saav did. For what he took from you. For Orielle. For all of it."

The elder set the Rootsong down carefully on the earth, and Ezra watched as the ground beneath it seemed to sigh with relief. The grass grew greener. The flowers nearby brightened. The land itself recognized what had been returned.

Then the elder pulled Ezra into her arms, holding her tight.

"You have nothing to apologize for, child," she said gently, fiercely. "You stopped him. You saved us all. And you brought our heart home." She pulled back, cupping Ezra's face in weathered hands. "Orielle would be proud of you. So proud."

Something inside Ezra shattered. She collapsed forward, sobbing into the elder's shoulder while grief for Orielle and Kireva and Torin and everyone they'd lost poured out in great heaving waves. The elder held her through it all, murmuring words of comfort in the old language, rocking slightly like she was soothing a child who'd skinned her knee rather than a woman who'd fought a god.

When Ezra finally pulled herself together, wiping her

eyes with shaking hands, the elder smiled through her own tears.

"The Rootsong will heal our lands," she said, gesturing to where the artifact rested on the earth. Already, new growth was spreading from it—small shoots of green pushing through scorched soil. "And we will rebuild. Just as you will rebuild your home, yes?"

She looked at all four of them—Ezra, Ash, Sela, Thorne—and her smile widened. "You are always welcome here. You are honorary Veyona now. Family."

"Thank you," Ezra managed, the word barely audible past the tightness in her throat.

The tribe gathered around them then, and they were pulled into the settlement proper. Food appeared—simple but nourishing. Stories were shared over the meal, Veyona voices mixing with theirs. The tribe spoke of those they'd lost, their grief raw but honest. In return, Ezra spoke of Torin. Of his steady strength. Of how he'd called her daughter even though she wasn't his blood. Sela added her own memories, voice breaking on the good ones—her father teaching her to track, to hunt, to see the world with clear eyes.

Ash spoke of the man who'd given his life so they could have theirs. Thorne, quiet as always, simply said: "He was a good man. Better than most. We'll honor him by living well."

The Veyona listened with the reverence such stories deserved, and when the meal was done and the sun began to set, the elder embraced each of them in turn.

"Visit us," she said, catching Ezra's hand one more time. "Often. You're family now. Don't be a stranger."

"We won't," Ezra promised, meaning it.

Veyar stepped forward, staff glowing faintly as he prepared to open the passage back to Vana'Sul. But he paused at the threshold, turning to look at Ezra with ancient, knowing eyes.

"The powers you're beginning to feel," he said quietly enough that only she could hear. "The Oracle gift, the Rootsong, the Fyr bleeding through your bond. Master them, Ezra. Learn what you're becoming. Because the world is changing, and you're changing with it."

Before she could ask what he meant—before she could demand answers about what she was becoming and why it mattered—the passage opened fully, reality folding around them.

They stepped through.

But they didn't emerge at Vana'Sul.

Ezra blinked in surprise as her feet touched ash and charred earth. The smell hit her first—smoke and ruin and old death. They stood in the ruins of Kireva, surrounded by blackened timber and collapsed walls. The village was gone. Truly gone. Just bones and memory now.

Veyar had brought them here deliberately, she realized. One last goodbye before they committed to their choice.

The silence was heavy. Oppressive. Ezra could almost hear the ghosts—Orielle's laughter, Torin's voice calling them in for dinner, the sounds of daily life that would never return.

"We could rebuild it," Sela said quietly, looking around at what had been their childhood home. Her voice was careful, testing. "If you wanted. The Tribunal said the land is ours. We could make it what it was."

Ezra was quiet for a long moment, feeling the weight of the ruins pressing down on her shoulders. She thought about Torin teaching her to fight in the training yard that was now just ash. Thought about Orielle's house where they'd studied symbols and visions, now collapsed in on itself. The marketplace where she'd bought bread every morning. The great hall where they'd gathered for meals. All of it gone. All of it reduced to char and memory.

She shook her head slowly. "No," she said softly, but with certainty. "Let it rest. Let the forest take it back. Let it return to the earth where it belongs."

She looked at her sister, saw the grief and understanding mixing in Sela's eyes. "Kireva was our home once. But it's gone now. The people who made it home—Torin, Orielle, all the Oracles—they're gone. And trying to rebuild it..." Her voice caught, but she pushed through. "It would just be chasing ghosts. Trying to resurrect something that died with the people we loved."

"Then where?" Sela asked, and there was no judgment in the question. Just honest curiosity. "Where do we go? What do we do?"

"Vana'Sul," Ash said, understanding warming his voice. He reached for Ezra's hand, and when their palms pressed together, Life Sigils connecting, she felt the familiar pulse of warmth. Of home. "Phoenix's house. It's already ours. Already home."

"And we'd be near the Veil," Ezra added, the pieces falling into place in her mind like a puzzle she hadn't known she was solving. "Near the sleeping gods. Near Phoenix." She looked at the others—at her sister, at Thorne whose loyalty had never wavered, at Ash whose brown eyes held only love and determination. "Someone needs to keep watch in our world, not just the Veil. To make sure Bastillion stays sealed. To make sure the gods sleep peacefully until the world is ready for them to wake."

"A sacred duty," Thorne said slowly, processing the weight of what she was suggesting. "Guardians of the Veil."

"A home," Ezra corrected, squeezing Ash's hand. "With a purpose, yes. But first and foremost, a home. We'll live there. Build our lives there. Love there. Train there. And if anyone needs sanctuary—survivors, refugees, people looking for a fresh start—we'll welcome them. We'll give them what Torin gave us."

"Not a tribe," Sela said, understanding dawning across her face like sunrise. "Not a formal structure with elders and rules and hierarchy."

"Just family," Ezra finished. "And anyone who wants to be family."

Kee appeared suddenly, perched on a fallen beam that had once been part of the Oracle house. Their usual irreverent grin was in place, but their eyes were softer than normal. "I like it. Cozy. Meaningful. Sacred duty mixed with domestic bliss and the occasional refugee in need of coffee and a safe place to sleep." Kee paused. "Speaking of coffee—the maker is at Vana'Sul, which is really the deciding factor here."

Despite everything—despite the grief and the ruins and the weight of what they'd survived—Ezra laughed. Real laughter, the kind that came from deep in the belly and left you breathless and lighter.

The others joined in, and for a moment, the ruins of Kireva rang with the sound of life and joy and people choosing to keep going.

When the laughter faded, Ezra took one last look around. She walked slowly through the ash, her boots crunching on charred wood. She paused at what had been the training yard, imagining Torin's voice: "Again. Faster this time. You're better than this, Ezra." She moved to where the Oracle house had stood, where Orielle had taught her to read symbols and trust her visions. Where they'd stayed up late talking about the future, neither of them knowing how little future they had left.

"Goodbye," Ezra whispered to the ruins, to the ghosts, to the past. "Thank you. For everything. For raising me. For teaching me. For loving me when I had nothing and no one." Her voice broke. "I'll carry you with me. All of you. Always."

Then she turned away. Turned toward Sela who stood waiting with understanding in her eyes. Toward Thorne who nodded once, respect clear in the gesture. Toward Ash whose hand found hers immediately, their fingers lacing together with the ease of seven lifetimes' practice.

She turned toward the future. Toward Vana'Sul. Toward home.

Veyar didn't need to be asked. He simply raised his staff, and the liminal passage opened—cleaner this time, more deliberate. When they stepped through, they emerged exactly where they belonged.

The Sanctum at Vana'Sul spread around them, peaceful in the gathering dusk. The Veil Pool glowed faintly in the center, its surface still as glass, a doorway to the realm where gods slept and Phoenix kept eternal watch. Somewhere beyond that water, in the golden-dark, her soulmate's divine half stood guard. Waiting. Watching. Protecting.

And behind them, built into the Sanctum itself with architecture that shouldn't exist but did, Phoenix's house waited. Their house now. Light glowed warm in the windows—Sela and Thorne must have lit the lamps earlier, or perhaps the house itself remembered how to welcome them home.

"Home," Sela breathed, and the word sounded like a prayer.

"Home," Ezra agreed.

They walked toward it together, all four of them, with Veyar and Kee following at a respectful distance. When they reached the door, Ash paused with his hand on the handle and looked back at Ezra. His brown eyes—fully human now, no trace of gold or god—held a question.

"Are you sure?" he asked quietly. "This is it. This is where we stay. Where we build our life together. All of us."

Ezra looked at the Veil Pool glowing softly in the twilight, a constant reminder of what they'd survived and what waited beyond. She looked at the house that blended modern comfort with ancient beauty, running water and captured-sunlight lamps coexisting with stone and wood that had stood for centuries. She looked at her sister, her face still marked with grief but also hope. At Thorne, steady and loyal and finally part of something that felt like family. At Veyar and Kee, gods and guardians themselves, who'd chosen to walk beside mortals through impossible odds.

Then she looked at Ash—at his brown eyes, at the face she'd loved across seven lifetimes, at the man who'd given up divinity to be with her. Her soulmate. Her anchor. Her choice.

"I'm sure," she said, and meant it with everything she was.

He smiled, and it was like sunrise after the longest night. "Then let's go home."

He opened the door, and warm light spilled out around them. They crossed the threshold together—Ezra and Ash first, hands clasped, followed by Sela and Thorne. The house welcomed them with the scent of wood smoke and something sweet that Sela must have baked before they left. The furniture was comfortable, worn in the right places. The lamps cast soft light across walls decorated with nothing yet, waiting for them to make it theirs. Waiting for them to fill it with life and memory and love.

Behind them, Veyar and Kee paused at the threshold.

"We'll leave you to settle in," Veyar said, but his smile was warm. Proud. "But we're not far. Never far. Family doesn't abandon family."

"Even the annoying immortal members," Kee added with a wink.

Then they were gone, fading into shadow and liminal space, leaving the four of them alone in their new home.

Ezra moved to the window that overlooked the Veil Pool. She pressed her palm against the glass, watching the water glow faintly in the darkness. Somewhere beyond that surface, Phoenix kept watch. She couldn't see him, couldn't touch him, but she could feel him—a distant warmth at the edge of her awareness, like the sun on a cloudy day.

"Thank you," she whispered. "For letting us live."

Ash's arms came around her from behind, pulling her back against his chest. "He made the right choice," he said quietly. "This is worth more than divinity."

Ezra turned in his arms and kissed him. Soft at first, then deepening, carrying the weight of everything they'd survived and the promise of what came next. His hands cradled her face, and she melted into the warmth and safety she'd found across seven lifetimes.

When they broke apart, both breathless, Ash rested his forehead against hers. "I love you."

"I love you too."

Before the moment could progress further, Sela's voice called from the other room. "Dinner's ready!"

Thorne's deeper voice answered immediately. "About time. I've been looking forward to that pie all day."

"It's not even baked yet, you impatient oaf," Sela shot back, laughter in her voice.

The sound was jarring after everything they'd been through—normal life, family banter, someone teasing about pie.

But it was beautiful.

Ezra took Ash's hand, and together they walked toward the kitchen. Toward the smell of food and the sound of family. Toward the life they'd earned.

Outside, the Veil Pool pulsed once with soft light. In

the golden-dark beyond mortal reach, Phoenix kept watch over sleeping gods. Bastillion remained sealed in chains.

But here, there was only dinner and laughter and the choice to keep living.

Seven lives had led to this moment.

Six deaths had earned them this chance.

And they would not waste it.

Bonus Scene

Veyar and Kee

Liminal Space

Kee dangled from a stone outcropping, one leg swinging, watching the viewing pool with unconcealed delight.

"They made it," Kee announced. "Both of them. In one piece. Mostly."

Veyar didn't respond immediately. He stood at the pool's edge, both hands gripping his staff, knuckles bone-white with the effort of staying upright. His robes hung in tatters, hem dark with something that might have been blood or might have been shadow. His face—gods, his face had aged centuries in the span of hours.

"Of course they made it," Veyar said finally, voice rough as stone grinding against stone. "They're too stubborn to do anything else."

"You look terrible," Kee observed. "Like death. Ironically."

"I feel worse." Veyar eased himself down onto the cold stone, legs giving out. His staff clattered beside him. "Do you know how much power it takes to hold a liminal bridge open while two gods battle underwater and the entire structure of divine imprisonment shifts around them?"

"Nope!" Kee grinned. "I just shepherd souls. Very low-stress. You should try it."

"I'm beginning to think death would be a vacation."

Kee's grin softened slightly. "You're not dying. You're just very, very tired."

"Same thing at my age."

They fell into companionable silence, watching the pool's surface. It showed Ash and Ezra in the modern world, sitting by the Hoh forest shrine, dripping wet, clearly overwhelmed by the returning memories.

"They remember now," Kee said quietly. "All of it. Every life. Every death. Every choice."

"Good." Veyar's eyes drifted closed. "They'll need those memories for what comes next."

Kee hopped down from the outcropping, landing in a crouch beside Veyar. Their shadows pooled around them both, less playful than usual. More thoughtful.

"So," Kee said. "You've been remembering too."

It wasn't a question.

Veyar's jaw worked. "Fragments. Pieces. When Bastil-lion woke, when his divine consciousness fully manifested, it... cracked something. The spell the Visionary used to lock away our memories. It's breaking down."

"What do you remember?"

"Not enough." Veyar opened his eyes, staring at the pool where Ash and Ezra sat together, choosing each other again. "I remember serving her. Remember the weight of her presence, the way her Ninth Eye could see every thread of fate simultaneously. I remember..." He stopped, throat working. "I remember loving her. Not romantic love. But devotion. She was everything good about divinity—wisdom, compassion, the willingness to sacrifice for the greater good."

"And?"

"And I remember her making the choice. Gathering all the gods. Explaining what she'd seen with the Ninth Eye." Veyar's hands clenched. "A future where the gods' love wars destroyed everything. Where Phoenix and Bastillion's rivalry over her escalated until entire civilizations burned. Where divine power, unchecked and untempered by mortal wisdom, became catastrophic."

Kee's expression went serious. "So she did lock everyone away. I wondered."

"She gave them a chance to learn." Veyar's voice dropped to barely a whisper. "Forced them into mortal bodies. Made them live and die and love and lose as humans do. Hoping that when—if—they ever woke, they'd have learned mercy. Learned restraint. Learned that love shouldn't destroy worlds."

"And then she locked herself away too."

"Because she knew if she remained, they'd eventually break free and come for her. Hunt her down for what she'd done." Veyar's eyes shone with unshed tears. "So she erased her own memories. Hid herself so completely that even I..." He stopped, shaking his head. "I can't find her. I don't know where she is. And now we wait for all my interference to settle."

Silence stretched between them.

"You're talking about the pact," Kee said finally.

"The pact." Veyar's voice turned bitter. "If only I'd remembered sooner. If only I'd known why she did what she did before I interfered." He looked at his hands like they'd betrayed him. "I made that pact with Ezra and Ash in their first human life. Offered them seven chances when they should have had one. Meddled with the natural cycle because I thought I was helping."

"You were helping," Kee pointed out.

"Was I?" Veyar's laugh was hollow. "I had no memories of the Visionary's plan. No understanding of why the gods were locked away or what she'd foreseen. I just saw two souls in love, cursed to die, and I thought—" His voice cracked. "I thought I was being merciful. Giving them chances. But my interference disturbed the balance she'd created. Twisted threads of fate she'd carefully woven. And it almost released a god who'd turned from light to darkness. Almost unleashed Bastillion's madness on the world two centuries early."

He pressed both hands to his face, shoulders shaking. "The Visionary foresaw catastrophe and built a prison to prevent it. And I, in my ignorance and arrogance, nearly tore it all down. Nearly undid everything she sacrificed."

Kee was quiet for a long moment, watching their old friend break under the weight of guilt.

"Or," Kee said thoughtfully, "maybe you did exactly what she needed you to do."

Veyar looked up, eyes red. "What?"

"The Visionary has the Ninth Eye," Kee said simply. "She sees every thread of fate. Every possible outcome. Every choice that could be made." They gestured to the pool where Ash and Ezra were choosing to return to the first life. "Do you really think she didn't see you making that pact? Didn't account for your interference in her plans?"

"I..." Veyar stopped, uncertainty flickering across his face.

"She locked away her own memories," Kee continued. "Hid herself so completely even you can't find her. But she left breadcrumbs. The symbols. The Life Sigil possibility. The way their souls kept finding each other across every life." They looked at Veyar with eyes that suddenly seemed far older than their playful demeanor suggested. "Maybe she knew you'd interfere. Maybe she counted on it. Maybe your pact was part of her plan all along."

"But the risk," Veyar whispered. "Bastillion nearly—"

"Nearly. But didn't." Kee's grin returned, sharp and knowing. "Because Ezra and Ash stopped him. Because they had seven lives to learn how. Because someone gave them that chance."

They stood, brushing off their clothes. "The Visionary sees all threads, Veyar. All of them. She knew what Phoenix would choose. Knew what Bastillion would become. Knew what you would do." They paused at the edge of the outcropping. "And she prepared for all of it. Left pieces in place for when the time was right."

"You think this was all her plan?" Veyar asked, hope warring with disbelief in his voice.

"I think," Kee said, "that the goddess with the Ninth

Eye doesn't leave anything to chance. Even her own disappearance." They winked. "Especially her own disappearance."

Then Kee was gone, fading into shadow, leaving Veyar alone with the viewing pool.

He stared at it for a long time, watching Ash and Ezra build something new from the ashes of what had been lost.

"Did you see this?" he whispered to the Visionary, wherever she was. "Did you know?"

The pool offered no answer.

But somewhere in the golden-dark where gods slept and Phoenix kept watch, perhaps a masked goddess dreamed. Perhaps she smiled behind her golden mask, seeing threads weaving together exactly as she'd foreseen.

Or perhaps she simply slept, waiting for the moment when the world would be ready for her return.

Either way, the gods remained sealed.

The curse was broken.

And two souls who'd loved across seven lifetimes finally had the chance to live.

Veyar closed his eyes and let himself believe—just for a moment—that maybe his interference hadn't doomed them all.

Maybe it had saved them.

THE END

Map of the Seven Tribes and Vana'Sul Overlaying
Modern Day Olympic National Park

Guide to Names and Places

A guide to names and places in *The Seventh Life* —
spoken as the characters would say them.

Characters:

- Ash – (*ASH*)
- Ezra – (*EHZ-ruh*)
- Saav – (*Sah*-v)
- Torin – (*TOR-in*)
- Sela – (*SAY-luh*)
- Thorne – (*THORN*)
- Orielle — *(Oh-ree-ELL)*
- Anok – (AH-nok)

Tribes & Realms:
Gods:

- Visionary

- Phoenix
- Bastillion

Minor Gods:

- Veyar – (*VAY-ar*)
- Kee – (*Key*)

The Seven Tribes of the Sacred Valley

- Fyr (*fye-er*)
- Kireva (kih-RAY-vuh)
- Kildra (*KEEL-drah*)
- Seyathi (*SAY-ah-thee*)
- Morilan (*MOH-ree-lahn*)
- Veyona (*VAY-oh-nah*)
- Nahrim (*NAH-rim*)

Outside of the Sacred Valley

- The Shrine (Veyar's shrine near Kireva)
- The Black Pool (Liminal Space)
- The Shattered Vale

Vana'Sul (VAH-nuh SOOL)

- The Sanctum
- The Veil Pool

Author's Note

Dear Reader,

Thank you.

Thank you for walking beside Ezra and Ash through every life they lived—every scar, every spark, every choice that brought them back to each other. Writing *The Seventh Life* has been a journey unlike any I've taken before. One full of questions about memory, sacrifice, and what it really means to be free.

If you're holding this book in your hands (or in your heart), it means you stayed. Through the myths and the magic, through battles and black flames, through uncertainty and love that refused to break.

Ezra and Ash were never just characters to me. They were voices that rose louder each time I tried to quiet them. And now, they live. Fully. Fiercely. Freely. Because of you.

This may be the end of *The Seventh Life*—but it's not

the end of their story. The Phoenix still burns. The visions still seek. And their world is still shifting.

I can't wait to show you what happens next.

With all my heart,

Kris Tenn

A Moment of Your Time

Enjoyed this book?

Please consider leaving a short review!

Reviews help indie authors like me reach new readers —and help readers decide if a story is right for them. Just a sentence or two makes a huge difference.

Thank you for your support. It truly means the world to me.

Flip the page to sign up to get Ezra and Ash's Journal.

Stay Connected & Read More — Free!

Haven't read your subscribers-only free gift yet?

*Subscribe today to download **The Forgotten Truth** and dive deeper into the world of **The Seventh Life**.*

Want more stories, exclusive extras, and behind-the-scenes content from my writing world?

When you subscribe, you'll get:
— Free Ezra and Ash Journal in an ebooks
— Character art, world maps, and playlists
— Early access to new releases, giveaways, and special surprises

Scan the QR code or visit: www.kristenn.me and click the subscribe button.
It's all waiting for you.

Also by Kris Tenn

The Seventh Life

Future books in the series:
The Eighth Flame
The Ninth Eye

About the Author

Kris Tenn tells the kind of love stories that stay with you, whether set in small towns, shadowed forests, or worlds touched by myth. With characters who fight for each other and the futures they dream of, Kris writes for readers who believe in magic, resilience, and the power of the heart.

facebook.com/kris.tenn.books

instagram.com/kris.tenn.books

tiktok.com/@kris.tenn.books

amazon.com/author/kris.tenn